TRUE LOVE

Toby stood. "I should head back to Charm before dark. Danki for everything."

Magdelena rose. "I'll go outside with you. But first I'd like to get something from my room."

Toby nodded.

Magdelena returned, and he bid her aunt and uncle farewell. They walked outside to the buggy.

She handed him a white handkerchief with the letter *M* embroidered on it. "Put this on your dresser. I want you to have it as a reminder my heart belongs to you."

He kissed her lightly on the lips and held her a moment. "I don't need anything to remind me of our love, but I'll cherish it." He kissed her cheek and then got in the buggy and waved goodbye.

He didn't glance over his shoulder. If she was crying, he'd never leave. . . .

Books by Molly Jebber

The Keepsake Pocket Quilt series

CHANGE OF HEART

GRACE'S FORGIVENESS

TWO SUITORS FOR ANNA

The Amish Charm Bakery series

LIZA'S SECOND CHANCE

ELLIE'S REDEMPTION

HANNAH'S COURAGE

MARYANN'S HOPE

MAGDELENA'S CHOICE

Collections

THE AMISH CHRISTMAS SLEIGH
(with Kelly Long and Amy Lillard)

AMISH BRIDES
(with Jennifer Beckstrand and Amy Lillard)

Published by Kensington Publishing Corp.

Magdelena's Choice

MOLLY JEBBER

ZEBRA BOOKS
KENSINGTON PUBLISHING CORP.
www.kensingtonbooks.com

ZEBRA BOOKS are published by

Kensington Publishing Corp.
119 West 40th Street
New York, NY 10018

All Kensington titles, imprints, and distributed lines are available at special quantity discounts for bulk purchases for sales promotion, premiums, fund-raising, educational, or institutional use.

Special book excerpts or customized printings can also be created to fit specific needs. For details, write or phone the office of the Kensington Sales Manager: Attn.: Sales Department. Kensington Publishing Corp., 119 West 40th Street, New York, NY 10018. Phone: 1-800-221-2647.

Zebra and the Z logo Reg. U.S. Pat. & TM Off.
BOUQUET Reg. U.S. Pat. & TM Off.

First Printing: February 2022
ISBN-13: 978-1-4201-5069-8
ISBN-13: 978-1-4201-5070-4 (eBook)

10 9 8 7 6 5 4 3 2 1

Printed in the United States of America

Mitchell Morris
The best brother and close friend
a sister could ever ask for.

ACKNOWLEDGMENTS

Thank you to:

Ed—The love of my life.

Dawn Dowdle, agent, and John Scognamiglio, editor-in-chief, for their support, kindness, and guidance. I'm grateful for you both.

Misty, my beautiful, talented, and smart daughter who lights up my life and helps me in so many ways.

Sue Morris, my mother. Beautiful, elegant, and amazing woman.

To Debbie Bugezia, Lee Granza, Mary Byrnes, Margie Sacnz, Elaine Saltsgaver, Kelly Hildreth, Connie Melaik, Barbara Visco, Mary Salan, Lynn Smith, Linda Schultz, Judy Brennan, Beverly Hancock, Cyndee Perkins, Ginny Gilmore, Donna Snyder, Melanie Fogel, Sigrid Davies, Shirley Madden, Margie Doerr, Ann Wright, Diane Winters, and my Southbridge, Quilt, and church friends. You know who you are and how much you mean to me.

Aunt Sharon Sanders, Beth Sanders, and Aunt Sheila Walters for their support, love, and memories.

Patricia Campbell, Diana (DJ) Welker, Marie Coutu, Friends of Southwest Florida Romance Writers' group, RWA Faith, Hope & Love Chapter, Keeping Up with the Amish Group, and Christian Authors Network for your advice, love, and friendship.

To Connie Lynch, you are such a blessing in my life. I appreciate you so much.

To Marilyn Ridgway and Carolyn Ridgway—You've lifted me up more times than I can count! You're such a blessing!

To Sandra Barela—Thank you for your friendship, advice, and encouragement!

To my readers—I couldn't do this without your encouragement. Thank you so much.

Chapter One

Charm, Ohio
July, 1914

Magdelena Beachy strolled to the dessert table and squinted against the hot sun. She scanned the sea of straw hats and bonnets for Toby Schlabach. He stood next to his daed, talking to Joel. She wanted to get better acquainted with him, but he worked long hours six days a week to provide for his family. He saved any spare time for his daed. She was determined to approach him later. She gripped the big spoon in the bread pudding and dropped a serving onto her plate, and then she grabbed the next spoon in a bowl of vanilla icing and drizzled the sugary mixture over her dessert. She grabbed a fork and some cotton napkins. It was considerate of her friends Ellie and Joel to host this casual, early Wednesday evening picnic. Hard to believe it was July first. Her favorite season was passing by too fast.

Her little schweschder grabbed her free hand. "Magdelena, hurry! I saved you a place by Ellie and her boppli, Emma." Charity dragged her through the crowd.

"Slow down! I'll drop my plate." Magdelena tripped over a branch and bumped into Toby. She gasped as the gooey mess slid down the front of his clean white shirt and black pants. Heat rose to her cheeks. "Oh no! I'm so sorry." She wiped the food from his shirt. This wasn't the way she had intended to get Toby's attention.

Charity winced. "Sorry, Toby."

He brushed more of the bread pudding and icing off his shirt. "No harm done, little one."

Magdelena's cheeks heated. "Charity, no more running."

"All right. I'll be with Ellie and Emma. I really am sorry, Toby." Charity avoided eye contact with her and Toby.

He squatted. "Don't worry. Accidents happen. Go have fun."

"Danki." She grinned and skipped away.

"Toby, do you mind if we find a spot together and talk?" She shouldn't be forward, but she didn't want to pass on this opportunity to have a conversation with him.

He smiled. "Good idea."

Magdelena set her plate on a nearby picnic table and gestured to the water pump. "Let's wet one of my cloth napkins."

He walked with her to the pump, accepted the cloth napkin, drenched it, and twisted it to get rid of the excess water. "It's all right. I should watch where I'm going." He dabbed the stains.

She handed him a dry napkin. "Here's another one to dry your shirt."

"The sun is blazing hot today. This gives me an excuse to use water to cool off."

Magdelena grinned. "Have you had dessert?"

He shook his head. "Your bread pudding looks delicious.

Kumme with me to get some, and then we can find shade under the willow tree by the pond."

She followed him to the dessert table and then to a bench under the willow tree, away from the crowd. She balanced her plate on her lap. "How's your daed? I'm surprised he joined you today."

"He doesn't complain. He fights through his pain on bad days better than I could. Always cold, he loves being outside in the warm sun. And he enjoys visiting with his friends." Toby glanced at his daed. "I'm not sure how long he'll last before we need to take him home." His smile faded.

She wished she could erase his sadness and worry. "Your daed is such a kind man. He's loved by many. Look at the crowd around him."

"He hasn't lost his sense of humor and love for telling stories." Toby glanced at his daed.

She admired his devotion to his daed, and it was another trait she found attractive about him. She talked to Toby any chance she got, and she'd never grow tired of looking into his light brown eyes. He had a square chin and high forehead. His thick brown hair had a natural wave and shine beneath his straw hat. He had a lanky build and a calm and kind demeanor. She wanted him to enjoy the day and his time with her. "These sunny days make me want to take long walks by the pond, fish out of the wooden rowboat we have, and wade in the shallow part of the pond with my bare feet. What do you like to do in the summer?"

"I like to play horseshoes, handcraft furniture and toys, and do all the things you named, but working at Andrew's place and on our small farm, and helping with Daed, fill my days and nights. I can't remember the last time I've done those things."

Charity and her friend Peter ran to them. "Will you both wade in the pond with us? Mamm said we aren't allowed to go by ourselves."

Peter swiped the sweat from his forehead with the back of his hand and smoothed back his chocolate-brown hair. He tossed his straw hat toward the nearby apple tree. "I'm hot. I want to wade in the water to cool off."

"Give us time to finish our dessert and we'll wade in the pond with you." Magdelena wanted Toby to herself for a couple of minutes.

Charity grinned. "Danki!"

Peter skipped after Charity.

"Toby, I'm glad you came today." She tensed. Her parents wouldn't approve of her being forward with Toby, but she wanted him to know she was interested in him. Maybe it would encourage him to carve out time for her. She'd be thrilled if he'd ask to court her.

Charity and Peter returned to them. Charity pointed to their plates. "You've both finished your dessert. Ready to wade in the water?"

"Almost. Will you give us a couple more minutes?" Magdelena finished her last bite of bread pudding.

"It's hot. We're ready to get in the water," Charity begged.

Peter waved Toby to the water's edge. "Kumme on."

Toby chuckled. "Wading does sound like fun."

"Yes, it does. Let's go." Magdelena swallowed around the disappointment in her throat. She set her plate on top of Toby's in the grass and stood. She would've liked to have had more time to talk with Toby without distractions.

Magdelena removed her shoes and socks and set them close to Toby's, Charity's, and Peter's.

She stepped into the shallow water. "It is refreshing."

When would Toby be ready to court? And was he interested in her?

Peter splashed Charity.

She splashed him back and laughed.

Magdelena shouted, "Charity and Peter, don't soak your clothes."

Charity giggled. "My dress is already wet. Peter's clothes are, too."

Toby swatted water at Magdelena and gave her a mischievous grin. "The sun will dry their clothes and ours in no time."

"You're right." She chuckled and splashed him back. The dimples in his handsome cheeks and the sparkle in his eyes made her heart skip a beat. She didn't know he had a playful side. Another reason to find him attractive.

Toby found some flat rocks, and he handed two to Magdelena. "I love to skim the water with the rocks and watch them skip across the surface."

"Me, too." Magdelena tossed a stone and watched it skip three times.

"Very good!" Toby smiled.

Peter held out his hand. "I want to try."

"Let me go first." Charity picked up a slender rock. She threw it. "Did you see it bounce on the water twice?"

"Watch me!" Peter spun his rock. "I did it. Mine skipped twice, too."

Toby didn't put much effort into his throw, and the stone sank right away. "You're all putting me to shame."

Magdelena liked his humbleness. He'd let the kinner outdo him. He was again thinking of others' happiness before himself. "It doesn't take much to get these two excited."

"They seem close. Do they spend a lot of time together?"

Toby offered Magdelena his hand to help her out of the pond.

She accepted, stepped out, and sat on the bench. "From the day they met, they've been close friends. Charity insists she'll marry Peter. He agrees. I envy their innocence and worry-free life at their age." She put on her shoes and socks.

Rachael joined them. "I'm sorry to interrupt, but Daed is ready to go home."

Toby finished putting on his socks and shoes. "I need to lift him into the back of the wagon. We've put blankets and a feather pillow in the back for him to get comfortable."

"I'll go with you and Rachael to say goodbye." Magdelena turned to Peter and Charity. "Get out of the pond, put on your shoes and socks, and play away from the water."

Peter cupped Charity's elbow, and they both left the pond and plopped on the ground.

Peter said, "We will."

"Wouldn't it be something if Charity and Peter's friendship blossomed into a future together in the years to kumme?" Toby glanced over his shoulder at the kinner.

"I would like for them to. They miss each other when they're apart. They defend each other when one is in trouble. And they talk about having a haus with three porch stairs and lots of rooms. They hope to have six boys and six girls. Charity and Peter are both definite about these things." She chuckled. "Liza and Jacob adopting Peter when his mamm died was such a blessing. And you'd never know he hadn't been born into their family. Ellie was excited to have him for a bruder. And he's been good for all of them. He's really good for Charity."

"They are adorable," Rachael said.

Magdelena smiled. "Charity isn't always adorable. She won't listen to us, but if Peter asks her to do something, she does it. I worry about her. She has a stubborn determination. She has her nose in the corner often at our haus for not minding."

Rachael limped between Toby and Magdelena. "The way you describe Charity reminds me of Ellie. She's outspoken, protective, and fearless. She's calmed since she married Joel and had Emma. I wouldn't change her. She's been a good friend to us."

"Ellie is a spitfire," Toby teased.

Magdelena and Rachael laughed. Magdelena loved Ellie's directness and how her friend defended her without hesitation. She knew Rachael and Toby felt the same about Ellie, too. She hadn't known Toby had such a good sense of humor and liked to tease. She was finding more things out about him she liked each time they were together.

"Are you both close to your daed?" Magdelena walked between Rachael and Toby.

"Yes. He's my best friend. He has a gentle soul and big heart. He was a hard worker before he became ill. But he'd always make time to take me fishing and hunting, and he taught me to swim. We'd go to town together to get supplies, and he and I loved lemon drops. He'd let me buy them, and then we'd share the candy with Mamm and Rachael. It seems like a small thing, but it meant so much to me as a little boy. I still buy them for us. I dread the day he's no longer with us. I don't know how much time we have left. I'm surprised he's lived this long." Toby's grin faded.

Rachael hooked her arm through Magdelena's. "I'm close to Daed, but Toby and Daed have a special bond. He doesn't let his sickness get him down. I'm not sure I would be as brave."

"Anytime I've kumme to your haus and delivered meals, he's been chipper and sweet. If I'm ever sick like him, I hope I'd have the strength to overcome my pain enough to show kindness to others like your daed and not want to hide from friends and family." Magdelena had visited and talked with Vernon Schlabach enough to recognize the resemblance in Toby and his daed. They both had gentle souls, strength to overcome adversity, and a happy heart. They might not have much, but she always left their home feeling like they had everything they needed. Love and each other. She wanted a future with Toby, and she'd be blessed to be a part of his family someday.

They approached Toby's daed. Mr. Schlabach's gray pallor concerned her.

He gave her a feeble grin. "Magdelena, danki for convincing my son to have some fun. It did my heart good to watch him relax. He works too hard."

Toby blushed. "Are you ready to go?"

"I'm tuckered out. I did love having the sunshine on my face and watching the kinner play and having conversations with my friends. Magdelena, don't be a stranger. We look forward to your visits. Right, Toby?" He winked at Magdelena.

"Time to go, Daed." Toby grinned at Magdelena and then helped his rail-thin daed to the wagon, where they'd stacked blankets.

Magdelena walked with Rachael and Eleanor.

Eleanor, Toby's mamm, clasped Magdelena's hand. "Danki for the meals you've provided for us. You're like a part of our family. We love you, Magdelena. And I'm sure my son does, too. I hope you'll be patient with him." She dropped Magdelena's hand and caught up with her son and husband.

Magdelena called out to Eleanor, "Danki. I love you, too."

Rachael pulled Magdelena back while Toby helped his daed into the wagon. "We've talked about this before, but I'm sorry again that Toby isn't ready to court you. I wish the circumstances were different. If you get tired of waiting on him, I'll understand, and it won't change our friendship. My bruder's heart is in the right place, but he does go overboard with what he surmises would be enough money to provide for our family and a fraa and kinner."

"I understand his position. I'll take every opportunity I can to talk with him, and I'm going to practice patience. Your bruder is worth the wait." Magdelena watched Toby as he helped his daed. He was a caring man.

Magdelena bid them farewell and watched them until their wagon disappeared onto the main road. Would Toby ever be free enough from his burdens to marry?

Toby drove toward home, and he winced each time his daed moaned when they hit a rut in the road. There were spots he couldn't avoid. Magdelena had brightened his day, along with Charity and Peter. What cute kinner. Charity's freckles across her nose and cheeks and curly light red hair added to her bubbly personality. His friends had found lovely fraas, they were having precious kinner, and they seemed happy. He would have a family someday, and he would court Magdelena when he was in a better financial position. Would she wait for him? It was a risk he'd have to take.

"Are you all right in the back with Daed, Mamm?" Rachael sat next to Toby and turned to look at Mamm.

"We're fine, dear."

Toby wanted a solid and loving marriage like his parents'. Mamm read the scriptures to Daed, and they said their prayers together each evening. In spite of his illness, she included Daed in their everyday decisions. She asked his advice and what to choose to cook for meals and bake for desserts. She hurried to finish her chores to be with him.

"We're home." He pulled the wagon close to the haus. He jumped out and stepped in the back. He lifted his father, scooted to the end of the wagon, and slid out. He carried him into the haus and lowered him to the chair. "Is the chair or bed more comfortable for you?"

"I'm not sure. I'll rest here for now." Daed closed his eyes.

"Patches, have you behaved while we've been gone?" Rachael bent and hugged the fluffy-haired dog. She opened the front door.

Patches ran outside to relieve himself and came back in the haus.

Mamm kissed Daed's forehead. "I'll empty the basket of dirty dishes in the kitchen. Call me if you need anything."

Daed opened his eyes and managed a weak smile and nodded at Mamm. "Toby, I didn't last too long in this chair. I'm sorry to trouble you. Please take me to bed. I'm ready to lay down. Danki, Son."

Toby lifted him and carried him to bed. "What can I get you?"

Patches settled on the floor beside Daed's bed.

Toby scratched the dog's back.

"Nothing for now. I suspect I'll be asleep in a matter of minutes."

Toby didn't want to move him to pull back the coverlet on the already made bed. He grabbed a sheet and quilt from the chest and draped them over his daed. "Are you too warm?" He didn't know how Daed could stand covers on this hot summer day. Daed had lost a lot of weight, and he appeared much older than forty-eight.

"No, I'm comfortable. Danki, Son." He shook his head. "Isn't it strange I'm cold when it's warm outside?"

"Patches is sure glad you're home. I'll check on you later." He closed the door partially behind himself, padded to the kitchen, and sat at the wooden scarred table with Rachael and Mamm. "Daed's lost more weight, and he seems weaker."

Rachael traced the rim of her glass. "Mamm and I said the same thing right before you joined us."

Mamm's eyes pooled with tears. "I'm not ready to let him go."

"I can't imagine him not being here with us." Rachael wiped a tear spilling onto her cheek.

"Daed and Patches are best buddies. The dog doesn't leave his side. Patches will be sad when Daed is no longer with us." He'd been afraid the dog he'd gotten from Magdelena's litter a couple of months ago would be a nuisance to Daed. It was the best decision he could've made.

"Let's change the subject. Daed wouldn't want us to dwell on his bad health." Mamm cleared her throat. "I noticed you and Magdelena had separated from the crowd and were talking. I wish you'd court her. She's lovely. And many of the unwed women who are bringing food to our haus are hoping you'll be here. You're at an age you need to consider a fraa. Magdelena is my favorite and, from what I observed, she's yours, too."

Rachael nudged him and gave him a mischievous grin. "Yes, Toby, why don't you court her? It's obvious you kumme to the bakery often to talk to Magdelena. Not me."

His cheeks heated. "Magdelena's beautiful inside and out. She and I are friends. I'd like to court her, but I'm not ready." Toby sighed.

Magdelena had captured his attention the first time they met. She was pretty with her coal-black hair and dark brown eyes. She had a cheerful disposition, and he loved being around her.

"I shouldn't nag you, but I'm your mamm and consider it my duty."

"I don't mind." He did stop at the bakery to talk to Magdelena whenever he was in town, and he enjoyed their conversations. She deserved more of his time, but he didn't have it to give, with taking care of his family's and Andrew's properties. He treasured his time with Daed. "I may not be Magdelena's idea of a suitor. She may want to keep our relationship as friends."

Rachael gave him a stern eye. "It's no secret Magdelena cares for you. Does her family's wealth from the cattle ranch have anything to do with why you won't court her? You shouldn't let their financial status stop you. Magdelena's interested in you and not what you can offer her."

Mamm leaned forward and placed a hand on his arm. "I agree with Rachael. Magdelena wouldn't be seeking you out at church services or the few socials you attend if she cared about your financial situation. Take her on a picnic or a ride through the country. She always asks if you're here and how you're doing. You and she could visit on Sundays."

"We could, but I'm not satisfied at present with what I

have to offer her. When I am, I'll ask her if I may court her. And yes, her daed's success does matter to me. She's accustomed to having more money than most of the Amish in Charm. I'm not in a position to offer her half of what she's used to."

Rachael crossed her arms against her chest. "You'd risk another man catching her eye? Are you willing to take that chance?"

"It's a risk I must take." Toby couldn't stand the thought of another man pursuing Magdelena, but he was set in his ways. He'd need enough money to build a haus for them and his family. Did God plan for him to marry or have a family? He didn't know yet.

Mamm stood. "You're a grown man and you have good reasons why the time isn't right for you and Magdelena to court. I appreciate all you do for this family, but I do feel bad about being a burden to you."

"You're not a burden. You and Daed have been good parents, and Rachael and I have always been close. Our riches may not be in wealth, but we're rich in love and devotion to each other." Toby stood and kissed Mamm's cheek.

"I love you, Toby." She hugged him.

Patches padded into the kitchen and barked.

Toby scratched the dog's perked ear. "What's wrong, boy?"

Patches barked and walked away from him and then looked back.

Toby's throat clenched. He followed Patches to Daed's room, with Mamm and Rachael close behind. Daed lay on his side facing away from them. Was he breathing? He seemed too still.

Toby gently shook his daed's shoulder. "Daed, are you all right?" He checked for a pulse.

Mamm paled. "Is he breathing?"

Daed rolled over onto his back and rubbed his eyes. "What's all the fuss about?"

Rachael gasped.

Mamm sat next to Daed on the bed and caressed his cheek. "Sweetheart, you scared me."

"Why?"

Toby blew out a breath. "Patches gave us a scare. He barked and looked back at us, as if he wanted us to follow him. We thought something was wrong." He'd been afraid Daed had taken his last breath. He loved him so much.

Stepping back, he watched Mamm, as she sat on the side of the bed next to Daed and caress his cheek. His parents had set a good example of how a couple should respect and love each other.

"I don't know what would have alarmed him. I did have trouble getting comfortable."

Mamm smiled. "We're sorry we disturbed you. Close your eyes and rest." She kissed his cheek.

Rachael hugged Toby's arm and whispered, "Each day we have with Daed is a blessing."

He nodded and motioned to the bedroom door. "We should give them time alone." He followed Rachael out of his parents' bedroom to the sitting room.

"I'm sure I would've had the same close relationship with my late fiancé, John, as Mamm and Daed enjoy. I miss him." She gave Toby a veiled glance.

"I have no doubt God has the right man for you. Be patient." He loved his schweschder.

She had been in love with John, who had been perfect for her, until robbers had chased them and caused a buggy accident wherein John was killed. Rachael had been fortunate, although she'd have a limp for the rest of her life. She'd let the limp damage her confidence. He wished she saw herself through his eyes. Her big green eyes and light brown hair made her pretty. She was average build. She was kind and a hard worker. She'd make a good fraa and mamm. He hoped the right suitor would kumme along for her. He was blessed to have her for a schweschder.

Rachael rested her head on his shoulder for a moment. "I'm content with my life. It's you we need to concentrate on."

Magdelena rocked in the porch swing. She'd had a wonderful time with Toby earlier today. It was eight-thirty in the evening and the sun wouldn't set until closer to nine. She'd asked Ellie if the new couple who moved in next door to her could kumme to the social, and she'd invited them. Why hadn't they kumme? The outing would have given them an opportunity to meet other Amish and make new friends. She went inside the haus. "Mamm, I won't be long. I'll take this plate of butter cookies left over from the food today to the new neighbors."

"Yes. I missed them today. I'd hoped to get better acquainted with them." Mamm shrugged. "They may have had too much to do to attend. I almost didn't get my chores done in time to go."

"Do you want to go with me?" Magdelena put her hand on the polished brass doorknob.

Mamm shook her head. "Charity's playing in the backyard. And your daed fell asleep in his chair. He could sleep through a thunderstorm. I better keep an eye on your schweschder."

Magdelena hitched the horse to the buggy and drove in

the direction of the farm next door. She breathed in the fragrance of the honeysuckle and admired the field of tall cornstalks. Daisies and wild purple flowers swayed in the gentle breeze. They had a modest white haus with a wraparound porch. A large gray weathered barn stood tall on one side of the haus, and a cornfield and garden of other beautiful vegetables grew on the other side.

She walked to the door with the plate of cookies and raised her free hand to knock but dropped it before knocking. She stared at the couple through the window in the door. Was Abram yelling at Annie? He towered over Annie and had his arm raised.

She had to do something. She didn't want to tell her parents. They'd tell her to mind her own business. She could trust Toby. She got back in her buggy and headed for his haus. She arrived and went to their door and knocked.

Rachael opened the door. "I'm surprised and happy you're here, but I hope nothing is wrong. You aren't smiling."

Toby entered the room, holding a glass of water. He held it up. "Can I get you anything to drink or eat?"

Magdelena held up the plate of butter cookies. "Please take these butter cookies and help yourselves. I'm still full from the food I had at the social. I'd like to discuss something with you if you have time."

"I'll give you two the room," Rachael said.

"You can stay." Magdelena sat and patted the settee's cushion.

"It's sweet of you, but there's a chair out back calling my name. Mamm's with Daed, and I wouldn't be surprised if she fell asleep next to him. I'd like to take a nap in my chair outside on this beautiful evening." She smiled and left them.

Magdelena wrung her hands. "I'm sorry to bother you with this, but you're the first person who came to mind." She set the cookie plate on the coffee table.

Toby helped himself to a cookie. "These are delicious. What's wrong?"

"Abram and Annie Hook moved into the farm next to us. I would guess their ages close to twenty-one, like us. I asked Ellie if I could invite them to the social this evening, and she liked the idea. I'd stopped at their home earlier today, introduced myself, and coaxed them to kumme. I met her, but not him." Magdelena wasn't sure she was doing the right thing. Maybe she was acting in haste. Since she was here, she might as well get Toby's advice.

"I don't remember meeting them."

"Abram and Annie didn't show. I went to take this plate of butter cookies to them, in hopes of getting better acquainted. It's not easy moving to a new community when you don't know anyone." Magdelena loved Charm, where she'd befriended the girls at the bakery soon after her family moved here. She'd been blessed to meet them sooner than later. Not everyone made friends as easily.

"Did something upsetting happen between you and Annie? You're not your usual happy self."

She gazed into his light brown eyes. He showed such concern. She wasn't surprised. She'd kumme to the right place. "As I was about to knock on the door, I overheard a man's loud voice and a woman crying. I peeked in the window, and Abram had his hand raised. He towered over Annie, and he looked upset. She appeared frightened. I left and came here to discuss this with you."

"I'm glad you came to me, but I'm surprised you didn't tell your parents or the bishop."

"Mamm and Daed would tell me to stay out of it. My parents wouldn't approve of me telling the bishop if they don't want me involved. And I'm positive it's what they would say. Am I poking my nose where it doesn't belong?" Magdelena couldn't let this go. Annie had said she appreciated the invitation. She had to do something.

"Would you like me to go with you to check on Annie?"

Magdelena nodded. "I hoped you'd offer. When I first met Annie, she had a bruise on her cheek. I asked her about it, and she said it was nothing. She told me she was clumsy and always had bruises from not paying attention to what she's doing. I wonder if she told me the truth."

"We'll visit and try to befriend them. They won't confide in us until we're better acquainted. And maybe she is clumsy and this is nothing more than a heated argument with no danger involved. But I'm glad you told me. You can kumme to me about anything, and I'm always here to help."

She relaxed. Toby couldn't have said anything better. Rachael had praised him for his work ethic and support of their family. Her friend had been right when she said he had much compassion for others. "I appreciate this. I still have these cookies to give them." She held them up and smiled.

"Let's step out back and tell Rachael we're leaving." He followed her to the back door and outside. "Rachael, we're going for a ride. We won't be too long."

"Take your time. I'll soak up the end of today's sunshine and enjoy the slight breeze. I wouldn't mind to steal one of those butter cookies." Rachael grinned.

Magdelena lifted the covering on her cookies and passed one to Rachael.

"Danki." Rachael broke the cookie in two and took a bite. "Enjoy your ride."

They bid her farewell and strolled to the front of the haus.

"Let's take my buggy." Magdelena stepped in the buggy and waited for Toby to untie the reins from the hitching post.

He got in and they drove to Abram and Annie's haus. "Rachael's right. The grass is thick and green, and the flowers are more vibrant. The trees and bushes are full of leaves. I love warm sunny days like this."

"Me, too. Danki for kumming with me. I shouldn't take you away from your daed."

"He was tuckered out from the social, but it was good for him. He'll probably nap a little while longer. And I'm enjoying spending time with you."

Magdelena's heart beat fast. She liked him, and their friendship was growing. "I hope you don't find me too forward."

"Not at all."

"We'll make this a short visit and keep in touch with them after this." Toby drove the short distance and pulled into the Hooks' lane.

Magdelena nodded, held her plate of cookies, and waited for him to tie the horse to the post. They walked together to the door and he knocked.

Annie answered the door, her eyes puffy and red, as if she'd been crying. "Magdelena, it's getting late. Is anything wrong?"

"No. This is Toby Schlabach. He's a friend I wanted to

introduce to your husband, Abram. I missed you at Ellie's social this evening. I brought a plate of leftover butter cookies from the supper social. Do you mind if we kumme inside? We promise not to stay too long."

"Who's at the door at this hour?" Abram joined his fraa at the door.

Magdelena looked at the tall and broad-shouldered man with a bushy beard and eyebrows. She wasn't sure if Abram's hands on his hips and serious eyes meant he was cautious or angry. He towered over short Annie. This might have been a bad idea.

Annie gestured for them to kumme inside. "Abram, this is Magdelena Beachy, our neighbor, and her friend Toby Schlabach."

Magdelena stepped inside the living room and stood next to Toby. She held out the cookie plate to Annie.

Annie accepted the cookies from Magdelena. "These won't last long. They're my favorite."

Toby held his hand out to Annie's husband. "Nice to meet you."

Abram didn't smile but shook his hand. "Have a seat."

They sat on the soft blue cushions on the oak settee.

"Annie, your haus is lovely," Magdelena said. "You've got everything neat and in order from just moving in last week."

A wedding-ring quilt of blue and white patches of material lay hung on an oak quilt rack. There wasn't a speck of dirt on the floors. It wasn't easy keeping dirt or grass off the floors during the summer.

Annie motioned for Magdelena to follow her. "I'll show you the rest of the haus."

Magdelena followed her to the big kitchen with oak

cabinets and a roomy dry sink. Pots and pans hung on hooks in order by size above the cookstove. A worn red dish towel hung on a hook near the dry sink. White curtains tied back at the window gave a clear view of the corn- and hayfields. "I love your large kitchen, and your window gives you a view of the fields."

"I like to cook, and I've already made good use of this large kitchen. At my parents' home in Berlin, Ohio, we had a small kitchen." Annie gestured down the hall to the bedrooms and led the way.

Magdelena admired the beautiful patchwork quilts on the beds in the four bedrooms. Each one was a different color, but she liked the blue and red one the best. "Your haus is lovely. How do you keep it so clean and neat after having moved in only a week ago?"

"Abram expects the haus to be in order at all times. My daed was the same way when I was growing up, so I'm used to cleaning a lot." Annie sighed.

"You mentioned Berlin, Ohio. Is Berlin where you're both from?" Magdelena liked Annie.

The girl was sweet. But she seemed uncomfortable. Why wouldn't she look Magdelena in the eye? Was she shy?

They sat at the maple kitchen table, with two matching chairs on each side, away from the men in the living room. Annie rose and opened a cupboard. "Yes, Berlin is where I grew up. Would you like anything to drink?"

Magdelena shook her head. "No, danki. We won't stay long. It will be dark soon."

"My parents were older when I was born, and I didn't have siblings. After they died, I wasn't sure how I was going to take care of the farm by myself. Abram was a widower. His fraa hadn't been gone long, and he suggested an arranged marriage. He wanted a fresh start, and so we sold his farm and mine. Abram always says I talk too much. I'm sorry to bore you with all these details."

Magdelena covered Annie's hand. She was glad to have time alone with her, away from Abram and Toby. "Don't apologize. Conversations help us get better acquainted and close. I work at the bakery in town. Kumme by tomorrow and I'll introduce you to my friends." She swallowed around the lump in her throat. She didn't know whether to admit she'd been there earlier. But she wouldn't leave until she knew Annie was all right. She moved closer to Annie and lowered her voice. "I was here earlier. I overheard Abram yelling and you crying. I peeked in the window and he had his hand raised. Annie, are you all right? I'm sorry to intrude, but I can't leave your home in good conscience if you're in danger."

Annie withdrew her hand from under Magdelena's. "You don't have to worry about me. Abram yells and he gets frustrated, but he would never harm me. We have harmless spats, like any other couple. And I'm truly clumsy. I bruise easily. I promise you I'm fine."

Magdelena didn't know whether to believe her or not. Annie seemed sincere but nervous. They'd just met. Annie had no reason not to trust her. She had to take her at her word. "I shouldn't have mentioned it, but I wouldn't rest until I did. I hope you'll forgive me for asking."

"I'm surprised you'd ask me this, but I'm not upset. You meant well." Annie gave her a weak smile.

Toby and Abram entered the kitchen.

"We should be going, Magdelena. The sun is about to set," Toby said.

Abram and Annie showed Toby and Magdelena to the door.

Abram clapped a hand on Toby's shoulder. "Danki for stopping by. It's been a pleasure."

Toby nodded.

Magdelena hugged Annie and they said their goodbyes. She strode with Toby to the buggy and he offered his hand as she stepped in and sat on the bench before he got inside.

"How was your conversation with Abram? He must be over six and a half feet tall, and he has the broadest shoulders. He towers over me, and Annie is a bit shorter than I am. I'd be afraid of him if he were yelling at me."

"Abram didn't warm up to me right away. He was direct and serious with his questions at first. Then he relaxed and we had a comfortable conversation. He said they didn't attend the social due to being exhausted getting their place in order. I believe he was telling the truth and not trying to avoid it. How was your visit with Annie?"

"Annie doesn't have parents or siblings. Abram was a widower who offered to marry her. Sounds like they have a marriage of convenience. I was bold. I confessed I'd been to their haus earlier and overheard yelling. She was shocked and embarrassed, but she insists he'd never harm her. She said he yells when he's frustrated." Magdelena didn't feel at ease about the situation. She hoped her doubts were unfounded.

"Did you believe her?" Toby glimpsed at her and then watched the road.

"I hope she's telling me the truth. She was convincing. I'll have to take her word for it. I shouldn't have dragged you over here on my silly suspicions and gotten you involved." Magdelena glanced at Toby and felt a pang of guilt for taking Toby away from his family on a suspicion something was wrong at the Hooks'. She cared too much about people sometimes. She was a fixer, and she couldn't stand for anyone to be afraid or hurt or sad.

"You're a compassionate and caring woman. Don't change. It's another reason I like you. And Rachael praises you for it. She said you've helped many women in need by giving them food and dry goods. You were right to bring this to my attention. At best, we made two new friends. He and I talked. He's a guarded man. It's difficult to tell much from one conversation with him whether I think he'd harm Annie."

"I appreciate you for not making me feel like a busybody. I am sincere in caring about Annie's well-being. I'm relieved you're comfortable she's safe after talking with Abram. Can you imagine if I'd told Daed or the bishop? They would have insisted I stop meddling in other people's business. They would have been so frustrated with me."

"I'm flattered you asked me. No one got angry and all is well."

Her instincts were right about Toby. She knew she could trust him to handle this in the best manner possible. He hadn't hesitated to accompany her and talk to Abram, relieving her mind. "Danki, Toby."

"Did you notice how everything was in its rightful place? They've been there a week, and their place looks like no one lives there. Our haus is clean, but we have clothes in the laundry basket, and Daed's blankets are thrown over the end of the settee. Sometimes the dishes don't get done right away." Toby chuckled. "Rachael says you can't stand for anything not to be in its place."

Magdelena sighed. "It's true."

. "I could tell when we were at Ellie's social. You couldn't stand for my shirt to be dirty. I saw you eyeing it when we talked."

She grinned. "You're right. It did drive me mad. I wanted to wash it in the pond. I can be ridiculous when things aren't neat and in order." She drove her parents and Charity mad at home straightening the towels in the kitchen drawer and in the closet. She had to have the dishes and glasses in perfect rows in the cabinets.

Rachael and Maryann teased her whenever she washed the dirty baking dishes too often, instead of doing them all at once at the end of the day, and when she mopped the kitchen floor three times a day, even though it would be soiled from flour and their baking ingredients minutes later.

"It's not a bad trait. You and Annie must have it in common. You and I should reach out to them at Sunday services and socials. You'll be better at it than me since I stay home to take care of Daed if he's not able to attend."

She nodded. "I'll do my best."

Toby drove her buggy to his haus. "It's getting dark. Maybe I should follow you home."

"You're thoughtful, but I've got my lantern, and home is close by. I'll be fine. Danki again."

"I'll stop in the bakery soon."

"I look forward to it." Magdelena left and headed home.

Toby hadn't disappointed her. He kept showing her more reasons to keep their friendship going and hope they might end up courting someday soon. She didn't want an arranged marriage or one of convenience, like Annie. She wanted to fall in love with the man she chose to wed. She couldn't wait for Toby to visit her at the bakery.

She wished she could talk with him every day. Rachael had commented a couple of times about women who had brought food to their haus asking to speak with Toby. Magdelena found herself getting jealous. He seemed interested in her, but he was nice to everyone. Was she reading too much into their time together?

Chapter Two

Magdelena ignored her family's chatter at the breakfast table Thursday morning. She couldn't quit thinking about Toby and her conversation and wading in the pond with him at the social yesterday. She was giddy around him. She'd been interested in him for months. They'd developed a friendship, and what better way to start a relationship?

Mamm slathered raspberry jam on a biscuit. "I heard you kumme right after dark. I couldn't go to sleep until I knew you were safe at home."

"Sorry. Time got away from me. Toby and I visited the Hooks. We had a nice time."

"Good." Mamm chatted about a new recipe she'd found for a chicken casserole.

Magdelena half listened. She liked remembering her evening with Toby. She hoped he would show at the bakery today.

"Magdelena!" Charity nudged her schweschder. "Why won't you answer me?"

She shook herself out of her musings. "I'm sorry. What was the question?"

Charity never ran out of questions to ask. "You and

Toby laughed and had a good time at the social, didn't you? Are you and Toby courting, like me and Peter?" Charity gave her a mischievous grin.

Mamm sighed. "Little one, you are too young to call your friendship with Peter courting. You're friends."

Daed grinned. "You may as well give up. She won't give in. It's harmless. They're kinner."

Magdelena took her dirty plate to the sink. "Toby and I are friends."

"You're not telling the truth." Charity crossed her arms.

"Be nice to your schweschder." Mamm gave Charity a stern look and then got up and poured herself and Daed another cup of coffee. "Go make your bed, and then you and I will make a butterscotch pie."

Charity drank the last of her milk and swiped her mouth with the back of her sleeve. "Can I lick the spoon after we're done pouring the mix in the piecrust?"

Mamm nodded. "But not before we're done, like you did last time. Understand?"

Charity stared at her feet. "All right."

Daed walked with Magdelena to the door. "Do you have your dinner?"

Mamm rushed to the counter and handed Magdelena a bag. "Here you go."

"Danki. I'll be home right after work." She was glad Mamm had put a stop to Charity's questions. Her little schweschder and Peter liked to talk, and they were the worst to get an idea in their heads and then tell whatever they'd dreamed up to all their friends. She didn't want anyone saying she and Toby were courting until it was true. Then they could tell the world.

Daed whistled a hymn while they harnessed the horse to the buggy. She stepped into the buggy, sat on the bench, and took the reins from him. Her daed was tall. He had piercing brown eyes and a thick build. And a confident stance on everything, which did annoy her sometimes. Mamm mirrored Magdelena's black hair and dark eyes. Her parents made a handsome couple. Mamm agreed with Daed on all things. Sometimes she wished Mamm would take up for her and Charity when he was too strict.

"Have a good day, Daed."

"You do the same, sweet dochder."

Magdelena left the farm and drove to town. She cherished her close relationship with her family. No one could figure how Charity got her light red curly hair. Charity could be a handful, but she wouldn't change her. Smart, inquisitive, and stubborn, she surprised them with her quick wit and how fast she learned to sew and crochet.

Magdelena pulled into the livery, passed the reins to Clyde, and lifted her bag. "Danki."

"Be careful crossing the road. We've got more wagons in town today than usual. There's a sale at the hardware store. People tend not to watch where they're going." He offered her his hand, and she took it and got out of the buggy. "Good day."

She waited for a wagon to pass, and then she dashed across the road to the bakery to avoid the next buggy. She opened the door and entered the bakery and walked to the kitchen. "Good morning."

Rachael clapped the flour from her hands. "I made blueberry muffins for Sheriff Williams and Dr. Harrison."

"They'll be delighted." Magdelena stowed her bag in a cabinet and then removed her apron from a hook and put it on. "Turnovers and pastries sell better for breakfast, and it's difficult to make time for muffins when we have pies, cakes, and cookies to whip up to display. You're kind to have them for our two special regulars."

The sheriff and doctor claimed their stools each workday and shared a paper and ordered something from the shelf. They'd become good friends. She looked forward to their visits.

Maryann hurried through the doorway to the kitchen. "I'm sorry I'm late. Betsy was grumpy this morning. And I burnt the scrambled eggs for breakfast. I had to make them over again, making me late dropping Betsy to Hannah. I was trying to do too many things at once."

Magdelena rubbed Maryann's back. "Would you like the day off? Rachael and I can manage the bakery." She'd noticed Maryann had been late and tired often since she'd gotten married again. Her first marriage had been to an Englischer, who'd gambled away their money and gotten himself killed over a debt he owed. She loved Maryann, and she was thankful Ellie had gone with Joel, Maryann's bruder and now Ellie's husband, to bring her back to Charm to live life as Amish again. She and her friends were thrilled to attend Maryann's marriage to Andrew. He was a devoted husband to her friend and loving daed to Betsy, and he had taught Toby handcrafting furniture and given him the job to manage his property. The two men had become best friends.

"I miss Mamm for many reasons. She made my life easier after I returned to Charm. She took care of Betsy while I worked here until she died. Now I have a home and husband to take care of again, and I'm having a difficult time adjusting." Tears dripped onto her cheeks. "I'm torn. I love working here with you both and the customers. It would be best for me to quit the bakery, but I don't want to let you or Liza down."

Rachael hugged Maryann. "Don't cry. We understand, and we want what's best for you and your family. You've taught both of us how to order the supplies and do the recordkeeping. Liza quit when she got married to Jacob. She'll be happy for you."

"You don't need to give notice. Stop at Liza's haus and tell her. Then get Betsy from Hannah and enjoy your day. If we need to hire another baker, we'll ask Liza and we'll find someone." Magdelena gave her a reassuring smile. "I don't like watching you struggle like this."

Maryann hugged them. "I love you both. I appreciate this. I really do."

Magdelena watched her leave and leaned on the counter. "I'm going to miss her."

"Me, too." Rachael sighed.

Magdelena followed Rachael to the kitchen and pulled her favorite white porcelain bowl out of the cabinet and set it on the worktable. "Should we hire another girl? What if one of us gets sick? Liza, Ellie, Hannah, and Maryann have all worked at the bakery and then quit to take care of their families. I don't want them to have to kumme in on a moment's notice."

"You and I have not gotten sick often. We can manage this place ourselves. We might not have the selection of baked goods as usual, but we'll get by." Rachael added a half teaspoon of salt to her dough. "Let's take the day to discuss and think it over and then discuss our ideas with Liza."

She and Rachael discussed the matter until it was time to open the bakery, and then Magdelena washed her hands outside at the water pump. She came back in to find Toby at the counter.

"Good morning." He tipped his hat and his gaze locked with Magdelena's.

Her cheeks warmed. "What a pleasant surprise! I thought I'd locked the door, and I was about to unlock it for customers. You're here early. We've got your favorite peach jam pastries."

"I'll take two." He sat on the stool at the side counter.

She served him two pastries. "Coffee?"

He nodded.

She poured him a cup and passed it to him. "Maryann won't be working with us. We're considering hiring another girl. We can manage both the baking and waiting on customers, but if one of us can't kumme in for some reason, it would be difficult for one to work alone. We don't foresee having this happen often, but two bakers and a girl at the counter is perfect."

"What about Annie?"

Magdelena raised her brows. "I doubt Abram would approve. I got the impression he wants her there taking care of the haus."

Rachael joined them. "Toby, did Magdelena tell you Maryann has decided to leave the bakery and stay home with Betsy?"

"Yes, she did. I suggest you consider Annie, Magdelena's new neighbor, as a replacement. I'm not sure she'd be interested, but it's a thought. She and Abram don't have kinner." Toby wiped peach jam from his lips. Toby took another sip of his coffee and stood. "I'd better be going. See you at home later, Rachael." He stopped at the door, smiled, and tipped his hat at Magdelena.

Magdelena's face warmed and she smiled and watched him leave. Then she recounted her visit to Annie and Abram's home to Rachael. "I wouldn't have considered her if Toby hadn't brought her up. I'm glad he did. Working here might be good for her, and it wouldn't hurt to ask. What do you think?" She'd be surprised if Abram let her work outside the home. He gave the impression he wanted meals and chores done at certain times, but she shouldn't judge him.

Rachael shrugged. "When the time is right, ask her. But if her husband isn't in favor of her working, then we won't pursue it."

"All right. I'll wait until I have a good opportunity to mention the job to her." Magdelena followed Rachael to the kitchen. She sniffed the air. "Do you have cookies in the oven?" She snatched a pot holder, opened the door, and removed the pan of browned butter cookies.

"Goodness! I almost burned them." Rachael put her hands on her cheeks. "I had all my ingredients together for a piecrust, and then I went to greet Toby and forgot about them."

Magdelena moved the cookies with a spatula from the tray to a large plate. "They're not burnt. A little crunchy, maybe. We'll discount them." She took them to the counter and put them on the shelf marked half price.

Dr. Harrison and Sheriff Williams strolled in.

Dr. Harrison took his favorite seat at the counter. "Good morning, Magdelena."

"Good morning, gentlemen." She served them each a cinnamon roll covered in white icing. "A favorite of yours. What do you think?"

Both men nodded and grinned.

Dr. Harrison smiled. "Perfect, Magdelena."

"Yes, you've made me a happy man." Sheriff Williams bit into the roll.

She poured coffee into two mugs and gave each of them one.

Sheriff Williams handed half of his newspaper to Dr. Harrison. Dr. Harrison opened his paper. "The actress Grace McHugh drowned while filming a scene for the movie *Across the Border* in Cañon City, Colorado. Such a tragedy. She was young."

The sheriff put his half of the paper on the counter. "Who would've thought acting could be dangerous? What happened, and did they recover her body?"

"As she was riding her horse across the river, the river was high and running fast. The horse stumbled, and she fell off and drowned. The cameraman threw down his camera and jumped in to save her. He also drowned."

Magdelena couldn't imagine being an actress and having to memorize lines. She didn't understand why they would risk their lives for an acting job. It didn't make sense to her. Ellie had seen films when she ran away from the Amish life. She was glad Ellie had come to her senses and returned. Ellie told her seeing a film was exciting and the story had seemed real. The actresses wore beautiful clothes, and the men were handsome. Toby was the only handsome man who interested her. Magdelena had no desire to watch any kind of film.

Dr. Harrison nudged the sheriff's arm. "Is it true what Gladys told my wife? Are you refusing to buy her the sofa table she wants from Andrew's furniture store?" He turned to Magdelena. "By the way, where is Andrew's wife, Maryann?"

Magdelena topped off his coffee. "She won't be working with us. She's decided to stay home and take care of her family."

"We'll miss her." The doctor sipped his coffee and

addressed the sheriff. "Andrew has some fine pieces in his furniture store. You should buy Gladys the table. You won't find one better to fit the space where you want to put it."

Sheriff Williams shook his head. "You're supposed to be on my side. The table we have is fine."

"You mean the one you had before you married Gladys? The one with the scratches and missing corner?" Dr. Harrison rolled his eyes. "You need to replace the eyesore. Don't you agree, Magdelena?"

Magdelena gave them each an extra napkin. "Gladys has told me she would love to replace the table. It would mean a lot to her if you would consider it." The best friends teased each other often, and she enjoyed their harmless banter. Since Amish weren't supposed to read the newspaper, she was glad they discussed interesting articles and the latest news about what President Wilson had to say and other happenings. The men both loved their wives, and they often gave each other good advice.

Sheriff Williams harrumphed. "I'll ponder it."

"Why wouldn't you want to please Gladys with this gift? You can afford it."

"My late wife and I bought the table Gladys wants to get rid of when we first married. It's the last piece of furniture I have from my life with her before she died. Gladys replaced all the other furniture after we wed."

"You didn't tell her why you don't want to replace the table, did you?" Dr. Harrison teased.

"No, I knew better. I don't want to hurt her feelings. I'm in trouble either way." He heaved a big sigh. "Are you finished? Let's go see if the table is still there. I'll need your help getting it into my wagon. Glad I brought the wagon to work today."

Magdelena grinned. The sheriff was a softy. He always gave in to whatever Gladys wanted. Their marriage was happy, and she hoped for one like it. She bid them farewell as they left.

An hour later, Mamm and Charity came into the bakery.

Magdelena stopped wiping the counter. "What brings you two to the bakery this morning?"

Charity pointed to the assorted cookie tray in the glass display counter. "We came to see you." She pointed to the cookies. "I sure would like to have a cherry jam cookie."

Mamm waggled a finger at Charity. "You'll have sticky fingers and jam on your clothes if you have one of those, Miss Messy. Pick another one."

"Stay for a minute and sit at the counter. She can finish it here, and I'll wipe Charity's face and hands before you leave." Magdelena pulled the tray of cookies off the shelf.

"Please, Mamm?" Charity gave her an impish grin.

"Don't dally. We don't have all day." Mamm took a seat at the counter beside Charity.

"What can I get you, Mamm?" Magdelena served her schweschder a cookie and a half glass of lemonade.

"I'll take a piece of the white cake with white frosting. Danki. I'd like to buy a sugar milk pie for supper tonight. I didn't have time to make one, and your daed mentioned he'd like one."

"I'll pay for it and bring it home. My treat."

"Danki, you sweet dochder." Mamm gestured to the coffeepot. "Mind if I have a cup?"

"I meant to pour you a cup." Magdelena served her mamm the coffee.

Toby entered. "Look who's here. Greetings, Mrs. Beachy. How are you, Miss Charity?"

Mamm smiled and nodded.

"I'm fine. Want a bite of my cookie?" Charity held it up to him.

"No, but danki for the offer." Toby grinned.

Magdelena smiled. Charity loved Toby. He was good with kinner. He played with the kinner for a bit whenever he attended the after-church meals or socials. "Toby, what has brought you back to the bakery today?"

"I wanted to surprise Andrew and bring him and Maryann some of your apple turnovers." Toby sat next to Charity.

"Toby, how is your daed? I was happy he came to Ellie and Joel's evening social." Mamm finished her coffee.

"He's not good. We're thankful for each day we still have him with us." Toby sighed.

Charity wiped her mouth with the back of her pudgy hand. "You should kumme to supper tonight. Mamm is buying a sugar milk pie for dessert. Magdelena wants you to kumme. Don't you?"

Magdelena's cheeks warmed. She could kiss her little schweschder for this. Toby would find Charity hard to resist. She had a cherubic face and won people over with her angelic smile.

"You're wilkom to kumme, but I understand if you have things to do." Magdelena wiped Charity's face and hands.

Mrs. Beachy stood and helped Charity off the stool. "Please join us, Toby. We'd love to have you."

Rachael came from the kitchen to the counter and hugged Mrs. Beachy and then Charity. "I had to kumme and say good morning to two of my favorite people."

"What about me?" Toby gave her a mischievous grin and held out his arms.

"You're my favorite, too." Rachael smiled and accepted his hug.

"Rachael, we invited Toby to supper tonight. Please kumme with him." Mrs. Beachy put her hand on the doorknob.

"I should stay home and help Mamm, but Toby would love to kumme. Right, Toby?" Rachael nodded to him.

He stood and stared at his feet. "Sure."

Charity got up and bounced on her toes. "Will you play pick-up sticks with me and Magdelena?"

He nodded. "How could I turn down a game of pick-up sticks? Of course."

Mamm grabbed Charity's hand. "Is five-thirty a good time for you, Toby?"

"Yes. Danki."

Rachael excused herself and returned to the kitchen.

Magdelena watched the others leave, and then she wrapped four apple turnovers for Toby. "The sheriff and Dr. Harrison left the bakery and were headed over to Andrew's store to buy a sofa table. Is it one of your pieces, by any chance?"

Rachael had mentioned Toby worked late into the night sometimes in Andrew's workshop handcrafting furniture and household items to sell.

He stood taller and grinned. "It is one of my pieces. The sofa table was one of my more difficult projects. I had trouble deciding what size legs to put on it. In the end, I was pleased with the results. I'm happy the sheriff is going to buy it for Gladys. They're such kind people and good friends. Andrew mentioned Gladys had made several trips to examine and mull it over."

Two women strolled in. One, a short and stocky woman, said, "Warm, fresh bread must be in the oven. The aroma in here is delightful."

Toby tipped his hat to Magdelena. "I'll get out of your way."

"Goodbye, Toby." She watched him leave and then faced the ladies. "How can I help you?"

The taller woman, who had orange-red hair, winked at Magdelena. "He's a looker. You better hang on to him." She gazed at the pies. "I'd like a strawberry pie, two loaves of white bread, and a dozen oatmeal cookies."

Magdelena managed a smile. Her eyes must've lingered too long on Toby for this woman to make such a forward comment. She'd have to be more careful. She packaged the goodies and accepted payment. She met the other woman's gaze. "Would you like anything?"

"I'll take two butterscotch pies."

Magdelena accepted her coins and passed her the wrapped pies. "Danki for kumming in."

At the end of his workday, Toby drove home to get ready for supper with the Beachy family. He entered the haus and ran into Rachael. "You have put me in an awkward situation with Magdelena."

"What do you mean? It's supper, not a wedding," Rachael huffed.

"I need more time before I go to supper alone with Magdelena's family."

"Friends have supper together often, and you're being silly. You can't take your eyes off her whenever the two of you are together, and she's smitten with you. Go and have a wonderful time." Rachael unhooked a skillet from the wall. "Mamm is outside taking sheets off the clothesline." She glanced at the clock on the shelf above the sink. "You better get going. You don't want to be late. I'll tell Mamm and Daed where you've gone for supper."

Toby gave her a heavy sigh and left. He got in the buggy and headed for Magdelena's haus. He smiled. The sun warmed his cheeks and added to his cheery mood. The oak, maple, and other hardwood trees were full of beautiful green leaves. He loved the dogwood, magnolia, and hibiscus trees. Most of the homes had plastic sugar-water holders to attract the hummingbirds. Rachael kept their feeder full of the mixture for the tiny birds who zipped through the air with such speed. They fascinated him.

He was happy Charity had invited him to supper. Magdelena had a hold of his heart, and the more he was around her, the more he cared for her. She had a wonderful mamm and schweschder. Her daed intimidated him. The man ran a successful cattle ranch business, and he was one of the wealthier men in their community. He'd always been polite to Toby, but he didn't linger for conversation. Toby wasn't ready to court Magdelena, but his heart wasn't cooperating. He found every excuse to go to the bakery or to seek her out.

He parked his buggy and strolled to the door.

Charity pushed the door open and yelled, "Toby's here!" She ushered him inside.

Magdelena came into the living room and wiped her hands on her white apron. "I'm helping Mamm with supper. It's almost ready. Would you like a glass of lemonade?"

Toby sat on the settee. The haus had two stories and was one of the largest Amish homes in Charm. You could fit twenty people in this room comfortably. "I'll wait and have a glass of lemonade with supper. Danki."

Charity dragged her box of pick-up sticks onto the

floor. "Ready to play?" She looked out the window. "Wait a minute. Someone is kumming down the lane." She got up and ran closer to the window. "It's Aunt Gloria and Uncle Otis."

Magdelena moved to stand behind Charity. "What a wilkom surprise. Mamm and Daed will be thrilled. Toby, my aunt and uncle live in Mt. Hope. We visit each other as often as we can. With work schedules, it's difficult. I can't wait for you to meet them."

"They will want time with your family. I should leave and kumme back another time," Toby said.

Charity looked at him with puppy dog eyes. "No. Please stay."

"You're not interfering." Magdelena gestured for him to sit. "You should stay. Aunt Gloria makes the best fudge. She always brings us some. I'll give you a piece."

"How can I resist?" He chuckled.

Gloria and Otis opened the door. "Greetings! I brought fudge," Gloria said.

Charity skipped to them.

Gloria and Otis came inside the haus and hugged her.

Toby stood while Magdelena made the introductions. "You're in time for supper."

Otis rubbed his stomach. "I'm hungry, and I love your mamm's cooking."

Gloria held her hands up. "What can I say? She is a wonderful cook." She pulled Charity and Magdelena to her and hugged them. "I have missed my girls. I had to kumme and visit." She smiled at Toby. "I look forward to getting better acquainted with you. Any friend of Magdelena and Charity's is a friend of ours. You're wilkom to kumme with them to our home anytime and visit. We'd love to have you."

"Danki, Mrs. Brenneman."

"Toby, call me Gloria."

"Danki, Gloria." Toby liked the sweet woman with rosy cheeks and dimples. He offered his hand to her husband. "Mr. Brenneman, it's a pleasure to meet you."

The tall, thin man's brown eyes sparkled. He didn't have a strand of hair on his head, and his smile was as friendly as his fraa's.

"Call me Otis." Magdelena's uncle clapped a strong hand to Toby's shoulder.

"Toby and I were going to play pick-up sticks. Want to play, Aunt Gloria? We'll put the sticks on a table so you can sit in a chair, and we'll sit in the settee across from you." Charity looked at her. "Please, Aunt Gloria."

"Maybe after supper, sweetheart." Gloria patted Charity's back.

"I'll play one game before supper." Toby sat on the brown cotton rug across from Charity.

Mrs. Beachy came into the living room from the kitchen, wiping her hands on her apron. "I recognized your voices. What a wonderful surprise." She hugged Gloria and smiled at Otis.

Gloria passed her the tin. "I couldn't kumme without bringing your favorite fudge."

Mrs. Beachy accepted the pan. "I won't be able to keep my hands off this. Danki."

"I hope you cooked enough food for us." Otis patted his growling stomach.

"I always cook enough food to feed five families. Gloria, your bruder will be glad you're here." She cocked her head to Toby. "Have you met Magdelena's friend?"

"Yes. He's such a gentleman. I'm looking forward to

getting to know him better this evening." Gloria grinned at Toby.

Magdelena's daed entered from the back door to the living room. "I was way out back chopping up a downed tree. I had no idea you were here. Good to have you both with us." Mr. Beachy hugged his schweschder and nodded at Otis.

He offered his hand to Toby. "Don't get up. You're keeping Charity occupied and out of Mamm's way. You should get an extra helping of dessert. Glad you're here."

Toby shook his meaty hand but didn't get up. "Danki, Mr. Beachy. She's beating me at pick-up sticks."

"Call us Mark and Bernice. Charity has a steady hand for such a little girl. I don't know how she does it. She is much better at it than I am."

"This is my favorite game. Even Magdelena doesn't win when we play." Charity beamed.

Magdelena's face warmed and she shrugged. "It's true."

Bernice hooked her arm through Gloria's. "Magdelena, kumme with us to the kitchen."

"Otis, I tore down the old smoke haus and built a new one. Kumme with me, and I'll show it to you."

Otis followed him outside.

Charity picked up a stick without moving the others. "Toby, you should marry my schweschder."

Toby chuckled. "Maybe I will someday, but I'd like to keep this secret between us."

Charity waited until she took her turn to answer. "I can't promise. I'm not good at keeping secrets."

Toby didn't want Charity to mention her suggestion at the table. "How about for tonight?"

"I'll try." She removed a stick he was sure would move the others, but she surprised him.

"You must've practiced this game with Peter." Toby moved all the sticks with his turn.

"He's going to marry me someday. He teaches me lots of things."

"You've got a while before you're old enough to get married."

"Peter says we're courting for a long time until we're sixteen, then we can get married."

Toby stopped playing the game for a minute. "What makes sixteen the right age?"

"I asked Magdelena if anyone gets married at sixteen. She said yes."

Toby doubted if Magdelena realized Charity was asking for her and Peter. He was amazed at Peter and Charity's close friendship. They were together as much as their parents would let them. Life was easy for them, at present. They didn't have to worry about parental approval or making adult decisions. He envied them.

Charity talked him into two more games.

Otis and Mark returned. "Who's winning?" Mark stood over them and observed the game.

"Me, and I've won two games of pick-up sticks!" Charity grinned.

Bernice stood in the open doorway between the living room and kitchen. "Supper's ready."

"We'll be right there, Mamm." Charity picked up the last stick. "Look, Toby, I won!" Charity beamed.

"Yes. You did. Congratulations." Toby followed her to the kitchen.

Otis and Mark were ahead of them and took their seats at the kitchen table.

Mark said, "Charity will keep you occupied as long as you let her. Don't feel obligated to entertain her."

"Sit by me, Toby." Charity wrinkled her brows. "Daed, he likes playing games with me. Right?" She looked at Toby.

"I sure do." Toby sat between Magdelena and Charity.

Everyone at the table filled their plates with steaming hot green beans, beef roast, and boiled potatoes. He breathed in the beef's aroma. It was a treat when his family had beef. Mark had given them generous portions of beef several times.

Mark took a slice of white bread from the basket. "Toby, I have some beef for you to take home later. And, Bernice, I told Toby to address us by our first names. I was sure you'd approve."

"Yes, of course." Bernice smiled at Toby.

"Danki to you both."

"Does cattle ranching interest you?" Mark slathered butter on his bread.

Magdelena cleared her throat. "Daed, he's taking care of Andrew's farm and making furniture. He doesn't have time for anything else."

"Let the man answer, Magdelena."

Magdelena's cheeks warmed and she stared at her plate.

"She's right. I love farming and handcrafting furniture and other household pieces. It doesn't leave much time for other interests. I admire your ranch and how you've grown your business. It couldn't have been easy."

"No. It's been hard work, but I love it. I'd hire you if you'd like to work as a ranch hand and learn the ropes. I'm sure Andrew wouldn't stand in your way."

Toby didn't want Mark to assume he was here vying for a job on the ranch. He did want to court Magdelena when he was ready, and he didn't want Mark to question his motives. He was happy working for Andrew, and they'd formed a close friendship. His friend was flexible and generous in allowing him to split the money for furniture he sold in the store and in his use of the workshop. He wanted to form a friendship with Mark. "Danki for your generous offer, but I'm not looking to change jobs right now."

"As you wish." Mark frowned.

Gloria handed her bruder the jam. "Bruder of mine, is peach still your favorite?"

Toby was grateful Gloria had rescued him from an awkward minute with Mark. Magdelena's serious face turned into a smile.

He didn't want to leave Mark disgruntled with him. "You've been generous to give our family beef, and we appreciate it."

"Don't mention it. I'm sorry your daed is ill. So often I take for granted what God has provided for our family, including our health."

Otis nodded. "It's true. Without good health, we can't work. I admire you, Toby, for what you're doing for your family."

"It's a pleasure to provide for them. We're blessed to have all formed a close bond."

Charity put her fork on the plate. "Is it time for dessert? I want to give Toby a chance to win at our next game."

"Yes. I'll give you a big piece." Mamm piled dirty plates and carried them to the sink. Magdelena helped her with the rest.

Charity glanced at Toby. "Toby needs a big piece, too."

Gloria cut the sugar milk pie and served Charity and Toby. "Are you sure you can finish your pie? It might be a little much for you, little one."

"Not for me. I love any kind of pie." Charity put a forkful in her mouth.

"Danki, Gloria." Toby loved sugar milk pie. He could've devoured three pieces.

Magdelena finished putting the dirty supper dishes into the washbasin to let them soak and sat at the same time as Gloria and Mamm to have her pie. "Charity, Toby and I are going for a boat ride. He won't have time for games."

"I'll kumme with you." Charity hurried to put another forkful of pie in her mouth.

"I'll play you a game of checkers," Gloria said.

"I'll play checkers after I ride in the boat," Charity said.

"Magdelena and Toby need time to themselves. We can play games after we help your mamm clean up the kitchen." Gloria winked at her. "You might have to teach me one of your new board games."

"Aunt Gloria, please play me a game after I go with Toby and Magdelena," Charity pleaded.

Mark finished his pie. "I'm sure Magdelena and Toby don't mind if Charity goes with them, unless Mamm would like her to help with the dishes. They're not courting. They're friends."

Charity clapped her hands. "Danki, Daed."

Toby held his breath a moment until the shock wore off. He was disappointed. He planned to court Magdelena in the future. She was the girl for him. He wanted to prepare them for a better courtship by saving money to build them a haus. It was clear Mark didn't approve of him as a suitor for his dochder. He was poorer than most Amish. But he'd started changing this by selling his furniture. He'd had time here and there to build bedroom and dining table sets. Englischers had bought them from Andrew's store, and he'd have more to sell soon. He'd increased his savings, and this brought him closer to asking Mark to court Magdelena.

Bernice grabbed the washbasin used for dirty dishes.

"Magdelena, Gloria and I will take care of the dishes. You go with Toby. Charity, you will not go on a boat ride right now. You can stay and help."

Charity stuck out her bottom lip. "Do I have to?"

Mark approached her. "You will have to forget about the boat ride. When your mamm asks you to do something, you don't question it. You do it. You help your mamm and Aunt Gloria with the dishes and don't argue or you won't be allowed to play with Peter for a week."

The men left.

Charity hung her head and grabbed a towel to dry dishes.

Magdelena motioned to him. "Toby, let's enjoy this beautiful evening."

They walked through the living room. Toby opened the door for her, and they followed the well-worn path to the placid pond. He turned the hardwood boat over and tossed in two oars. He shoved it half into the water. "You get in, and I'll push it off."

Toby removed and threw his socks and boots on the ground and then jumped in and picked up the oar and paddled away from the haus and then let the boat drift. "Danki for having me over. I feel as if I've known your aunt and uncle for a long time. I'm glad they're here. They are wilkoming and easy to talk to."

"Unlike my daed. I'm sorry for his abrupt behavior. He assumes every man wants to be a cattle rancher." Magdelena shook her head and looked out over the large number of grazing cattle.

"Your daed offered me a job. There's no harm done and no need for you to apologize."

She shouldn't feel responsible for her daed's opinions. He understood her daed wanting the best for his dochder, and it was clear Toby didn't meet his expectations. He hoped to show him he was worthy of Magdelena in the kumming months.

"Charity loves you and Gloria and Otis, too. I don't understand anyone who wouldn't like you." Magdelena's face warmed.

"I like you, Magdelena. You're sweet and such a good person. I'll add *beautiful* and *smart* to the list as well."

"I hope Daed's comments haven't damaged our friendship." Magdelena met his gaze.

"Not at all. I respect him, but I'm saving money to buy a haus." He gazed into her eyes. "I'm not as poor now that I've been selling furniture. It's something I will continue, and I enjoy it." Since the day they met, he'd been smitten. He hadn't had eyes for any other girl.

He tried to lighten the mood. "Patches and Daed are inseparable. I can't danki enough for giving the dog to us. Daed may love the dog more than us. What happened to Patches's parents and the other puppies?"

"Charity was supposed to provide food and water for them. Daed threatened to give them away if she kept forgetting. The third time she forgot, he kept his word. They were gone the next day. He gave them to an Englischer family."

"Do you miss them?" Toby understood Mark's reasoning. But what about the rest of the family's attachment to the dogs?

"I do. Daed could've punished her some other way. Mamm and I loved the dogs, and we'd given all the pups from the last litter away. Charity is brokenhearted. She learned a valuable lesson, but the rest of us got punished for her neglect."

"It must be hard being a parent. Disciplining your kinner wouldn't be a pleasant thing to do, and you have to be effective. I hope to be a daed in the future, and I pray God will give me the wisdom to do the right thing when making decisions for them." His parents hadn't been hard on him and his schweschder. They were sent to their rooms if they misbehaved when they were younger. But maybe Charity required a harsher punishment.

Mark and Otis came to the water's edge a couple of yards away from them.

Mark cupped his mouth. "Time for you and Toby to kumme in. It will be dark soon."

Magdelena gritted her teeth and forced a wave. "We're kumming."

Toby got the message. Mark didn't want him to get any ideas about courting his dochder. He prayed he would change Mark's mind someday soon. He jumped out in the shallow end and pulled the boat to shore. He was glad the men were heading to the haus.

Magdelena stepped out of the boat onto the ground. "I would've liked another half hour with you. It's a warm, peaceful evening to be out on the water. No bugs tonight."

He finished putting on his socks and boots. He'd enjoy being anywhere with Magdelena. "It was nice. Danki for inviting me." He accompanied her to the haus.

Charity hugged his legs. "Daed let me out of my room. I'm not in trouble anymore. Want to play another game with Aunt Gloria and me?"

He tousled her hair. "It's time for me to go home, little one."

Charity looked at him. "Please kumme back soon, Toby."

He nodded and smiled. "Take care, Charity."

Mark handed him a package. "Here's the meat I promised you. Give your daed my best."

"This is very kind of you. Danki." Toby appreciated the

gift, but this was the first time he'd been given the meat. Rachael or Mamm had been home and accepted it when Mark brought the beef over for their family. Mark's attitude at the supper table made him feel as if he needed the handout, and it hurt his pride. A trait God said was a sin, but he was human. The humiliation wasn't going away anytime soon. Had her daed used this opportunity to remind Magdelena he was poor? He wouldn't consider himself poor anymore, but it would make things worse if he didn't take the package. His family would enjoy the beef. He thanked him and bid them farewell again.

Magdelena walked him to his buggy. "Will you kumme to the bakery this week?"

He wanted to take her hand, but he knew he must not until he was ready for a commitment. She gazed at him with those pretty dark eyes and his frustration earlier with her daed dissipated.

"Yes. I look forward to seeing you, and danki again for tonight." He got in his buggy and waved goodbye.

On the way home, he had mixed emotions. He'd enjoyed his time with Magdelena, but her daed's comments disturbed him. Mark hadn't given him the warm reception he'd hoped. Getting his approval to court his dochder wasn't going to be easy.

Chapter Three

Magdelena tossed and turned during the night. Daed had insulted Toby. She was relieved Aunt Gloria and Uncle Otis had been with them to deter Daed's attitude from getting too harsh toward Toby. He made it sound like Toby was poor and foolish and not worthy of her attention. Daed had been raised on a cattle ranch, and he'd been spoiled by his daed.

She didn't want anything to discourage Toby from asking her to court him. She prayed he would ask her soon. She got up, said her prayers, and did her early Friday morning chores and headed for the kitchen. "Good morning. Aunt Gloria, it's wonderful you're here with us, and I'm glad you met Toby."

Aunt Gloria kissed Magdelena's cheek. "Charity sure likes him, and if she does, I'm sure I will, too. He's also quite handsome."

Magdelena's face burned. "He liked you and Uncle Otis, too." She glanced around the kitchen. "Where's Charity? I assume the men are outside."

Mamm served her scrambled eggs. "Charity had to show Uncle Otis her favorite chicks and cats. We all finished breakfast a couple of minutes ago. Your daed's meeting with the cattle hands. Did Toby have a good time last night?"

"Toby's polite, so he wouldn't say otherwise. I apologized for Daed's directness, and Toby said there was no need for me to apologize. Daed gave the impression he was insulted Toby didn't quit his job with Andrew and work for him. Toby emphasized we're friends, but I sense he wants us to court. I suspect Daed's wealth intimidates him. I would accept Toby's offer to court me if he asked." She gripped her skirt, waiting for Mamm to answer. She needed her support.

"Daed has your best interests in mind. You've been raised not wanting for anything. You can buy any selection of fabrics, yarn, and sewing notions you desire. We employ Amish men who depend on us. He doesn't want you to regret your decision to marry any man. He wants you to live in the way you're accustomed."

Aunt Gloria sat next to Magdelena. "My bruder is set in his ways. He doesn't consider Toby the best partner or provider for his dochder. He also doesn't realize a good provider doesn't have to match this family's wealth to be a worthy suitor for you."

"Danki, Aunt Gloria." She glanced over her shoulder at Mamm. "Amish aren't to cherish things. I appreciate what we have and how hard you both work to provide for us. I'm proud Daed provides jobs for men to financially care for their families. And I'm grateful for the life he's given us. But I care about Toby, and he's the special man who has caught my attention. I have no doubt he can provide a good living for us if our friendship should grow into a courtship. I'd like your support if he should ask me." She couldn't tell if Mamm understood her desperation. "Mamm, please."

"I'm not convinced, Magdelena. It's easy to say you'd be content with Toby, since you haven't experienced a life with him. He's poorer than most Amish. Don't get me wrong. I like Toby. Trust your daed's opinion. Why are you sure he'd be the right man for you?"

"I've liked him for a long time. From the moment we met, he captured my attention. Anytime he's around, I'm smiling. He makes me laugh, and I can discuss anything with him. He's smart and gives wise advice. He's not lazy, by any means. Maryann said Andrew can't understand how Toby can do the work of two people on his farm. She wonders if Toby ever sleeps, with as many hours as he works. Rachael said he kummes home for supper and goes back to Andrew's workshop after their daed goes to bed."

"Toby is a kind and honorable man, but it's clear he doesn't have time to court and plan a future. Most of your friends are married. You should give other men interested in you a chance."

"Toby is my choice." Magdelena glanced at the clock. "I should go to work. Danki for breakfast, Mamm." She swallowed her rising disappointment. She had hoped Mamm would be on her side about Toby.

Aunt Gloria rose. "I'll walk you outside. I want every minute I can with you until we leave. I wish we lived in the same town."

Magdelena bid Mamm farewell and went outside with Aunt Gloria. "I'm worried my parents won't give their blessing if Toby asks to court me. We care for each other, and I don't have interest in any other man. What am I going to do?"

Aunt Gloria clasped her hand. "Pray about this, Magdelena. Ask God to intervene. I believe Toby is the one for you. The way he looks at you is hard to miss. It's like when your uncle Otis started looking at me in a star struck way, and I was happy like you. Our love has grown deeper over the years, and I treasure each day we're together. I want the same for you, and I trust your judgment. If you say Toby's the one, I support you. You always know where to find me if you need help convincing your parents."

"I love you, Aunt Gloria. I can always share what's in my heart with you more easily than with my parents. I love them, but we don't always agree."

Money wasn't as much a concern for her as it was for them. Aunt Gloria had always understood her better than Mamm and Daed.

"They have good intentions. Your mamm sticks by your daed in all things, and you shouldn't be upset with her. He's her husband, and they have a strong bond. It's wonderful your parents love and support each other."

Magdelena rested her head on her aunt's shoulder. "I want her to take my side when I need her."

Aunt Gloria kissed and patted Magdelena's cheek. "I understand. My mamm could coax Daed into agreeing to let me go with my friends to an outing or stay overnight with a friend when we knew he may not approve. Every marriage is different. Your mamm chooses not to go against your father's decisions. It's not wrong."

Magdelena hugged Aunt Gloria. "I'm blessed to have two parents who get along as well as they do. I'm also blessed to have you and Uncle Otis here with us for a couple of days."

Aunt Gloria shook her head. "Last night I sat straight up in bed and remembered I had told my friend Louisa I'd help her with a social. We have to head back today. I'm embarrassed to have forgotten. At least we spent time with you. Write when you can, and I'll do the same."

Magdelena was sad her aunt and uncle had to leave so soon, but she understood. "I will. Give Uncle Otis a hug for me. Travel safe."

Daed had harnessed her horse to the buggy. He and Otis and Charity weren't in sight to say goodbye to. Aunt Gloria returned to the haus. Then Magdelena drove to the bakery.

Rachael stood in the kitchen and greeted her with flour on her nose. "I've mixed ingredients for sugar cookies."

Magdelena wiped the flour off Rachael's nose with her forefinger. "I can tell." She giggled. She put on her apron and followed Rachael to the kitchen. "I'm sorry I'm late. Aunt Gloria and Uncle Otis made a surprise visit and had supper with us. Did Toby say anything about last night?"

"Toby came home with a smile on his face. He had a good time at your haus with you and your family."

"Charity dropped her pick-up sticks on the floor and invited him to play the minute he walked inside the haus, and he accepted. I don't know who had more fun. Aunt Gloria and Uncle Otis liked him on sight. She's always been my best supporter and encourager. Aunt Gloria isn't judgmental and is open to discussing any question or concern. I love my parents, but they aren't open to questions about the world or matters of the heart."

Daed and Mamm's matter-of-fact attitude about Toby wasn't fair. It should be her decision as to how long she was willing to wait on Toby.

"You've always spoken about your aunt Gloria and uncle Otis with love. You're blessed to have Gloria as an aunt and close friend. Toby said Charity was fun. He loved playing games with her. And he enjoyed his time with you most of all. I'm happy Toby had a night off. He doesn't take enough breaks from work."

Magdelena removed a metal bowl from the kitchen

cabinet and set it on the worktable centered in the room. She opened the molasses and poured a fourth of a cup in her bowl. "I'm glad he had a good time. Tell me more about Toby's likes and dislikes, flaws, and what he was like as a little boy."

Rachael chuckled. "You do like him a lot. Your smile couldn't grow any wider. And he beamed last night talking about you." She gave Magdelena an impish grin. "Half the fun of falling in love is asking your suitor these questions. I don't want to reveal too much."

"No harm in telling me some of what I asked. What are friends for?" She grinned.

"Keep in mind he's twenty-one and I'm twenty-four. All I know is what our parents have told us until I was about six. As we grew older as kinner, I remember he got in trouble a lot for leaving his clothes and shoes where they didn't belong."

Magdelena grinned. "What else?"

"He would rather work with Daed than play with his friends. When he was too young to do the more dangerous projects, he sulked until Mamm told him to get outside and play or she'd have him clean inside. He and I liked to play board games before bed. We didn't fuss much. His room may be a mess, but a project must be perfect." Rachael's tone grew serious. "Do your parents approve of Toby?"

"Daed and Mamm have reservations about him as a suitor for me. Daed considers a man's wealth in regard to a man I'm interested in. I don't care if Toby doesn't make a lot of money. Whom I choose to court should be up to me."

"Isn't it important for you to have your parents' approval of Toby?"

Magdelena stopped mixing her cookie batter. "Please

don't agree with my parents. I need your encouragement where Toby's concerned."

Rachael's friendship was important to Magdelena. Another benefit of she and Toby marrying would be to have her as a schweschder-in-law. Why would she insinuate that if her parents didn't approve of Toby, she shouldn't consider him?

"I didn't mean to offend you. I love you, and there's nothing more I'd like than to have you and Toby marry someday. Other girls have tried to catch his attention, and he's politely turned them away. You're the first girl he's made an effort to show interest in. But I don't want your liking Toby to cause trouble for you at home." Rachael limped around the worktable and took Magdelena's hand. "And I worry you'll be upset and frustrated with him. His best quality of wanting everything right in his life, including having the right sum of money saved to court you, can also be his worst flaw. I didn't mean I don't support the two of you."

Magdelena heaved a big breath. "You scared me. You and Aunt Gloria are the ones I can talk to about anything. I don't want our being able to talk about anything to change. I'll keep what you've said in mind, but don't worry about me." She loved Rachael's openness, kind heart, and infectious laugh. They'd become close.

Magdelena admired the tarts and cookies lined on trays and ready for the counter. "I'll display these on the shelves in the café and unlock the front door for customers." She slid open the door behind the counter and arranged the desserts for customers to view. She centered the bell and sign on the counter, asking customers to ring for service if no one was present in the front of the store.

Jed Byler came into the bakery clutching his hat to his

chest. "Magdelena, I've been wanting to have a private conversation with you, but you're always surrounded by your friends at socials. I came the minute you opened, hoping we can talk."

Magdelena tensed. She was aware Jed had asked several available women in the community to agree to marry him. He'd been turned down by them. She suspected it was her turn. She didn't have anything against the widower, but he wasn't what she was looking for in a suitor. His sweet fraa, Addie, had died and left him with three kinner. He was short, stodgy, and had two front teeth missing. She had her heart set on Toby. She also wanted to raise a family of her own and not someone else's kinner. "What's on your mind, Jed?"

"I'd like to ask your daed for your hand in marriage. I thought I would approach you first. We don't know each other well, but I need a fraa and a mamm for my household. Addie and I had a happy life together, and I'm sure you and I would, too."

Magdelena gripped her apron. Jed was bold.

"I'm sorry, Jed. I'm interested in another man."

Jed's smile faded. "Has this man asked you to court him?"

She stiffened. It wasn't any of his business. She'd given him her answer. Why wouldn't he accept it? The last thing she wanted was for Jed to approach her parents and for them to think this was a good idea. Jed ran a successful dairy farm. Her daed might consider him suitable because of his financial status. "I consider this a private matter, Jed."

"Are you or are you not courting this man?" Jed crossed his arms.

Magdelena didn't like his determination. He didn't intimidate her, and she didn't owe him this conversation. She was being nice, but now she would be more direct. "Jed, again, I'd rather not discuss this with you. I'm working, and customers could kumme in any moment. My answer is a firm no. I wish you well in finding the right woman. Please excuse me."

He didn't budge. "I should've approached you at your haus." He sighed. "Do you mind if I kumme by your place this evening? You may be waiting for the man you're interested in to propose, and he may never do so. I'm offering you a marriage proposal."

She inhaled a deep breath to calm herself. "I don't want to hurt your feelings or be disrespectful, but I won't change my mind." She took out a dozen butter cookies, packaged them, and passed the bag to him. She wanted him to leave. Maybe this would end their conversation on a cordial note. "Please take these cookies home for your kinner at no charge."

He accepted the package, shrugged, and finally went on his way.

She shuddered. Before Jed might approach her parents, she'd have to make it clear to them that he wasn't an option for her to marry. Hopefully, Jed wouldn't pursue the idea with her daed while she worked at the bakery today. She couldn't tell if he would honor her wishes. She'd be uneasy the rest of the day.

Magdelena served tea and blueberry tarts to two customers, waited for them to leave, and then joined Rachael busy baking in the kitchen. "I received a marriage proposal this morning from a man I would never marry."

"What!" Rachael froze. "Who would ask you such a question at the bakery and not wait until you were home?"

"Jed Byler, and I'm glad he chose not to kumme to my haus. I don't trust Daed not to accept his offer. Daed and Mamm have said to me I should consider a man's financial standing when I'm choosing who to marry. I want to fall in love, and as long as the man can provide for us comfortably, I don't need him to have a lot of money like Daed." She never wanted her daed to arrange a marriage for her unless it was with Toby.

"Can you coax your mamm to agree with you?"

"No. She goes along with Daed." Her mamm didn't cross her daed. She wished she would defend her and Charity when his punishment seemed harsh, like making them give away all the dogs.

Rachael heaved a big sigh. "Jed is looking for a mamm to care for those two younger unruly kinner. He and Addie let them run wild. The older girl, Christina, is nice, but she's eleven. The two younger kinner took pies from the table at the last after-service dinner and used their hands to eat them. I found them eating what was left and scolded them. But my words fell on deaf ears. They grinned and ran off."

Magdelena sighed. "I hope he finds the right woman." She didn't have anything against Jed. She felt sorry for him, but not enough to wed him.

Rachael spooned cookie batter onto the tray until she had a dozen. "I miss my late fiancé every day. We fell in love, and we couldn't wait to get married. We were talking about our wedding plans, and then those robbers came after us to steal the money Daed asked us to deliver to the bank. I'll never forget John trying to outrun them and our wagon flipping over. Here I am with a limp, and John was killed. I often relive the day I lost him."

"Would you get engaged again?" Magdelena's eyes pooled with tears.

"I don't know. I'd rather be a spinster than to have an arranged marriage. Jed and Addie were happy. She sang his praises, and he adored her. She was a sweetheart. I miss her." Rachael cocked her head to the café. "The front door shut. We might have customers."

"I'll take care of them." Magdelena hurried to the counter. "Annie, wilkom. What would you like?"

"I don't need anything, but I wanted to visit a minute with you. You've both been so kind to me. Abram doesn't allow me out of his sight too often, but he needed nails. I offered to buy them." She held up the small bag with a bandaged hand.

Magdelena smiled. "Let me get Rachael. I want you two to meet." She went to the kitchen. "Rachael, Annie Hook is here. She's new in town. Kumme and greet her."

"Sure." Rachael washed her hands in the bowl of water she kept for this purpose.

Magdelena hooked her arm through Rachael's, and they walked to the front room. "Annie, meet Rachael."

Rachael grinned. "I'm pleased to meet you. Are you settled in your home?"

"Yes. There's nothing I need to unpack or put away. I have a routine for my chores, and I needed conversation with someone other than Abram."

"You're in the right place. Would you like tea, coffee, or lemonade?" Magdelena opened the cabinet behind the counter and above the small cookstove.

"Lemonade, please."

Magdelena poured lemonade in the glass and set it on a small café table. "Let's sit."

Rachael dragged an extra chair over to the table. "I have

a couple minutes left until my raspberry tarts are ready to kumme out of the oven. This will give me a chance to rest my feet."

Magdelena touched the wrapped bandage on Annie's hand. "What happened?"

Annie shrugged. "It's nothing. Me being clumsy again. My hand got caught in the door." She glanced away and chewed on her bottom lip.

Magdelena wasn't sure she believed Annie, but she wouldn't pursue it. She wanted Annie to trust her and to enjoy her time at the bakery. "I forgot to ask if you'd like anything from the shelves. How about a piece of peach pie?"

"I'd love a piece." Annie beamed.

Rachael popped up. "I've got to take my tarts out of the oven. Annie, I'm sorry I don't have more time to talk today. Please visit us again soon." She headed to the kitchen.

"I understand. I don't want to keep you from your work." Annie grinned and held her wrapped hand next to her stomach.

Magdelena served Annie the pie and sat across from her. "Rachael would've had more time to visit, but we're managing the bakery with two, instead of three, people these days. We had another friend of ours working here, but she's decided to stay home and take care of her husband, Andrew, and her toddler, Betsy."

A young couple opened the door and entered. The girl wore a calico dress, with her beautiful blond hair in a ponytail, and the tall handsome man held her elbow as they approached the counter.

The young woman grinned. "Greetings. We're passing through this delightful town, and we couldn't resist the sweet aroma of fresh bread as we passed the window.

We'll take a loaf of white bread." She glanced at the selection of other baked goods. "Please add a rhubarb pie. It's my husband's favorite."

Magdelena packed their requests and accepted payment. "May I interest you in our tarts or cookies?"

"Sweetheart, would you like anything more?" The young man beamed at her.

"You're so good to me, Alan." She shifted her gaze from him to Magdelena. "Everything looks delicious, but we'll stick with our choices. Thank you."

He placed his arm around the girl's waist as they left.

Annie sighed. "There's a couple in love. I wish I would've waited to fall in love with a man before I married." She put a hand to her mouth. "I shouldn't have said such a thing." She stood. "Danki for the lemonade and pie. I should go." Annie put her coins on the table, cradled her injured hand next to her body, and rushed out the door.

Magdelena stood. Arranged marriages weren't uncommon, but her friend stating she wished she would've waited to marry for love sounded like a regret. She hoped Annie would fall in love the longer she was married to Abram and have the happily ever after most women desired.

Toby walked into the bakery minutes later. "Magdelena, what's wrong? You're as pale as the white apron you're wearing. Are you ill?" He hurried to her.

She shook her head. "I'm fine. Annie was here. We were having a pleasant conversation, and then she made a comment and rushed out before I could say goodbye." She slid the coins from the table into her hand. Then she removed the cashbox, deposited the coins, and returned it to the cabinet.

"What did she say?" Toby sat at a table.

"A couple came in to order bread and a pie, and it was

obvious they were in love by the way they acted. Annie said she wished she'd have fallen in love before she married. Then she hurried out."

"Sit with me." He gestured to the other chair at the table. "I'm sure Annie spoke without thinking. We've all said things we regret."

"You may be right." She veered to the coffeepot, filled a mug, and served it to him, and joined him at the table. "I'm concerned for her."

"Did she act sad or upset?"

"No. She was pleasant, and she met Rachael. She seemed comfortable until the couple left and she said what was on her mind." Magdelena slapped the table. "I should've offered you something from the counter. We've got fresh custard pastries."

"I'll take two, danki. Back to the subject of Annie . . . I'd forget about Annie's abrupt departure. She may have been embarrassed, but she'll be fine the next time you run into her."

She slid the two fragrant pastries on a plate and passed it to him. "Annie had a bandage on her hand. She said she slammed it in a door. She seemed nervous when she explained what happened."

Rachael carried a tray of cinnamon sugar piecrust rollups to the counter. She grinned. "Toby, are you here to see Magdelena?"

He held up his coffee and grinned. "Yes. I am."

Rachael chuckled and set the tray on the shelf. "Where's Annie?"

Magdelena recounted to Rachael what she told Toby. "I've been building a friendship with her. I don't want her to worry about what she says to me. If she needs help, I want her to tell me."

Her friends were open about their happy marriages. She wanted the same for Annie, but she wanted Annie to share what was on her mind without reservation.

Rachael limped to a chair and sat. "She tensed when you asked her about her hand?"

"She may be uncoordinated." Toby sipped his coffee.

Rachael headed to the kitchen. "After Annie gets comfortable with us, she may confide more about her marriage to Abram. Until then, we have to do our best to show her we care."

"Good point. I want to check on her. I'll stop at her haus on my way home." Magdelena respected Rachael's opinions.

"I'll meet you at your haus, and I'll drive you over to the Hooks' place. I don't want you going there alone. Abram might decide to come home early. Until we know more about him, it's not wise for you to visit Annie without me." Toby held open the door to leave. "I'll pick you up at your haus about five-fifteen."

Magdelena nodded.

The bakery was busy all afternoon, and she and Rachael worked until five. When the day was over, Magdelena took off her apron and stuffed it in her clean flour sack to take home to wash. "Ready?"

Rachael took off her dirty apron and draped it over her arm. "Let's go."

Magdelena locked the door, and they crossed the road to the livery and retrieved their buggies. She drove home with a smile of anticipation at spending more time with Toby. She pulled her buggy next to Toby's in front of the barn, hopped out, and handed her reins to the stable hand who worked for her father. "Lyle, please tell my daed I'm going to visit Annie Hook next door."

"Will do." Lyle took the reins.

Magdelena stepped into Toby's buggy.

With a nod to Lyle, he drove away from the barn to the Hooks' farm. "You're kind to concern yourself with Annie. Even if she's not in trouble, she still needs friends."

"I'm glad you offered to accompany me to their haus. I didn't think about Abram coming home early." She didn't want to assume he was hurting Annie, but she was glad for the extra protection Toby provided. She wanted to be wrong.

They arrived at the Hooks' place. Toby jumped out of the buggy, helped her out, and tied the horse to a new hitching post. "Abram sure did put his place in order fast. The garden has perfect rows with no weeds. His woodpile is stacked neat, and he must've installed this hitching post. I'm impressed."

They crossed the yard and Magdelena knocked on the door.

Annie opened the door with a surprised countenance. She lowered her eyes then glanced from one to the other. "Kumme in please. Magdelena, I'm embarrassed how I acted earlier. And, Toby, good to see you."

"There's no need to apologize. You didn't say anything I would repeat. I wish you had stayed and we could've talked longer," Magdelena said.

Annie led them into the living room and indicated the beautiful oak carved settee with pretty daisy embroidered pillows. "You're gracious. I shouldn't have run out on you."

"Don't think anything of it. I hope you'll visit the bakery often." Magdelena grinned and sat.

Annie patted her stomach. "Your desserts look delicious. I couldn't stay away from the bakery if I wanted to."

Toby chose to sit beside Magdelena after Annie seated herself. Toby leaned back against the gray cushion. "Is Abram around?"

Annie sat ramrod straight in a high-backed hardwood chair across from them. "No. He's out of town. He'll be back tomorrow."

Magdelena smiled. "I'm looking forward to growing our friendship."

"I'm blessed you're giving me another chance. I acted childish at the bakery earlier. I get embarrassed when questioned about my bruises." Annie stared at the floor. "And I never should've mentioned such a personal statement about my marriage." She gave them a weak smile. "I'll not stay away from the bakery, and I'm grateful to you for reaching out to me."

They conversed about the weather and the crops, and then Magdelena glanced out the window and noticed the sun was low in the sky.

"We should go. If you'd like to stay with me tonight while Abram's away, you're wilkom."

"I'll be fine. Danki." Annie rose and walked with them to the front door.

Magdelena bid her farewell.

Toby tipped his hat. "Give Abram our best."

Annie escorted them outside and waved goodbye as they got in the buggy.

Magdelena couldn't help but watch until Annie went back inside the haus. She wasn't as relieved as she should've been about Annie and Abram.

Toby drove onto the main road. "It's none of my business, but I wonder why Abram wouldn't take Annie with him this weekend. She doesn't know anyone except you and me. I wouldn't leave you alone if we were married and new in town."

Magdelena beamed. "You wouldn't?" She was falling in love with him. She couldn't help herself. Having him refer to her and use married in the same sentence made her day.

Toby's cheeks reddened. "I misspoke. We're not officially courting. I'm rambling, and I need to stop talking before I get myself into trouble."

Magdelena grinned. "I wouldn't be opposed if you suggested we court." She held her breath for a moment. She might have overstepped to make such a statement. It wasn't appropriate. She'd been too outspoken, but patience wasn't her virtue.

"I would do anything for you. I care for you. I would like nothing better than to court you, but I'm not in a position to ask you yet. I have a plan, but it may take a while. Can we enjoy our friendship for now?"

Her heart sank. "I don't care how much money you have. Our courtship can go on as long as we would want it to. The purpose of courting is to find out if you want to have a future together. I would be proud for our friends to know we were officially courting. I don't understand why you shy away from this."

"Please trust me. Your parents will want to know what my financial standing is to make sure I can provide for their dochder. Right now, they wouldn't be happy with my answer, and neither am I. I have an excellent start on savings. My furniture is selling fast. I will get there if you can be patient with me."

She knew he was right. Her daed would pepper him with questions, and his expectations didn't match hers where money was concerned. "I'm happy you admit you care for me and want to court. I respect your wishes, and I'll wait." She grinned. "You're worth it, Toby Schlabach."

He covered her hand. "Danki, Magdelena. I wish things were different. I really do." He pulled in front of her haus.

"I understand." She managed a smile and swallowed her disappointment. "Want to kumme inside?"

He shook his head. "I need to check on Daed, and I plan to stay up late and work in Andrew's workshop on his property to finish a desk. Please give your family my best."

Magdelena hopped out of the buggy. "Danki for taking me to Annie's. Don't be a stranger and give your family my love." She went inside the haus but watched from the window until Toby drove away.

Mamm dozed in her rocking chair in the living room, her knitting needles in her lap. She stirred when Magdelena entered. "How was your evening?"

"Wonderful. Toby and I had a good visit with Annie. Abram's out of town."

"I'm glad you checked on her. Your supper is still warm on top of the stove." She rubbed her eyes. "Your aunt and uncle left and they give you their love. Your daed had a visitor today."

"Danki for my supper." She raised her brows. "Who?" Her stomach clenched. She hoped it wasn't Jed.

"Jed. He said he wanted your daed to arrange a marriage between you and him."

"Please tell me Daed told him no." Magdelena gulped.

"Your daed wouldn't approve of Jed. He'd rather you marry someone who hasn't been married. I'm not sure he will mention it to you, so I wanted to tell you. Jed said he'd asked you at the bakery and you'd turned him down. I'm surprised he didn't ask you here, where it would've been more appropriate. Has he approached you to court him before today?"

Magdelena shook her head. "No. He's in a hurry to have a woman take care of his kinner, cook, and clean. I don't blame him, but he's going about finding a fraa the wrong way. I feel sorry for him, but not enough to accept his proposal. I'm frustrated he approached Daed after I told him no."

Mamm nodded. "I understand. He was persistent. He left here and drove to Sadie Yoder's haus and asked her. Her mamm dropped off a blouse for me to repair, and she said Sadie accepted Jed's proposal. She's excited to plan the wedding. He may have hurried to find a fraa in a surprising way, but he found one. I'm happy for them. Sadie is almost thirty. Her mamm couldn't wait to tell us. I didn't have the heart to tell her he'd been here about you right before he went to their haus."

Magdelena plopped in the chair next to Mamm. "Thank goodness." She didn't know what she would've done if Daed had said yes to Jed. She went to the kitchen to have supper with a throbbing headache.

Toby drove home and went over his conversation with Magdelena. Sadness filled him over her disappointment in his not being ready to court her. He had to prove to her father he could provide a nice living for her. She might not like it, but she seemed to understand. But for how long? And how long would it be until some other Amish man approached her daed? Their friendship would have to suffice for now. He took care of his horse and then went inside the haus. "Good evening."

Mamm sat in her rocking chair with a brown ball of

yarn in her lap with her crochet hook moving faster than he could keep up watching their motion. "I wrapped a ham sandwich and put it on the table for you in the kitchen." She stopped crocheting. "Rachael told me about Annie running out of the bakery earlier in the day. She said Annie seemed embarrassed about something. She said you and Magdelena visited her. I hope it went well. You are both kind to befriend this new couple, but I'm glad you didn't let Magdelena go alone. Rachael said her husband, Abram, may not be a nice man."

"Danki for fixing a sandwich for me. I don't know what to make of Abram. When I talked to him on my first visit to his home, I found him serious and cordial. Annie's kind and wilkoming. Magdelena and Rachael befriending her is a good idea. Abram wasn't home when we stopped by the Hooks's place. I was eager to talk with him again in hopes he'll become comfortable with me."

"I'm proud of you for not giving up on Abram."

He glanced at Daed's empty chair. "How was Daed today?"

"Rachael's at his bedside reading him verses from Proverbs. He finished one scrambled egg and half a piece of white bread. He loves butter, so I slathered a thick layer on it for him. I'd say he had a better appetite than yesterday. He said his pain wasn't any worse."

"Danki. I'll leave Daed and Rachael alone, grab the sandwich, and head out to Andrew's workshop and stay for a couple of hours."

Mamm held her crochet hook. "Please don't stay out too late. I worry you're working too hard."

"You don't need to worry about me. I'm happy with my life. I love you, Mamm." He took his sandwich and drove to Andrew's. He wouldn't intrude on Andrew and

Maryann's time. He had Andrew's permission to use the workshop anytime. The haus was far enough away from the shop as not to disturb them. He stepped inside and polished the table and chairs he'd finished.

Andrew opened the door and surprised him. "I have something for you." He handed him an envelope.

Toby opened the flap and grinned, "Danki for the money. What sold?"

"The bedroom set, dresser, and two chairs. You must have enough to buy land and build yourself a haus. I and our friends will help you."

"I'll add this money to my savings. I'll be ready to buy land and a haus sooner than I've anticipated. I appreciate you letting me sell my furniture and household items in your store. Are you satisfied with how the store is doing?"

"I'm blessed beyond measure. Englischers have spread the word about our store, and we've had many of them travel to Charm to buy furniture, hope chests, potato boxes, and more. You've become an excellent craftsman, and your fancy spindles on chairs have made them popular." He dragged a stool closer to the worktable. "My bruder and his fraa, Gracie, are kumming for a visit. They should arrive tomorrow. Why don't you and Magdelena kumme for supper?"

"I'm not officially courting Magdelena, but I would like to bring her. I haven't asked her daed for his permission. I suspect his financial expectations for the man Magdelena considers a future with are high. I want to be in the best position to show him I can provide a good life for her when I ask him. It won't be long."

"You're wise. Magdelena's daed is set in his ways, and he's proud of his ranch and standing in the community.

It will be difficult for any man to meet his standards. I don't envy you."

"She's important enough to me to try to win him over. I'll need more money to build a haus and have a substantial savings to impress him. Magdelena and I want to move into courtship, which is all the incentive I need to also work hard at establishing a friendship with her daed."

"I'll pray for you and Magdelena. Bring her to supper. Rachael is also wilkom."

"Rachael will want to stay home with Mamm. She and Daed have a special time reading him the Bible. Mamm knits or sews while Rachael takes over his care."

"Tell me about your daed. How is he feeling?"

"He had a better day than most for him." Toby blew the dust from the top of the table where he'd sanded it. "I'll ask Magdelena about tomorrow night. What time?"

"Six, and don't bring anything, and tell Magdelena not to. Kumme, relax, and enjoy good food and conversation." Andrew slapped him on the back.

"Sounds like a good time. Do you mind if we include a new couple to Charm, Annie and Abram Hook?" He liked Gabe, and he was glad Andrew's bruder had returned to Amish life and reestablished his relationship with Andrew. Gabe had taken over their late uncle Luke's furniture store in Millersburg, and Andrew had bought the local Charm furniture store and expanded it. They were easy to talk to, and he was sure Annie and Abram would like them.

"No, bring them." He stood. "I should leave you alone to work. The rectangular oak table and chairs are perfect for a large kitchen."

Toby loved this particular oak table and chairs. The set should bring in a substantial sum. "Danki. I learned from the best. Do you mind helping me load them in my wagon? I'll bring them tomorrow morning to the store."

Andrew lifted one end of the table. "Yes. I'll display this kitchen set in the window tomorrow morning when you drop it off."

Toby and Andrew loaded the table and then carried the additional pieces to the wagon and threw a cover over them. Toby tied the cover down with a rope. "Danki for the extra pair of hands. I'll ask Magdelena in the morning about supper. I'm sure she'll want to kumme."

"We'll look forward to having you both join us. I also hope your friends, Annie and Abram will kumme. Don't stay up too late. I worry you don't get enough rest." Andrew gave him a concerned look.

"I won't. I'm heading home, and I'm looking forward to our time with you. Good night." Toby headed home. Andrew had given him the job of managing his property and livestock and working in the store when he had time, which was mostly in the winter months. The wages he earned took care of his family and enabled him to build a modest savings. This latest sale happened fast, and it brought him closer to meeting his goal. All he needed was Magdelena, and he was weeks away from approaching her father.

Toby arrived home, got a good night's rest, and woke Saturday morning. He skipped breakfast and drove to town. He delivered the furniture to Andrew, and then he crossed the road to the bakery and knocked on the door since he was there before it opened.

Magdelena answered the door. "Come in. Have a seat." She poured him a cup of coffee and served him a warm peach pastry.

"Danki. Andrew invited us and the Hooks for supper

tonight at six. Gabe and Gracie will be at their haus for a couple of days. Are you free to go?"

She bobbed her head. "I'd love to."

"I'll pick you up. Andrew said to not bring anything. I asked if Annie and Abram could kumme, and he said yes. I'll go to her haus and ask them. Hopefully, Abram will be home in time to go."

"What a wonderful idea to include the Hooks, and what a treat to spend time with Gabe and Gracie. I enjoyed meeting them at Andrew and Maryann's wedding."

Toby would be happy to have more time with Magdelena. "They're a nice couple. I should head to Abram and Annie's place later and invite them to Andrew's. I look forward to being with you tonight." He gazed into her beautiful brown eyes as she blushed. Then he tipped his hat. He went to Andrew's and did some chores until about eleven in the morning. Then he departed and drove to the Hooks' haus. He stepped to the door and knocked.

Annie's eyes widened. "Toby, did you kumme to speak with Abram? He's not here."

"I wanted to invite you to supper at Andrew and Maryann Wittmer's haus tonight. They are close friends of Magdelena and me. Andrew is also my boss. I mentioned Magdelena and I are getting to know you, and he said to invite you and Abram. His bruder, Gabe, and Gabe's fraa, Gracie, will be there. Magdelena and I would love it if you and Abram would join us. It's a good way to get better acquainted with more people in Charm."

"If Abram returns home in time, we'll kumme together. He's been gone a couple of days. He's supposed to kumme sometime today. If not, I'll attend, and leave Abram a note to join us when he gets home. Danki for the invitation. What can I bring?"

Toby shook his head. "Andrew gave strict instructions to not bring anything. He doesn't want us to worry about a dish to bring. He said to arrive at their haus about six." He gave her directions to Andrew's haus.

Annie grinned. "Sounds fun. Danki for including us."

Toby said goodbye and traveled to Andrew's to finish his chores.

After a full day, the old maple clock hanging in Andrew's barn struck five, and Toby put his tools away, drove home, changed clothes, and picked up Magdelena at her haus.

"Did you talk to Abram and Annie? Are they kumming tonight?"

Toby recounted to Magdelena what Annie told him. "I'm glad she's kumming for sure, and I hope Abram will get home in time to join us."

"Me, too." She grinned. "I can't wait to catch up on Gabe and Gracie's news and find out how they're doing in Millersburg. You must be anxious to visit with Gabe again." Magdelena sat next to him in the buggy.

"Andrew keeps me posted on what his aunt Doris, Gabe, and Gracie are doing. Gabe sends him letters. Andrew is pleased Gabe is keeping in touch with him since they had lost contact when Gabe lived in the outside world. Since Gabe has committed to Amish life and taken over their late uncle's store and married Gracie, Andrew said Gabe's matured and made him proud."

"I'm not sure Maryann would've married Andrew if Gabe hadn't intervened. She was hurt when Andrew never mentioned Gabe. I might be upset if you had a bruder and didn't tell me about him. You want to think your suitor would be open and honest at all times. I'm glad Gabe returned to Amish life and took over their uncle's store so

Maryann and Andrew could stay in Charm. Gabe's timing couldn't have been better."

"He's a funny and likable man, much like Andrew." Toby hoped Abram would kumme and be more open. He parked the buggy and helped Magdelena step out.

Betsy ran to greet them and held her arms out behind the glass in the front door. "Oby and Eena!"

"Betsy, you're a doll." Magdelena opened the door and then picked her up.

Maryann entered the room. "Kumme in, Magdelena. Toby, the men are in the backyard. Since the weather is beautiful, the men set tables and chairs in the back for us to have supper outside."

"Excellent idea. I'll join them." He strolled to the back of the haus to join the men.

Gabe dragged another chair over for him. "Toby, sit by me."

Toby plopped in the chair. "What a nice surprise to find you're staying with Andrew for a couple of days. How's life in Millersburg?"

"The store is successful, and Aunt Doris spoils both Gracie and me. She cooks, cleans, and sings her hymns. We're blessed to have her with us. How about you? Andrew tells me you're gathering up courage to speak to Magdelena's daed. I can't imagine he wouldn't be happy to have you for a son-in-law."

"He's a wealthy rancher who wants his dochder to marry a man who can provide what he has for his family." Toby sighed.

"Amish aren't supposed to measure a man's worth by his wealth. I'm surprised." Gabe furrowed his brows.

Toby shrugged. "We all have our flaws. Pray for me.

He's been less friendly since Magdelena and I have been spending more time together."

Gabe had put on a little weight. He looked good, and he still had the ornery gleam in his eyes Toby remembered. He'd missed him.

"I invited Annie and Abram Hook. I'm disappointed they're not here."

"Annie's inside. She said she left a note for Abram to drive over here when he gets home. She said not to wait on him. He may be too tired from his short trip to join us. She came early and insisted on helping Maryann and Gracie with supper." Andrew got up and added a chair to the circle. "This chair will be for him."

Toby plucked a blade of tall grass and ran it through his fingers. "How are James and Matt?" The two men who had worked and became friends of Andrew's when he took over his uncle's store and before Gabe returned had impressed him when Toby met them. He wished they lived in Charm. They had handcrafting in common and were easy to get to know. Gabe had been fortunate James and Matt had been hired by Andrew and trained before Gabe took over the store.

Gabe chuckled. "James does anything his new fraa, Lena, tells him to. She's nice but bossy. He doesn't mind. The man is smitten and happily wed. Matt and Katie are married and doing well. I can tell when they've bumped heads. Matt's grumpy and tells me. But they don't fuss often, and they're a good couple. We have supper together once a week, and Gracie and I feel fortunate to have such close friends. They send their best."

Annie came from the haus with dishes on a tray and added them to the other food offerings on the long table, with place settings for the couples. "Supper is ready."

Maryann slid Betsy into her high chair, which had already been placed at the outside table.

Gracie followed her with a pitcher of fresh lemonade. "This should do it. Take your seats."

Andrew waited until everyone was seated, and then he offered a prayer to God for the food. Then he passed the sliced ham to Maryann. "Annie, we're happy you could join us."

Abram came around the corner to the table minutes later. He gazed at Gabe and hesitated, kept silent, and then stepped closer to the group. "Greetings, everyone."

Toby stood and shook his hand. "Abram, I'm glad you could make it. I'll let Andrew make the introductions, since we're at his haus."

Andrew stood and also shook Abram's hand and then introduced him to the rest of his friends and family. "Your timing is perfect."

Annie poured him a glass of lemonade. "Abram, I'm happy you made it."

Gabe studied him. "You look familiar, Abram. Have you spent any time in Massillon?"

Abram cleared his throat. "Not much." He passed the fried potatoes to Annie.

Maryann tilted her head. "You're familiar to me, too. I lived there with my late husband, Gerald Harding. I met Andrew when I returned to Amish life." Maryann mashed fried potatoes for Betsy and placed them on her dochder's tray.

Abram kept his gaze on his plate. "No. You both must be mistaken."

Toby noticed Abram's jaw tighten, and the man's eye twitched. He doubted he was telling the truth. The mystery about this man baffled him. Why would Abram deny being in Massillon? What did he have to hide? He didn't want Abram to bolt. He had to find another topic to discuss. "Abram, do you have any hobbies?"

Abram looked Toby in the eyes. "I enjoy fishing off the bank, although I'd like to build a simple fishing boat for access to the whole lake."

Annie beamed. "I'd enjoy paddling down the lake and fishing with you."

"I prefer fishing alone." Abram slathered butter on a slice of wheat bread.

Annie's cheeks pinkened, and she sucked in her bottom lip.

Toby hadn't expected Abram's response to Annie, and he was at a loss for words.

Gracie spooned another helping of buttered carrots onto her plate. "Annie, do you like to knit or sew?"

"I stitch quilts, but I'm not good at making clothes. I crochet, but one pattern is all I know."

Magdelena grinned. "I'd be happy to teach you more stitches, and if you need a dress or bonnet, Rachael and I are seamstresses."

Annie beamed. "What a relief. I didn't know what I was going to do after moving to Charm. I had a friend Dottie, in Berlin, who made dresses and kapps for me. I can't cut a straight line on fabric, and I don't like to sew. I could help at the bakery now and then in return for your generous offer to make me dresses."

Abram shot her a stern glance. "We'll need to discuss this. Your duties at home kumme first."

"Of course. You're right." Annie stared at her plate and didn't touch the rest of her food.

"Rachael and I don't expect anything in return for making you dresses. It's what friends do for each other."

Annie blushed. "Danki."

Betsy had potatoes on her face, hands, and dress. "Cookie."

"You'll have to wait a couple of minutes, Betsy," Maryann said.

Toby gazed at Betsy. Nothing like a boppli to bring a smile. "Abram, I don't know about you, but I always leave room for dessert. What's your favorite?" He wanted him to relax.

Abram sighed. "I like simple butter cookies with no fruit or nuts added. Annie makes the best."

Annie smiled. "Danki. I like all desserts."

"I love this butter cookie recipe from my late mamm. I'd be happy to share it with you if you like them." Maryann stood. "Would you girls mind bringing in the dirty dishes with me, and then I'll serve the cookies." She turned to Betsy. "Child of mine, you are a mess." She took her napkin to the pump and got it wet. Then she returned and wiped her dochder's face and hands. "Andrew, please watch her for me."

He reached over and caressed Betsy's cheek. "We'll be fine. Take your time."

Toby stacked plates and carried them with Magdelena behind Maryann, Gracie, and Annie. He was concerned about Annie. He was sure Magdelena would ask if she was all right, but he wanted to show his support. He was determined to help this couple.

Toby and Magdelena approached Annie on the porch after the other girls had gone inside the haus. Toby faced Annie. "Are you all right?"

Annie glanced from Toby to Magdelena. "I'm having a wonderful time with you and Magdelena and your friends." She cast her eyes to her shoes. "I'm embarrassed by

Abram. He treats me like a child much of the time. He may be aggravated with me for asking him to have supper so soon after he's been out of town. I shouldn't have accepted the invitation without clearing it with him first. He would expect me to make supper and let him rest. I was selfish to want to visit with you and your friends."

Toby kept his voice low. "Now they're your friends, too. Have you told Abram you'd like him to address you as an adult? He might not realize you're upset about this." He would give Abram the benefit of the doubt. He seemed like a decisive and serious man, and he hoped, for Annie's sake, Abram didn't mean to kumme across like a stern taskmaster.

Abram stepped onto the porch and crossed his arms. "Annie, what is taking you so long? We should go. I've had a long day, and I'm tired. Magdelena and Toby, I've told the others danki for their hospitality and danki for thinking of us. Enjoy the rest of the evening."

Annie, wide-eyed, looked at her husband. "I thought we were staying for dessert."

Abram gave her a curt nod to the door. "I've changed my mind. We can have some of your cookies at home."

"Good night to you both. Magdelena, I'll visit you at the bakery soon." Annie's cheeks pinkened.

Toby had been surprised at Abram's fast denial to Gabe's comment he recognized him from Massillon. Abram's set jaw and annoyance at the mention of him in Massillon seemed odd. Why did Gabe's comment that he may have seen him there frustrate him? Toby thought it best not to approach Abram about it. He gestured for Annie to pile the dishes she held onto the ones he had in his hands. "I'll take them to the kitchen for you. Danki for kumming. Have a good night."

Magdelena nodded. "Take care."

Annie rushed after Abram.

Toby waited until Abram and Annie had reached their buggy and were out of sight. "I'm curious why Abram seemed uncomfortable when Gabe said he thought he recognized him from Massillon."

"He wouldn't make eye contact with Gabe, and he was adamant Gabe was wrong. He acts like he's hiding something. But what?"

Toby shrugged. "He's hard to figure out. Let's take these dishes inside, and then we'll join the others."

She nodded and managed to open the door with her free hand, and they took the dishes into the kitchen.

Maryann held a tray of cookies. "Danki for helping with the dishes. Where's Annie?"

Toby set the dishes in the big metal dish basin full of water. "Abram and Annie left. He's had a long day and wants to get home." He moved to let Magdelena put her dishes in the sink.

"I hope they enjoyed the evening. Toby, will you take this tray of cookies to the men?"

"Sure." Toby smiled at the women washing the dishes and then returned to the men. "Maryann sent me with cookies. The women are washing dishes." He walked the tray around to each of the men, and they each took one. He put the cookie tray on a small table by his chair and took a cookie for himself.

Gabe looked at Toby. "I have some information about your friend, Abram, you should know. I played cards with Abram in Massillon. I'm sure of it. Did he leave Amish life like I did, and return?"

"What? Are you sure?" Toby sat ramrod straight. "We

don't know much about the couple. They're from Berlin, which is about twenty-one miles from Massillon."

Gabe nodded. "I'm sure."

Andrew's smile turned to a frown. "Bishop Fisher won't tolerate gambling. Abram must know this. And he took a big risk to gamble in Massillon. Many of us in our community go to Massillon for things we can't buy here. One of us needs to approach him before someone else sees him there."

"Magdelena and I are making an effort to befriend them. I'll talk to him." Toby moved his chair next to Betsy. He picked up a napkin and wiped her hands and face.

Gabe rubbed his chin as if in deep thought. "Toby, Abram bragged the one time I gambled with him about partaking in his Englischer friend Bucky's moonshine. I knew Bucky, and I visited his still a couple of times while I lived in the outside world. Also, Abram had on Englisch clothes. He may have dressed Englisch when he was in Massillon and then changed into Amish clothes when he returned home. I have no idea what his story is now. I didn't know he was Amish until tonight." He shrugged. "He may not take part in either of those things anymore."

Gracie joined them and nudged Gabe. "I caught your story on my way out here. You left out your visits to the still when you told me about your life in the outside world, Gabe Wittmer."

Gabe chuckled. "All in the past, honey. You have nothing to worry about. I returned to Amish life because I could give up gambling and buying moonshine. I didn't allow these things to become priorities in my life. Where are your friends?"

Gracie grinned. "They told me to join the men and they'd be out as soon as they put away the dishes."

Toby liked how Gracie and Gabe jested and exchanged endearing looks. He had a twinge of envy over their happy marriage. He wanted what they had with Magdelena someday, but he'd have to wait until the time was right to ask her daed's permission to court her. "They haven't been in town long. Let me approach Abram. If he is dabbling in the outside world with these things, I'd like to help him find his way back to our Amish lifestyle and traditions."

Andrew nodded. "You're a good friend to want to help Abram. Let me know if you need me."

The rest of the ladies joined and greeted them.

Toby recounted to the women what they had been talking about concerning Abram.

"Toby and I really like Annie and Abram. We're ready to help any way we can," Magdelena said.

"You and Toby are good not to shy away from them because Abram may be doing something he shouldn't. It's when friends need us the most." Maryann took Betsy out of the high chair. "I need to put this little girl to bed. I'll be back. Magdelena and Gracie, you can kumme if you like or you can stay outside."

Magdelena yawned and covered her mouth. "We should head home, Toby. Danki for having us. Gabe and Gracie, it's been a pleasure." She hugged Gracie and Maryann and kissed Betsy's forehead.

Toby bid his friends good night, then he and Magdelena went to the buggy and headed to her haus. He raised his brows. "This was an interesting evening."

"I'll say." Magdelena shook her head. "When do you plan on talking to Abram?"

"I'm not sure. I want to pray about it, and then I'll let you know when I plan to approach him."

"I'm glad you're willing to help him." Magdelena scooted closer to him.

"We all make mistakes."

"I hope Abram appreciates your offer to listen and help." She sighed. "I like Annie, and I want to be the shoulder she can lean on."

"All we can do is offer." He covered her hand. "On a better note, I had a good time with you. I'm falling in love with you, Magdelena. It isn't proper for me to say this and not have approached your father about us courting, but I can't help myself."

"I'm falling in love with you, Toby Schlabach. I like to avoid my daed when I don't think he'll agree with my way of thinking. After the way he was rude to you at supper at my haus, I'm afraid of what he'll say."

"I've changed my mind. I've got enough money saved to ask your daed if we can court. I'm ready to ask your daed to court you, but it wouldn't be appropriate to ask him on Sunday. I'll ask him on Monday."

"Toby, I'm excited."

"Me, too. Are Gloria and Otis still at your haus?" Toby wouldn't mind their support.

Magdelena frowned. "They had to cut their visit short. Aunt Gloria forgot she promised to help her friend plan a community social. She forgot to tell the woman she was going out of town. I'm a little worried about her. She doesn't forget such things."

"When we get older, we tend to forget things. I don't always remember to do what I had planned for the day. I'm sure it's nothing." Toby sighed.

"You're right. I forget things, too. I depend on Aunt Gloria. Daed listens to her. They've always been close as bruder and schweschder. I wish they would be here with us when you speak with Daed on Monday." Magdelena shivered.

Toby nodded and pulled in front of her haus. "I would've liked for them to have been here, too. I'm nervous about what your daed will say." He took her hand. "Let's pray together." He bowed his head. "Dear Heavenly Father, please give me the words to say to Mark. Help him to understand I have the best intentions toward his dochder. You can move mountains. If this is Your will for us, please help us. Danki, and we love You. Amen."

He kissed the back of her hand. "Sleep tight, sweet-heart."

Magdelena's face burned. "You, too, Toby."

He helped her out of the buggy and watched her step onto the porch and go inside the haus. He couldn't imagine his life without her. But would he have to?

Chapter Four

Magdelena rode with her parents to the Yoders' for Sunday service. She wished they had services each Sunday instead of every other. She liked the bishop's messages and having time with Toby when he attended. It would depend on his sweet daed's condition and if he chose to stay home with him in lieu of his mamm or Rachael.

Charity poked her side. "You're too quiet. Why?"

"Tired, I suppose." Her stomach churned. She loved Daed, but she was afraid he expected the man she married to be like him. She wanted Toby, who was strong but humble. A man who listened to her and cared about what she had to say and one who took wise advice from others to heart. Daed provided for his family, loved them, and was faithful to God, but she didn't think he had a humble bone in his body, and he seldom accepted advice.

"You look sad, and you should be happy." Charity gave her a mischievous grin.

"I'm not sad, but you're up to something. You have an ornery look. What is it?" Magdelena was glad her parents were discussing the weather and not paying attention to them. She never knew what Charity was going to say, and it could be embarrassing.

"Wait until we get out of the buggy, and then I'll tell you."

Her parents walked ahead of them, and she waited until they were out of earshot. "Tell me before we go inside the haus."

"Toby told me he wants to marry you someday, but I'm not supposed to tell." Charity covered her mouth and chuckled.

"You shouldn't have told me his secret, but I'm glad you did." Magdelena faced her. "Did you tell Mamm, Daed, or anyone about this besides me?"

"I told Peter, but he said he wouldn't tell anyone. He keeps secrets better than me."

"Charity, don't tell another soul. Promise me." Magdelena put her hands on her schweschder's shoulders.

"I won't. Why can't I tell?"

"Toby asked you not to, and he may ask Daed if we can court. I'd rather Daed be surprised. It's a special occasion for us. It's not your surprise to tell. You'll disappoint Toby and me if you do. I'm glad you like Toby, and he thinks you're pretty special, too. But let him tell Daed."

"All right. I won't tell."

Magdelena took her little schweschder's hand, and they sat on one of the benches inside, next to their parents. The Yoders went to a lot of trouble to move out their living room furniture to make room for the benches each time they hosted Sunday service. Charity warmed her heart with her joy over Toby's secret. At least she had her support. She scanned the sea of straw hats and kapps. Toby, Rachael, and his mamm weren't there. She had a sinking feeling something was wrong. Her family had arrived a little late, and everyone was seated. She nodded to her friends Ellie, Liza, Hannah, and Maryann. She smiled at Gracie and Gabe. Annie sat in front of her, and she tapped her shoulder.

Annie looked back at her and whispered, "I'm glad to see you."

She leaned close to Annie's ear. "Is Abram here?"

"He stayed home with a bad stomachache. He's better this morning and I left him sleeping. Danki for asking."

What was the real reason Abram wasn't there? She shouldn't judge him until she knew the facts. She glanced over her shoulder. Had Toby kumme in? She didn't see him anywhere. Was he all right? She couldn't get her mind off Toby.

Bishop Fisher took his place in front of them. "Before we start, I'd like to wilkom the Hook and the Hilty families to our community. I understand Abram Hook is home ill. Please introduce yourselves to these newcomers at the after-service dinner. Please bow your heads for prayer." He prayed to God and then asked them to open their Ausbund to page five.

Charity lifted the Ausbund next to her, opened it, and shared it with Magdelena. She sang "Faith of Our Fathers" off-key.

Magdelena didn't mind how her schweschder sang. It was sweet music to her ears. The slight breeze on this hot sunny day brushed past her cheeks as she sang.

The bishop then opened his Holy Bible and delivered a message on not being too quick to judge others. She had been guilty of judging Abram. She hoped she and Toby could help him if he was in any kind of trouble.

Bishop Fisher finished his message two hours later. He prayed for the food and then asked them to stay seated.

"You may have noticed the Schlabachs aren't with us today. Vernon Schlabach died early this morning."

Magdelena gasped and tears filled her eyes.

"Toby came to my haus, and we went together to take his daed's body to the undertaker for preparation before today's service. The undertaker will deliver Vernon to the family's home later today, and they will accept visitors tomorrow between one and three. Then we'll have the service and the burial will follow. The family didn't want to have the viewing and funeral on separate days, and these were Vernon's wishes as well. Ladies, please prepare your favorite dishes to take to the Schlabachs' home tomorrow."

Magdelena wiped tears dripping onto her cheeks. She couldn't concentrate. Her mind swirled with heartache for the man she loved, her best friend, and their mamm.

Charity tugged on Magdelena's sleeve. "Did Toby's daed die?"

Magdelena nodded.

Charity's eyes filled with tears, and Magdelena hugged her.

The bishop offered another prayer to God and then dismissed them for the after-service meal.

Magdelena clasped Charity's hand.

Charity stood quiet.

Mamm squeezed Magdelena's arm and gestured for Charity to take her hand. "I'll make food tomorrow to take to them."

"I'll go with you. I'm sure Liza will close the bakery. Danki."

Maryann, Ellie, Hannah, and Liza approached her.

Liza circled an arm around her waist. "It goes without saying we'll close the bakery tomorrow. I'll take care of it."

"I appreciate it, Liza. I'd like to go there today and early in the morning to do all I can for them." She couldn't imagine the pain they were going through. Her heart ached at never talking to Vernon again. She loved his strength in the midst of his weak body. She understood where Toby acquired all his good qualities once she got better acquainted with Vernon.

"Magdelena, what can we do? We want to help. You must be in shock," Maryann said.

"I want to be with Toby and his family. Since this happened early this morning, Toby or Rachael didn't have time to tell me, and I'm certain they're shocked and bereft with grief."

Hannah gestured to her buggy. "I'll take you there, but I won't stay. You can have Toby take you home whenever you're ready to leave."

"I would appreciate it. Danki." Magdelena glanced at her parents. "Let me tell my family I'm leaving." She went to Mamm and told her and then returned to Hannah and the girls. "Toby's family will be happy with anything you bring tomorrow. I'll see you all tomorrow at the viewing."

Hannah gave a curt nod in the direction of her husband. "While you told your family where you were going, I ran over to Timothy and told him I'll drop you at the Schlabachs' place and be right back. He said to pass on his regards to Toby and his family."

Magdelena got in the buggy, and Hannah drove to the Schlabachs'. They talked about what a sad time this would be for Toby's family.

Hannah looked at Magdelena once they arrived. "You go in. I'll speak with them tomorrow. This will be a difficult day, and you're closer to them. Give them Timothy's and my regards."

Magdelena's tears stained her cheeks. "Yes. I'll ask

Toby to take me home. I love you, dear friend. Danki for bringing me here." She hugged Hannah and got out of the buggy. "Goodbye, and danki again."

Hannah's lips quivered as she nodded and drove away.

Magdelena crossed the yard to the haus, and the front door opened.

Rachael ran outside and into her arms and wept.

Magdelena stood outside, holding her as they sobbed together.

Moments later, Rachael pulled back and removed a handkerchief from inside her sleeve and wiped her eyes and nose. "Toby went to Andrew's workshop. He's made a marker with Daed's name and he wanted to engrave it with the date. He should be back any minute. Kumme and sit with me."

"I can't imagine what you're going through. What can I do for you?"

Rachael gave her a weak smile, walked with her inside the haus, and motioned for her to sit. "You're doing it by being here. The viewing will be here tomorrow then the funeral, and the burial will follow. But I take it the bishop made the announcement at the church service. Where's your buggy?"

"Yes. Bishop Fisher did make the announcement, and our friends are concerned and send their love. Hannah has always been the mamm of our group. She takes good care of us. She offered right away to bring me to your haus, and I accepted. She dropped me off, and she wanted to give us time alone. She and Timothy send their love, and they'll arrive early tomorrow."

Rachael wrinkled her forehead. "What should we do about the bakery?"

"Liza said she'll go to the bakery and post a closed sign

on the door with a note we will reopen on Tuesday. Where is your mamm? How is she holding up?"

"Mamm is resting. Daed passed away around four this morning. We could tell a big change in his breathing around nine in the evening. His breathing sounded rattled, and he didn't open his eyes or move. He stopped breathing and had no pulse at around four. We stayed with him until he died." Rachael let tears drip onto her cheeks. "I miss him."

Magdelena pulled her into her arms and held her again as she wept. Patches's sad eyes touched her heart as the dog lay by Vernon's empty chair. The dog might never be happy again. He loved Vernon so much. The man was an inspiration with his pleasant moods, conversation, and kindness. She wanted to snatch the pain out of the man she loved, her best friend, and their mamm, and Patches.

Toby entered the room and sat across from them, his shoulders slumped.

Rachael lifted her head and sat back. "Toby, Mamm's still resting. May I get you anything? What about you, Magdelena?"

Toby shook his head. "Nothing for me."

"I'm fine." Magdelena gazed into Toby's eyes, feeling bad for him.

Rachael stood. "I'm going to lie down in my room and give you time together. Do you mind kumming in the morning to help us greet guests and stay with us throughout the day?"

"Of course. I want to do anything I can for you." Magdelena nodded, and Rachael left the room.

"Let's go onto the porch and sit in the swing. I need some fresh air," Toby said.

Magdelena stepped outside and sat next to him on the

worn white swing, thankful for the sunshine and the wilkom breeze.

"I'm sorry about your daed. He was a kind man I'd grown to love." She winced at the pain on Toby's face.

"This has been one of the most difficult days of my life. I keep reminding myself he's no longer suffering. But I miss him. We've always had a close relationship. We could discuss any subject. I'll miss his counsel and smile and our discussions. He was an excellent example for showing me his faith in God. Sunshine, a soft blanket, his family, and other little things were most important to him. He taught me to appreciate the little things as well as the big things in life."

"Your daed put me at ease the first time we met. He was a gentle soul. You're blessed to have had such a close bond with him. I love my parents, and I appreciate them, but I don't have the close bond you share with your mamm and daed. I'm freer to say what's on my mind with Aunt Gloria or Rachael than I am with my parents." She wasn't bitter or angry about this. Her parents were good to her, but she wished they were less stubborn and rigid.

"Daed liked you. He told me I shouldn't let you get away."

Her face warmed. "I hope you'll listen to him. You're tired, and you should rest. I'll kumme early in the morning to help. Do you mind giving me a ride home?"

"I'd be happy to." Toby walked her to the buggy, harnessed the horse to it, and drove her home. "Danki, Magdelena, for kumming today."

She smiled and got out of the buggy. "Of course. Take it easy, Toby. You've a long day ahead tomorrow."

He tipped his hat. "I will."

She watched his back until he was out of sight. Another

buggy was parked in the yard. Who did it belong to? She went inside the haus. Ida, Ethan, and their son, Zach, were there from the Sunday service at the Yoders'. Ida was average height and pretty with her strawberry blond hair and nose and cheeks peppered with light freckles. Ethan was short, thin, and had the warmest smile. Zach, she guessed was about her age. He had the broadest shoulders. He was handsome with his sandy blond hair, structured jawline, and muscular arms outlined by his tight sleeves.

"Greetings."

Daed introduced the Hiltys. "They were at the service today. They bought the large farm next to the Yoders'."

Zach stood. "Pleasure to meet you." He gazed into her eyes.

Magdelena's face warmed. "Wilkom to Charm."

His gaze lasted too long.

"You'll like Charm. It's small, but our town has almost everything you need. You'll make friends in no time."

Mamm motioned to the tray of peach tarts and pitcher of lemonade and motioned to a chair. "Please help yourself and visit with us a while, Magdelena. Charity went home with Liza and Jacob to play with Peter. How are Toby and his family?"

"They're in a fog and going through the motions of preparing for the viewing. The undertaker will return Vernon's body to their home this evening. They're grief-stricken over his death but glad he's no longer in pain. He was a kind and strong man not to complain. I'll miss him." She blinked back tears.

Ida addressed Magdelena. "I'm sorry for their loss. Your parents said you're close friends with their family."

Daed shook his head. "Don't misunderstand. Magdelena works with Rachael, the dochder of Vernon, and they're best friends."

Magdelena held her breath a moment. Why was Daed going out of his way to make sure this family didn't think she and Toby cared about each other? She opened her mouth to say she was close with their entire family. But she shut it. It didn't matter at the moment, but it would when Toby approached Daed to court her. Her stomach grew queasy thinking about Toby's important conversation with her daed when he was ready.

Zach smiled at her. "Would you mind taking a stroll with me? It's a beautiful day to sit on the bench under the maple tree by the pond."

Daed rose and opened the door. "Sure she will. Take the boat out on the water if you wish."

Magdelena took obedient steps to the door. The last thing she wanted to do was be alone with Zach. Her heart ached for the pain and suffering Toby was going through with the loss of his daed. She was grieving Vernon's death, too. She'd rather be alone right now. But her daed hadn't left her much choice. She went onto the porch with Zach.

He walked beside her to the bench and sat. He patted the space next to him. "Instead of a stroll, let's sit by the pond. I hope you don't mind me asking you to accompany me outside. I thought you might like some air. This can't be easy for you."

Magdelena sat and stared out over the calm water. "Forgive me for not being the best company for you and your family today. I'm sad about Vernon Schlabach's passing."

"What can I do?" Zach picked a tulip from around the tree and gave it to her. He sat next to her again.

"The men from our community will go early to their

home to move furniture and bring benches from the large shed on the Yoders' property for guests to sit in the home and in the yard. Mamm and I will take dishes of food and help Rachael and her mamm arrange it on tables."

"Daed and I will go and pitch in. Which farm is theirs?"

"It's the sixth farm on the left on the main road." Magdelena rolled her shoulders back and relaxed.

Zach seemed to understand.

"Your daed said you work at the bakery in town. I'll have to stop in. I love desserts. Please don't take this the wrong way, but why are you working there?"

She wasn't offended. She had been asked this question before, since it was obvious her family didn't need the money. "It's not about the wages for me. I like baking and waiting on customers. Most of them I know from our community. The best thing about the job is being with my friends each day. The owner, Liza, is the sweetest woman, and she trusts Rachael and me to manage it on our own. Other friends have worked with us, but they've left when they wed or were with child." She shifted and faced him. "Why did your family move to Charm?"

"Daed's parents died last year. Mamm's parents had already passed three years ago. He wanted to buy a larger farm and raise hogs. He got a good price for our farm. He visited here and noticed a posting in the general store about the Keims' farm for sale. He made an offer, and Mr. Keim accepted it. It's much larger than the farm we had in Berlin, Ohio."

"Were you sad to leave your friends?" Magdelena wouldn't want to leave Charm for any reason. She loved her friends, the beauty of the quaint town, and her job at the bakery. She hoped she and Toby's courtship would end in marriage and they'd build a life in Charm.

"Yes, but I worked hard with Daed on the farm, and I had little time to socialize. You're the first person I've met since moving here. I hope we can spend more time together. Daed is hiring some men to help manage the farm. I'll be busy, but I'll make time for you."

Magdelena stood. She hadn't minded their conversation until now. She didn't want to encourage him. The bench had become too close for comfort. "Let's take a walk. My back is getting stiff on the bench."

They strolled across the yard to the big corral of cattle and walked along the fence line. Zach glanced at her and back at the cattle. "Did I say something wrong?"

She didn't want to hurt his feelings or give him the wrong impression. "I'm interested in Toby. We're good friends, and I'm hoping he'll ask my daed to court me soon. He's a farmer and builds furniture and useful household items."

"Your daed mentioned Toby and his family to me. He said not to misunderstand your closeness to Toby. He insists you're friends and nothing more. From what you and your daed have told me, I assume you and he have different opinions on your relationship with Toby. He would prefer you and Toby remain friends. Am I right?" Zach stopped and faced her.

Magdelena kept her distance from him. "You're making a lot of assumptions for not knowing Toby or me. I'm sure you misunderstood Daed. He likes Toby."

A buggy came down the Beachys' lane and stopped near them. Liza, with Peter and Charity, all greeted them.

Charity jumped out of the buggy and ran to Zach. "I met you at the service today."

He smiled. "Yes. You did."

Liza held the reins and stayed in the buggy. "Please give

my best to both your families. I should get home to little Lorianne and Jacob."

Peter waved goodbye to them.

Charity held up a picture. "Peter and I made this card for Toby and his family."

Magdelena took the paper from her schweschder. On the card were a heart and the words *I love you*, with Charity's and Peter's names at the bottom. "You and Peter did a wonderful job with this. Toby and his family will love your card."

Charity gazed at Zach. "Want to play a game on the picnic table?"

Zach shook his head. "I'm not much of a game player."

Charity frowned. "How about a boat ride?"

Magdelena would like for Charity to stay with them. Her company would deter Zach from asking more about Toby. She was worried his interest in her would delight her parents. Their financial means would especially please Daed.

Zach tousled Charity's light red curls. "Why don't you go inside the haus and talk to my mamm? She likes to play board games."

Charity shrugged and skipped to the haus.

Magdelena hadn't expected him to not include her schweschder. She didn't want to get in the boat with him. "We don't have to take a boat ride."

"What a relief. I don't much feel like it today." He scanned the grounds. "Your family has a lot of beautiful land to accommodate a cattle ranch. I've always wanted to be a cattle rancher. I'm hoping your daed will take me under his wing and teach me the ropes." He resumed walking with her. "Your daed may like Toby, but it may not be in the way you'd like him to."

"Zach, I'm not comfortable discussing Toby with you. It's been a sad day for me, his family, and many of our friends who love them and his daed. Please, let's not talk about him."

Zach held up his palms. "I didn't mean to upset you. We don't have to have any further conversation about him. I'd rather learn more about you."

Magdelena shielded her eyes from the sun. "Your parents and mine are heading this way. We should meet them halfway." She had no intention of telling him more about her.

Their parents' timing couldn't have been better.

Ida held a container. "Magdelena, your mamm gave us some of her peach tarts to take home. They're the best. We've had a wonderful time getting to know your family."

Magdelena managed a weak grin. "It's been a pleasure meeting you, Mrs. Hilty."

"Call me Ida, dear. We hope to spend a lot more time with your family. We've enjoyed our visit so much today."

"Danki, Ida." Magdelena didn't mind her parents befriending the Hiltys, but she was uneasy about Zach.

Mamm grinned. "Kumme visit us again soon. We've enjoyed your company as well. And you, too, Zach."

Daed clapped a hand on Zach's shoulder. "Kumme by tomorrow. We'll discuss a job for you."

Zach's eyes widened. "I look forward to it."

Magdelena pressed a hand to her temple. She had the beginnings of a headache. Zach working for Daed? She didn't like where this was going. Daed's smile was much too broad and his behavior toward Zach was different than the way he treated Toby. Thank goodness she had the bakery to keep her busy, since Zach would be working with Daed. She'd keep her distance from him.

Ida clasped Magdelena's hand. "Dear, please call my husband Ethan. We hope to spend a lot more time with your parents and you and Charity."

Magdelena smiled and nodded. She wasn't keen on the idea of Zach hanging around their haus, much less working for her daed. He seemed way too interested in her for her liking.

Charity ran to them. "Goodbye. Danki, Mrs. Hilty, for playing a game with me."

Ida hugged Charity. "Sweetheart, you can call me Ida and my husband Ethan."

Charity nodded and hugged her. "Danki, Ida."

Magdelena noticed Charity didn't address Zach. He must've hurt her feelings when he refused to include her in a game or boat ride. Her little schweschder didn't miss a thing, and she would be upset he didn't want her around.

Their guests left, and the family went inside the haus.

Daed sat back in his chair. "Magdelena, did you enjoy Zach's company?"

The hairs on her neck prickled. "He's nice enough."

Charity harrumphed. "He isn't as nice as Toby."

"I agree." Magdelena kissed Charity's forehead.

"Listen, both of you. Be kind to our new friends. Give Zach a chance, Magdelena. He'd be a worthy suitor for you."

Mamm nodded. "He's such a gentleman. No harm in finding out more about him."

Charity narrowed her eyes. "Magdelena likes Toby, not Zach. Toby's her special friend."

Daed waggled a finger at her. "Charity, this is none of your business. Toby and Zach can both be Magdelena's friends."

Mamm fidgeted her hands. "We should discuss what to

take tomorrow to the Schlabachs', Magdelena. Let's go to the kitchen and write a list. We'll get up extra early and get started on the food."

Magdelena was thankful for Mamm's intervention. She couldn't get to the kitchen fast enough. Daed's support of Zach made her uneasy. She'd feel better when Toby spoke to Daed. Or would she?

Toby helped Mamm wash and dress Daed's body early Monday morning. Vernon had been a bag of bones by the time he passed away. Mamm left to help Rachael in the kitchen. Toby stood alone by the box and gazed at Daed's lifeless body. He refused to remember him like this. His memories would be more precious since there would be no new ones. He'd miss his daed's wise counsel, silly jokes, and stories about his childhood. Daed had been his best friend. He'd give anything to listen to his daed's loving voice again.

An hour later, a knock sounded and Rachael answered the door. She called to him. "Toby, the men are here to move furniture and add benches where we need them. I put Patches in Mamm and Daed's bedroom."

Toby directed the men where to put the benches. He scanned the sea of men and women pouring in to the haus and filling their yard, all busy to make this day as easy for his family as possible. He loved this community. Magdelena, her mamm, and Charity were heading toward him.

Magdelena's mamm, Bernice, carried a picnic basket. "Your daed will be missed, Toby dear. I will take this food to the kitchen." She headed inside.

Magdelena stayed next to him. "Don't hesitate to ask if

you need anything. I can't imagine how difficult this day must be for you, Rachael, and your mamm."

"You being here with me makes it easier." He met her gaze and smiled. Magdelena had become important in his life. She was the calm he needed to get through this day.

Charity clasped his hand. "Toby, Peter and I made you a card." She handed it to him.

His heart swelled with gratitude. He loved this little girl. She had a big heart, and she was always showing him she cared. "Danki. I'm keeping it on my dresser."

Charity beamed. "Peter will be here soon. He said I could go ahead and give it to you."

"Danki." Toby squeezed her hand.

A new family came to the door, and Toby greeted them. Magdelena introduced Ida, Ethan, and Zach Hilty.

Toby shook their hands and thanked them for kumming before Ethan and Ida went back outside to help where needed.

Zach faced Magdelena. "I'd like to chat with you more. Would you mind if I came to your haus later?"

"No. I'm sorry, Zach. I'll be here most of the day, and I'm expected at the bakery very early tomorrow." Magdelena gave Toby a worried glance. "I should check on Rachael." She left the room.

Toby didn't miss that Zach ignored him and focused on Magdelena. Did he understand Toby's interest in her? He had too much on his mind to deal with Zach today. "Danki for kumming."

"I'm sorry our introduction isn't under better circumstances." Zach didn't make eye contact with him and moved to the window. "I should join the men. Looks like they could use a hand." He went outside.

Gracie, Gabe, Andrew, and Maryann came into the haus. Andrew put his hands on Toby's shoulders. "We're all sad for your loss. Gabe and I will help you carry your daed's body to my wagon, and then we'll help you lower him into the ground at the burial site. On a brighter note, Maryann brought chicken and dumplings. She knows how much you like her recipe. If you want to take tomorrow off, please do."

"Danki, Andrew and Gabe. I appreciate it. No, it's kind of you to offer me a day off, but I'll want to work to occupy my mind. Work is enjoyable for me. Danki for kumming. And, Maryann, it was sweet of you to bring chicken and dumplings. Gracie, it's nice to have you and Gabe in town visiting."

Toby watched them go outside to talk with other friends, and then he turned and stood at the open door and looked outside. Friends had brought and lined up benches and long tables to the side filled with covered dishes. He went to the kitchen, and women carried more covered dishes to the outside tables. He moved to the living room, where his daed lay in the simple pinewood box. Magdelena gripped the side of the box, as tears dripped onto her cheeks.

He came alongside her and choked around the threat of a cry in his throat. "I keep telling myself he's with God in Heaven. It relieves the pain of missing him."

She wiped her eyes and nose with her thin, white hand-kerchief. "I wish I had the perfect words to say. But you know my heart. I want to be the one you lean on."

"You are the woman for me. I told Daed you were special, and he urged me to not let you go. He told me not to wait and to ask your daed's permission to court you. I plan to by the end of this week. Daed always did give me the best advice."

She looked at him. "Your daed treated me like I was already part of your family. I loved him for it."

Bishop Fisher approached them. "I'd like to start the service if you're ready."

Toby nodded.

Bishop Fisher told everyone in the haus to move outdoors to the benches. Then he went outside.

Toby and Magdelena walked outside together.

Toby whispered in her ear, "I'll talk to you later."

"Mamm and I offered to stay behind and organize the food dishes and prepare for mourners to return for the meal," Magdelena said.

"Danki. I'm sure Mamm and Rachael appreciate it. I do, too. I'd better join them." He moved to where his family was sitting.

Magdelena took her seat with her parents.

Bishop Fisher took his place in front of the benches and called to the guests to take their seats. The others already outside sat. He waited for the crowd to settle. "Please bow your heads." He offered a prayer to God for Vernon and asked for comfort and peace for the family. He led them in the singing of two hymns, and then he presented his message on Heaven where there will be no more suffering. "I had a close friendship with Vernon, a faithful follower of God, and one of the most compassionate and caring men I have known. I'll miss him."

Toby blinked back tears, as Rachael clutched his arm. Mamm, her lips quivering, sat on the other side of Rachael. Would this pain last a long time? He took good care of his family, but he couldn't erase Mamm's and Rachael's grief.

His ache to talk with his daed once more would be a desire he'd carry to his grave.

The bishop closed his Holy Bible and prayed again to God and then dismissed them to the burial site and instructed the crowd to return for dinner at the Schlabachs'. Toby helped carry the pine box containing his daed's body, along with his friends, to Andrew's wagon. Then he drove Mamm and Rachael in his buggy to the burial site. He disliked this part of the process the most. They arrived, and he, along with Andrew and Gabe, lowered the pine box into the hole in the ground.

Bishop Fisher delivered another message on faith, hope, and love. "I visited Vernon often, and we became close friends. Although he was the one sick, he made me laugh and I always left his haus with a smile. He will be missed. Let's all remember he's in a better place and his suffering is over. Schlabach family, we're here for you for whatever you need. Let's sing." He led them in a hymn.

Toby stared at the deep hole where the box now lay at the bottom. Mamm squeezed his hand, and Rachael gripped his other one. He looked at the puffy white clouds and blue sky. God had promised never to forsake him, and it was true of this day. He'd prayed for strength when this day came, and he'd been more stoic than he'd anticipated. God had answered his prayer, and, although it was sorrowful, he could concentrate on being the one his family could lean on.

The bishop offered a prayer to God to give the family peace in the kumming days and for the food.

Toby had constructed a wooden cross for a marker with his daed's name and date of birth and death on it. He'd given it to Andrew to take care of today. Toby didn't want to wait for the men to cover the body. He'd leave Andrew and Gabe to do this for him and to place the marker on the appropriate spot. He walked with Mamm and Rachael to the buggy, and they drove home in silence.

Mamm stepped out of the buggy and peered at him. Her watery eyes had dark circles underneath. "Rachael and I will go inside the haus to help Magdelena and Bernice. It was thoughtful of them to stay behind and prepare for our guests."

Toby nodded and got out of the buggy. "I'll take care of the horse. I'll join you soon."

Toby unharnessed the horse and led the animal to its stall and secured the door. He dragged over Daed's weathered hardwood chair and plopped in it. He needed time alone before he could face his guests again. He held his head in his hands and wept. His best friend was gone. The many times they'd spent in this barn before Daed had gotten sick were over. He dried his eyes and checked the clock he'd kept in the barn. He'd been there for over forty-five minutes as he'd reminisced about Daed.

The barn door opened and Andrew stepped in. The burial site was close and Andrew and Gabe had muscular arms. He wasn't surprised they were back so soon. Gabriel must've gone inside the haus.

Andrew held his arms wide and they embraced.

Toby's throat ached with all the emotion of the day. Andrew's shirt, wet with sweat and spotted with dirt from where he'd filled in the hole above his daed's coffin, brought his mind back to the burial site. Tears flooded his eyes, and he hugged his close friend for a moment. "You've always been there for me, Andrew. Danki."

"Likewise, Toby."

"I guess we should join our friends." Toby mopped the tears from his face, and then they crossed the yard.

Abram and Annie approached Toby.

Abram said, "I'm sorry about your daed and for our hasty exit the last time we were together."

Annie looked at Abram then nodded.

"I appreciate you both kumming today. Magdelena and I don't want to intrude. We'd like to build a friendship with both of you."

Abram smiled. "Do you like to practice archery? I have two bows and plenty of arrows. I make the arrows."

Annie's eyes widened, and she grinned.

Her surprise matched his. Toby expected he'd have more work to do to win over Abram's trust before the man would be willing to do anything with him. He'd make the time. "I haven't shot a bow and arrow. I'd like to learn if you'll teach me."

Abram nodded. "Let's schedule a time for you to kumme over to our haus."

Annie beamed. "Thursday at six. Please bring Magdelena and join us for supper. I'll mention it to her."

"I'll speak to her about picking her up." Toby glanced over Annie's shoulder at Gracie and Gabe, who stood back, waiting to speak to him. He didn't want Abram to leave because Gabe and Gracie were here.

Abram glanced at Gabe. "Gabe."

"Greetings." Gabe and Gracie moved closer.

Abram motioned to the food table. "Annie, we've taken enough of Toby's time. We should allow others to speak with him."

He and Annie walked away.

Gabe faced Toby. "I remember when Andrew and I lost

our parents and uncle. You go through the motions, as if you're walking in a fog."

"Yes. You said it best. I've enjoyed you and Gracie being in town. When do you go back to Millersburg?"

"We're packed and leaving now. We'll be praying and thinking of you, Toby. Please be careful around Abram. I have no doubt I gambled with him in Massillon. And you don't know what else he may be hiding. I apologize for bringing this up today, but I couldn't leave without giving you this advice."

"I've heard many compliments about your daed today. It's obvious he was loved by many. A lot of your friends shared fond memories of him. And it's kind of you and Magdelena to go out of your way to befriend Annie and Abram. We care about you, so we want you to proceed with caution," Gracie said.

"Danki for staying for the service, and I'll heed your advice with Abram. Please be careful going home. I'll look forward to your next visit."

Toby searched for Magdelena and found her pouring lemonade in glasses lined on the table. "May I steal you away?"

She passed the pitcher to her mamm. "Would you mind doing this?"

Her mamm accepted the pitcher. "Toby, how are you holding up?"

"I'm fine. Danki for asking." He gestured to the willow tree with two weather-beaten chairs beneath it.

She turned one chair to face him. "Rachael and your mamm are working to feed the guests right along with us. Even when they're hurting, they want to help others."

"Busying ourselves keeps our mind off this morning's service. I want to wipe out this day and remember Daed when he was vigorous and healthy. Even the days when he was sick, he managed to laugh, and we had good conversations. Not this day."

"I would want to do the same. Annie said she invited you and me to supper at their haus Thursday. Will you spare the time? I realize the service has interfered with your work."

"Andrew, Gabe, Joel, and Timothy helped with my work at Andrew's farm and here. I won't be as behind when I return to work as I had anticipated. I'll make time for Abram and Annie. I was encouraged when he offered to teach me archery. We're making progress with them. I'd like to keep it going."

"I'm thrilled. Annie said she was happy Abram invited you. He hadn't said a word to her about it."

Toby opened his mouth to answer, but friends surrounded them and expressed condolences to him. He and Magdelena stood and got separated.

Two hours later, most of the visitors had left. Men loaded benches in wagons to take them to storage on the Yoders' property, and the women finished washing and drying the dirty dishes.

Magdelena's daed approached him. "Toby, if there's anything I can do for you or your family, please don't hesitate to ask."

Toby wanted his blessing to court his dochder, but this wasn't the appropriate time. "Danki, Mark, for everything you've done already in putting out the benches."

Ethan, Zach's daed, came alongside Mark and gave him a friendly slap on the back. "I'll follow you home and help with putting up the long shelf in your barn." He turned to

Toby. "I wish I'd known your father. I enjoyed the memories friends shared this afternoon."

Toby tamped down the fear and uneasiness consuming him. The camaraderie was evident between the two men. Mark was kind but distant with him. Ethan was more outgoing, bolder, and he had a louder voice. He wished he could have Mark's favor. "Those are kind words. Danki. He was a loving father, husband, and friend to many."

Magdelena and her mamm carried picnic baskets and joined the group.

Toby took the baskets. "I'll put them in your buggy."

Bernice nodded. "How kind of you. Danki." She separated from them and headed to the buggy.

"They are heavy." Magdelena smiled.

Zach walked with Mark, Magdelena, and Toby. "Magdelena, I'll ride with your family. I'm going to your haus to put up a shelf in the barn with your daed. It will give us a chance to talk."

Magdelena nodded.

Mark gestured to Zach. "Great idea. I appreciate the help."

Magdelena pinched her lips and didn't look at Zach.

Toby gripped the baskets and listened.

Zach ignored him and got into the buggy.

Magdelena stood back from the buggy and glanced at Toby. "Rachael is insisting on kumming to the bakery tomorrow. If it's too much for her, please tell her to stay home and rest."

"She's like me. We like to stay busy. Being with you will make her happy." Toby put the baskets in her parents' buggy.

Mark gestured to Magdelena. "Time to go."

Magdelena got in, onto the back bench next to Zach. She called out to Toby, "Please stop in the bakery if you get a chance."

"I will," Toby said. He noticed Magdelena's coolness to Zach, and understood that she didn't want Zach close to her. The man was persistent. He watched their buggies leave, and then he went inside. The furniture had all been moved back in its place, and the living room table was minus the coffin. His eyes lingered on the empty chair.

Patches raised his head and then returned to his vigil.

Rachael swiped her forehead with the back of her hand. "I'm tired." She plopped on the settee. "Patches hasn't left his usual spot by Daed's chair. I was sure he'd be playing with the kinner, but he had no interest."

"Is Mamm all right?"

"She's exhausted. She's rocking on the back porch. I'll go sit with her. I'm sure we both may doze since the overhang provides shade this time in the afternoon. Do you want to join us?"

"I'll feed the livestock and tinker in the barn." Toby wilkomed the friends to take his mind away from this sad day, but he was ready for some quiet. He patted his leg. "Patches, kumme with me."

Patches raised his head and whined. He didn't budge.

Toby understood. They each had to grieve in their own way. He noticed Daed's favorite patchwork quilt was missing from Daed's chair. He had caught a glimpse of it on Mamm's bed. He hoped it comforted her. The yellow and brown material in the tattered quilt reminded him of his favorite memory with Daed when they made a kite of using fabric for the tail of similar colors. They'd had the best success flying it high in the sky until it got tangled in a tall oak tree. They'd had fun putting it together. It was the first and last time he'd made a kite. Daed said they'd make another one, but he'd gotten ill soon after their special day.

He shook his head. Funny how the simplest thing could stick with you and mean so much. He strolled to the barn, opened the doors, and fed the livestock. Then he opened an old weathered chest and found a half-finished wooden heart. Daed must've whittled it for Mamm and then hadn't had a chance to finish it. He found a knife, whittled the rest of the heart, and sanded it until the wood was smooth. He carried it into the haus and left it on Mamm's dresser.

He bumped into her as he was leaving her bedroom. "Excuse me. I found a small gift in the barn to you from Daed. It needed some finishing touches. I left it on your dresser."

She circled around him and picked up the heart. "Danki. God must've had you find this for me. I love it." She clutched the treasure to her chest. "My routine revolved around him. I'll have to create a new one. Our friends tell me the ache I have in my chest will lessen as time passes. I don't think it ever will."

Toby hugged her. "He wouldn't want you to live your life without him in sadness. He'd want our family to hang on to our happy memories and to be strong for each other. I keep telling myself this and maybe it will help you."

Mamm wiped her tears. "I'm blessed you and Rachael are with me. Together, we'll get through this." She sat on the bed. "I'm going to stay in here awhile."

"I'll be in my room if you need me." Toby passed Rachael's room on the way to his.

He poked his head around the open doorway. She was

asleep. He retreated to his room, knelt by his bed, and prayed for the strength to get through his grief. Tears sprang in his eyes. Daed would've wanted to attend his wedding. He'd miss him not being there. Assuming there would be a wedding someday with Magdelena. He had a bad feeling about what Mark would say when he got the chance to speak with him.

Chapter Five

Magdelena pinched the fluted edges of the crust and put the peach pie into the oven Tuesday morning. She glanced at Rachael. Her heart ached for her best friend. "What can I do to make your day easier?"

"You being here makes my day better. Amidst the grief, I have remembered precious times with Daed. He made me a small wooden doll when he was able to whittle. I found it in my dresser drawer last night. I pulled it out and set it on my bedside table." Rachael dipped her measuring spoon in the canister of sugar and gazed at Magdelena, blinking back tears. "Mamm showed me what had originally been a half-finished wooden heart from Daed. Toby found it in the barn and finished it for her. He made time for Toby and me separately. He was such a fun-loving and giving man."

"I'm blessed I got to know him before he passed. I admire how his illness didn't dampen his ability to laugh. He had the best sense of humor." Magdelena walked around the worktable and circled her arm around Rachael's waist. "I can't imagine losing a parent. I'm here to listen or hold you if you need to cry."

Rachael added the sugar to her batter. "I'm doing better today. It was hard to watch him suffer, so I'm happy for him to be with God. When I get sad, I concentrate on happy memories. Being here with you and baking helps keep me focused on the good things in life."

"How did your daed and your fiancé, John, get along?"

Rachael put a pinch of salt in her batter. "He liked him. He said if I was happy, he was happy. He wanted me to find love like he and Mamm had together. He trusted me to pick the right man. Daed was grief-stricken and blamed himself for the robbery and buggy accident causing John's death and my limp. It took a long time before Toby could convince him it wasn't his fault. Mamm and I tried, but to no avail. I'll always be grateful to Toby for this. I still ache when I think of the day John died."

"You've suffered a lot of tragedy in your young life. You're blessed your daed supported your decision to marry John. I'm sorry you didn't get to have your wedding. I believe God has the right man for you when you're ready. Although a man may sweep you off your feet and capture your heart when you least expect him to."

"I'm not sure any man could fill John's shoes, dear friend." Rachael measured three tablespoons of molasses and poured it in her bowl.

A rap on the front door of the bakery startled them.

"I'm late opening for customers. I'll go and take care of it." Magdelena moved to the front, unlocked the door, and turned the sign.

Zach stepped in. "I brought you some flowers." He held five yellow roses in a large mason jar.

Magdelena moved behind the counter. She didn't want to encourage him, but she also didn't want to offend him. "I'm not comfortable accepting them."

"No harm in giving flowers to a friend. I asked your daed if it was all right with him before I brought them to you. He said yes." Zach held them out to her again.

Gladys, the sheriff's fraa, entered the bakery and stepped to the counter. "What beautiful flowers. There's nothing like a pretty bouquet to brighten one's day."

Zach set them on the end of the counter and introduced himself. "I'm Zach Hilty. It's a pleasure to meet you. Magdelena, enjoy your day and the flowers." He tipped his hat and left the shop.

"He's handsome with his big broad smile, and those muscles are about to tear his shirt. He has his eye on you." Gladys gave her an impish look.

"His parents and mine are becoming fast friends. I'm not interested in him for other than a friend." She loved Gladys. The woman was cheery, and she stopped in often to chat. Gladys showed she cared about her and Rachael with her frequent visits to talk with them and ask how they were doing. "I have my sights set on Toby Schlabach."

"Smart girl. Know what you want and don't settle. Marriage is for a lifetime. You want to make the right decision. If Toby is the one for you, then Zach will have to find another girl to court. I've never understood how any woman could agree to an arranged marriage." She pointed to the kitchen. "Is it all right if I speak with Rachael? My heart breaks for her losing her father. He was such a sweet man. I embroidered a hanky for her." She held it out to Magdelena.

Magdelena fingered the fine linen. "Absolutely. How thoughtful. She'll love the handkerchief. We can never have too many of those."

Gladys grinned and bustled to find Rachael.

Magdelena stared at the flowers. She would leave them

at the bakery and not mention them to her parents. She didn't want to give them any reason to push her toward considering Zach.

Gladys returned to Magdelena minutes later. "Have a wonderful day, sweet girl."

An hour later, Mrs. Hilty strolled in and stuck her nose in one of the roses. "Zach asked me to pick these for you this morning. He couldn't wait to bring them to you. They're beautiful."

"Danki, Mrs. Hilty." Magdelena didn't know what else to say.

"Dear, remember, you must call me Ida. Our families are growing a close friendship, and I couldn't be more thrilled." She gazed at the display case. "I came to buy a loaf of cinnamon bread and a half-dozen wheat rolls."

Magdelena wrapped her purchases and accepted payment. "Enjoy."

Ida winked. "I'll look forward to having you over to spend time with Zach. He's not one to give up on you."

Magdelena's cheeks warmed. "Did he tell you I'm interested in another man?"

"He did, but he's not worried. He's far from a quitter. We always encourage him to strive for what he wants. Give him a chance. You won't be sorry. Zach's a confident, happy, and caring man. I've said my piece, and now I'll go." She made a hasty exit.

At the end of the workday, Magdelena glanced at the flowers.

Rachael joined her. I've had a long day working in the kitchen. She pointed. "Pretty flowers."

"Zach brought them to me. He's too interested in me.

I've tried to deter him, but he doesn't get the message and neither does his mamm. I told them I'm interested in someone else, but they dismiss it. I'm leaving the flowers at the bakery. I don't want my parents or Zach to think I'm taken with them." She locked the door and left with Rachael.

"It's pushy of Zach and his mamm to ignore your interest in Toby and to encourage you to like Zach. I hope they don't make things awkward for you with your parents." Rachael gave her an empathetic smile.

"Yes. My daed seems taken with Zach. I'm worried the Hiltys will gain Daed's favor."

"I'll pray for you and Toby, Magdelena." Rachael waved goodbye and got in her buggy at the livery.

"Danki, Rachael." Magdelena turned and stepped in her buggy and also left the livery and drove home.

Zach and Daed were standing outside the barn.

Zach rushed over to take her reins. "I got to witness a cow have a breach birth today. Your daed was amazing."

Daed helped Zach unharness the mare. "Zach is a natural-born rancher and a quick learner. I've asked him to stay for supper."

Zach looked inside the buggy. "Where are your flowers?"

"Yes. Zach told me he delivered roses to you at the bakery." Daed glanced at the buggy.

"I left them at the bakery for everyone to enjoy." She stared off at the pond to avoid looking at both of them. She had no intention of encouraging him by putting the flowers in her room.

Zach nodded. "I like the idea. You'll have more time to enjoy them there."

Daed frowned and stared at her for a moment. "I'll take

care of the mare. You and Zach go take a gander at the cow and her new calf."

She walked with Zach and rested her arms on top of the gate to observe the cow and the wobbly calf in the stable. Magdelena laughed as the boppli frolicked around its mamm. "She's a spunky one."

"Your daed's an excellent teacher, and he makes ranching fun and not like a job. Cattle ranching has been a dream of mine for a long time. To find your daed and have him train me, as well as treat me like a friend, is a blessing."

"Daed said most of the men who work for him like the money and do a decent job, but they don't have a love for cattle ranching. Having you express a genuine interest in it makes it fun to teach you what he knows." She stepped away from him.

He came closer to her. "How about a game of horseshoes?"

She dropped her gaze and stepped away again. "I should go inside and help Mamm with supper."

"I told your mamm I'd like to have time with you when you got home. She gave me permission to kidnap you." He chuckled.

Daed strolled into the barn. "Magdelena, I heard Zach ask you to play a game of horseshoes. Your mamm has all the help she needs. It won't hurt you to play a game. Go ahead."

Hairs on Magdelena's neck prickled. Zach had her parents conspiring to bring them together. She had made her wishes known. Why wasn't anyone listening? She hadn't challenged her elders. There may be a first time if they kept coaxing her to consider Zach. She glanced at Daed. His curt nod told her she didn't have a choice. Now wasn't the time to ask Daed to consider what she preferred. "I'll play."

Zach led her outside and picked up the horseshoes. He handed her one. "Ladies first."

She threw and it circled around the post.

He threw one and missed. "I'm out of practice."

She suspected he was letting her win. He didn't understand. There was nothing he could do to win her heart. They finished playing the game, and she won by a couple of points.

Mamm shouted out the window, "Supper's ready."

Magdelena glanced over her shoulder and smiled at the buggy kumming toward them.

Liza, with Charity and Peter in the buggy, pulled the mare to a halt. "Greetings. The kinner had a great time together as always." She hugged Charity.

"Goodbye, Liza and Peter. Danki for having me over." Charity jumped out of the buggy and ran toward her and Zach.

"Liza and Peter, danki for bringing Charity home." Magdelena grinned.

Liza nodded, and Peter waved to them. She then directed the mare away from the haus.

Charity lifted a horseshoe. "These are too big for me. Daed has some smaller ones. Will you play a game with me?" She looked at Zach.

Zach pointed to the haus. "No. Your mamm said it's time to go inside and have supper."

Charity pinched her lips and marched to the haus.

Magdelena watched Charity run inside the haus. Zach didn't make much of an effort to get better acquainted with her little schweschder. Toby was sincere in his enthusiasm to play games with Charity, and it was another reason she was drawn to him.

Zach's parents, Ethan and Ida, arrived and got out of the wagon. Ethan tied their mare to the hitching post. "We came to visit. Do you mind?"

Daed greeted them. "Not at all. Your timing is perfect. You can join us for supper. The food is on the table."

Ethan grinned. "Danki. We'd be happy to stay for supper."

Magdelena went with Daed, Zach, and his parents inside the haus and to the kitchen. She was surprised Zach and his parents were joining them for supper.

Zach sat next to Magdelena. She instinctively leaned away from him.

Daed offered a prayer for the food.

Mamm stood and each of them handed their bowls one at a time for her to serve them ham and bean soup. The aroma filled the room. She filled her bowl last. "A little birdie told me you received flowers at work." She raised her brows at Magdelena.

"Who gave them to you?" Charity wrinkled her brow.

"Zach. They are yellow roses."

"Toby won't be happy you gave my schweschder flowers." Charity glared at him.

"No harm in giving a lady flowers." Zach shrugged.

Daed slathered butter on his cornbread. "Charity, mind your manners."

Charity was right. Toby would be put off by Zach's attention to her. She wished Zach would focus on any other woman. Someone who would wilkom his attention. There were plenty of unmarried young women in Charm who would look kindly on him.

The men discussed what Zach had learned from working with her daed all day. She didn't mind Zach enjoying his job on the ranch, but she didn't want him to set his sights on her. She'd made herself clear when he expressed his interest in her the first time.

Charity beamed. "Peter and I waded in the shallow end of the pond while Liza hung her clothes to dry. We skipped rocks like we did with Toby at Ellie's social. It was fun. We should have Toby over and wade and skip rocks in the water again."

Magdelena nodded. "I'll ask him soon, and you can ask Peter to join us." Her schweschder had given her the right time to remind her parents and the Hiltys about Toby.

Zach cleared his throat. "We can wade in the pond after supper is over." He gazed at Magdelena.

Charity glowered at him. "I'd rather wait for Toby. He's my friend and he always wants to play with me." She picked up her spoon and finished her bean soup. A brief, uncomfortable silence descended on the gathering.

Mamm cleared her throat. "She will go. Ida and I can visit while we wash and dry dishes." She pinched her lips and sent Magdelena a stern look.

She lowered her eyes. Mamm sided with Daed. Zach was their choice for her. Their push for her to be with him at every turn this evening had been obvious. She'd speak to them after the Hiltys departed. "Charity, you can kumme with us."

Daed stood and pushed back his chair. "Charity's kumming with me. I'll let her pet the newborn calf."

Charity clapped her hands. "I can't wait!"

Magdelena dragged her feet to the pond with Zach. She settled on the bench.

He took off his socks and boots. "The water will cool us off from this heat." He glanced at her shoes. "You're not kumming in?"

She shook her head. "Zach, please respect my wishes. I am not the girl for you. There are other available girls who are ready for courtship. I could introduce you to some of them."

"If you had not met Toby, would you have given me a chance?"

"Why does this matter?" Magdelena crossed her arms.

"Please answer the question. Your answer makes a difference to me."

"I don't know." She watched the two ducks dipping their heads in the water and avoided eye contact with him. "Please understand. I don't dislike you, Zach, but I'm set on Toby as my suitor."

"Your parents are in favor of us having an arranged marriage or they wouldn't insist you say yes to my suggestions. Your daed and I are working side by side, and he doesn't have a son to run this ranch when he's ready. All the puzzle pieces fit. It makes sense for us to court and ultimately marry."

Magdelena covered her mouth with both hands and closed her eyes for a moment to hide her displeasure and frustration with him. She took a deep breath. "What you propose is more of a business arrangement with no regard for my desires. I take back my answer to your earlier question. No, I would not consider you. You're self-centered, arrogant, and money hungry." She stood and turned her back to him.

He shifted to face her. "I'm none of those things. I'm patient and smitten with a beautiful and kind girl I'd like to know better. Yes, the ranch is work I enjoy. Yes, I'm fond of your daed and mamm. I should've started with the fact I'm drawn to you. I don't deny I enjoy monetary rewards from hard work. I pointed out the pluses to a marriage between us to show you why our parents are in favor of our union." He lifted her chin and met her gaze. "I asked your daed for permission to marry you, and he said yes."

Magdelena paced. "Why didn't you tell me this when we first stepped outside? How absurd. You don't even know me. I won't agree to an arranged marriage with you. I don't understand why you don't find a woman who is available." She had feared this would happen, but she wouldn't be forced to marry a man she didn't love. She'd have to make her parents understand. She should appeal to Zach first. It would be better if he would tell Daed he had changed his mind. "Please. I want to choose my future husband. You can still work with Daed and one day run this ranch without marrying me. You will cause tension between me and my family if you pursue this."

"Your daed mentioned you may be stubborn and for me to overlook it. I'll treat you like a queen, Magdelena. I promise. I'll show you I'm the man for you. In time, you'll thank me for pursuing you in spite of your rejection."

Magdelena opened her mouth to protest.

Charity ran to them. "Magdelena, the boppli calf let me hug her. She's pretty with big eyes and black fur."

Magdelena smiled and smoothed her curls. "She's beautiful, isn't she?"

Charity bobbed her head and grinned.

The Hiltys and her parents came outside.

Ida circled an arm around Magdelena's waist. "Your daed's given his permission for you and Zach to marry. Arranged marriages are wise. We, as parents, know more about what our kinner need than they do. I'm thrilled you'll be my dochder-in-law."

Magdelena swallowed the bile rising in her throat. She

was sick about this. She couldn't pretend to agree. "I haven't said yes."

Daed narrowed his eyes at her. "Magdelena, your mamm and I have made our decision. The sooner you accept it, the better it will be for all of us. I'm sure, given time, you and Zach will fall in love and thank all of us for making this arrangement."

She froze.

Both families said their goodbyes, and Magdelena followed her parents inside the haus and went to her room. This was ridiculous. She wouldn't marry Zach Hilty. Toby needed to ask Daed for permission to court her as soon as possible. He hadn't stopped in the bakery today, and she missed him. He would pick her up on Thursday to go to the Hooks' for supper. She'd speak with him about what transpired tonight, but her heart sank. What would she and Toby do if Daed said no?

Toby drove to the bakery Thursday morning. He'd missed Magdelena the last few days while he'd gotten caught up on chores. "Magdelena, you are as lovely as ever. I stopped by to let you know I'll pick you up at ten until six this evening for supper with the Hooks."

"I'm looking forward to going to the Hooks' place with you. I've missed you, too. Each time the bakery door opened, I was hoping you'd kumme in. Rachael said you and your family are keeping busy plowing through the grief of losing your daed. I was worried about you."

She had a compassionate heart. Another thing he liked about her.

"I'm doing better than I anticipated. I find myself wanting to tell him things about my day and, in a split second,

I realize I can't right now. But I'm getting through it. Danki for asking. I had to catch up on chores these last couple of days, but I've been thinking about you." He pointed to the yellow roses. "Who brought the pretty flowers to the bakery?"

"Rachael didn't tell you?" Magdelena poured him a glass of water and served him a blueberry tart.

"No, why?"

"I overheard my name." Rachael joined them. "It's Magdelena's place to tell you."

Toby lifted his brows. "Magdelena, what's she talking about?"

"The flowers are from Zach Hilty to me. He brought them on Tuesday. My parents have taken to the Hiltys, and they're becoming best friends. Daed hired Zach to work for him. He's teaching him everything he needs to know about running a cattle ranch. Toby, Zach asked to marry me, and Daed gave his blessing. You have to talk to Daed as soon as possible."

Toby's chest tightened. This was a nightmare. Zach hadn't wasted any time making his claim on Magdelena. It hadn't entered his mind Zach would ask for an arranged marriage. Mark didn't know the Hiltys well. Zach must've won him over being all excited about the ranch. "I'll ask him tonight after we return from the Hooks' place. This is shocking."

Rachael took an empty tray out of the display cabinet. "You two belong together. You have to fix this. I've said my piece, and I'll leave you two to work this out."

Magdelena nodded to Rachael. "Danki for your support, dear friend."

Rachael disappeared into the kitchen.

Magdelena pulled the flowers out of the mason jar and

threw them in the trash. "I wanted to throw these flowers away as soon as he gave them to me, but I was afraid his parents or mine would ask about them if they came to the bakery. I haven't encouraged him. I was going to tell you about Zach this evening, but I'm glad you're here. I'm angry and sick about this."

Toby brushed her hand with his. "I'm sorry this happened. It's my fault. I shouldn't have waited to speak with your daed. You're the one for me. Magdelena. Will you marry me?"

"Yes! I'll marry you."

He took her hands in his. "I love you. We can talk about a date and arrangements later. I'll have to convince your daed I'm the man you should wed."

"I pray he'll say yes." Magdelena gave his hands a gentle squeeze.

"I've saved enough money for a future for us and to take care of Mamm and Rachael. I hope I can convince your daed I can provide for you."

"I want to go in with you when you ask Daed," said Magdelena.

Toby returned to his stool on the other side of the counter. "I don't mind." He had to gain her daed's favor. Magdelena being by his side would show Mark they were committed to each other.

Two Englisch women bustled into the bakery. The gray-haired round woman put her nose close to the glass case. "I want one apple pie and one dozen ginger cookies. Myrtle, what do you want?" The customer stood and glanced from Magdelena to Toby. "You both seemed in serious conversation when we walked in. I hope we didn't interrupt. Don't they make a striking couple, Myrtle?"

Myrtle had the same narrow brown eyes and pointed nose. Toby assumed they were schweschders.

He smiled. "Yes, you're right. Magdelena is striking, and I am mad about her."

Magdelena's face warmed. "I care about him, too. But we shouldn't be wasting your time talking about us. You came in to shop. Would you like some of our delicious fudge?"

"You're not wasting our time. We have nothing but time these days. Yes, give us half a pound, please." Myrtle grinned. "We're sisters, and we both have always loved fudge. We try to watch our waistlines, so it's a treat when we buy it. Right, Clara Jane?"

"I must confess, I've bought fudge and several times finished it before I got home. I'm past caring about how much weight I gain. I can always buy bigger clothes." Clara Jane chuckled. "Oh, to be young again and in love and caring about my waistline. It's obvious you're in love by the way you look at each other. I envy you both."

Magdelena grinned. "You're both kind."

"I agree with her. The two of you are adorable. And seeing the two of you reminds me of when Clara Jane introduced me to Lawrence, the love of my life. My father was set on me marrying another man until Clara Jane convinced him Lawrence would be the better choice for me. It took months. Don't wait. Get married and enjoy your life together."

Toby couldn't agree more. "Danki for the advice."

Myrtle and Clara Jane each paid for their purchases.

Clara Jane put her coin purse back in her reticule. "No. Thank you for letting us old biddies take up your time dredging up memories. Best wishes to you both."

Magdelena held their purchases. "We've enjoyed your visit. Here are your packages. Please kumme back soon."

Clara Jane grinned and accepted them. "We're passing through town, but we'll kumme by this way again next month. We're on the way to Mt. Hope to visit our brother, Calvin. We try to visit him once a month. But this fudge will be gone before we get there. He'll never know." She winked.

Toby watched the schweschders. Seeing them together reminded him of his close bond with Rachael. He and Rachael confided in each other, and they gave each other good advice. He couldn't ask for a better schweschder. The two women were strangers to them, and even they recognized the connection between him and Magdelena. He waited for them to leave. "We have a big night ahead. I'll be prompt at five-fifty. Enjoy your day, sweetheart."

He drove to Andrew's and worked in the garden until time to leave. He went home and washed and changed clothes, and then he picked up Magdelena at her home to go to the Hooks' place.

She sat on the buggy's bench next to him. "Are you nervous about speaking to Daed tonight?"

"I am, but excited, too." He reached over and gave her hand a gentle squeeze.

They arrived, and Abram invited them into the haus. "Magdelena, Annie's in the kitchen. Toby, let's get in some target practice before supper while we have good daylight. Follow me to the shed."

Magdelena left them and headed for the kitchen.

Toby and Abram strolled to the shed. On one side of the shed was a worktable with tools hanging on hooks, and shelves lined the other wall. On additional hooks, two fur quivers, two leather ones, and two exquisite bows.

"This is impressive. Do you make the bows and arrows here?"

"Yes." Abram removed a quiver from a crate. "I make these out of wood, leather, or fur. I've sold a few."

Toby accepted it from him. "This one is amazing." He pulled back the fur to examine it. "This is a perfect size and your stitches are nice and even."

Abram took back the quiver and handed him another one with arrows and then a bow. "You can use these." He chose another set for himself. "Let's go to the backyard and in the woods. I have tin cans I arranged earlier in the day for target practice."

Toby listened as Abram explained and showed him how to properly use the bow and arrows.

They went together to the spot Abram had cleared and prepared for them. The cans were on a long fallen oak tree, spaced about a foot and a half apart. Abram shot his arrow first and knocked off and spun the can in the air.

"Great aim. Let's see how well I listened to your instructions." Toby pulled back the arrow with the bow, aimed, let it go, and missed. He shook his head. "I need practice."

Abram reset the cans on the tree, and they kept taking turns and enjoyed target practice. "We should check on the girls. Supper may be ready."

Toby put a hand on his arm. "Do you mind if we sit a minute?"

"Sure." Abram sat on a tree stump.

Toby sat on the ground near him. "The other night, Gabe said he's certain you gambled with him in Massillon. He left Amish life and traveled for a while before he returned. If you're in trouble or need a friend, I want to help. You can trust me."

Abram stared at the tall cedar and oak trees around the clearing. "I don't want to talk about this. I have a plan, and everything will be fine by the end of the month. If I need help, I'll ask you. I appreciate the effort you and Magdelena have made to befriend Annie and me."

"All right, but don't hesitate to ask me for what you may need. I don't want you shunned. Amish from our community travel to Massillon for supplies unavailable in Charm. If they should notice you going in or kumming out of the saloon, they would have questions. Amish have their share of gossips. Be careful." He didn't want to preach or scold Abram. He hoped he'd conveyed his sincerity.

"I may take you up on your offer. But right now, I'm fine. I hope this won't hinder our friendship. My plan is to right my wrongs." Abram cleared his throat.

"Our friendship won't change. Remember, if you need help, ask. And I pray your plan works." He didn't want to badger Abram. His friend seemed to be on the right path to change his ways. He held up the bow. "Have you ever sold the bows?"

Abram shook his head. "One or two. I've never asked to consign with a store to sell them. I don't want to fill orders and have to make them by a certain time."

Toby stood and shouldered the quiver rope over his shoulder and carried the bow. "Ready to go in?"

"Yes. Annie may have supper on the table."

He and Toby strolled to the shed and hung the two bows and quivers containing arrows.

They entered through the back door and strolled to the kitchen.

Toby sniffed the aroma of fried chicken. Not something he had for supper often. "Annie, the chicken is quite a treat."

"Abram brought me the chicken this afternoon, plucked and ready to prepare. We are thrilled you're here. Please find your seats."

Magdelena set a bowl of steaming mashed potatoes on the table. "She's outdone herself."

Abram sat at one end of the table. "She's a talented cook and baker."

Annie lifted the water pitcher and dropped it.

Magdelena caught it before it hit the floor.

"There I go. Clumsy me. Danki." Annie's cheeks pinkened.

"No harm done." Magdelena filled the water glasses for her and put them on the table.

Annie opened a cabinet door and took out a platter for the chicken. She arranged the meat on the platter and carried it to the table. She went back to grab the breadbasket and bumped her forehead on the cabinet door she'd left open. "Ouch." She rubbed the spot.

"Did you cut your forehead?" Magdelena examined her head. "It's not bleeding, but you might get a bruise." She closed the cabinet door.

"I'll add it to my many bruises and cuts from accidents I've had for a while." Annie grimaced.

The girls took their seats, and Abram offered a prayer for the food.

Toby poured gravy on his mashed potatoes. "Do you have siblings and are your parents still alive, Abram?"

"My parents died about five years ago. I had a bruder and a schweschder. They were older than me. My bruder got with the wrong crowd during rumspringa as a teen and robbed a bank. He was shot in the crossfire between the deputy and other robbers. He died. My schweschder died last year. She'd been ill most of her life. The doctor suspected it was her heart."

Annie darted a glance at Abram. "His fraa passed away from the fever about two years ago."

"You've suffered a lot of tragedy, Abram." Magdelena sipped her water.

"I had a good marriage, and I loved my family. It was difficult, but Annie agreed to an arranged marriage with me. She's been a lifesaver."

"What about you, Annie? Any siblings?" Magdelena reached for the butter dish.

"No. I'm twenty-two, and Abram's twenty-three. I'd not married, and when Abram asked me, his timing couldn't have been better. My parents had died in a train wreck. Dad took Mamm to Canton for a little trip. I stayed home to take care of the livestock. I don't have siblings, so I was alone."

"How terrible." Magdelena clutched her napkin to her chest.

"We've kumme to Charm to start life anew. We're happy to have met you and Toby, and we look forward to having more fun together." Annie beamed.

Magdelena finished her last bite of food and stood with Annie to clear the dishes. She carried and slid them into the basin for washing.

Annie uncovered a beautiful tea ring made with cinnamon and drizzled with honey. Crushed nuts decorated the top. She served them each a piece.

"This is superb. We haven't made these for the bakery. It would be a great idea." Magdelena forked another bite. "Would you give me the recipe? I understand if you'd rather keep it for yourself."

"I'd be happy to give you the recipe. My grossmudder

died before I was born, but Mamm said it was her creation. It's always been my favorite."

"Mine, too." Abram grinned.

Toby cleaned his plate. "Delicious."

"Would you kumme to a social at the bakery? I'd like to have it Saturday around four. We'll close the shop early and invite our friends. You can get better acquainted with them." Magdelena stacked the dessert plates and dirty utensils and carried them to the counter.

Annie followed and dropped the glass in her hand, which she aimed to put on the counter. It shattered on the floor. She bent to gather the shards. "I go through a lot of glasses."

Abram rose. "I'll get it for you. I don't want you to cut yourself." He returned with a broom and dustpan.

Toby got up and dragged over a trash can for Abram.

"Danki. I don't know how Abram puts up with me." Annie covered her face.

"Easy. You're a wonderful fraa and partner." He dumped the last of the glass in the trash. Abram stowed the broom and pan. He returned the trash can to the corner of the room. "Toby, let's go sit in the rockers on the porch."

Toby had enjoyed his time with the Hooks, but he was nervous about speaking with Mark. He should give Magdelena more time with Annie and not rush her to leave. Both of them had made headway with their friendship with the Hooks. He didn't want to spoil it. "You have a large farm, and you've got a fair amount of livestock for the short time you've been in Charm. It's impressive."

"I had the financial means to buy the farm and livestock. I enjoy the farmwork. Annie takes good care of our home and me. So far, we're happy here."

Magdelena and Annie entered the porch. "This has

been a wonderful evening. Danki for the delicious food and conversation."

Annie clasped her hand. "I hope this will be the first of many visits you and Toby will make to our home."

Toby stood with Abram and shook his friend's hand. "Great time this evening. Danki." He nodded to Annie.

They bid the couple goodbye and retrieved their buggy. Toby guided the mare toward Magdelena's home. "Did you enjoy your time with Abram and Annie?"

"Yes. I no longer suspect Abram of harming her. She does have quite a few mishaps. She seems nervous. I don't know if it's her nature or if she is nervous for a reason. I believe she has told us the truth about her bumps and bruises. I'm wondering if she needs spectacles or if she is clumsy. It appeared she meant to set the glass on the counter and missed."

"She does have a lot of accidents. Did you mention to Annie she should consider spectacles, or detect any reason she may be nervous?"

Magdelena shook her head. "I didn't want to embarrass or insult her. I will consider how to broach the subject and then maybe ask her the next time we're together." Magdelena shifted to better look at him. "Did you enjoy your time with Abram?"

Toby had had a pleasant time, but he wished he knew more about Abram's plan. His friend's evasiveness made him uneasy. He hoped Abram's plan didn't put his friend in danger. Gambling could lead to owing scary men money. "I did. I told him Gabe insisted he'd gambled with him in Massillon. I made it clear I wasn't passing judgment on him. I offered my help. He said he has a plan and he'd rather not discuss it. I warned him many Amish from our community go to Massillon for supplies not plentiful here and they may recognize him. He needs to remember if someone tells Bishop Fisher they suspected him of gambling, it would turn into a big problem."

"Did he open up to you?"

"He has a plan, but he didn't elaborate. I hope he'll ask for help if he gets in trouble. I like him."

Toby turned into Magdelena's lane and parked the buggy near the haus. "Your daed is with Zach on the porch." He had hoped to catch Mark alone. He didn't blame Zach for being attracted to Magdelena, but he did question whether Zach's intentions were honorable. Did Zach view Magdelena as a way of securing his spot to someday take over Mark's cattle ranch? Toby's sole motive was his love for Magdelena.

"Zach spends more time here than at his haus. He will say or do anything to gain Daed's favor. I find it downright sickening. Daed laps up Zach's attention and desire to learn from him. Daed treats him as if they've known each other all their lives. Forgive me for my unkind rant. Zach's too presumptuous, and he unsettles my nerves."

Toby grinned. "I understand, and I'm glad. I'll ask if we can speak to your daed in private."

He tied the reins to the hitching post, and he and Magdelena approached the two men. "Good evening, gentlemen."

Mark nodded.

Zach smiled at Magdelena. "I waited until you came home. I didn't want to go all day without talking to you. Toby, we haven't had a chance to get better acquainted. You'll have to kumme over more often and spend time with Magdelena and me."

Magdelena sucked in her bottom lip and stayed quiet.

Toby knew from the way she sucked in her bottom lip

that she was frustrated. He pushed his annoyance with Zach out of his mind. He had to focus on why he was here. He shouldn't give in to Zach's attempt to rile him. He stepped closer to Mark. "Do you mind if Magdelena and I have a word with you in private?"

Mark raised his brows. "Very well. Let's go inside."

Zach gave them a curt nod. "I'll catch up with you tomorrow, Mark, and my beautiful Magdelena. Goodbye, Toby."

Magdelena frowned.

"You can stay, Zach," Mark said.

Magdelena's eyes widened and she exchanged a worried glance with Toby.

Toby gave her an assuring nod and waited for Zach's response.

Zach shook his head. "I should go home and be with the folks. Take care." Zach proceeded to his buggy.

Toby was relieved Zach didn't take Mark up on his offer. He didn't want this conversation to be any more difficult than it might be already.

Mark smiled. "You, too, son."

Son? Toby and Magdelena exchanged concerned expressions and followed Mark inside and sat together on the settee. Mark sat across from them.

Magdelena raised her brows. "I'm surprised Charity didn't kumme running to greet Toby. Where is she?"

"She's staying overnight at Liza's to help with Lorianne and play with Peter. She and Peter are glued at the hip." He chuckled.

Bernice entered the living room. "Toby and Magdelena, how was your visit with the Hooks?"

"We enjoyed their company, Mamm. Toby has asked to

speak to Daed, but why don't you join us?" Magdelena searched Toby's eyes.

Bernice darted a glance from Magdelena to Toby. "What's this about?" She sat in the chair beside her husband.

Toby cleared his throat. "Yes. Bernice, forgive me for not including you. I'd like you to hear this news. I love your dochder, and she loves me. We'd like your blessing to marry."

Magdelena pressed a hand to her rapidly beating heart. "Please, Daed and Mamm. This is what I want."

Toby smiled at her and then looked at Mark. "I've saved enough of my earnings to build or buy a haus and farm and to provide for us. I promise to love, respect, and be a good husband to her. With my father's passing, I have more time to devote to work and to Magdelena."

"Please, Daed and Mamm, grant us your blessing."

Toby couldn't read Mark's or Bernice's expressions.

Mark settled back in his chair. "This has kumme as a surprise. We like you, Toby. You're a good man, but Zach asked me first to court Magdelena, and I gave him my blessing."

Magdelena paled. "I don't love Zach. This shouldn't be a surprise. You're aware we've spent time together. It's no secret I'm smitten with Toby. I love Toby. He's my choice. Mamm, please help me."

"I agree with your daed. The Hiltys have become good friends. It wouldn't be right." She addressed Toby. "We care for you, but you can understand why Mark won't withdraw his blessing."

Toby's heart hurt. Frustration and disappointment raged through him. He shouldn't have waited. Rachael had warned him not to lose her over having to save the right amount of money. He'd overcompensated, and he might have cost himself Magdelena. Mark should want his dochder to be happy in marriage. Didn't she have a say? He had to remain respectful. "What can I say or do to change your minds?"

Mark stood. "There's nothing you can do. Zach and Magdelena will soon be wed. Bernice and I and the Hiltys have agreed to their arranged marriage. It's done."

"No!" Magdelena's jaw dropped. She stood. "I should have a say in who I will marry. Why are you doing this?"

Toby didn't stand. He reached for her hand to calm and guide her to sit. He wouldn't leave until he'd given his all to convince Mark and Bernice to change their minds. "I'm open to whatever change you'd like me to make to gain your approval. There must be something I can do."

Magdelena dropped to the chair next to Toby, and tears pooled in her eyes.

"Toby, again, I've given my word to Zach and his parents. I don't have anything against you," Mark said.

Toby understood the situation all too clearly. Zach and Mark had cattle ranching in common. The man had captured Mark's interest, and no doubt this played into his decision. "If you'd like the man Magdelena marries to work with you on the cattle ranch, I will change jobs."

"I filled the last open position when I hired Zach, and he has a genuine love for ranching. You like working for Andrew. There's no need for you to change jobs."

Magdelena's tears stained her cheeks. "You're not giving Toby a fair chance. He's willing to do anything you ask. Please reconsider. We're adults, and we are in love. Please don't force me to do something against my will I'll have to live with the rest of my life."

Bernice remained seated. "As parents we know what is best for you."

Mark stood next to her. "We've made our decision. You both need to accept it. Toby, I admire your work ethic and your family values. We wish you the best in finding the right woman for you."

He and Bernice made a hasty exit.

Magdelena motioned to the front door. "Let's go outside where we can have some privacy."

Toby followed her in silence to the other side of the barn. Her parents hadn't given an inch. What could he have said to gain their approval?

She turned to him and wept.

He couldn't think of another thing. He held her in his arms and kissed her hair.

She raised her head, her watery eyes sad and worried. "What are we going to do?"

He reached for her hands. "I'm out of ideas at the moment, but I'm not giving up. God can move mountains, and I believe He can change your parents' minds. Let's pray together."

They bowed their heads, and Toby offered a prayer to God. "Dear Heavenly Father, forgive us for any sins we've committed. We praise You for Your almighty power. We ask You to change Mark's and Bernice's minds and give us their approval. We love You, and we trust You. Amen."

Magdelena wiped her eyes. "I don't understand why my parents are so adamant."

Toby had to hold his emotions in check for Magdelena's sake. His muscles tensed and his head throbbed. "I don't know. We must trust God to work this out for us. I'll buy land and a haus or build one, and then I'll approach them again."

"Maybe you're right. If you have a place for us to live, then it will prove to my parents we're ready to marry. Zach still lives with his parents."

He managed a smile. Hope sprang in Magdelena's voice. He'd accomplished not leaving her defeated. What if it wasn't God's will for them to marry? *No.* He didn't believe this. Zach hadn't bothered to better acquaint himself with Magdelena or respect her wishes. "I love you. Let's take one day at a time."

She nodded. "Will you stop by the bakery tomorrow?"

"Yes. Your daed didn't ask me to stay away from you, thank goodness. I should leave. He may kumme looking for you." He took her in his arms and kissed her.

She stayed in his arms a moment and then walked with him to his buggy. "I love you so much. Don't ever doubt it."

"I won't." He got in the buggy, watched her walk inside the haus, and then drove home.

Dark gray clouds gathered overhead. Much like his mood. Daed had been right. He'd told him to not overthink things. He'd warned him not to pressure himself to have the perfect amount of money to court Magdelena. His flaw had been wanting to have things too perfect. He could've courted Magdelena and kept saving money. He thought he'd had all the time in the world. Tonight, he'd learned this wasn't true. He'd look for homes for sale starting tomorrow. Would a haus and property change her parents' minds?

Chapter Six

Magdelena dragged her feet into the haus and to her bedroom after Toby left. She shut the door. Would Zach expect her to go to suppers and activities with him? She shuddered. This evening should've been filled with joy and excitement. A day she'd never want to forget. Instead, her stomach churned. She changed her clothes and slipped into her gown. She got into bed and pulled the sheet to her chin. The storm outside matched the turmoil raging within her.

She woke Friday morning earlier than usual to escape breakfast with her parents. She yawned and rubbed her eyes. She'd tossed and turned most of the night. Tired, her emotions roiled. She hoped she wouldn't say something she'd regret. She tiptoed to the kitchen, made her dinner for noon, and exited to harness her mare to the buggy. She frowned at Zach waiting for her.

"Magdelena, I've got your mare ready." Zach handed her the reins.

She startled and then snatched them from him. "Danki. Where's Daed?"

"He's out with the cattle."

She glared at him. The sight of him raised her temper. "You have some nerve asking my parents for my hand in marriage. We haven't even formed a friendship. You haven't been in Charm long enough to know which Amish girls are available. I love Toby. Why do you want to marry me when you know I love him?"

Zach got in the buggy beside her. "I have no doubt we'll fall in love and live a happy life together. Our families have formed a fast friendship. I love cattle ranching, and I've bonded with your daed. You're the only one who doesn't realize we're a good match. And maybe Charity." He chuckled. "She's almost as difficult to win over as you."

"I don't find any part of this conversation humorous. Be friends with Daed. Enjoy your work here. But don't involve me. Please inform Daed you want to withdraw your request to marry me, and please do it today." Magdelena pinched her lips.

"Toby can't give you what I can. Our daeds have more money than most Amish men in Charm. To have our families become close friends is a blessing. I belong here with you. Give me a chance."

She scowled. "You don't respect anything I say. You've explained our life together as a puzzle where all the pieces fit. The biggest and most important piece is missing. Love. Something I insist on before agreeing to marry. I always said I'd never agree to an arranged marriage, and this hasn't changed." She had to make him understand. He could fix this if he would bow out of his request to wed her. "Please, Zach. Tell Daed you no longer want to marry a woman who loves another man."

He shook his head and jumped out of the buggy. "I'll be here when you get home from work, Magdelena. And

I'll be staying for supper tonight. It's time you gave me a chance." He turned and disappeared inside the barn.

She cried angry tears from the ranch to the livery, and then onto the bakery. The lanterns were lit in the kitchen. Rachael had arrived earlier than usual. "Rachael, I'm glad you're here early."

"Toby told me what happened when he came home last night." Rachael set her bowl aside and opened her arms wide.

Magdelena hugged her and sobbed.

"My heart aches for the two of you."

Magdelena pulled her handkerchief out of her sleeve. "I'm furious with my parents and Zach."

"Did you discuss your conversation with your parents any further before you went to bed?"

She wiped her damp eyes. "No. I didn't want to say anything I shouldn't, and I didn't trust myself. I'm full of frustration."

"Have you told Zach you're in love with Toby? Ask him to speak to your daed and take back his request to marry you."

"I did tell him again this morning. He won't budge. In my opinion, he wants to marry me to be sure he gets a piece or all of the cattle ranch when Daed retires. He could still have this even if he marries another woman. The man is single-minded and infuriating."

"There's no question he'd position himself better to take over the cattle ranch if he was your husband. Toby is upset with himself. He thinks if he'd asked for your hand earlier, all of this could've been avoided. I'm not sure. I told him not to waste time on regrets."

"I agree with you. Daed may have had it in his head I should marry a man with similar means or he may have been waiting on a man he liked to groom for taking over the ranch someday and to marry me. The ranch is his life. Money is too important to him. We all have our flaws, and his is placing too much importance on wealth." She didn't like her daed making decisions for her. Why couldn't he have a relationship with Zach and leave her out of this? Was she nothing more than a game piece to be moved at the will of her father and Zach Hilty?

Rachael added a teaspoon of honey to her sour cream apple cake mixture. "Maybe in time Zach will give up."

"If I didn't love Toby, I still wouldn't choose a man like Zach. He's pushy, arrogant, and using me to get what he wants from Daed. I'm hurt no one is listening to Toby or me. I don't know how to get through to any of them."

"God tells us to have faith in all things. We don't know why this is happening. There's a lesson to be learned, but we aren't seeing it. We'll all continue to pray and ask for God's direction. You've got our family's support. We'd like nothing better than to attend your and Toby's wedding."

"We'd be schweschders." Magdelena sighed. "Let's change the subject. We can't fix this right now."

"Toby said you had a good visit with the Hooks, but he told me about what happened and what Gabe said about seeing him gamble. Tell me more about your time with Annie and Abram."

Magdelena rooted through the drawer to find a round scalloped cookie cutter. "I invited Annie for a social here tomorrow at four. I want her to get better acquainted with our friends. We can invite Hannah, Ellie, and Maryann. I don't want to overwhelm her."

"Wonderful. We can make jam cookies. They'll go perfect with coffee or lemonade. I'll go to each of their places on the way home and tell them about it."

"We're not giving them much notice, but we'll take who shows." Magdelena liked Annie a lot, and she was sure her friends would, too. "We had the best time with Annie and Abram. Archery is a hobby of Abram's, and he crafts bows and arrows. Toby enjoyed target practice with him." She and Toby had made progress growing their friendship with the couple.

Magdelena chuckled. "Abram adores her. She is the clumsiest girl. I lost count of how many times she dropped things or tripped. I'm convinced she's telling the truth about her bruises and bandages. It's a relief."

"Toby said Gabe, Andrew's bruder, insisted he'd gambled with Abram. He said he broached the subject with Abram, and Abram said he didn't want to discuss it. Toby is determined to help him. I'm not sure I want my bruder involved," Rachael said.

Magdelena mixed her dough, dumped it out of the bowl, sprinkled flour on it, and reached for her rolling pin. "I'm worried about what Abram may be into. I also don't want Toby to get hurt or to get into trouble helping him. For now, Abram wants to handle whatever it is he's doing alone."

"Yes. I pray he does, too." Rachael stopped what she was doing and pulled out a heart-shaped cookie cutter from the drawer. "Wouldn't heart-shaped jam cookies be cute for the social?"

Magdelena accepted the cookie cutter. "I love the idea. I'll bake a batch today to sell, and tomorrow, I'll make them again plus an extra dozen for the social and spoon strawberry jam in the center of them. These always sell out fast." She baked with Rachael until it was time to open.

* * *

Minutes later, Toby opened the door and greeted her. "I didn't sleep much last night. I spoke with Andrew about buying a place. Andrew suggested I talk to his neighbor, Mr. Umble, who has his farm for sale. He has a two-story haus on the property. Andrew and I are going over there today. If the place is right for us, I'll negotiate a price with him. Do you want to tour the haus with me first?"

Magdelena shook her head. "I've been there, and I loved the white clapboard exterior of their haus. The family wants to move to Nappanee, Indiana, to care for Mae's parents. I like the layout of the haus. There's a big kitchen, four bedrooms, a sitting room, and living room. Mr. Umble kept adding on rooms after they bought it. There's land enough for crops and space for you to build a workshop. It would be perfect for us." His idea gave her hope her daed would be more comfortable considering her wishes once the haus and land were in place.

"Andrew uses his workshop at the furniture store, and I've been using the one on his property. The workshop could wait, but it is an added bonus I'll have room on the property for one."

"This will help sway Daed's decision. It has to." She wouldn't give up. She could envision a happy life with Toby. Zach had no place in her heart.

Magdelena and Toby exchanged a surprised look and stopped talking.

Zach swaggered in, stared at Toby, sat next to him, and then smiled at Magdelena. "Sweetheart, I'd love a cup of coffee."

Magdelena gripped the coffeepot. "I'm not your sweetheart, Zach." She set a mug in front of him and poured his coffee. She glanced at Toby's clenched jaw. He wasn't happy.

Toby rose and tipped his hat to Magdelena. "I'll check

on you later." He didn't want to leave her. He wanted to defend her and to tell the man to leave her alone. But it wouldn't bode well for him to cause an argument and give Zach ammunition to disparage him with Mark.

He left the bakery and went to Andrew's to work. He worked on the farm and fought to erase his encounter with Zach until quitting time.

Andrew arrived home and gestured for him to get in the buggy. "Ready to meet with Mr. Umble? I'll drive us over there."

"I am. Danki for going with me." Toby grabbed a small can from under his buggy seat, and then stepped into Andrew's buggy and sat next to Andrew. He shoved the can under his seat.

"Nervous?" Andrew glanced at him with an understanding smile. "I take it you have money in the can for a deposit. Good to be prepared and positive."

"Very nervous and for several reasons. This is a large purchase. I'm hoping Mr. Umble will accept my offer. I brought more than enough for a deposit." He drew in a deep breath. "Most of all, I hope Mark will be impressed enough to change his mind."

"You've got a lot you want to accomplish. I'm disappointed Mark is adamant about Magdelena marrying Zach when she's against it. She must be miserable."

Toby stared out over the meadows as they traveled. "We're both upset. Zach came to the bakery this morning while I was there. He's determined to marry Magdelena. I'm sure it's to secure his position on the cattle ranch. And Magdelena is one of the prettiest and kindest girls in our community." His family had been poor, but his life had changed when Andrew provided him with a generous wage and taught him how to craft furniture to sell in his store.

"I wish you'd let me discuss you and Magdelena with Mark."

"I appreciate your offer, but I suspect he'd think I sent you to do my bidding. I doubt it would make a difference."

Andrew and Toby arrived at the Umbles' farm. They approached Mr. Umble on his porch.

Andrew shook the man's hand. "Greetings, neighbor. This is Toby Schlabach, the man I told you about that might like to buy your place if the price is right. Do you mind giving us a grand tour?"

"Greetings, Mr. Umble." Toby nodded.

"Wilkom. Yes, I'd love to show you around. Please follow me." Mr. Umble was short and had to look up at them. He had a round stomach and a jolly face. Mr. Umble gave them the grand tour of the haus, barn, smoke haus, and corn- and hayfields. He showed Toby his garden of vegetables without a weed in sight.

Toby studied the property, and he was pleased the place was in much better shape than he'd anticipated. His stomach clenched. He hadn't made a transaction the size of this one. He had sense of pride and excitement about having land and a home of his own. He and Mr. Umble went back and forth on price. If Mr. Umble accepted his last offer, he'd be getting the place lower than he'd predicted. He appreciated Andrew throwing in his supportive comments.

Mr. Umble stroked his beard. He then smiled and shook Toby's hand. "You've got a deal. But I'll need two months before you take possession." He requested a down payment sum.

Toby's heart soared. In two months, he'd be a homeowner. He hadn't had to wait to build a haus. This was perfect. Toby walked back to the buggy and retrieved his lard can and returned to Andrew and Mr. Umble. He opened the lid, removed and counted out the exact amount he owed him. He passed the money to Mr. Umble.

"I'll go inside and get the paperwork. Make yourselves comfortable on the porch chairs. We'll use the table between them to sign the paperwork. My fraa's not here. She's visiting a friend." He went inside and returned with a pen, ink, and the paperwork. "Here you go, Toby."

Toby read the paperwork, dipped the quill in the ink, and signed his name. "Danki, Mr. Umble."

Mr. Umble accepted the paperwork he'd had already drawn up for the sale. "Here's a second set of paperwork for your records." He passed Toby the papers. "I'm happy to sell to a young man who is purchasing his first home. Andrew sang your praises when he stopped over to chat with me yesterday. He's given me more than reasonable prices on furniture, and this is a way I can show him my appreciation. You're blessed to have such a close friend as Andrew."

"I agree." He exchanged a smile with Andrew.

"If you both keep giving me compliments, my head is going to swell." Andrew chuckled.

Toby would pay the balance and take possession in two months. Toby couldn't wait to tell Magdelena all the details.

An hour later, Toby and Andrew arrived back at Andrew's place, where Toby'd left his buggy. "Danki for everything, Andrew."

"I'm thrilled for you, Toby." Andrew waved goodbye.

Toby drove to Magdelena's to tell her and her daed the news. He frowned. Zach stood with Mark piling wood from a tree they must've chopped down. He'd wait until tomorrow. He had to speak to Mark soon. Zach had Mark's blessing to marry Magdelena. Toby was sick about it and determined to change Mark's mind.

* * *

Magdelena went to work Saturday morning. "Rachael, I wish I could move in with you. Zach is everywhere I turn at my haus. You would think he was glued to Daed. Last night at supper, Zach prattled on about the cattle and didn't stop praising Daed for all he was learning." She couldn't stand the sound of Zach's loud voice and his constant need to impress Daed, and she resented him kumming between her and Toby.

"Did he ask for your time after supper?"

"Yes. I begged off with a headache and went to my room." She didn't know how many excuses she could make before her parents would insist she stop avoiding Zach. She'd take her chances and decline his invitations for as long as she could.

Rachael rolled her dough and used the heart-shaped cookie cutter. She placed the cookies on the tray, pressed her thumb in the center of each cookie, and put a half spoonful of strawberry jam in the middle of each one. "I'm making the jam cookies. I didn't think you'd mind. I hope Zach doesn't drop in on our social. Liza and Maryann can't attend the social, but Ellie and Hannah and Annie will be here. We haven't had a social with our friends in a while. This will be fun."

"Yes. I'm looking forward to the social. No. I don't mind about the cookies. I don't want Zach here either. I'm afraid Zach will push me for a wedding date. I've got to stall him. Toby needs time to show Daed we're ready to marry and we have a place to live."

"I'm sad your parents chose Zach and refuse to listen to you." Rachael opened her mouth and shut it. She glanced at Magdelena. "I want to tell you something, but it would be wrong. It's Toby's news to tell."

"What?" Magdelena washed her hands and went to Rachael.

"I can't." Rachael avoided eye contact.

"Please. I don't know when Toby will be in here again. Did he talk to Daed? Did he buy the Umbles' haus?"

"I shouldn't have said anything. I will say you'll be pleased." Rachael ignored Magdelena and put her tray of cookies in the oven.

"All right. I'll leave you alone. But I'm dying to know what has happened." She hugged herself. "I don't care if I live in a shed if it means Toby and I can be together."

Dr. Harrison and the sheriff were their first customers of the day. Magdelena served the two friends cherry pastries and coffee.

Dr. Harrison nudged the sheriff. "Dottie came to my office right before I closed last night with a gash on her head. She'd fallen off a stepladder reaching for a basket on a high shelf. The woman is always up on the latest gossip and can't wait to tell anyone who will listen. She said Duke pointed a shotgun at Clay until he agreed to marry his daughter, Denise. Do you know anything more about this?"

The sheriff harrumphed. "Clay and Denise have been courting. Then Denise's cousin, Sharon, came to visit. Clay decided he liked Sharon better than Denise. Clay and her father got in a scuffle, and Denise came and got me. When I arrived, Duke had a shotgun aimed at Clay but dropped it when I approached him. Clay came by my office today and told me he was leaving town to go after Sharon. Thankfully, I don't know anything more."

"Clay shouldn't be forced to marry Denise. Maybe he

and Sharon had a better relationship. I'm glad Clay didn't let Duke bully him into doing something he didn't want to do."

The sheriff gave the doctor an exasperated grunt. "I don't like getting involved in love disputes, but I agree with you. And why would Denise want him if he loves another woman? They are a rough bunch. Nothing they do makes sense."

Dr. Harrison pointed to an article in his half of the newspaper. "On a better note, George Herman, Jr., known as Babe Ruth, is making his debut with the Red Sox. The coach has high hopes for this young left-handed pitcher since he's been excellent pitching during practice. A friend of mine observed him in practice and said he's quite a slugger with the bat, too."

"I'm anxious to find out how he does and if he's worth the praise he's been getting from practice."

Magdelena remembered Denise from her visits to buy desserts from the bakery. She didn't kumme in often. The girl had worn overalls and had a wad of chewing tobacco in her cheek each time she'd visited. She was a kind woman but bold. She believed there was a mate for each type of person. She didn't know Clay, but she did agree with Dr. Harrison. Clay should marry whom he chose. Like her and Toby. At least her daed wouldn't threaten to shoot Toby. Things could be worse.

Zach whistled a tune as he entered the bakery. He brought her daisies. "I figured the flowers I gave you the other day would be wilted by now. I brought you fresh ones." He dropped the flowers in a jar. "May I take you to dinner around noon?"

Dr. Harrison and Sherriff Williams bid her farewell.

She said goodbye to them and addressed Zach. "No. I don't want to leave Rachael by herself."

"We're making progress. You sound as if you would go if you weren't leaving Rachael alone. I'll meet you at five and we'll go to the ice cream shop for a sandwich and dessert. This is their day to serve chicken salad. We've got some important matters to discuss."

Magdelena's stomach churned. She had to get out of this. "We're closing the bakery early to have a social here today. There's no time for supper, and I'm not interested in spending time with you."

"If you keep avoiding me, I'll have to enlist your mamm's and daed's help. Please don't make this difficult. I have a lot to offer you."

Magdelena splayed her hands on the counter. She glowered at him. "Leave me alone. Find another woman. Be a cattle rancher. I don't care. But leave me out of this plan of yours."

He frowned. "Toby is an all right fellow, but he kummes from a poor background. I wish him the best. You'll thank me and your parents a year from now when you're living in a big haus wanting for nothing. I promise to be a good husband. I'm attracted to you, and I'm sure we'll fall in love the more time we spend together."

The door opened, and a hunchbacked woman used her cane to take slow steps to enter and to approach the counter. "The aroma of fresh bread drew me in this shop. You're smart to leave the window open. I'd like two loaves of cinnamon bread and the two-layer vanilla cake with tiny roses on top."

Magdelena could've hugged this woman for kumming in. She'd been the perfect excuse for not continuing her conversation with Zach. She wrapped the woman's purchases and passed them to her. "Danki for shopping with us." She faced Zach, where he sat at the counter. "I've got a lot to do before the social."

He stood. "I'll leave, but please stop being so negative about our arrangement. I don't want this to be unpleasant or to make you miserable. Please open your heart. You like my family. I like yours. You don't know me well enough to say no to this arrangement. I'd like to set a wedding date soon." He didn't wait for her to respond and left.

Magdelena huffed and rolled her eyes. Zach eliminated Toby's name from any part of this last comment. He acted as if Toby was a beggar and not worthy of any of them. Zach infuriated her. She wouldn't let him ruin the social. She was disappointed Liza would miss it, but she understood. Liza's young son, Peter, and toddler, Lorianne, kept her busy. She hoped Zach wouldn't show up at the bakery insisting she go to supper with him.

Toby hurried inside the shop. "Magdelena, I've got wonderful news. Mr. Umble sold me his property. We don't have to worry about building a haus. He'll be handing his place over to me in two months."

Magdelena's heart soared. "You made this happen fast. I'm proud of you. I can't wait to call you my husband. When will you tell Daed?" She had to believe her parents would be impressed, be surprised, and understand there was no reason for them to deny her and Toby having a future together. If they didn't, she'd crumble. She pushed away the doubt clouding her joy.

"I was going to tell him right away, but I'd rather share this news with him once I have possession. It will make a bigger impact and show him we have nothing holding us back."

A chill went through her. "We may not have much time.

I avoid my parents and the Hiltys as much as possible. Zach wants to set a wedding date." Magdelena disliked the division Zach had put between herself and her parents. They'd been strict disciplinarians, but they didn't hesitate to tell her and Charity they loved them. Their decision she should spend the rest of her life with a man she didn't love had hurt her heart.

Toby straightened. "I plan to talk to Zach when I can find him at his haus and not yours. Do you have any idea when he leaves from work?"

Magdelena didn't want their problem to grow worse. She wouldn't discourage Toby. They needed to do whatever they could to win over her parents and urge Zach to withdraw his request. "I'm home by five-thirty and sometimes he's still there. Seven would be the best time. He'd be at his home by then after working with Daed on the ranch, even if he stays for supper at our haus."

"We don't have Sunday service tomorrow. I'll miss talking with you. But don't worry. I'll be at the bakery sometime Monday and tell you about my conversation with him."

"The Hiltys will probably visit us on Sunday. I dread it. I pray your meeting with Zach will discourage him from pursuing me any further. We shouldn't have to struggle this much to be together. I'm sorry for all this turmoil my family has caused." She loved Toby for his fortitude. He hadn't wavered in his devotion to her. Daed could demand he not speak of marrying her again. She feared Daed may reject Toby's proposal to marry her. And worse, then he may demand Toby never speak of marrying her again. Then what would she do?

His loving gaze held her eyes. "Don't apologize. One of the best days of my life was meeting and falling in love with you. We'll talk again Monday. Enjoy your social this afternoon."

She watched him leave the bakery. She'd had her eye on him long before they fell in love. He'd always been the one for her. His handsome face, warm smile, and devotion to working hard and taking care of his family touched the surface of why she loved him. He was wise and reasonable, like his late daed. And not like her daed. She'd do whatever it took to have a future with him.

She waited on customers and helped Rachael bake goodies until four, and then she posted a sign on the door the bakery had closed early for the day. Minutes later, Hannah and Ellie arrived. Magdelena hugged each one. "We've got strawberry jam cookies and lemonade or coffee. Help yourselves."

Rachael joined them and hugged them. "I'm happy you all could kumme. Ellie, you look terrific for giving birth to Emma a month ago. How is the angel? I would imagine Peter loves to visit her."

Ellie chuckled. "Emma sleeps through the night, and she doesn't cry unless she's hungry or needs her nappy changed. You're right. My stepbruder loves to hold her, and he is a big help when he kummes to our haus. Peter's a lot more patient than I am. The way he thinks and talks you'd think he was an adult instead of a child."

"Emma's beautiful, like her mamm. And Charity acts twenty and not seven, so I understand what you mean about Peter." Magdelena gestured to two of the tables pulled together with chairs surrounding them. "Take your lemonade and cookies from the serving table and make yourselves comfortable. Ellie, my schweschder, Charity, insists she will marry Peter. As close as they are, I wouldn't doubt it."

The group giggled and nodded.

Hannah set her glass and small cookie plate on the table. "Maryann and Liza won't be here. They had a prior commitment to go to supper at the Yoders'." Her eyes twinkled. "I'll be disappointed if Peter and Charity don't get married when the time is right. They are adorable."

Annie entered the shop and tripped. She grabbed the edge of the counter and righted herself. "I'm sorry I'm late."

Rachael rushed to her side. "Greetings, Annie. There's no need to apologize. Go ahead and find a chair. I'll bring you your lemonade and cookies."

Magdelena made the introductions. "Annie likes to bake. She made the most beautiful tea ring with nuts and a delicious glaze. The dessert was almost too pretty to cut."

"Annie, we're glad you're here. Please tell us about yourself." Ellie grinned.

"I'm married to Abram, a widower who needed a fresh start. Hence, our move to Charm. Toby and Magdelena have become good friends of ours."

"Where are you from?" Hannah asked.

"Berlin, Ohio. I had no family left, and Abram's fraa had died from the fever, and his bruder, schweschder, and parents had all passed away. Charm has been a good choice for us. Better to leave all the sad memories behind. I'm thrilled Magdelena and I have become friends, as well as Abram and Toby. I'm waiting for the announcement of Magdelena and Toby's wedding." Annie covered Magdelena's hand.

Magdelena blushed. "Toby and I want to marry."

The girls clapped their hands and said, "Yay!" in unison, except for Rachael. Ellie crossed her arms. "Aren't you happy for Toby and Magdelena?"

Rachael heaved a big sigh. "I would be, but Magdelena's daed refuses to give them his blessing."

"What?" Ellie shook her head.

"My daed has arranged a marriage between Zach Hilty and me." Magdelena could use her friends' advice.

"Why, if you're in love with Toby?" Ellie frowned.

Annie covered her open mouth. "I'm surprised by all this."

Hannah leaned forward. "Have you and Toby spoken with your parents about you and he getting married?"

"Yes. My daed refuses to change his mind. He's impressed and elated Zach wants to learn about cattle ranching. Like our family, the Hiltys have more money than most Amish families. Zach's parents bought a thoroughbred horse and they have a big home and a new large barn. They have become fast friends with Mamm and Daed." Magdelena's heart ached talking about this.

Hannah frowned and shook her head. "Toby is one of the kindest and most dependable men in Charm. He's admired for his work ethic, faith in God, and devotion to his family. Why on earth would your daed not consider him? What are you and Toby going to do?"

"Toby bought the Umbles' place, and he takes possession in two months when the Umbles are packed and ready to leave. He wants to approach Daed again when they have left and he has possession of the property. I'm not sure we have the time."

Ellie raised her brows. "What do you mean?"

"Daed and Zach are rushing things. Zach wants to make plans. He knows I love Toby, but he doesn't care. He and my parents insist their plan is best. It's more about the ranch and the two families being friends than a loving marriage. The arrangement suits them and not me or Toby." She had no say. She didn't like feeling invisible, as if her choice didn't matter. She'd been an obedient dochder, and she didn't deserve this.

Ellie moved her chair closer to Magdelena's. "Don't give up. You don't want to spend your life with a man you don't love. Do whatever it takes to marry Toby, even if you two must run away."

Hannah clutched Ellie's arm. "Ellie, your advice can be forceful at times. God already knows how He's going to work on her parents' hearts. You and I had difficult circumstances to overcome before we married and everything got ironed out for us. He can do the same for them without Magdelena having to go against her parents."

Annie gave her a weak smile. "I agree with Ellie. Magdelena, don't settle. Do what you must to be with Toby."

Ellie met Magdelena's gaze. "Maryann says Andrew brags about Toby's work at their property to anyone who will listen. I'm sure he'd speak to your daed on your and Toby's behalf whenever you're ready."

"I'm sure he would, and I appreciate it. But it would have to be Toby's decision to ask him. Toby plans to speak to Zach sometime this afternoon or evening. Zach's glued to my daed's hip most of the time. He sometimes stays for supper, and I told Toby to try finding him at his haus after seven. Maybe he can reason with the man. We'll keep Andrew in mind. I'm not marrying Zach under any circumstances. Enough talk about me."

For the next two hours, Magdelena and her friends chatted about their sewing projects, recipes, and cleaning tips as they enjoyed their cookies.

Hannah stood. "We should all head home. We've kept Rachael and Magdelena after work long enough, and our husbands are waiting on us." She put a hand on Magdelena's shoulder. "We're all here for you and Toby. We'll be praying for you both. God never promised our lives would be easy, but He never leaves us or forsakes us."

Magdelena hugged the girls, thanked them for kumming and for their support.

Rachael bid them farewell. She gathered the dirty plates, and Magdelena put the glasses in the sink.

Rachael yawned. "Let's let these dishes soak in the water overnight. I'll wash them early in the morning."

"Yes. I'm tired, too. I'm sorry the conversation focused on my problems. I planned to have a cheerful time. Annie and our friends were supposed to get better acquainted. I should've kept my mouth shut." Magdelena sighed.

Rachael patted Magdelena's back. "Annie acted like she enjoyed herself. We all care about you and Toby. This is a life-changing decision your parents are making for you, and they aren't listening to you. I'm losing sleep over this, too. I've been praying for God's intervention. I need to have faith things will work out for Toby. We aren't going to solve it tonight. Let's go home and get some rest. We've got time."

Magdelena hoped she was right. At least Zach hadn't shown up at the bakery to take her to supper after the social. But each day it became more difficult to fend him off.

Chapter Seven

Toby hoped Magdelena's social this afternoon brought Annie closer to her friends. He had compassion for the Hooks, and their interest in the couple had brought him closer to Magdelena. They both had the desire to help those who might not be easy to like. Most Amish were close, but not with those who were brusque and secretive. He'd gotten a glimmer of a softer and kinder side of Abram when they practiced archery. For now, he had to convince Zach to respect his and Magdelena's wishes. As he came close to the Hiltys' home, he slowed his mare. He had chosen to visit Zach around seven as Magdelena had suggested.

He pulled over and prayed for God to give him the words to say and to control his frustration. He then proceeded to the haus, tied his mare to the hitching post, and approached Zach on the porch. The big white barn had a fresh coat of paint, and the wraparound porch to the two-story home, which was almost as large as Magdelena's home, had an overhang with high posts. In the distance, sows and hogs filled the fenced-in area on the hillside. "Beautiful place your parents have here."

Zach didn't stand. "If you're here to discuss Magdelena, you're wasting your time. Let's not argue about this. Our families and I are doing what's best for Magdelena. Her daed will need a son to take over the ranch. You can't break the bond of friendship our parents have formed."

Toby's neck hairs prickled. "Zach, don't you want to marry for love? There are plenty of available girls for you to wed. You can work at the cattle ranch."

Zach huffed. "I get it. You want to marry Magdelena and then take over the cattle ranch when Mark's ready to retire. Then what? I'd work for you? No. I like the plan already in place. You choose one of those available girls and stay away from Magdelena. You'll never meet Mark's expectations. I do. Accept his decision. You don't have any choice."

"Magdelena is adamant she won't marry you. She's rejected you at every turn. Do you want the ranch enough to wed a woman who can't stand you?" He scanned the property. "You already have a business to run and own when your daed is no longer able to. I don't get it."

"You have a simple mind. I have bigger plans. Both places together will bring in a bundle of money, which will benefit both families and our future kinner. I'll keep a steady staff of dependable and well-trained men to keep the businesses thriving. You should've sealed this deal before I came along." He smirked.

Toby flexed his hands at his sides. He didn't remember ever getting this angry, and he couldn't let his emotions ruin what he wanted to accomplish. "I don't notice a haus being built for you and Magdelena. If you have the money you claim, why don't you build one? You plan to live with your parents after you're wed?"

Zach glowered at him. "It's none of your business, but

I predict Mark will give us land and a big haus for our wedding present."

Something was awry. Zach had dropped his stare to his shoes and backed away. He'd let his guard down for a moment. Why? "You wouldn't build near your family? You've got plenty of acreage here."

"No. Being close to the ranch makes more sense. I'm done having this conversation with you. We can be cordial but don't kumme here again. And I will be relaying your interference to Mark. Maybe you should consider relocating. Make it easier for all of us."

Toby shook his head, turned his back, and went to retrieve his wagon.

The front door slammed. Toby glanced over his shoulder.

Mr. Hilty marched to Zach. "I'm tired of telling you over and over again to do things around here. You're an adult. Act like one. Mark says you're an excellent addition to the cattle ranch. Show me the same respect."

Toby left and drove home. He wished he had his daed to ask for advice. He didn't accomplish anything appealing to Zach to leave him and Magdelena alone, but he had learned Zach wasn't giving his daed the same respect he gave Mark. And the haus question unnerved the man. He didn't fully understand why, but it was something to ponder. His visit hadn't been a waste of time.

Mamm ushered him to the kitchen. "Son, you've got to keep food in your stomach. You work all hours. You don't sleep much, and you skip meals. I'm worried about your health. Now, with your daed gone, you've got more time to work. I understand you have goals, but you could ease off your hectic schedule."

Rachael entered and plucked a strawberry from the small bowl on the counter before sitting at the table.

"Magdelena is beside herself with the pressure Zach and her daed are putting her under. She told the girls at the social what is going on with Zach and her daed, and we're all rooting for the two of you."

"I spoke to Zach and got nowhere." Toby uncovered the plate of ham salad and fresh fruit his mamm set before him.

"What about asking the bishop for his opinion?" Rachael leaned back.

Mamm shook her head and patted Toby's arm. "He'd advise you to accept Mark's decision. To cause dissension would go against Amish traditions."

"Even if Magdelena and Toby plead their case?" Rachael tilted her head.

"Yes." Mamm sighed. "Kinner are to obey their parents. Toby, you may have to accept the circumstances. I'm sad for you and Magdelena, and for Rachael and me. We are disappointed not to have her become family."

Rachael covered Mamm's hand. "You and Daed wouldn't have forced us to marry someone for any reason. You've both supported and encouraged us to marry for love. Magdelena's wishes shouldn't be dismissed."

"Don't misunderstand. I despise what Mark and Zach are doing. Amish strive to not lay our treasures on earth but in Heaven. We need enough funds to live and help others but not to stockpile and center our lives on. Mark's ruining his dochder's life, and he's let greed take first place in his life. She'll find it difficult to trust her parents again."

Toby appreciated his mamm's understanding. Magdelena didn't have this luxury. If Zach hadn't moved to Charm, would Mark have given him and Magdelena his blessing? He had assumed if he acquired enough money to show he could provide for Magdelena, Mark would've given his permission for them to wed. Or maybe he would never measure up in Mark's expectations, regardless of Zach being in the way. He was certain God had put Andrew in his life. Andrew had given him a job, taught him a skill to earn a substantial living, and offered to speak to Mark on his behalf. He could depend on Andrew for anything. He'd consider Andrew's offer if he exhausted all possibilities with Magdelena's daed. "What advice can you give me?"

Mamm stared at him for a moment. Then she reached over and caressed his cheek. "I'll support whatever you and Magdelena decide to do. Please be careful. You both have compassion and need to exercise your faith in God when making decisions. Be patient. Pray and read the scriptures. Don't do anything you'll regret later. I shouldn't have asked you to accept Mark's rejection. Your daed and I would never had asked you or Rachael to marry someone you didn't want to wed. I'm sorry you're both having to go through this."

Rachael's eyes pooled with tears. "I remember how excited John and I were to marry. I'm grateful for the time we had together before he died. But I'm thankful to have known what it felt like to have been in love. I want you and Magdelena to have the future we didn't get to experience. An arranged marriage is cold and indifferent. The opposite of what you and Magdelena have together. We have to stand by her. Listen. Hug her. And speak to anyone you think will help."

Toby nodded. "John was an exceptional man. I pray you'll fall in love again. Magdelena is comforted by you. I'm glad you're close friends. She needs us to support her. I wish we had church tomorrow. I don't want to wait until Monday to tell her about my conversation with Zach, and to discuss what to do next." Church was important to him, but he hadn't minded having tomorrow off to rest and be with family and friends until now. Magdelena mentioned she thought the Hiltys would visit her family. A full day of having Zach at her home might be a struggle for Magdelena. There was nothing he could do about it. He would go to the bakery to talk to her first thing Monday morning.

Toby chatted a couple of minutes and then went to his room. He didn't understand why he and Magdelena were going through this turmoil with her daed.

Magdelena washed her face Sunday morning. The Hiltys would be here soon, and she dreaded their visit. She supposed they'd stay until evening. Their fast friendship with her parents wouldn't irritate her if Zach and she weren't the topic of each conversation. And he'd insist they take a walk, boat ride, or something. He didn't stray far from her daed, so at least she wouldn't have to worry about him being with her all day. She needed church today. She needed Toby.

Charity skipped into her room and climbed on her bed. "Mamm said you and Zach will marry soon. What about Toby? I like him much better."

"Did you ask Mamm why I'm marrying Zach?"

"She said Toby isn't right for you and Zach is and there would be no further discussion about it. I started to say Toby was my favorite and yours. She gave me the mean look and said to find something to do."

"Our parents insist I marry Zach, and I don't want to. Even if I didn't want to marry Toby, I still wouldn't want Zach for a husband. I'm heartbroken they won't listen to me." Magdelena plopped on the bed beside her.

Charity snuggled close to her. "Don't worry. I'll tell Peter about this. He's smart. He'll think of something."

"I'll take all the help I can get." Magdelena wanted the world to know she didn't want this wedding. Charity and Peter couldn't change her aggravating circumstances, but their outlook and sweet nature was refreshing.

Charity stood and tilted her head to the door. "The Hiltys are here. Zach's loud." She covered her ears and left the room.

Magdelena closed her door with a gentle shove. She'd hide in her bedroom and prolong having to greet them.

She jumped at the hard rap on her door.

Daed's voice boomed. "Magdelena, we have company. Kumme and greet them."

"I'll be there in a minute." She pulled out a handkerchief from her dresser drawer and held it to her cheek. Aunt Gloria had given the embroidered handkerchief to her two years ago. She tucked it in her sleeve. She liked to keep one there in case she needed it for any reason. She wished Aunt Gloria were here. Her aunt would understand her side of things. She took a deep breath and went to obey her daed. "Greetings."

Ida engulfed her in a hug. "My dochder-in-law. I'm anxious for this wedding to take place."

Magdelena's throat clenched. She didn't respond to Ida. Mamm's smile and nod didn't set well with her. The two mamms must've been making plans behind her back. How far had they taken things? She stepped back and sat in the farthest chair from the group.

Zach plopped in the chair next to hers. He leaned close. "Toby paid me a visit. Did you know about it? Has he said anything to you about our discussion?" His tone was intense.

She narrowed her eyes. "He said he was going to speak to you on our behalf." She hoped Toby had made progress with Zach. His tone said otherwise.

"I told him I'm done with his interference. Nothing he can say will change our arrangement. I've spoken to Bishop Fisher. Our wedding is scheduled for September second."

Magdelena huffed. "No. Call it off."

"Please don't fight me on this. God would not want you to disobey your parents, treat me this way, and go against our Amish way of arranged marriages."

"Step outside with me right now." She gave him a curt nod to the back door. She'd had enough of him. Outside, she walked a good distance from the haus before speaking. "God has a plan for my life. You're not in it. You'll never convince me otherwise. Nor would He want you to insert yourself between Toby and me. God wouldn't want you to force me into a marriage against my will. Your motives aren't pure."

"Any man would want to marry you. You have it all, and I'm not talking about the ranch. If I hated the ranch, I would still want to marry you. I'm sincere in my interest and fondness for you."

Charity ran and interrupted them. "Mamm said it's time to read the scriptures."

Zach tousled Charity's sun-kissed light red curls. "Where were you when I arrived?"

Magdelena was surprised at his gesture with Charity. Was he now trying to get closer to her? He'd avoided her until now. Was his gesture genuine?

"I was in Magdelena's room, and then I went out the back door to play. You better kumme with me, or we'll be in trouble." She slipped her sweet pudgy hand in Magdelena's.

They walked to the porch and Magdelena chose a chair in the circle between Ida and Charity.

Ida patted Magdelena's knee. "You'll be happy with Zach. You'll see."

Magdelena crossed her arms. The words stung. She listened to Daed's prayer and reading of the scriptures on kinners' directive to obey their parents. Daed glanced at her too often while he spoke. They asked too much of her.

Daed finished the devotion and offered a prayer for the food.

She hurried to her feet and dashed to the kitchen. Food didn't interest her, but putting distance between Zach and herself did.

Ida circled an arm around her. "I pray you'll give Zach the chance he deserves. He needs a fraa like you. Someone who is responsible and is wise in giving advice. A partner he can depend on."

She didn't have anything against Ida, but the woman had given her more reasons why she wouldn't consider Zach a suitable husband. Magdelena wanted a husband who could be a spiritual leader, a partner she could count on for advice, a man who knew and loved her with his whole heart. Ida had verified Zach's immaturity. He was obsessed with having his way. Cattle ranching was his first love. She doubted God or a woman would ever be first in his life. She gave Ida a weak smile and set the full gravy boat on the table.

Mamm called the men inside for dinner. She'd warmed

mashed potatoes, beef bits, and gravy she'd prepared yesterday. "Charity, give Zach your seat. Kumme over by me."

"Magdelena wants me to sit here." Her sweet schweschder sipped her lemonade and then picked up her fork.

She didn't want Charity to get in trouble. "Zach doesn't mind. Do you?" She glanced at him.

He was half out of his chair and righted himself. "I have the rest of the day with her. It's fine."

Mamm squinted at Magdelena, her lips pinched.

Magdelena darted her gaze away from Mamm and forced a half spoonful of mashed potatoes in her mouth. She'd been happy with her family until now. Her biggest worry had been helping a friend in trouble or waiting on a rude customer. She'd been upset with her parents at times, and they with her, but they'd never let anything kumme between them. She didn't like displeasing them. How could she make them understand what they were asking of her was wrong?

Charity pushed her plate aside. "Is Toby kumming over today? I miss him."

The conversation stopped.

Magdelena stiffened. Daed wouldn't like this.

Mamm dabbed her mouth with her napkin. Magdelena was sure it was to gather her thoughts for a moment. "It's not appropriate for him to kumme to supper unless Zach would like to include him, since he'll soon be Magdelena's husband."

"Why can't I invite him? He's my friend, too. Zach doesn't live here. Why is everything up to him?"

"Watch your tone, young lady." Daed glared at her schweschder. "Toby is a friend to us. But Zach will be your bruder-in-law soon. There's a difference."

Zach sat back and put his arm over the corner of the chair.

The position showed another example of his arrogance. "I don't have any siblings. I need a little schweschder."

Charity stayed silent for a moment and then stood. "May I be excused?"

Magdelena couldn't miss the relief screaming from Daed's face.

"Yes. You may." Daed resumed his discussion with Zach and Ethan about a bull he was contemplating buying.

In the kitchen, Magdelena unfolded a dish towel to dry dishes with Ida as Mamm washed them. Then she strolled outside to sit with Charity at the picnic table by the water. Her schweschder had drawn a monkey, dog, and cat. "You've got talent."

"Which do you like the best?"

Magdelena tapped the paper. "The monkey. I can't draw a straight line. Your drawings are improving all the time."

Charity withdrew a paper she had underneath her drawing and showed it to her. "I made this for you. It's you and Toby."

Magdelena held the picture closer to her face out of Zach's view, and then turned it over on her lap. "Danki."

Zach sat next to Magdelena. "Charity, I need to speak with your schweschder. Do you mind leaving us alone?"

Charity heaved a big breath and looked at Magdelena.

Magdelena gave her a forced smile and nodded.

"I'll take the picture inside and lay it on your dresser." Charity rolled her eyes at Zach and then clutched her picture and headed to the haus.

Zach reached for Magdelena's hand.

Magdelena dropped her hands to her lap.

"You shouldn't spend time with Toby. It wouldn't be proper. I understand he will attend socials and services and visit with your friends here. I ask you to respect our impending wedding. I'm sure your parents would agree."

She couldn't argue this arrangement would make meeting with Toby more difficult. Her reputation and Toby's would suffer if they weren't careful. She refused to succumb to Zach's wishes. She'd never snuck around behind her parents' backs. They'd have to if she and Toby wanted to discuss their options. She had to mind her words. Zach would repeat anything she said to Daed. "Toby and I have the same friends. Rachael is my best friend. We're in the same social groups."

Zach frowned and cast her a veiled glance. "I suppose, but don't make it too often. There is no hope for you and him. This wedding will take place September second. I'd like you to be happy about it. I'll prove to you what a good man I am. You won't regret it."

September second wasn't far away. Magdelena wanted to scream. She struggled to muffle a scoff. Why couldn't he get it through his thick head? She didn't care if he was tall, short, fat, skinny, mean, or nice. She wouldn't have a thing against him if he weren't standing in the way of her and Toby having a future together. But she doubted she'd be interested in him if she were available, with his arrogance, obsession with Daed's ranch, and still living with his parents. He hadn't even mentioned building a haus. "Why aren't you building a haus on your parents' land? I'd assume, given your family's wealth, you'd want a haus of your own. You obviously came to Charm ready to find a fraa."

Zach's face reddened. "Mamm takes care of me. Why should I have a haus until I have a fraa to manage it and help with outside chores? Besides, I'd rather build a haus on your property. Your mamm and daed have more property, and I'm hoping we can build here."

She nodded. Lazy? She'd add this trait to the list of ways he was the opposite of Toby. She endured another couple of hours of Zach's account of what he'd accomplished working for Daed. Boring conversation, but better than him discussing their future.

Charity returned with her little hands on her hips and a satisfied smile on her face. "Time for you to go home, Zach. Your parents wanted me to tell you to untie the horse." She darted a glance at Magdelena and gave her an impish grin.

Zach didn't appear to notice. "Will do, little one."

The Hiltys and Beachys strolled out to meet them. Ida put her hands on Magdelena's shoulders. "I can't wait to show you your wedding dress. Your mamm was kind enough to give me the measurements and allowed me to stitch it. I went right to work on it, and I stayed up late to finish it. I love to sew, and it's easy to create."

Magdelena's chest tightened. She hoped never to put it on. Something had to give before then. Mamm, standing behind Ida, gave her a harsh stare. "You finished the dress in a short time. We can change the wedding date. Wouldn't you like more time to help us plan the wedding? We don't need to be in such a hurry." She didn't like how Ida was rushing things.

"How sweet of you, but it was my idea to have the ceremony early. I know about Toby. But Zach will prove to you he's the right husband for you, given time. Besides, I've got plenty of time to make it special." Ida patted Magdelena's cheek.

The woman was patronizing. Why not give her a choice? Everyone was forgetting about Zach proving himself to her. Toby didn't have to prove anything. And she wanted nothing to do with Zach. They weren't giving in. His mamm appeared anxious to get Zach out of their haus and on with his life. Another indication the man may be a tad lazy. Magdelena had an inkling he wanted to run the ranch for Daed so he'd have men doing the actual work for him. Maybe Daed would realize Zach wasn't the ideal man for his future plans after all. She wasn't sure about any of this. She might be reaching for any excuse to make herself feel better.

Ethan gestured to Ida. "Time to go." He rolled his eyes. "She'd stay longer if I didn't remind her we need to get home."

Magdelena smiled at the interruption. The man had saved her. She'd had enough of this day with them.

Mamm gripped her elbow and escorted her away from the rest of her family. "You've never given us a minute of trouble or embarrassed us in front of others. I've been proud of your obedient behavior and sweet disposition. Straighten up, Magdelena. Don't disappoint us." She marched into the haus.

Mamm's grip on her elbow had let her know she shouldn't respond. She could cut the tension with a knife in her home. She felt insignificant. They ripped her heart out and stomped on it. She needed to talk to Toby tomorrow.

Toby woke Monday morning and drove to the bakery before it opened.

Magdelena unlocked the door, let him in, and fell into his arms and wept.

He held her, and his heart ached. He didn't have good news for her, and he didn't have answers.

She stepped back and wiped her eyes. "The Hiltys stayed way too long at our haus yesterday. Zach said he talked to you, but I'd like to hear your side of the conversation."

"I asked him to step aside. He refused, and there's no glimmer of hope with him. He's forging ahead, no matter what you or I say. We don't know Zach well. As I left Zach at his haus when I went to talk to him, I overheard Ethan demand Zach do chores and chastise him as if he was a five-year-old child. Zach may be motivated to do his best for your daed at present, but what about the future? Is he counting on the men he'll manage to do all the work? Your daed wouldn't approve."

"If he's lazy, he could disguise his plan to get out of as much work as possible. Once he has a fraa to take over from his mamm, then he'll consider building a haus. September second is way too soon for us to count on him disappointing Daed. Ida has my wedding dress already made," Magdelena said.

"September second! This is getting all too real. I don't know what we can do." He couldn't walk away from her. "I'm wrong to ask this, but should we leave and start a life away from here?" He shook his head. "We shouldn't. Your parents may never speak to you again. Our reputations would be ruined in Charm. Bishop Fisher would shun us from kumming back here to visit my family, but they could visit us. Maybe they'd move with us. I'm throwing out ideas, and I'm not sure any of them are good."

"I consider a life away from here with you often." Magdelena raised a brow and waited.

He took her hands in his. "Communities nearby may have friends or relatives who know us and tell the bishops not to accept us. None of them would condone us going against your daed's wishes. I'm sure the farther we move away from Charm, the better chance we'd have of being wilkomed to our next home. Are you ready to destroy your relationship with your parents?"

"What would your daed say to us if he were still alive? I love my parents, but I was envious of the deep love your daed had for you and Rachael. Your opinions and desires mattered to him. I'm certain your daed or mamm never made you or Rachael feel insignificant."

Toby gently brushed back a stray hair on her cheek. "Your parents love you, and I'm sure they'd be devastated if you left. What kind of man would I be if I took you from them? Daed wouldn't have approved. He'd have said for me to have faith and be patient. Mark and Bernice would never forgive me if I went forward with this. My family would have to move with us. Your parents would blame them because of your closeness with our family."

"I agree. Hannah told me Liza didn't love her late husband, Paul, but married him with the promise he'd provide for her and her family. She was the happiest when he bought her the bakery and she could be away from him and manage it. She didn't tell anyone until after he passed away how unhappy she'd been in the relationship. I was happy her story ended with her falling in love with Jacob. I never expected to relate to her experience in any way. She sacrificed her life to give others financial security. I'm not sure I can be as noble."

Rachael walked in from the kitchen, wiping glaze from her fingers with a towel. "I listened to part of your conversation. I shouldn't have, but I care and want to help. I've worried you may choose the option to leave. I haven't asked Mamm, but I'm sure she would agree to move. Me, too."

Magdelena shook her head. "Your lives would be ruined in Charm. You shouldn't have to risk your reputations and change your lives for us. I don't know how far my parents would take their frustration out on us and you if we carried out this plan. I won't have you do it."

Toby gazed into her eyes. "I believe we are meant to marry, have kinner, and live happily ever after. God hasn't let me down, and He won't now."

Rachael gave him a playful snap with her towel. "You should go. We open in ten minutes, and I'm sure word is getting around town about Zach and Magdelena's wedding. The gossips love to spread the news. Watch out for Zach or Ida when you visit from now on. You don't want him to make trouble for Magdelena with her daed. It's bad enough as it is."

He nodded.

Rachael returned to the kitchen to bake.

He kissed Magdelena's cheek. "Try and enjoy your day, sweetheart." He headed for the door and opened it for Liza, Lorianne, Charity, and Peter. "It's good to see you." He shut the door and stayed inside the bakery to talk with Liza and the kinner.

Magdelena greeted them.

Liza balanced Lorianne on her hip, and Charity and Peter were in front of her.

Charity looked at him. "Peter asked his mamm if you and Magdelena could kumme to his haus and teach us how to make a crate. Liza wants us all to stay for supper."

"Liza, you're so kind to offer this." Magdelena smiled.

Liza switched Lorianne to her other hip. "I'm sorry about what you and Toby are going through. I agreed to an arranged marriage. Magdelena, you shouldn't be forced into one. This is my way of helping you to have time together."

Peter nodded. "Charity said you can't visit Magdelena at her haus. Mamm suggested you both kumme to ours."

Toby loved Charity and Peter. They were the sweetest kinner. And he didn't expect this from Liza, but he wasn't surprised. Her husband Jacob's dochder, Ellie, had put her in danger and been a handful, but Liza hadn't given up on the girl until they'd formed a bond of mutual trust. Liza didn't hesitate to put herself in jeopardy to help others.

"Her parents may be upset about you asking us over to your haus. I don't want to cause you any trouble." He reached out to Lorianne, and she squealed as he took her in his arms.

Charity tugged on Liza's skirt. "We're going to visit Rachael in the kitchen."

"Behave yourselves," Liza said.

Peter and Charity went to the kitchen.

Liza gave Toby and Magdelena a mischievous smile. "I love you both. I don't support Magdelena's or Zach's parents' decision, and I'm not afraid to be truthful with them if asked. Charity is at our haus often. These kinner are wiser than most their age. They're innocent, but they know more about what's going on with your situation with Zach than your parents might guess. They're not in favor of Zach. This man shouldn't insert himself into your relationship. Please kumme to our haus."

"This means a lot to me. It's very kind. When, and what time?" Toby grinned.

"Tomorrow night at six. Grab a crate, and you can tell them how you built it. The rest of the time is for you and

Magdelena. I'll cook my chicken and rice casserole for supper."

"Danki, Liza. We really appreciate it," Magdelena said.

"When you bring your dish to socials, I leave lots of room for it on my plate. Any food I've tried of yours has been delicious." Toby passed Lorianne back to Liza.

Rachael, Charity, and Peter joined them. Rachael greeted Liza and Lorianne.

Toby beckoned to the kinner. "I look forward to being with you tomorrow."

"Yes. I do, too." Magdelena beamed.

"What are you up to today besides kumming to town?" Toby grinned.

Peter opened his paper sack. "We got two boxes of Cracker Jacks. Mamm says we have to wait until we get home to have them. I'm hoping to get baseball cards. Rachael gave us each a sugar cookie."

Charity opened her sack. "I got a new rubber ball for my Jacks game. Jacob said when he played it, they called it Knucklebones. I like Jacks better. Peter saved his cookie, but I ate mine."

"You beat me at Jacks most of the time. Now you'll have a new ball. I wanted to have a chance." Magdelena chuckled.

"Do you play Jacks, Peter?" Toby couldn't believe how much taller Peter had grown in the last six months. He turned eight this year.

Peter grinned. "I play to make Charity happy, but I'd rather play baseball or kickball."

"I used to love to play Jacks." Rachael smiled.

Lorianne rubbed her eyes and whimpered.

Liza rubbed her dochder's back. "We'd better go. I'm

on borrowed time with Lorianne's temperament staying pleasant. She'll need a nap soon. Charity and Peter have plans to play at our haus again tomorrow. She can stay at our haus until you're ready to take her home with you tomorrow."

"Danki again, Liza," Magdelena said.

Rachael bid them farewell and returned to the kitchen.

Toby thanked Liza again and said goodbye to all of them. He didn't like having to go around Magdelena's parents to speak with her. But this would have to do for now.

Chapter Eight

Magdelena finished work on Tuesday evening. She couldn't wait to go to Liza and Jacob's to be with Toby. Her schweschder and Peter were little schemers, and she loved them for it. Hannah and Ellie had been keeping Liza up to date on her dilemma, and she wanted to help. Magdelena wouldn't discourage Charity speaking her mind.

She and Rachael locked the shop and parted at the livery to retrieve their buggies and drive home. As she arrived home, Zach stepped in front of her buggy. She stiffened. Zach gestured her to park in front of the barn.

"I'll take your reins. How was your day, sweetheart?"

She cringed. Her day had been good until now. "Don't call me sweetheart."

"Mamm brought over your dress for the wedding. She wants you to try it on. Then we'll take a stroll before supper."

He acted like she should be the obedient bride-to-be without a care in the world. He was getting what he wanted, and it didn't matter if she was not in agreement or miserable. She wanted to scream at him to leave her alone. But she had to play along. She wouldn't give up her evening with Toby. "Liza invited me to her haus. She is my boss and friend. I'm cutting it close to be at her haus by six."

"Just you?" He quirked his brows and bore his eyes into hers as they arrived at her haus.

"And Charity." Magdelena jumped out of the buggy and hurried inside. She didn't give him a chance to ask another question.

Ida met her at the door and held up the dress. "I can't wait to have you try this on."

Magdelena forced a smile. Beautiful, but it was hard to get excited about the dress due to the woman's reason for making it. Ida had made it clear she approved of the arrangement, no matter what Magdelena had to say. She couldn't be honest and appeal to her to understand her side of things. A tiff with Ida was out of the question. She wouldn't disrespect her, and her parents would be furious if she spoke her mind. She had no time to deal with this. "Danki, Ida. Do you mind leaving the dress, and I'll try it on tonight when I get home. I'm heading to Liza's."

"How nice, dear. Zach would love to get to know your friends better. Take him with you." Ida cocked her head and grinned.

Magdelena swallowed the bile rising in her throat. She had to get out of this haus and leave Zach behind. "I'm sorry. Liza's invitation was for Charity and myself. Danki again for the dress. Please tell Mamm where I'm going. Have a good evening." She hurried to her room, redressed, and tiptoed to the front door. Mamm must've been in the kitchen. She or Daed hadn't been in sight. She listened for Ida's chipper voice. She must be in the kitchen with Mamm. She walked fast to the front door and left. She was glad Charity had gone to Liza's earlier to play with Peter and was already there.

Driving there, she blew out a breath of relief. She'd gotten out of the haus without speaking to Zach again. She hoped Ida wouldn't tell Zach she wanted Magdelena to take him to Liza's with her. This might raise her parents' suspicion about Toby maybe being at Liza's with her and Charity. She wouldn't worry about what she'd face later tonight at home. This would be precious time with Toby.

Toby met her in the yard at Liza's. "I came early to show Charity and Peter how to make a crate. They're drawing pictures on it, and Peter will use it to put their special games in. Those two are a hoot. They banter, laugh, and say the cutest things to each other. I wish you and I had formed a friendship as kinner like them."

"Me, too." She studied his loving brown eyes. "I almost had to bring Zach."

"Does he know I'm here?" Toby helped her out of the buggy.

"No. I told him I had plans with Liza. He asked if I was the only guest. I said Charity would be here and hurried to leave the haus. He wasn't in sight when I left. Ida greeted me with my wedding dress. She wanted me to try it on. I told her I would later, but I want to tear it to shreds. She's dismissed my feelings, knowing I don't want to marry her son. She suggested I bring Zach here with me. I told her the invitation was for Charity and me only."

Toby snorted with disgust. "Now they've set a wedding date, Bishop Fisher will make the announcement, and women throughout the community will plan for the big event. There will be questions, gifts, and counseling sessions. I'm sick about all of it. Do you mind if Andrew speaks to your daed on our behalf?"

"No, I don't mind. I'm ready for anyone to talk sense into my parents, but I dislike putting our friends in the middle of this. I would appeal to my parents again, but I'm worried they'll keep me from socializing with my friends and suspect you're a part of them."

"We have to discuss how far we can take disguising visits with our friends to be together." Toby frowned and sighed. "We're being deceptive and lying by omission."

"I don't want to face what you're suggesting." Magdelena's lips quivered.

"Don't get upset. Let's enjoy tonight."

They chatted with Charity and Peter and then had supper with Liza and her family. Charity helped serve butterscotch cake. "Maybe Liza will make you and Toby a wedding cake like this. It's the one Peter and I want for ours."

Toby forked a bite. "I'll have any cake Magdelena chooses."

She blinked back the water pooling in her eyes. She had to act. God gave her free will and a brain, and she would use it. Zach wasn't the man she was supposed to wed. She had a plan. One she'd tell Liza in confidence, but not her family, friends, or Toby. The less they knew, the better. It broke her heart to implement it. She'd take in every minute with Toby tonight. "I'd love this cake. You've got excellent taste, Charity."

Charity lifted her chin. "Danki. May Peter and I go finish coloring our crate?"

Liza pulled Charity to her for a hug. "Yes. You may."

The two kinner scampered outside.

Jacob and Toby chatted about farming, and then Jacob said, "Toby, I'm upset Mark has refused to give his blessing to you and Magdelena. I would ask him to give you his support if I thought it would do any good, but he's a tough one. I could do more damage because I'd find it difficult not to defend you to the point of an argument. Amish aren't supposed to let discussions grow to anger, but we are human."

Liza caressed Magdelena's cheek. "You and Toby are special to us. Jacob and I had Ellie's opposition to our marriage, but, at the time things seemed impossible, God worked it out. I pray the same for you." She patted Magdelena's hand. "I fed, bathed, and put Lorianne to bed before you arrived so we could have a nice supper together. Now, you and Toby go to the backyard where you can have some private time. It's a beautiful evening to take a stroll along the creek's edge."

"Danki, sweet friend. You have a heart of gold. May I speak to you in private for a minute?"

Liza clasped her hand and took her to the sitting room. She shut the door. "What is it?"

Magdelena crossed her arms tightly. "I will not marry Zach under any circumstances." She told Liza her plan. "Please don't tell anyone until tomorrow morning. I've left my parents a note on my dresser. They don't ever go in my room, but I'm sure they'll check it for a note when I don't go inside the haus tonight with Charity and they find the buggy gone. You've been good to give me a job, and I didn't want to leave Rachael alone. I don't want to tell her. My parents may show up at her and Toby's haus tonight and pepper them with questions, and it's better if Toby and Rachael don't have to hide anything."

"This is a very serious step, my dear, but I do understand. I can work for you while you're away. Hannah and Ellie can fill in for me when needed. I won't hire anyone until we give you some time to figure things out. Are you sure about this?"

She nodded. "I'm sorry to disappoint my parents, but

they've refused to consider my side of things. This is my life. They act like this decision is as easy as what to fix for dessert. I am miserable, and I'm not even married to Zach. Imagine if I did become his fraa. He's not a bad person, but he's not for me under any circumstances."

"Maybe you should reconsider and tell Toby."

Magdelena shook her head. "If he doesn't know, he won't have to lie to protect me. I'm not sure what I'm facing with Daed. He may hunt me down or disown me. I'll wait for his reaction, and then I'll have more to go with what to do next."

"You may be shunned from returning to Charm. Are you ready to accept this?"

"My heart breaks at the idea, but the risk is worth it to avoid marrying Zach. I'm hoping it doesn't kumme to my never being able to return home."

Liza hugged her and opened the door. "I'll honor your wishes."

Magdelena swallowed the sob threatening to take over. She took a deep breath and followed Liza from the room and joined Toby. "Sorry to keep you waiting."

He strolled with her outside along the creek. "Everything all right at the bakery?"

"Yes. She's wonderful to me as a friend and boss." She didn't want to discuss the reason she spoke to Liza. "Did you have a nice chat with Jacob?"

"He isn't afraid to state his opinion on a matter. He has this in common with Andrew and Gabe. Amish will oppose our being together at socials or hearing we've had suppers together at friends' homes now that Zach has scheduled a wedding date. I don't want to tarnish your reputation. I don't want to sneak around and dishonor you or your family. But we have to see each other. I'll stop in the bakery. I can be a customer."

"Ida having the dress ready and Zach questioning me about tonight brought this reality to light. I don't like it, but you're right. We have to be careful. And I don't want to compromise our friends. They could be shunned for going against my family's wishes by aiding us."

Toby faced her. He took her in his arms and held her.

Magdelena rested her head against his chest. Insects and frogs sang in the background. The orange hue of the sun peeked through the oak trees. The water's calm added to the beauty of the evening. She wanted to remember this romantic moment with him for the rest of her life. Would it be their last? "I love you, Toby." She lifted her head and gazed into his eyes. "Never doubt it."

He kissed her. "I love you, Magdelena Beachy, with all my heart. No matter what we face, I will honor your wishes."

Magdelena nodded. "You've said all the right things, and I don't ever doubt you."

"Good." Toby clasped her hand and they walked in silence back to Liza and Jacob's haus.

Magdelena bid Toby and her friends good night. She and Charity got into the buggy, and they headed home.

Charity fidgeted her hands. "Peter snapped at me when I said Snuggles and Cinnamon were getting fat."

"Snuggles, his pretty bunny, and Cinnamon, his cute dog, are special to him. You shouldn't say things about them that may hurt Peter's feelings. Did you apologize?" Magdelena cocked her head at Charity. She sometimes liked Charity saying what was on her mind, but this wasn't one of those times.

Charity shrugged. "Yes. I wouldn't want him to call me fat. I felt bad."

"His pets are his friends. He loves them, and he'll defend them. You hurt his feelings."

"I didn't mean to. I love Snuggles and Cinnamon."

"Sometimes we hurt those we love with our words unintentionally. As soon as we realize it, we need to apologize." Magdelena patted Charity's knee. "I'm proud of you. You cared about what he thought and said you were sorry." She darted a glance at Charity. "I'd prefer you didn't tell anyone Toby was at Liza's tonight. You can go ahead and tell Mamm and Daed after tomorrow if they ask."

"I wouldn't tell. Daed would be mad. He doesn't seem to like Toby. I don't understand why. Should I lie if Mamm or Daed ask me?"

"No. But don't offer the information. If they ask you a direct question, you must be truthful with them." Magdelena cringed at putting Charity in the middle. She would have to hope they wouldn't ask Charity who was at Liza's tonight. She had to go through with her plan tonight, and then Charity could say whatever she wanted to.

"All right." Charity held the lantern. "We didn't need the lantern. It's getting dark. Maybe Mamm and Daed will let me catch fireflies."

"No. It's time for you to go to bed."

"Maybe tomorrow night?"

She nodded. "You can go out at dusk tomorrow evening, and there will be fireflies."

"Will you catch them with me?" Charity climbed out of the buggy and waited for her.

Magdelena got out of the buggy. She didn't want to say no and have Charity plead with her. She couldn't handle the emotion of what was ahead of her. She had no energy to argue with her schweschder. "We'll see. You should go inside. Our parents may be upset we weren't home an hour ago."

Charity covered her open mouth. "I hope not. We'll be in big trouble. I'll tell them we're here and you're taking care of the horse." She passed Magdelena the lantern and ran to the haus.

Magdelena bent over and braced her hand on the buggy. She sobbed. This would be harder than she'd predicted. She may not hear Charity's sweet voice again for a while. She didn't unharness the horse. She got into the buggy, checked the oil in her lantern, and headed to Mt. Hope. She'd be there in an hour.

She kept her eyes on the road, and she was glad not to pass anyone. Not many Amish would be out after dark. She shouldn't take the risk to travel alone, but she couldn't think of a better plan to escape. Her parents and the Hiltys had made it unbearable. She couldn't stay and plan the wedding they wanted for her and Zach. She risked cutting off her relationship with her parents, Bishop Fisher, and her friends. Becoming a runaway bride wouldn't bode well with many people in Charm. But she had to end this forced marriage.

She arrived at Aunt Gloria and Uncle Otis's haus. She tied her horse to the tree. Her aunt and uncle came outside. Aunt Gloria wrapped her arms around Magdelena. "We couldn't imagine who had kumme to visit us this late. What's happened? Is your daed or mamm sick? Charity?"

"No." Magdelena shook her head. "They're healthy. I had to leave town. Aunt Gloria, in a short time, the Hiltys, who are newcomers to Charm, became fast friends of my parents. Their son, Zach, has bonded with Daed over cattle ranching, and Daed is teaching him the ropes. Zach envisions taking over the ranch and, to seal the deal, he asked Daed if he could marry me. Toby also asked for Daed's blessing, and he refused him and me. I don't want to marry Zach Hilty. I love Toby. It's been a nightmare. I'm a runaway bride."

Uncle Otis untied the reins to her mare. "This is quite a predicament. I'll take care of your horse. You go inside and tell Aunt Gloria how we can help. You can stay as long as you like."

Magdelena kissed Uncle Otis's cheek. He reminded her of Vernon, Toby's daed. He had a gentle soul, but he stated his opinions without hesitation when needed. She followed Aunt Gloria inside the haus and settled into a comfy high-back chair. Aunt Gloria had beautiful mahogany furniture. Her quilts she'd handmade hung on two racks. Magdelena's favorite was a tattered and faded wedding quilt Uncle Otis kept draped over his chair. The aroma of ginger cookies drifted in the air. "I've missed being here with you. It's been a while since we've kumme to visit you."

"I'm thrilled you're here, but this is a distressing turn of events, my dear. Did you leave your parents a note?"

"Yes. I told them I was kumming here and I wouldn't marry Zach. I told them Toby has no idea I left and not to blame him. Liza had Toby and me for supper tonight. She empathizes with our dilemma. Charity was there playing with her son, Peter. I took Charity home after our evening with Liza's family and Toby. I dropped her off, and she ran inside. I hurried here the minute she shut the door. I didn't tell anyone I was leaving except Liza. She is a supportive and understanding friend, and she would need to fill in for me at the bakery or ask one of my friends. She went through with an arranged marriage with a man who made her miserable. He's passed away, and now she's happy with her husband, Jacob."

"You didn't tell Toby?"

"No. I wrote the note to my parents so they wouldn't harass Toby. They'd assume we ran off together, and I'm sure they'll be surprised to read in my note he is still in Charm. My parents left me no choice but to leave Charm. You're the person Daed will listen to. I'm sure he'll kumme and have a few choice words for me. I'm hoping then you can reason with him. I shouldn't put you in the middle of this, but you're my last hope."

Aunt Gloria motioned her to the kitchen. She poured her a mug of hot tea and gave her two cookies. "Your parents will be worried sick about you traveling by yourself and at night. I'm glad you're here safe."

"Ida, Zach's mamm made a wedding dress. She brought it over for me to try on. I couldn't stomach it. I wasn't rude, but I can't go along with my parents, the Hiltys, and Zach by pretending this is a happy time for us. It's to the point where Toby and I can't find excuses to be together because this wedding has become a foregone conclusion. They've set a date of September second. We've run out of options."

"Did Toby ask Zach to withdraw his proposal and allow the two of you to marry?"

Magdelena nodded. "Zach won't listen to him. He's greedy. He represents the son Daed didn't have, and Zach wants to run a ranch. Both families are close and they get together whenever they can at our haus. Zach, working for Daed, is at our haus when I get home from work. Then he stays for supper and wants to take a stroll. I can't face him anymore. And I won't marry him."

"Magdelena, if you refuse to marry Zach, your daed may insist your family shun you. Are you prepared for this?" Aunt Gloria covered Magdelena's hand with hers. "If so, you can live with us and you can marry Toby in Mt. Hope. But I don't want it to kumme to this. I'll do everything I can to change your daed's mind."

"I'm ready to face the consequences should Daed declare I be shunned. I wouldn't marry Zach even if I were available. He's nothing like Toby, and Toby has all the qualities I'm looking for in a husband and partner. I'm a means to an end for Zach. He doesn't see me, hear me, or know me. Toby does."

"You've been obedient to your parents until now, and you've had a wonderful relationship with them. I don't want you to regret this."

"I love them, and I'm grateful for all they have provided for me. I admire Mamm's devotion to Daed, but I wish she was free to speak her mind. I want my husband to seek my counsel and to take my advice into consideration. There have been times I haven't agreed with Daed's decisions, but I could live with them. Now, he's being unreasonable."

"I agree. But tomorrow I'll have to send Otis to let them know you're safe. Otis will find out where your daed stands, and then we'll plan from there. I'd rather your daed came to me to hash this out away from any interference by Zach." Aunt Gloria straightened in her chair. "I'm going to give this my best effort, Magdelena, but I'm not sure he'll bend."

"Aunt Gloria, you've rescued me several times with Daed. I don't know what I'd do without you. I cherish Mamm, but you're the one I've confided in. I could always trust you would keep my secrets and help me with Daed."

"You were curious about the outside world growing up. Do you remember when your parents found you reading a newspaper, and your daed snatched it from you and tore it in pieces without giving you an explanation?" Aunt Gloria raised her brows.

Magdelena nodded. "I was eleven, and I decided to only ask you about the outside world from then on. I'd found the paper, and I was fascinated with the beautiful dresses and hats for sale. Then I read about a train accident, and I wanted to read the details. They overreacted. You're always patient and understanding. I also remember asking why I couldn't have the beautiful doll with a face in the general store. You explained we don't have dolls with faces to keep us from wanting us to look a certain way leading to vanity, and I understood. I always accepted your answers and lived by them."

"Your parents misunderstood your questions about such things. They were certain you would leave the Amish life one day if they addressed your interest. Your parents are of the mindset kinner don't deserve an explanation. If they say what you are doing is wrong and don't do it again, that's it. I've always believed being open with you and Charity builds trust and understanding."

"I'm glad both of you took this approach with us. I want to do the same when I have kinner." Magdelena hoped she'd be as wise and patient with her kinner as her aunt and uncle had been to her.

"When Otis and I didn't have kinner, I doted on you and Charity. Mark's a decent man, but he can't get out of his own way on this. I won't let him ruin your life or Toby's for his stubborn reasons." Aunt Gloria squeezed her fingers. "Why don't you get some rest? Your room is ready for you as always. You didn't take a bag out of the buggy. Do you want Otis to get it?"

She shook her head. "I didn't bring one. Charity may

have asked me why I had one. She's inquisitive and doesn't miss a thing. Can I borrow a gown?"

"Yes. I have dresses and two gowns for you. I was your size once, and I hang on to everything. I can stitch you another one if we need to. You wait here." She returned with the clothes and hung them over Magdelena's arm.

Uncle Otis came inside the haus and joined them. "Your horse is taken care of."

"Danki, Uncle Otis. Aunt Gloria, these clothes will be perfect." She bid Aunt Gloria and Uncle Otis good night and proceeded to her room. She poured water from the blue porcelain pitcher into the matching basin on a small table in the corner, washed, and dried her face. She shed her clothes and slipped the gown over her head, and climbed into bed. The breeze from the open window cooled her.

She didn't know what lay in store from her parents in the days ahead, but she was glad she took the risk. Her once-happy home had become a place of turmoil and tension. She got out of bed, knelt, and folded her hands. "Dear Heavenly Father, forgive me for worrying my parents and for my disobedience to them. Please give me clarity of what You would have me do. I plead with You to intervene on Toby's and my behalf. Please show me Your will for my life. All these things I ask and pray in Your name. Amen."

She got back in bed and stared at the dark ceiling. Toby would be upset. She didn't discuss her plan with him, but she hoped he'd understand. She'd ask Otis to tell Toby she was in Mt. Hope, and she'd ask Aunt Gloria if Toby could visit. She shuddered. She'd never gone against her daed like this. She wouldn't sleep a wink tonight.

* * *

Magdelena rubbed her eyes early the next morning, threw her legs over the side of the bed, and stood to change her clothes. She followed the bacon aroma to the kitchen. "Good morning."

Otis was at the table holding a coffee mug. His plate was dirty with smudges of scrambled egg and bread crumbs. He pushed it aside. "You're up way early this morning. You should've slept in. I'll be on my way to Charm in a couple of minutes. The stallion is harnessed to the buggy. Do you have any special requests for me to pass on?"

"Would you mind going to this address?" She passed him a note. "Toby will be at Andrew's place most of the day. I'd like him to know where I am after you speak with Daed."

Aunt Gloria spooned scrambled eggs and sliced bacon onto her plate. "You and I will stitch you more undergarments, and I've got a couple more socks and bonnets you can have." She rubbed her husband's back. "Otis, if my bruder doesn't run you out of town, please ask Bernice to pack a bag for Magdelena."

"I'll ask." Otis sat his mug in the sink. "I'm off." He hugged them both goodbye.

Magdelena forced a bite of eggs down her throat. She had no appetite. "I've put Uncle Otis in an awkward position. I'm selfish for doing so."

"It isn't the first time Otis and your daed had words. Your daed insisted we live in Charm, and if Otis didn't agree, he didn't think we should marry. I love Mark, but he's a bully. Otis told him we'd marry and live in Mt. Hope and he could visit or not. Otis told him he'd like to be friends and what could he do to mend this fence. I told your daed he better think twice before answering. He huffed for a day or two, and then he gave in. I'd supported him marrying Bernice."

"Has Daed always been hardheaded?"

"Yes. But he can be kind and giving. Think about all the people he's given meat to who couldn't afford it. He basks in the attention it gives him, but he's still providing a generous gift to others. He's given you a good life, and he's convinced he's always right. I surmise he has never accepted you're a grown woman and capable of making your own decisions."

Toby answered the door. "Mark, would you like to kumme inside?"

"No. I'd like to discuss something in private with you. Please step outside." Mark frowned.

Toby stepped out onto the porch.

Mark crossed his arms. "Toby, I came here this morning to find out what you know about Magdelena leaving Charm. She didn't kumme in the haus after she dropped off Charity last night. We went outside and she was already gone. Then we went to her room and found a note from her saying she had left to go to my schweschder's haus in Mt. Hope. She claims you don't know anything about her leaving. Is this true?" He tipped his hat to Bernice and Rachael. "I'm sorry to bother you this morning."

"Mark, she's telling you the truth. I didn't know she planned to leave Charm."

"This is all your fault." Mark turned his back to Toby and left.

Toby went inside the haus. Mamm and Rachael were waiting for him. He didn't want to argue with Mark. He could tell by the man's tone he wouldn't listen to anything Toby had to say.

Rachael cocked her head. "Did Mark say Magdelena left town? Why wouldn't she tell me?"

"She knew Mark would ask us about Magdelena. This way, we didn't have to lie. She was protecting us. Her daed and Zach won't listen to her. She must've been desperate." He was hurt she hadn't confided in him. What did this mean for the two of them? He wanted to talk to her.

Rachael sighed. "I suppose you're right."

Mamm sighed. "Magdelena's a grown woman. She's made her choice, and she did what she thought was necessary. Maybe her actions will get her parents' attention."

Rachael opened the door. "I'm late. I'm running off to work." She left the haus.

"I should get started on my chores, too." Mamm patted Toby's arm.

"I'm going to visit Andrew, Mamm." Toby worried about Magdelena and what he should do next.

He drove to Andrew's and caught him before he left for the furniture store. "Andrew, can you spare a couple of minutes?"

"Yes. What's on your mind?" Andrew put his dinner in the back of the buggy.

"Magdelena left her parents a note she was going to Mt. Hope to her aunt Gloria and uncle Otis's haus. They're proceeding with plans for her to marry Zach. She must've gotten desperate after Mark wouldn't grant us permission to marry."

"I don't blame Magdelena for leaving. It should be her choice whom she weds. I'm sorry you're having to go through this, Toby." Andrew clapped a hand on Toby's shoulder. "I'm here for you, friend, for whatever you need."

"Danki. I appreciate your support." Toby bid Andrew farewell.

Andrew got into his buggy and drove to his store.

An hour later, Toby finished weeding the garden and stopped to pump water onto his rag and cooled the back of his neck. He wiped the sweat off his face. He squinted against the hot sun to make out the man in the buggy kumming toward him. *Otis.*

Otis pulled the buggy near the pump. "Toby, do you have time to talk?"

"Otis, what a pleasant surprise. Mark came to my haus and said Magdelena left a note she is staying with you and Gloria. How is she?"

"She's upset her daed won't let the two of you wed. She's at a standstill with her parents over this arranged marriage with Zach. She ran to us, and we're on her side, as well as yours."

Toby shook his head. "I don't understand why she didn't tell me she was going to Mt. Hope."

"She was afraid Mark and Zach would accuse you of being involved. This way, you're not."

Toby's throat constricted. She'd driven in the dark alone. She could've been hurt or had an accident. "She should've let me drive her to your home."

"Mark, Bernice, and Zach overwhelmed her. She had to get away. I spoke with Mark and Bernice before kumming to talk to you. He's furious and Bernice is frustrated and worried. Mark said she has embarrassed the family, and he has cut her out of their lives. They weren't interested in anything I had to say. Gloria assumes Mark will show up at our place, and she hopes to show him the error of his ways. If not, we've told Magdelena she has our support to marry you and move to Mt. Hope."

Toby would do what he had to. Magdelena was his priority. Andrew would understand, and he'd bring Rachael and Mamm if they didn't want to stay in Charm. They had many friends. Maybe they would still be happy here. He didn't want to uproot them after having lost Daed so soon. And he had a haus in Charm he didn't want to sell unless he had to. "You and Gloria are generous to offer. I'll follow Magdelena's lead. When can I visit her?"

"Wait a few days in case Mark or Zach kumme to Mt. Hope to talk to her. I pray he calms down, misses Magdelena, and travels to Mt. Hope to work this out."

Magdelena had left Charm. Left him. Left her parents. Gossips would spread this news like a forest fire. Zach wouldn't take being jilted well. He'd better brace himself for a confrontation from the man. "Tell Magdelena I'll do whatever she asks."

"She's worried about you. I am, too. Mark and Zach may ruin you in this town and blame you. You have endured pain with your daed's passing away. You don't need this. Should I stay in town for a couple of days to support you until Mark simmers down? I may not know you, but I trust Magdelena's judgment. She's like a dochder to me. None of us know what he'll do. He's not a violent man. He won't raise a hand to anyone, but he has a temper and he won't be quiet about this. He'll want to cast blame onto someone other than himself."

"Mark said this is all my fault, but I'm not worried about what he or Zach will say. I have a lot of friends who will support me. You don't need to stay, but danki for the offer. You've gone beyond what Magdelena or I would've asked. I understand why Magdelena is so fond of you and Gloria. I'll be all right."

"Gloria and Magdelena will be anxious for me to tell them what transpired. I look forward to you kumming to Mt. Hope to visit sometime next week."

"I'll be counting the days until then. Please give her my love."

"I will." Otis shook his hand and headed home.

Toby removed the ax from the tree stump and sat. What did Magdelena's leaving mean for the two of them? Should he make arrangements to relocate to Mt. Hope? Should he wait? He had big decisions to make. He'd honor Otis's request before going to discuss with her what was next for them. He should check on Rachael.

He drove to the bakery. "Liza, greetings!"

Liza came from around the counter to face him, her eyes sad and apologetic. "Rachael told me about your visit from Mark. I'm sorry for what you and Magdelena are going through with her parents and Zach."

"Danki. Her uncle Otis arrived in town this morning to tell me Magdelena was with him and Gloria in Mt. Hope. Otis had been to Mark's before talking to me this morning, so he knows about Mark's conversation with me last night. I wish Mark would understand how much Magdelena and I love each other and give us his blessing."

Liza blew out a breath and smiled. "My heart breaks for you and Magdelena. When you and she were at our haus for supper, the love between you was evident in the way you couldn't take your eyes off each other. I pray her daed realizes the seriousness of what his demand on her could do to their family."

Rachael joined them. "I'm still hurt she didn't tell me.

I'm her best friend. I wouldn't have said anything. I'm proud of her. She can't live her life for her daed."

Toby gave her an empathetic look. "We'll get questioned by her family, our friends, the gossips, and Bishop Fisher. We'll speak the truth. We didn't know her plan."

Liza passed him a cup of hot chocolate. "Rachael, your bruder's right."

"I would've told her it didn't matter. I would've done the same and ran away, too." Rachael twisted the towel in her hands.

"Otis asked me to wait a week to visit Magdelena. I'll take you to visit her sometime soon after I go first."

Rachael grinned. "I look forward to it."

A customer entered, and Liza stepped to the counter to wait on her.

Toby shrugged. "I should go. The bakery is getting busy." He said goodbye to Rachael and went to the furniture store to talk to Andrew again.

"Toby, any more news on Magdelena?" Andrew dragged over a stool for him to sit.

"Her uncle came to visit me at your place after you left. He invited me to their home to visit her. He asked me to wait a week. She took a big risk, and we don't know what Mark will do after he's had time to contemplate all this. And she needs time to accept what happens should she stay in Mt. Hope to avoid Zach."

"Will she marry you in Mt. Hope?"

"I believe so, but there may be complications for us there. I don't know if Bishop Fisher or Mark will contact Bishop Hershberger in Mt. Hope and express their opposition to us marrying against her parents' wishes. Her aunt and uncle are one of the kindest couples I've met. I imagine they are loved in their community. They support us.

This week will be telling after her family's initial shock settles over what she's done."

"Do you expect trouble from Zach or Mark?" Andrew nodded to the door. "Be prepared. Zach is here with Mark. We're about to find out."

Mark and Zach came inside the store. Mark approached him. "Toby, I noticed through the window you were in here. May I have a word with you outside?"

Andrew stepped next to Toby. "I'll go with you."

"Danki, but I'll talk to them. I don't want you to miss any customers who may kumme in to shop."

"Use my workshop area. You'll have more privacy." Andrew motioned to the back.

Mark nodded.

Toby walked with the two men to the back and closed the door to the workshop. He kept silent. He wanted Mark to speak first.

Mark crossed his arms. "Are you going to continue to pursue my dochder?"

Toby nodded.

Zach stood next to Mark with narrowed eyes and pinched lips.

"I'm asking you to stay away from her." Mark stepped close to Toby.

"I love her. I support whatever decisions she makes." Toby didn't want trouble, but he wouldn't lie. He had every intention of speaking with Magdelena.

Zach crossed his arms against his chest. "Do you and she have plans to marry in Mt. Hope?"

"Until I speak with her, I don't know what she has in mind. If you're asking if I would marry her in Mt. Hope, the answer is yes." He backed away. "Mark, I'd like to have your blessing. Magdelena and I would like to stay in

Charm. She doesn't want to sever ties with her family, but she wants whom she marries to be her choice. You're forcing her to marry a stranger."

Zach huffed. "She knows me enough. Arranged marriages are between strangers most of the time. I'm convinced you and she planned this together. You're to blame for separating her from her family."

Mark held out his palm to Zach. "Wait, Magdelena is to blame as much as Toby." He took off his straw hat and raked a hand through his thick brown hair. He set his hat back on his head and turned to Toby. "Would you be willing to tell Magdelena it would be best for her to marry Zach to repair the wrong she's done in running away?"

Toby shook his head. "I don't understand why she should agree to a decision at the cost of a lifetime together. I purchased a home and farm to prove I have the financial means to provide for Magdelena. I'd like to become a part of your family, and my family loves Magdelena. What would ease your mind about me marrying her?"

Mark relaxed his tightened jaw. "You can't provide for her like Zach can. You're not a rancher. I need a son-in-law to take over for me. Zach has the drive and interest. Between his family and mine, we have the finances to build both businesses. Magdelena is young and used to having more than most Amish women. She will resent you when you can't provide the same level of living she's accustomed to."

Zach wore a satisfied grin.

Toby sighed. "You underestimate us. Magdelena and I are happy to manage a farm, and my furniture sales will give us extra income. I'm doing better than you think, but you discount it. You will always consider me poor, which is untrue. And Magdelena lays her treasure in Heaven, not on earth, as I do. I ask you to trust us. We're responsible adults. Stop fighting two people who love each other."

Zach scowled. "Why should we stand here and listen to this liar? He'll say anything to soothe his conscience. It's not right he's ripped your dochder from you and from me."

"Toby, I'm ashamed of you." Mark scoffed. "You've had a good reputation in Charm, and you've ruined it by shattering our family. You've poisoned Magdelena's mind with your empty promises of a good life with you."

"It's sad you don't accept Magdelena ran away from you of her own free will. She's desperate. She risked her relationship with you because you forced her hand. If I had a dochder, I'd listen to her and want to repair our relationship. I hope you will, too." He had to appeal to Mark to change his attitude for Magdelena's sake. She would be heartbroken if her parents rejected her forever.

Mark turned on his heel and left with Zach close behind.

Andrew waited on two customers. He glanced at Toby and then to the men leaving the shop. "Toby, please stay. I'll be with you in a couple of minutes."

Toby nodded. He hadn't been surprised at the confrontation. He'd expected it would be worse. Mark had kept calm, although it was apparent he was angry. He stood firm on choosing Zach for Magdelena. Toby felt chagrined. He'd have to sell the haus he bought and buy one in Mt. Hope. He'd sell his family home, too, if Rachael and Mamm wanted to relocate with them. He could continue to sell furniture in Andrew's store, but it would be a farther drive. He could make it work, but what could he do about Magdelena's broken heart over losing her family? Would this wound ever heal?

Andrew sold the couple a side table, and Toby helped the man carry the small table to his wagon. He returned.

"Did you accomplish anything with Mark and Zach?"

Toby shook his head. "Mark's outraged because Magdelena defied him. I'm not sure their relationship can be repaired. He's stubborn. I'm not worried about Zach. He's embarrassed by her action, and he's determined to get his way. Nothing I can say or do is going to change their minds about me, but I care more about Magdelena and how she feels."

"The Hiltys and Beachys will paint you as the villain. It's not true or fair."

"My friends will understand." Toby had planned to raise a family with Magdelena in Charm. They'd have been surrounded by close friends and had a good life here. But they could build a new life in Mt. Hope, if it's what they had to do.

Andrew handed him his portion of the sale. "Your things are selling. Would you still bring your pieces to me if you marry Magdelena and move to Mt. Hope?"

"Yes. It will give me a chance to visit you." Chances were his sales would suffer. Amish bought his pieces, as well as the Englischers. If he were to be shunned by the Amish, they'd stop buying his pieces, but he'd worry about this issue later.

Chapter Nine

Magdelena pulled weeds from her aunt's garden Tuesday mid-morning. It had been a week today since she'd left Charm. Uncle Otis had told Toby to wait a week before visiting to give her time to contemplate her decision. She missed him and couldn't wait to talk to him. They had much to discuss. She hoped he'd kumme today.

Her heart sank. Daed or Mamm hadn't had a change of heart or they would've kumme to talk to her. She grieved the laughter and fun they'd shared. Her friends could visit, but it wouldn't be the same as working next to Rachael every day or driving minutes to her friends' homes. But she'd have Toby, and the rest they could work out. She'd never get over her parents' rejection, but she'd have to live with their decision. It didn't seem possible it had kumme to this. She shielded her eyes from the sun. A buggy was kumming down the lane toward the haus. Two men sat in front. It got closer. *Daed and Zach.* She took a deep breath and wished her knees would quit shaking.

Daed pulled the buggy under the shade of the willow tree. He got out and secured the mare. Zach followed him. She met them on the porch and kept silent.

"I'm furious you ran away. You're kumming home today, and you'll stay away from Toby. You've shamed our family by your actions. Get your bag and get in the buggy." Daed narrowed his eyes and crossed his arms against his chest.

Aunt Gloria came around the side of the haus from the backyard. "Mark, I'm glad you're here." She smiled at Zach. "I'm Magdelena's aunt Gloria, Mark's schweschder."

"I'm Zach Hilty, Magdelena's husband-to-be."

Uncle Otis came from the corral and joined them. Aunt Gloria introduced him to Zach.

Uncle Otis motioned for all of them to sit on the swing or rocking chairs. "We want unity for our family. How can we accomplish this, keeping in mind Magdelena's wishes?"

Magdelena wanted to hug Uncle Otis. He'd said what she wanted to say.

Mark took off his straw hat and put it in his lap. "I'm sorry Magdelena involved you in our difference of opinion. She was wrong to run away and cause turmoil in our family. I'm here to take her home where she'll marry Zach as planned."

Zach grinned. "We'd love to have you at the wedding and anytime you'd like to visit us."

Magdelena stared at Zach. He spoke as if she wasn't present. She didn't understand why Zach insisted on this arranged marriage after she'd run away. Her rejection of him had made her opposition known to the community. She was sure gossips had spread the news. She wanted a partner who cared about her opinions. She was a woman and not a servant or a pet.

Aunt Gloria sat next to Magdelena on the swing. She squeezed Magdelena's fingers. "Magdelena is more like a dochder to me than a niece. She wants to marry Toby Schlabach, and I don't understand, Mark, why you won't grant them your blessing." She gazed at Zach. "You, young man, should remove yourself from this triangle you've created. Magdelena has declined your proposal. Work for Mark and leave her out of it."

Zach glanced from Aunt Gloria to Mark and kept silent.

"Gloria and Otis, this matter is of no concern to you. You shouldn't allow Magdelena to stay here while she's going against our wishes. She's disobeyed us, and I won't have it. She's to leave with us right now." Mark stood.

Zach rose, too, as if imitating Mark's every move.

Magdelena stood straight and faced her daed. "Daed, please don't make me do this. I love you. I want unity in our family, but I won't return to Charm with you if you won't consider my feelings." She turned to Zach. "I refuse to marry you. Please leave me alone."

Mark scoffed. "You don't know what you want. Toby is all right, but Zach's better."

Aunt Gloria stood and stomped her foot. "Better for who? You? The son you want to run your ranch? Dandy. Go ahead with your plan, but leave Magdelena out of it. I happen to remember when you wanted to marry Bernice and her daed wanted her to marry another man. I helped convince him you were the right husband for Bernice. She and I were close friends, and he listened to me. Our parents spoke on your behalf as well."

"Daed, I haven't heard this story." Magdelena covered her open mouth.

Uncle Otis nodded. "Your daed was miserable thinking Bernice was lost to him. Gloria was instrumental in changing Bernice's parents' minds. They respected her opinion, and they didn't want Bernice to be miserable in the end.

They granted their blessing and the young man they'd arranged for Bernice to marry bowed out with dignity." He shot a stern glance to Zach.

"Daed, why would you do this to me after going through the same thing with Mamm?" Her heart sank. In spite of his experience, he had no regard for her and Toby and the turmoil he was causing them.

Mark shifted his feet and avoided eye contact. "This isn't the same."

"Why not?" Gloria stood with her hands on her hips.

"Magdelena has never wanted for anything. She'll never have to worry about finances with Zach, like she might with Toby. She's not considering the future."

Magdelena took a deep breath. "Toby bought a haus on a decent-sized farm. He sells beautiful furniture he handcrafts. You've discounted his talents and the hard work he did to provide for his family while his daed was ill. Now he'll have more than enough money to take care of me and his family. Zach has had the comfort of his parents' money, and now he works for you. He's been given these opportunities, and I'm not saying that's wrong. Toby has had to work for what he has, and he deserves your respect for doing so."

Uncle Otis slapped his leg. "I couldn't have said it better myself."

"Let's not fuss about this. Zach, you're a handsome fellow, and you seem nice enough. I want you to fall in love with a woman who feels the same about you. Mark, let Magdelena wed Toby. Stop putting her through what you had to endure with Bernice's parents. Now, let's have supper together," Aunt Gloria said.

Zach took off his hat and traced the brim, staying silent.

Mark waggled a forefinger at Magdelena. "You kumme

back with me, young lady, or you'll be shunned by your family. When your friends find out you've disobeyed me, you'll be shunned by them. You'll no longer be wilkom in Charm. And this will be your doing, not mine."

Zach reached for Magdelena's hands. "Please, Magdelena, I don't want this for you. Kumme back with us. I care about you. You'll get over Toby. I promise."

She jerked her hands from his grasp. "Please, Daed. I love you, Mamm, Charity, and my friends. We've had a good relationship until now. I'm upset you won't take my wishes into consideration. Please don't force me to choose. And if I must, then I choose Toby."

Mark marched off the porch. "Gloria, we'll not be staying for supper. I wish you wouldn't interfere, but so be it. Zach, let's go."

"You'll regret this, Mark. You're the one tearing your family apart." Aunt Gloria engulfed Magdelena in her arms and rubbed her back. "It's all right, sweetheart. You always have a home with us."

Magdelena wept in Aunt Gloria's arms, and then she wiped her eyes on her sleeve and stared after her daed. Would this be the last time they'd be together? She envisioned Mamm and Charity. Would they visit her? She pressed a hand to her heart. She ached at not being with them again. But she wouldn't give in to pleasing them at the cost of her future. She believed it was God's will for her and Toby to wed. But was she thinking this because it was what she desired? Her head throbbed. What was the right thing to do?

Uncle Otis called out to Daed. "Mark, don't cut her off. She's your sweet dochder who has brought you such joy all her life. Don't turn your back on her. She needs you."

Mark and Zach got in the buggy. They didn't leave right

away. Mark gazed at Magdelena for a moment, and then he coaxed the horse to gallop away.

Uncle Otis took her hand. "It breaks my heart to have you at odds with your daed, but I understand. You will always have a home with us."

Magdelena nodded. "I never intended to split forever with my family. This is the first time I've taken a stand like this with them. As I've grown from a child to an adult, I've learned my parents aren't always right, but I've accepted their decisions. This ultimatum is too high of a cost for me to succumb to. Is it wrong for me to resent them for putting me in this position?"

Aunt Gloria nodded. "Don't resent them. Forgive them and go on with your life. They'll kumme around or they won't. I hope they'll ponder this and realize they made a mistake. God has a plan for your life. You believe you're following it. He'll intervene when you least expect it. Stay here. After this week, Toby will kumme and you'll make plans together."

"Danki for standing up for me. I don't know what I'd do without both of you." She'd run to them knowing they'd understand and wilkom her without reservation. They hadn't let her down. She had a pang of guilt over the argument she'd caused between Daed and Gloria. Their close relationship as bruder and schweschder might never be the same. The decision she made had caused more than her life to change. Was she being selfish or determined?

Toby crossed off the last day on his calendar. He'd honored Otis's request to give Magdelena this last week to contemplate what to do. She hadn't returned, and he couldn't wait to wed her. Had her daed and Zach been to

Mt. Hope this past week? Where did she stand with them? He hadn't run into Mark or Zach. Rachael had told him they came to the bakery and questioned Liza. She'd told them Magdelena had asked her to remain silent until after she left town. She told them where to find Magdelena. He was glad she was with her aunt and uncle if they had.

He drove to Gloria and Otis's haus. He made good time and arrived close to an hour later.

Magdelena ran to his buggy. "I'm glad you're here. I've missed you."

He jumped out of the buggy and took her in his arms. "It was difficult to stay away this past week. How are you?"

Her eyes had dark circles beneath them. She'd been trim, but she'd lost weight. Her face was thinner. He worried this emotional upheaval would make her ill.

"Aunt Gloria and Uncle Otis are at the neighbor's checking on Mr. Girod. He's been ill, and they took over some food. We've got privacy to discuss our plans. I have a lot to tell you."

His heart jumped. She'd said *our* plans.

"Want to go to the porch or take a walk?"

"Porch. I love the swing." She took him to the swing, and they sat together. "Daed and Zach demanded I return to Charm. I told them I wouldn't marry Zach. I pleaded with Daed and Zach to consider my wishes. Aunt Gloria and Uncle Otis defended me. They left in a huff, and Daed said my ties with them would be severed if I stayed."

"I'm glad I didn't kumme and complicate things further for you while they were here. I'm sorry our situation is causing you such distress, sweetheart."

"Your timing is good. Marry me in Mt. Hope. We can stay with my aunt and uncle until we can sell your haus in Charm and buy one here, if you're in agreement."

"Of course. I'll go back and put a sale sign in the yard and advertise it at the general and hardware stores. I'll have to give Andrew time to find someone to take my place." His mind spun with a laundry list of changes he'd have to make. But he didn't care. He'd gladly make any personal sacrifice to marry her.

"I haven't asked Otis, but I'm sure he won't mind if you build a workshop in his old barn, and there's a furniture store in town. You could talk to the owner about selling your items."

Toby's heart raced. She'd considered what would make him happy. He loved her for it. "All of your suggestions are good. I suppose we should speak to the bishop. Your aunt and uncle should go with us."

"I'll mourn my lost relationship with my family for a long time. I may never get over it, but I'm certain I want to marry you. Aunt Gloria and Uncle Otis are sad like I am about this mess, but they're excited to help and proud to host our wedding. They'll agree to go with us to ask the bishop for his blessing and schedule a date."

"I'll wait until after we speak with Bishop Hershberger in Mt. Hope before I make arrangements to ask Mr. Umble to find another buyer and return my deposit on the haus I am to pay for in full soon."

Magdelena nodded.

"I would much prefer your family was as happy about our union as my family and our friends. Maybe one day they'll kumme around. I pray so. Maybe when Zach finds another woman to wed and his work with your daed is un-interrupted, they'll calm and want a relationship with us," Toby said.

"I pray this happens, and I'll write to them often. They may throw my letters away, but I'll keep trying to reconcile."

Gloria and Otis returned home. They greeted and joined Toby and Magdelena on the porch and sat in the rocking chairs.

Gloria grinned. "Have you set a date? I'm anxious to plan. We'll have to check the bishop's schedule."

Otis chuckled. "Don't let her rush you. The latest happenings have brought a lot of change to both of you. You're invited to live with us as long as you like once you marry until you're ready to build or buy a place here."

Toby nodded. "Danki. You're being very gracious and we appreciate it."

Gloria and Otis reminded him of his parents. Their love and devotion for Magdelena ran deep, and they had protected Magdelena from her parents forcing her into doing something she or they didn't think was right. It was a bold stand. But his parents would've done the same for him or Rachael.

"Yes. We do. Danki doesn't seem sufficient, considering all you're doing for us." Magdelena beamed. "Would you and Uncle Otis go with Toby and me to ask the bishop for a date on his calendar since we're new to Mt. Hope?"

Gloria and Otis nodded.

Gloria clapped her hands. "I'm excited and ready to plan. I'll stitch you a dress and Toby a new shirt and pants. When can you visit again, Toby?"

Toby wished he had time tomorrow. He didn't want to wait to set plans in motion any longer. But he had a lot to do before they wed and moved. "A week from today? I'll return next Tuesday, and we can meet with the bishop."

"I'll alert the bishop tomorrow and have him put us on his calendar." Gloria clapped her hands to her open mouth. "Toby, I should've offered you food and drink. Are you hungry? I can make you a ham sandwich or I can warm vegetable soup if you'd like. Let's all go to the kitchen and have some supper. I'm hungry. We didn't have anything at the neighbors'. We didn't want to trouble them, and I left food for their supper."

Toby followed the family to the kitchen, and they all pitched in and put supper together and set the table.

Gloria said, "Danki for everyone's help. Let's sit. Otis, please offer a prayer to God for our food."

Otis prayed and then lifted his sandwich. "Toby, did Mark and Zach approach you this past week?"

"They did, but they weren't listening to reason, no matter how hard I tried. This isn't the ideal situation for Magdelena and me. I'm surprised Zach, a newcomer, is so persistent."

Gloria shook her head. "He's got his eye on the ranch and Magdelena would be a good catch. He should've backed away the minute she said she had an interest in you. I don't blame him for wanting to put this nice package together for himself before he knew about you. Now that he does, I don't approve of his strong persistence to pursue her."

Magdelena nodded. "I'm still not over your story about Mamm and Daed having a similar circumstance as Toby and me. You'd think they would relate and be more understanding after what they went through." She recounted to Toby what Gloria had relayed to her about her parents.

Toby had his sandwich to his mouth but set it on his plate. "I would've thought he'd be more empathetic with how we feel after what he went through with Bernice's parents. This week, he and she may reminisce about the past Gloria brought to the forefront. They could soften over remembering this part of their past."

"I doubt it." Gloria harrumphed. "Mark didn't flinch

when I reminded him of it. I've been the one he'll listen to when he's being stubborn. This time, he has his heels dug in the ground, and he's not budging. I love my bruder, but he's putting his needs before Magdelena's. And it's not necessary."

Otis smiled. "Let's change the subject." He got up and brought back the wall calendar. "Let's pick a date for this wedding."

Magdelena rose and stood over his shoulder. "How about September tenth. I don't want to wait any longer than we have to."

"September tenth it is." Toby gazed into her beautiful dark brown eyes. He'd been worried they'd never marry. It was a reality, and he couldn't be more pleased.

They chatted about having the wedding in the yard, and Uncle Otis had built an extra barn for special occasions and church services. The men in the community had helped him build it for this purpose.

Gloria went to her sewing basket and returned with her tape measure. "Hold your arms out for me, Toby. I need your measurements to make you proper wedding attire." She chuckled. "This is so much fun."

Toby rose and moved when she told him to. He'd like having new clothes. Gloria was a wonderful aunt. She oozed with kindness and made him feel like he'd known her forever. "Danki for this, Gloria."

"I'm tickled to be such a large part of this wedding process." She penciled her last measurement on her pad of paper. "I'm finished."

"I'm sorry, but it's getting late. I should head back before dark." Toby didn't want to leave. The day had been a big success and one he'd never forget. He'd be a husband to the love of his life on September tenth.

Magdelena headed for the front door. "I'll walk you out."

He hugged Gloria and Otis and thanked them for everything. He went to his buggy with Magdelena. He pulled her into his arms and kissed her lightly on the lips. "I love you, and I will count the days until I say, 'I do.'"

"Me, too. Danki for accommodating me. I'm sorry you have to sell our haus and leave your job with Andrew."

"I'll do anything for you." He twirled her around. "We have a wedding date! I'm the happiest man alive!"

She laughed. "No wonder I fell in love with you. You make me laugh, and you wipe away my worries."

He kissed her cheek, bid her farewell, and drove home. They'd been through a lot of turmoil to get to this point. He didn't foresee anything standing in their way since they had Otis's and Gloria's support. Her family chose to shun them, and they were on their own to marry. He was sure this would overshadow their special day. Magdelena would miss having them there, but he'd do his best to make their day a happy one. He still held out hope they'd reconcile with Magdelena and attend.

He was almost home when thunder clapped and lightning struck in the meadow. Rain pelted the buggy top. He was surprised at the rain, since the day had been filled with sunshine. The clouds moved in fast, and he shuddered. He'd learned to expect the unexpected.

Chapter Ten

Magdelena and Aunt Gloria went to town to the general store and bought a new mop and bucket Wednesday, and they ran into the bishop.

Aunt Gloria clasped Magdelena's hand. "Bishop Hershberger, this is Magdelena Beachy, my niece. She's staying with us, and she'd like to marry her suitor, Toby Schlabach, in Mt. Hope. Do you have time to meet with us and Toby next Tuesday at two in the afternoon?"

"Magdelena, it's a pleasure to meet you." Bishop Hershberger checked the bag he carried with him and smiled. "I'd be delighted to meet with you and Toby." He pulled out a small pad of paper. "I always carry a list of my scheduled meetings and a pencil along with my spectacles in this bag. I run into friends who want to schedule one thing or another with me while I'm in town, and my memory isn't as sharp as I'd like. I forget what I had for breakfast by lunch." He chuckled.

Magdelena grinned. Bishop Hershberger had unruly gray hair and a kind face. His round and dimpled cheeks and the sparkle in his eyes made him approachable. She loved her bishop in Charm, and she'd pictured him officiating her wedding ceremony when the time came, but Bishop Hershberger appeared to be a good substitute.

"Will you reserve September tenth for our wedding date? We can change the meeting date if you're booked," Magdelena said.

"Yes. I have September tenth open. I'll make a note of it. We don't need to change the meeting date, but I can't agree to marry you and Toby until we talk more next Tuesday. I look forward to it. Wilkom to Mt. Hope, Magdelena. Gloria, always a pleasure. Give my best to Otis."

"We understand. Danki." Aunt Gloria smiled.

Magdelena hooked her arm through Aunt Gloria's. "He seems like an easygoing fellow." She was glad he wasn't too serious and authoritative. She'd heard her parents mention this about their friends' bishops in other Amish communities. She hoped she was on her way to becoming Mrs. Schlabach. Would the bishop be sympathetic to her and Toby's situation with her parents? Would Mamm coax Daed to understand she didn't run away from her family but from his unyielding demand? Would her mamm remember what she went through with her parents? Magdelena loved them so much. To have them at her wedding would mean the world to her.

"Let's go to the dry goods store. I need white fabric for your dress and Toby's shirt." Aunt Gloria toddled along to the store.

Toby went to the furniture store Wednesday afternoon delivering a small desk he'd handcrafted. He carried it to the shop's door, and Andrew held it open.

Andrew whistled. "What a beautiful piece. Mahogany was a good choice. How was your visit with Magdelena?"

"We set September tenth for the wedding in Mt. Hope. If the bishop agrees to marry us in Mt. Hope, I'll need to sell the property I bought and use the money to buy a home there. I'll have to find a job there. I want to give you plenty of time to find someone to take my place. I don't want to do anything until we've met with the bishop in Mt. Hope, but I wanted to let you know what was going on." He looked forward to work each day at Andrew's farm. They'd become best friends, and he'd miss him. They'd visit when they had time, but it wouldn't be the same.

"If you get permission from the bishop in Mt. Hope to marry, work for me until your wedding. I'll find someone by then, and you won't have any problem finding work in Mt. Hope. I'll contact the furniture store owner there and give you a good recommendation. I've been to the store, and the owner has a workshop in the back like I do. Then you'll have a relationship with the store owner to sell your pieces after you no longer need the job and will have your farm to manage. The place you bought in Charm will sell fast."

Andrew had given this some thought. He should've known his friend would have a plan in mind. He'd always looked out for him.

"Danki. I appreciate it. I'll take you up on your offer."

Mrs. Miller and Mrs. Mullet, two older Amish women, came inside the shop. One was hunchbacked and had a cane to balance her. The two ladies were the biggest gossips in town, and Toby avoided them whenever possible.

Mrs. Miller nodded and frowned. Her companion did the same.

Toby's cheeks heated, and he arranged the small desk he brought onto the sales floor. He knew better than to say anything to the women. They always had to have the last word and no explanation would satisfy them. They were never wrong, according to them. He didn't need to fuel their fire with trying to defend his position to them and have them say he'd been rude to them. Amish weren't supposed to spread untruths or confront each other.

Andrew stepped to them. "How may I help you ladies, today?"

Mrs. Miller pointed her cane to the desk Toby set in the corner. "I like it. Did you make it, Andrew?"

"No, Toby did. It's a lovely piece."

"Do you have another?" Mrs. Miller scanned the shop.

Mrs. Mullet scoffed. "Mary, you can't buy anything Toby has made. It's an abomination for what he's done to the Beachy family."

Mrs. Miller stared at Toby. "You're right. Let's kumme back after he leaves. Any man who would separate a dochder from her family is a dishonorable man." She scowled.

The two women huffed their way out of the store.

"Andrew, I'm sorry. I didn't mean to drive business away from your store. I don't know what to say. Is this the attitude of most of the Amish in Charm?"

Mark had a lot of influence in this town with his money and generosity in helping others. Bernice also did her share of making food for the sick and stitching clothes for those less fortunate. Toby admired them both for it.

Andrew waved a dismissive hand. "You held your tongue better than I would have. You're wise. It would've made matters worse. They would've twisted anything you said because they are never wrong, according to them. Those old biddies should mind their own business. They do more harm than good by disparaging others with their negative remarks. They've hurt reputations with untruths about some of our friends' misfortunes. We've ignored them, and we should forget what happened with them today. They'll move on to another target tomorrow. I can't wait to attend your wedding, and I'm sure many of our friends will agree with me."

"No matter what I say, they wouldn't listen. Danki again for your offer to work for you until the wedding. I may have to take off early some days to go to Mt. Hope for our counseling sessions. I'm hoping to meet with the bishop there next Tuesday."

"Take off early any days you need to." Andrew smiled. "You can work out your schedule without checking with me."

Toby would miss his conversations with Andrew. He was glad they wouldn't be too far apart to lose touch. And he still wanted to sell furniture in Andrew's store. He wouldn't be free to make enough trips on a regular basis when he had a farm to manage. He hoped the storeowner in Mt. Hope would be open to selling his pieces. "Andrew, I appreciate everything you've done for me."

Customers came into the store, and Andrew nodded and went to help them. Toby strolled outside, got in his buggy, and then went to visit Abram. He didn't want to dismiss the friendship he'd built with him, and he needed to tell him what was going on with himself and Magdelena. And maybe Abram would be ready to tell him why he was going to Massillon so often. He drove to Abram and Annie's.

Annie carried a basket of peaches. "Toby, I went to the bakery and Rachael said Magdelena's in Mt. Hope. She told me about her father and Zach insisting she go through with the arranged marriage. What does this mean for the two of you?" She blushed. "I'm sorry. I shouldn't pry, but I've kumme to care about you both."

"Don't apologize. Magdelena and I care about you and Abram, too. We have pleaded with her daed and Zach, but they don't take us seriously. Zach says he's interested in Magdelena, but he wants to secure his future on the ranch. Being a rancher is his top priority. He and Mark have become friends, and it's an advantage for both of them to have Zach involved in the ranch as a member of the family."

"Do you think she'll return? It must be hard for her to leave her family and friends. Will you marry her in Mt. Hope against her daed's wishes?"

"Magdelena's aunt and uncle in Mt. Hope are in full support of our marriage. Her aunt Gloria is Mark's schweschder, and she can usually persuade him to reconsider his decisions, but not this time. Our desire is for her parents to bless our union, but we don't hold much hope for this. He's demanding Magdelena make a lifelong commitment to a man she doesn't love. We have no choice. We'll reside in Mt. Hope after we're married."

She sighed sadly. "I'm sick about this."

"Since we'll be an hour away, we can make day trips to visit each other. You're invited to the wedding. We chose September tenth for the date. But we have to ask the bishop if this date is free on his calendar. I'm going there Tuesday."

"I'm happy for you." Annie rolled her eyes. "You've kumme to speak to Abram and I've peppered you with questions the minute you got here. He's not here." She cast her eyes on the peaches. "He said he'd be back in tomorrow."

"Is everything all right? You seem worried." Toby took the basket from her. He set it on the porch step.

She frowned. "I'm not sure. I don't know why he makes these mysterious trips to Massillon. He said everything's fine. He has business there and not to badger him about why he goes there. I'm tense while he's gone. When he returns home, I'm always relieved he's returned safely. It can't be good if he won't talk about it. I was hoping he'd tell you what he's up to."

He shook his head. He didn't want to reveal anything Abram had told him, even though it wasn't much about why he was going to Massillon. After what Gabe had told him about playing cards with Abram in Massillon, Toby suspected gambling was what drew him there. "He's not revealed to me why he's taking these trips. I'm hoping, as we grow our friendship, he'll share this with me." He lifted the basket and put it by the front door. "If you need anything, please don't hesitate to ask. I'm at Andrew's or my haus. And you can find Rachael at the bakery."

"Danki. There may be a day when I kumme knocking."

"My offer is sincere, and Rachael is more than willing to also help." He nodded and left. He headed to Mr. Umble's place and passed Bernice in her buggy. He waved.

She yelled and gestured to him to pull over.

He did, and he got out of the buggy to talk to her. She stayed seated in hers. He had no idea what to expect. "Greetings."

Bernice was alone. She stared at him for a moment, silent.

He waited, looked away, and then back at her.

"Toby, how is my dochder? I assume you've been to Mt. Hope."

"Yes. She's upset. She loves you and Mark and misses being with her family. She's sad about all this. It's not what she or I want. We'd give anything to have your blessing." He had to try again to win them over. Maybe through Bernice, Mark would understand Magdelena's side of things.

"Toby, please step away from Magdelena. If you do, she'll kumme back to us. Mark will never give his blessing for her to marry you. The ranch has always been a priority for him. Zach's the perfect son in his eyes because of his love of the ranch. Please, Toby. I don't want to lose my dochder."

"But what's your opinion, Bernice? Do you agree with Mark? It would mean so much to Magdelena if you would speak to him on our behalf. Even if I wasn't an option, Magdelena won't kumme home. She won't marry Zach regardless of whether we marry or not."

A tear escaped her eye. "My opinion doesn't matter. I wish it did. Mark's a good provider. But when he makes up his mind about something, he won't budge." She wrenched her gaze from his, stared out at the road ahead, and then left.

He wiped the dust from her horses' hooves going past him on the road. He dreaded telling Magdelena about this conversation. Their marriage wouldn't be the one he'd envisioned with their families and friends, moving into their new home, and keeping their roots in Charm. He wouldn't have expected all this resentment, bitterness, and pain associated with it. Zach's interference had changed their lives. Zach, like Mark, had made ranching the top priority. Magdelena had beauty and all the qualities any man would want in a fraa. Toby felt like the villain tearing

Magdelena apart from her family. His heart ached thinking about it. His reputation was important to him.

He drove to Mr. Umble's place.

Mr. Umble met him at the buggy. "Toby, what a pleasure."

Toby got out of the buggy. "Greetings, Mr. Umble. Do you have time for a chat?"

"Sure." He motioned to the picnic table under the shade of the three tall maple trees.

"I've had a change of plans. I may need to sell the home. I didn't know if anyone had inquired about it before or after I talked to you."

"No, the gossips leave no stone unturned. Mae told everyone we sold the place to you. She also heard Magdelena's parents arranged a marriage with Zach Hilty. Is this true?"

"They did, but Magdelena won't marry him. She's in Mt. Hope living with her aunt and uncle."

"I have good news for you. A man approached me the other day and asked if my place was still for sale. I'd forgotten to take the advertisement down at the general store. He's staying in town with friends and left the address. I'll contact him and make the sale. He was just by here yesterday. Let me return your deposit. Stay here a minute." He went inside and returned with Toby's deposit and handed it to him. "I'm sorry you and Magdelena are having such a difficult time with her parents."

"Danki. Your letting me off the hook for this haus is a big help. I believe God wants us to marry. I'm having a difficult time justifying our actions against Mark's will. But the cost is too high to honor his demand. I've chosen to support Magdelena. I pray God will intervene. But we don't have a lot of time. We've set the date as September tenth for our marriage if the bishop in Mt. Hope has it open on his calendar."

"Listen, there's power in prayer, and your friends are praying for you. We want you and Magdelena to be happy."

Toby grinned. "Danki." He tapped the brim of his hat as he returned to his buggy with his refunded deposit in his pocket. What a fortunate turn of events this had been.

Toby headed out of town Tuesday morning to go to Mt. Hope. Full from breakfast, he didn't have to worry about getting hungry on the way. He'd fed the livestock at home and at Andrew's place. He'd been relieved not to run into the Beachys or Hiltys after his encounter with Bernice this past week. He liked church services, but he wasn't unhappy this past Sunday had been their regularly scheduled week off. He passed his friends' farms as he drove through Charm to Mt. Hope. He and Magdelena would make new friends, but they'd wanted a future together with their present ones. He wished they could have it all.

Magdelena ran to him when he arrived. She clapped her hands and bounced on her toes. "You're back! I've missed you. Aunt Gloria and I have been planning our wedding. She's already made my dress and your shirt and pants. She's stitching your jacket. I've met some of her friends, and I'm starting to grow roots here."

He held her hand for a moment. "Your smile is radiant. It thrills me you're having a great day. Wherever you are is where I want to live." He wasn't sure what mood she'd be in when he arrived. Nothing had changed with her family, and she had so much to lose leaving Charm. He wanted her to have it all without compromises.

She hooked her arm through his as they walked to the

haus. "Are you hungry? We have leftover fried chicken, mashed potatoes, and a mixed berry pie from last night's supper. I can warm it for you."

"Maybe a little later. Mamm made me cheesy eggs and crisp bacon early this morning." He patted his stomach. "I had more food than I should have."

"You don't have to worry. You never gain an ounce. Aunt Gloria is bound to make me chubby." She laughed. "The woman cooks the best food."

"You're beautiful, and you don't gain any weight. And if you did, it wouldn't matter to me." Toby kissed the back of her hand.

They went to the kitchen.

Gloria wrapped her loving arms around him. "Wilkom." Her eyes sparkled. "I've got a surprise for you. I'll be right back." She left the kitchen and returned with his clothes she'd made for him. "Go try these on in the guest bedroom." She ushered him down the hall.

He chuckled. Her smile couldn't get any broader. He wished everyone was as happy as Gloria for them. He undressed, put on the new clothes, and went to show them his outfit. "The shirt and pants fit. You did a superb job. Danki."

Magdelena held her hands to her cheeks. "You look so handsome in them."

Gloria waved him down the hall. "Go take them off for now. I don't want them to get a speck of dirt or a wrinkle in them. You do look striking, Toby."

He returned, dressed back in his clothes, and joined them in the living room. He teased Gloria. "When are you going to show me Magdelena's dress?" He winked at Magdelena.

"Not until she wears the dress on her wedding day." Gloria grinned.

Magdelena's smile turned to a frown. "Daed won't be walking me down the aisle. I'd always assumed he would be there on my special day giving me away."

"Don't fret. Uncle Otis will fill in if your daed doesn't kumme through. I'm praying my bruder will realize he doesn't want to ruin his relationship with you. I can't imagine he'll let this wedding go through without him."

Magdelena glanced at Toby. "Did you run into Zach or my parents since you were here last?"

He nodded. "Not Zach or your daed, but your mamm. We passed each other on the road, and she asked me to pull over. Which I did."

Gloria stood ramrod straight. "What did Bernice say to you?"

Toby took a deep breath. How much should he say? He didn't want to dampen Magdelena's mood. He had to be honest with her always. It's what he wanted for them. "She asked me to step aside and free Magdelena to marry Zach. I asked for her opinion."

Magdelena gripped her skirt. Her knuckles white. "What did she say?"

Gloria sat on the edge of her chair. "Yes, I'm very interested in her answer."

"She avoided the question and told me what Mark wouldn't do. She wants her dochder back. She thinks my stepping aside will allow Magdelena to marry Zach, and she'd have her family back together. I told her Magdelena wouldn't marry Zach whether I was in the picture or not. I reminded her we'd like nothing better than their change of heart."

"How did she respond?" Magdelena sucked in her bottom lip.

"She left me standing in the road. Please understand she wasn't nasty. She didn't raise her voice or glare at me. She had tears in her eyes. She's in pain over this. I don't believe she's against us. She wants harmony, and she is asking you to marry Zach to create this. She doesn't hold much hope Mark will listen to her or anyone. I may be wrong, but it's what I think."

Magdelena sprang to her feet. She paced the floor. "Why can't she stand up for me this once? She went through this very thing before her marriage to Daed. She knows how heart-wrenching this situation is for us. It doesn't make sense. I miss Charity. I wonder what they are telling her."

Gloria moved to the settee and patted the cushion next to her. "Charity loves you and Toby. If you and Toby marry in Mt. Hope, maybe your parents will finally accept it and bring Charity to visit." She gestured to the settee. "Sit, Magdelena. You're expecting your mamm to go against her husband. I'm certain she's as upset as you. She may have pleaded with him. But don't blame her. She's powerless in this if Mark won't listen to her. And you don't want your parents to have strife in their marriage for any reason."

"If we have kinner and I disagree with Toby, I'll speak my mind." Magdelena stared at her hands shaking in her lap.

"I will always consider what you have to say. We'll compromise." Toby didn't expect their marriage would be perfect.

Magdelena stared at the ceiling. "It's true. I don't want to cause trouble between my parents. I wish Daed would value Mamm's comments about things more than he does.

Especially now. She wants to keep the peace with him to a fault. He loves her. It's evident. He may surprise her and listen. She doesn't know if she doesn't try. I hope she won't quit expressing how she feels."

Gloria patted Magdelena's knee. "Marriage is complicated. You are like me. Bolder. Your mamm wouldn't go against your daed for any reason. It's natural for Bernice. She's devoted to him, and their relationship works best if she doesn't oppose him on any matter. But don't forget. God is still in control. This isn't over. We'll keep planning, and we'll pray. It's all we can do."

Magdelena rolled her shoulders back. "I can't let go of this tension. We've got some time before we have to go to the bishop's haus. Let's get in the canoe, Toby. The water is calm, and it's a cloudless day. We can get our feet wet and paddle down the river."

"Perfect idea. You two skedaddle." Gloria ushered them to the door and outside.

They strolled to the canoe, removed their shoes and socks, turned it over, and then threw in the paddles. Toby pushed it in the water, and he held it while Magdelena got in. He got in and paddled down the river. "What a beautiful day. Listen to the birds. They have a singsong chirp."

"Oh no." Magdelena yelped. "The eagle swooped in and clamped its claws onto a bunny." She pointed to the sky. "I love bunnies. I wish the eagle would take a snake instead. I don't like those."

Toby had a soft spot for bunnies, too. Even if they did like to devour his vegetables. "Look at the sunflowers. They're getting taller." He wanted her to enjoy the day with him and to take her mind away from unpleasant thoughts.

"They are pretty." She beamed.

"Have you met the bishop?" Toby stopped paddling and let the canoe drift.

"Yes. Aunt Gloria and I were in town and he was, too. She asked if we could meet with him today, and he agreed. He left a good impression on me, but we only had a couple of minutes with him. Aunt Gloria and Uncle Otis like him. Did you speak with Mr. Umble about the haus? I didn't want to sell it." She stuck out her bottom lip.

"Great news. Mr. Umble has another buyer for the haus. He returned my deposit."

"How did he have another buyer? He sold the haus to you."

Toby recounted his conversation with Mr. Umble.

Magdelena gasped. "I believe God intervened on our behalf and found the buyer for us. That's a relief, isn't it?"

"Yes. A big relief."

Magdelena snapped her fingers. "On another subject, I didn't want to forget to ask. Have you been to the Hooks'?"

"Yes. Annie was alone, so I didn't stay long. Abram was on one of his jaunts. Annie said he won't tell her why he's making these trips."

"You didn't tell her Gabe gambled with him in Massillon, did you?" She gripped the sides of the canoe.

"No. It's not my place. It's Abram's, when he's ready. I plan to speak with him again. I don't want to leave Charm and abandon them. I feel like God wants us to help them. They're beginning to trust us. I'll keep trying. Annie is concerned for us. She also supports our decision. She's sure they'll attend our wedding."

Magdelena smiled. "I'd love to have them here." She sighed. "I suppose we won't be wilkom in Charm. Our friends will have to kumme here."

He reached for her hand. "You can always write to your parents, and we'll not give up asking them to reconcile with us. When we have kinner, they'll want to know them." He'd never want to have this kind of turmoil with his family. He wished her parents would understand how difficult this was for Magdelena to be in opposition with them. She'd never be content as long as she was apart from them. Plus, they had Charity to consider. He loved her like a little schweschder. He didn't want her to think they'd abandoned her. She had to see they were trying with her parents.

"I shouldn't have to make them understand their demand for me to marry someone I don't love should be my choice."

Otis came to the bank and called out to them. "Time to go to the bishop's haus."

"We'll be right there." Toby paddled to where they'd put the canoe in the water. He jumped out and held it steady for Magdelena to get out. He dragged the canoe onto land and turned it over and tucked the oars underneath. They hurried to put on their shoes and socks.

Gloria toddled to the buggy carrying a container. "I made Bishop Hershberger his favorite blueberry tarts."

Otis chuckled. "You're trying to sweeten the man."

"A little encouragement never hurts." She got in the buggy.

Magdelena and Toby sat in the back seat and grinned at the couple. Magdelena held a calendar on her lap. "I bought a wall calendar, and I'm marking off the days until we reach our wedding. What kind of cake do you want? I'm sure Liza and the girls will want to make a special one for us."

"Rachael will want to decorate it with her special roses for you."

"Oh yes. I love those. Let's have vanilla cake with strawberry filling and white icing." Magdelena steepled her fingers under her chin.

Toby chuckled and squeezed her hand. "Sounds delicious. Should I tell Rachael or do you want to? I'll bring her with me to visit. She's homesick for you." Toby didn't want to encourage Mamm and Rachael to make arrangements to move to Mt. Hope. He wanted to wait. He wasn't sure what would be best for them. They had the haus and roots there. Rachael thrived at the bakery.

Gloria glanced over her shoulder. "Bring your schweschder next time you kumme to visit. I'd love to meet her."

Magdelena widened her eyes. "Would you, Toby? Hannah would fill in when she knows what day you want to kumme. I need to hug Rachael. I miss her so much. I didn't like leaving without confiding in her, but it would've put her in the middle of you and me. I don't want any misunderstanding between us."

Toby clasped her hand again. "I'll arrange it."

Rachael had blossomed as she formed a close friendship with Magdelena. And Magdelena had been instrumental in growing his schweschder's relationships with her other friends in Charm. It had been years in the making. The more this move became a reality, the more he realized what they'd taken for granted. He couldn't forget the two women who disparaged him at Andrew's furniture store. Being the center of hurtful gossip wasn't the way he wanted to leave Charm.

They arrived at the bishop's haus. He had a small farm and the barn had a fresh coat of paint. Sheep grazed in the corral. The bishop opened the door. "Kumme in." He had a tray with a pitcher of lemonade and empty glasses on the coffee table. "Help yourselves."

Gloria passed him the blueberry tarts as she introduced Toby to the bishop. "I brought your favorite dessert."

He opened the container. "Any friends of Gloria and Otis are friends of mine. Take a seat, and I'll get some plates." He sniffed the tarts. "Danki, Gloria. Blueberry. Can't wait to take a bite." He returned and passed them each a plate. He put the container on the table. "Please take one. Gloria may have told you I'm a widower. We didn't have kinner. The Yoder family bought my farm, and they look after me."

Toby sat on the lumpy brown cushioned chair. A tattered wedding quilt lay over the back of the chair the bishop chose. The haus lacked the touch of a fraa. No other quilts or baskets of yarn were in sight. His shoes were lined up by the door and the haus was quiet. Too quiet. Too absent of warmth. It was neat, clean, and lonely.

The bishop had his Holy Bible and calendar with a pencil on a small table beside his chair. "Before we begin our conversation, I'd like to pray. Please bow your heads.

"Dear Heavenly Father, we seek Your will in all matters. Please direct our paths and help us to do what is pleasing to You. We praise You for Your power, and danki for Your love. Amen."

Gloria sat next to Magdelena on the settee. "Magdelena is like my own dochder, and we loved Toby the minute we met him. We're pleased they want to marry in Mt. Hope."

The bishop cocked his head to Toby. "Tell me why you want to marry in Mt. Hope."

Toby shifted in his chair to better address him. "We live in Charm, but we plan to reside in Mt. Hope. Magdelena's daed has arranged for her to marry another man who has the same interest in ranching as him. He foresees this man taking over the ranch when he retires. Zach, the other man, is interested in Magdelena and agreeable to the arrangement. Magdelena is not."

"Have you and Magdelena spoken with her daed?"

Toby had known the bishop would ask these difficult questions. He'd tried to put this unpleasant part of the conversation out of his mind. Now he had to answer whether he wanted to or not. Would the bishop understand their plight? "Magdelena and I are in love. I asked her daed for his blessing, and he wouldn't grant it."

Otis held up his palm. "If I may interrupt?"

The bishop and Toby nodded.

"Magdelena's daed, Mark, is determined to set aside the love this couple has for each other. Toby is a hardworking and God-fearing man. His flaw in Mark's eyes is not having a love for cattle ranching. We support this couple. We're asking you to stand with us."

Gloria covered Magdelena's hand with hers. "My niece shouldn't be forced to wed a man she doesn't love to satisfy her daed's plans for his operation of the ranch when he retires. I've spoken with my bruder, and he refuses to listen. This couple is at a crossroads, and they've kumme to us for our support. Will you please schedule a date on your calendar to wed them?"

The bishop didn't lift his calendar. "Mark Beachy came to my home. He made the trip solely to speak to me. He was afraid Magdelena and Toby would want to marry in Mt. Hope. He told me he's opposed, and he asked me to decline should you ask. I kept our appointment because I wanted to listen to your side of the story."

They gasped.

Toby stole a surprised glance at Magdelena. She had tears pooling in her eyes. Mark had thought of everything to prevent them from being together. Could he and Magdelena be wrong to push having a future together? Was God telling them their union wasn't His will for their lives? He didn't believe this. "Do you agree with him?"

The bishop settled back in his chair. "I wasn't sure, so I rode over to Charm and met with Bishop Fisher yesterday. He said Mark had discussed with him his wishes for whom Magdelena should marry. He had no disparaging remarks about Toby. Your bishop said he asked Mark to let you and Magdelena be together and have Zach continue to work at the ranch. Mark refused. We went to speak with him together. He insists Magdelena marrying Zach will keep their families close and create the best life for her."

Magdelena had tears staining her cheeks. "Please, Bishop, I won't do as my daed asks under any circumstances. Not to rebel for the sake of opposing him, but for the reason I can't commit to a man I don't love. Zach's not a bad man, but he's not for me. Whether Toby and I marry or not, I'll stay in Mt. Hope to avoid doing what my daed demands. Please understand I love my parents. This breaks my heart."

Toby gazed at her then the bishop. "I covet Mark's blessing. This isn't how Magdelena and I want to begin our lives together. What would you advise us to do?"

Gloria circled her arm around Magdelena's shoulders. "Bishop, I realize this puts you in a precarious position, but these two don't deserve the turmoil Mark is causing for them. Won't you give them this way out? Marry them, please."

Otis reached over and clamped a hand on Toby's arm. "This young man has done everything he can to show

Mark he's worthy of his dochder's love. Mark's blinded by his own personal benefits to Magdelena's union with Zach. Won't you help them?"

"Your bishop and I have prayed together for guidance for you and your families. Kinner are to obey their parents. Mark may be wrong in this, but he's her daed. Your mamm is an obedient fraa, and she's standing by her husband. We should keep praying for God to change Mark's heart. It wouldn't be right for me or your bishop to agree to go against your parents' wishes. God wouldn't honor it."

Magdelena wiped her damp eyes. "Are you saying Toby and I should go our separate ways?"

Toby's heart sank. He wouldn't let her go. He was sure God chose Magdelena for him. He would never love another woman. He held his breath while he waited for the bishop's answer.

"No. I'm saying it's not the right time. Give God a chance to intervene. He may be using this situation to teach one or all of us a lesson. Your bishop and I are praying for you and your families. We are sympathetic to what you're going through. God tells us to be still and listen. Be patient." The bishop addressed Toby. "Why didn't you go to your bishop in Charm and ask his advice?"

Toby sighed. "Mark and Bishop Fisher are close. I'd be putting Bishop Fisher in an awkward spot to ask him to go against her parents. I don't want to go against her parents. I have the utmost respect for our bishop and you. It was easier kumming to you since you were outside our community. We were out of options. I'm sorry if you find this inappropriate. And I agree I should've discussed this with our bishop."

Bishop Hershberger nodded. "He understood why you

didn't talk to him for the reasons you've mentioned. I'm glad you came to me."

Magdelena sat on the edge of her seat. "Bishop Hershberger, are you opposed to me living and worshipping in Mt. Hope?"

The hair on Toby's neck prickled. Magdelena would have to stay away from Charm or she'd be doomed to marrying Zach. Why couldn't she live here with her aunt and uncle protecting her?

"You're an adult, Magdelena. You can choose where to live. Toby, I'd advise you to stay away from Magdelena for a few days. Magdelena's division from her parents isn't God's will. If you visiting forces your plans, it will further advance Mark's frustration with her. The best outcome is if Mark changes his heart and mind and repairs his relationship with her. Her mamm will follow his lead, from what your bishop has said to me."

Magdelena darted a glance at Toby and back to the bishop. "Please, don't ask us to end our pursuit of happiness together. I need Toby now more than ever."

"You need to pray and to heal your relationship with your parents. It will take effort on both sides. This would be the best outcome for your future with you and Toby. Separate for now. Again, pray and be patient." He offered a prayer to God, and then they thanked him and bid him farewell.

They got in the buggy and headed home. Gloria sniffled and wiped her nose with a handkerchief. "I'm sorry this meeting didn't turn out like we'd hoped. I don't agree with the bishop. Toby, you're wilkom at our home anytime."

Otis kept the mare at a slow trot. "I'm sorry, Toby and Magdelena. I agree with our bishop. Toby should give

Mark time to miss his dochder and want to mend their relationship. I'm talking a few days. He's angry, and time may soften him. If Toby keeps kumming here, Mark will center his frustration on Toby. Let's not upset him."

Gloria stared at her husband. "I don't agree, Otis. Why should we tiptoe around Mark? He's in the wrong."

Magdelena put her hand on Gloria's shoulder. "Please don't argue over us. We've caused enough trouble. We'll honor Uncle Otis's wishes. I may not like it, but it makes sense."

"I'll wait for as long as Magdelena asks. I want to do the right thing for all of us." Toby dreaded being apart from her. The days seemed long before he came to visit her this time. A month? But he would do whatever it took.

Otis halted the buggy, and they got out. He held the reins. "Toby, take Magdelena on a stroll. I'll unharness the mare."

Gloria huffed. "He's staying for supper. I refuse to send this lovely man off without a full stomach."

Otis smiled at his fraa. "A wonderful idea, dear."

"Danki, you both," Toby said.

Magdelena ran to the porch and grabbed the folded quilt on the swing and returned to him. "There's a path through the woods to a beautiful cleared spot overlooking the water. Let's go there. We need to talk."

He clasped her hand, and she led him to the spot. He spread the quilt on the ground, and they sat. "Sweetheart, what are your thoughts about what happened today?" Toby wanted open communication between them about everything. They were up against a lot of turmoil, and he didn't want any misunderstandings between them. He didn't want to assume he knew what she was thinking.

"I love you, Toby. I always will. No matter what anyone

wants me to think or do, it's a fact. I don't understand why God would allow this to happen to us. We've both been devoted to Him and to our families. I don't doubt you're the man God has put in my life to wed. What does He want to teach us from this?"

"Maybe the lesson is not for us." Toby took her hand in his. "Maybe it's to teach your daed something. I don't know. I'll honor Otis's request, although I'll miss you very much. As much as I don't want to, Otis and our bishops' thoughts are right. It's not wise for me to pursue you right now, knowing Mark's opposed. I'm not leaving you for good, but we'll give him time. One or two months isn't too bad. And then we'll reassess."

"Will you write?"

"I'd like to, but no. If your daed should visit and ask you if we've been in touch, you'd have to say yes if I wrote to you. I'd like him to know we're staying apart for a short period to respect his, our bishops' in both Charm and Mt. Hope, and your uncle's wishes. I'll be counting the days until a month is over. I'll visit then, and we'll talk and decide if we need to wait another month."

"I'm impatient. Two months seems too long." She gazed into his eyes.

His heart dropped in his chest. He wanted to take her hand and run far away. Somewhere they could be together and leave all their woes behind. But there was no place to hide. And it wouldn't be the right thing to do. They had to walk through this turbulent time and wait for God's intervention. "I believe we'll get through this. We have to wait and see what God has in store. I believe this ends with us together."

They walked back to the haus and had supper with Gloria and Otis.

Gloria kept the conversation light and told funny stories about her and Otis. "When we were first married, I wanted a hope chest, and Otis refused to buy the one I wanted. I couldn't understand why."

"Why didn't you want to buy it?" Magdelena tilted her head.

Otis chuckled. "I had a pretty one being built by a friend. By the time he finished it, Gloria was barely speaking to me."

Gloria grinned. "Then when he gave it to me, I cried and begged for his forgiveness. It was much prettier than the one I had picked out."

Otis and Gloria exchanged an endearing look.

"Gloria and I learned to not keep anything from each other, and then there's no misunderstanding. We talk things through. It's the best advice I can give you. I'll be surprised if the two of you don't get married at the end of this. I feel in my heart God has put you together. It's not for us to question but to have faith and believe. He'll do what's best for each of you. Toby, kumme in a month. Let's talk then."

Toby stood. "I should head back to Charm before dark. Danki for everything."

Magdelena rose. "I'll go outside with you. Wait a minute. I'd like to get something from my room."

Toby nodded.

Gloria hugged him tight. "I have kumme to love you, and I'm rooting for you." She handed him a container. "These are maple butter cookies." She winked. "I'll need this container back. So I expect you here in a month and not a day later."

He kissed her cheek. "You and Otis have been so good to me. I'll miss you. And you can mark it down. I'll be back."

He held his hand out to Otis, and Otis pulled him into

a hug. "This hurts us as much as it does you. You're like family. You take care and be well."

Magdelena returned, and he bid her aunt and uncle farewell. They walked outside to the buggy.

She handed him a white handkerchief with the letter *M* embroidered on it. "Put this on your dresser. I want you to have it as a reminder my heart belongs to you."

He kissed her lightly on the lips and held her a moment. "I don't need anything to remind me of our love, but I'll cherish it." He kissed her cheek and then got in the buggy and waved goodbye. He didn't glance over his shoulder. If she was crying, he'd never leave.

Magdelena watched his back until he was no longer in sight. She crossed her arms and proceeded to the bench by the river's edge. "Dear Heavenly Father, forgive me if I'm disappointing You. I don't want to. Why is this happening? I miss my parents. I want them to be pleased about my choosing Toby and have them in our kinners' lives if we're blessed to have bopplin. Please help us. I beg You. Amen." She picked up a stone, threw it, and watched the circle of ripples until she could no longer discern them in the twilight. What was her family doing right now? Did they miss her? What did they tell Charity?

She crossed the yard, stepped inside, and grabbed a dish towel to dry dishes. "Toby left and took half my heart with him. I miss him already. I can't believe Daed spoke with both bishops. He's leaving no stone unturned."

"Your daed is used to getting his way. You've never challenged him until now. He's not sure what to do. Charity questions him, but she's too young to pose a threat. You're grown. Your mamm stands by him, no matter what. I wish

I knew what he'll do. I pray he makes the right decision and doesn't ruin his life and yours."

"No bishop will marry Toby and me unless Daed gives his permission. It's apparent after our discussion today. Toby and I knew they wouldn't, but we didn't want to face it. We'd have to leave our Amish lives to marry and live in the outside world as Englischers if Daed won't kumme around to our way of thinking. Toby or I wouldn't make this choice. Our faith in God and living the Amish life is too important to us." The possibility of being with Toby became bleak. She couldn't accept it. She wouldn't accept it. A month. She'd have to wait.

"Continue to pray about this, but let's not dwell on it. It breaks my heart to have you sad. We need a project. Let's knit an afghan for the elderly couple who live three farms over from me. The last time I was there I noticed the ones they were using were worn." Aunt Gloria sorted through her knitting basket for the right colors.

Magdelena loved Aunt Gloria for trying to distract her from her somber thoughts, but her mind was elsewhere. If she didn't marry Toby, she'd settle in Mt. Hope and her friends could visit. What would Toby do? Stay in Charm? Marry another woman as the years passed? She couldn't fathom it. She had a love so deep for him she couldn't imagine giving her heart to another man in the future. Why had she and Toby fallen in love? Why had they connected in a big way the first time they met? Why did they know early on they wanted to have a future together if they weren't meant to be? She pounded her fists on her legs. "Why, God? Why?"

Aunt Gloria gasped in alarm. She circled her arms around Magdelena and held her. "I'm so sorry, Magdelena. I wish I could make all your heartache go away. Please tell me what to do."

Chapter Eleven

Toby had missed Magdelena this past week. He listened to the bishop's message on pride and selfishness. Both were keeping him from Magdelena. Maybe this message would penetrate Mark's heart. He prayed so.

Bishop Fisher directed them in another hymn and then offered a prayer to God for the food the women had brought for the after-service dinner.

Toby bumped into Zach going to the picnic tables set up buffet-style. "Greetings."

"Toby, are you making trips to Mt. Hope?" Zach faced him. "I sincerely want to know."

"Magdelena and I have agreed not to talk for at least a month. We'd like a peaceful resolution with you and her family. I don't want to provoke you or Mark."

Hands on hips, Zach faced him. "Good." He turned on his heel and walked away.

Toby wasn't sure what to make of Zach's response. A month wouldn't change Magdelena's mind.

Abram slapped his back. "Friend, you look perplexed."

Toby shrugged. "Zach is still vying for Magdelena's

heart. I'm not worried she'll change her mind, but I wish he would change his."

Abram pulled him away from the crowd. "What's the latest news?"

"We're giving her daed and Zach time to reconsider Magdelena's wishes and staying apart for a month as to not provoke them. There isn't a day I don't want to ride over there, but this is best for now. But let's talk about you. Why the mysterious trips to Massillon?"

Abram scanned the area around them.

"No one is listening or around us. Confide in me, Abram. You can trust me." Toby gazed at Abram in silence.

"I wish Gabe hadn't told you about my gambling or being involved in the moonshine business." Abram stared past Toby.

"But he did." Toby didn't want to repeat what Gabe had said and question him about the moonshine involvement. He wanted Abram to tell him.

"I'm surprised you're talking to me. You're in enough trouble with Magdelena's daed and Zach. I'm sure if you asked their friends, they consider you at fault for pursuing her against their wishes. If my gambling and moonshine involvement is discovered, they may question why you're friends with me and wonder if you knew."

"Magdelena chose me long before Zach came along. I love her, and she's the woman God chose for me. I'm sure of it. What kind of friend would I be if I turned my back on you? Do you plan to quit?" He would have to distance himself if Abram insisted on continuing these behaviors.

"I've got one more batch of moonshine to sell. I'm one of six who are part of the business. Two of the men left Amish life years ago. They don't have any problem with my leaving the business. I owe one more payment to a man who lent me money to gamble. I can pay him and have money left over for Annie and me." Abram swatted at a fly and cast his eyes to the ground. "Are you going to tell anyone?"

"No. I'm glad your plan is to put an end to it. Do you want me to go with you to make the last payment? Is this man a threat?" Toby shouldn't be with Abram. Amish may be there and assume he was a gambler. But he didn't shy away from friends who needed him.

"Larry Greene wouldn't hesitate to injure me or end my life if I didn't make this payment. I'll be all right. I'll have what he wants. And then, I promise to obey God as best I can and follow our Amish traditions." Abram sighed and managed a weak grin.

"What's making you stop?" Toby wondered how long Abram had been keeping these secrets.

"I was friends with the two men who left the Amish life, and they invited me to join them in the business. I got greedy, and I loved the extra money. My late fraa begged me to quit, and I didn't. I married Annie and moved here for a fresh start, but I had to sell moonshine to make enough money to pay off Larry. It was the first time I'd lost and then borrowed money to keep playing. He was at the table and gave me a loan. I won't put myself in this position again. Annie is the reason. I've fallen in love with her."

"How dangerous is Larry Greene?" Toby didn't like Abram going to face this man again alone.

"My friends claim men have disappeared who haven't paid Larry on time."

"Are you late with this payment?" Toby feared for Abram's life. Liza's late husband had been murdered for being late on his gambling payment. He didn't want this to happen to his friend.

"I hope not. If the buyers for the moonshine kumme through as planned, I'll be fine."

"Abram, when are you going to Massillon again?" Toby didn't want any part of the moonshine sale, but he would want to accompany Abram to pay his debt. He didn't want anything to happen to his friend.

"I'll leave Friday around six in the morning. The trip will take me about seven and a half hours. I'm sure I'll be fine. You don't need to worry about me. I'll get a room at the boarding haus and then go with my moonshine buddies to make this last sale, collect my portion of the money, and tell them this will be my last involvement in the business. They should be fine with it. Then I'll meet Larry at the saloon and pay him off. He makes it a point to be there Friday afternoon and through the evening to collect whatever anyone owes him. I'm ready to do God's will and follow the rules we agree to live by as outlined in the Ordnung."

"Have you told Annie any of this?"

He shook his head. "I tell her when I'm leaving on a trip and when I'll return. I get short-tempered with her if she asks any questions, so she doesn't inquire anymore. She's innocent, and I don't want her to know or be dragged into this. I've been edgy and abrupt with her when she's asked about my trips. I've also been short-tempered about the silliest things with her because of my worry about being discovered or this meeting to pay Larry going wrong. The sale of the moonshine could be canceled or the men may not want to pay and ambush us. None of it's good. I'm ashamed. I will get this done, and then I will turn my life around and treat her better. I promise."

"I'll go with you to Massillon on Friday, and I'll stay and kumme back with you on Saturday. You shouldn't go alone."

Abram rubbed the back of his neck and cleared his throat. "Toby, you can't kumme with me. You can't be involved. You're having enough trouble with Magdelena's daed. I'd never forgive myself if you got hurt."

"Listen, Abram. I'm not thrilled about going, but you owe it to Annie to have me go with you. What is she supposed to do when you don't kumme home? Magdelena and I care about both of you."

Abram frowned. "Does Magdelena know?"

"She does, but she hasn't told Annie. You will have to tell Annie when all this is over. She's your fraa and the person you should trust the most. You owe her an apology and the promise you've made to me to treat her better should be said to her." He was relieved Abram wouldn't gamble or sell moonshine anymore after this. Would Annie forgive him? He hoped this would be the start of a happy marriage for both of them.

"You've been a better friend to me than I deserve. Danki." He stepped closer to Toby. "The meeting is at six at the saloon."

Toby nodded. "Pick me up. I'm going with you."

"All right. If you insist. I'll pick you up at six in the morning on Friday."

Charity ran to Toby. "Mamm said Magdelena's at Aunt Gloria's, and she doesn't know how long she'll be gone. I miss her. Will you kumme and play a game with me at my haus sometime? I've missed you, too."

Abram smiled at Charity and then walked across the yard to join Annie.

Toby squatted to look into Charity's eyes. It must be

difficult for her to have Magdelena gone. "I miss her and you. I'm not sure when we can play a game again."

"Because of Zach?" Charity crossed her arms.

"Zach's all right." Toby gently squeezed her hand.

"No, he isn't. Mamm told Daed Magdelena ran away to Aunt Gloria's so she wouldn't have to marry Zach. Why won't Daed let her marry you?"

Toby's heart plummeted. Charity shouldn't have to worry about adult problems. "This will all work out. You don't worry your little head about a thing. God will take care of all of this for us. We have to be patient. Do your parents know you were listening to them?"

"No. They were in their room with the door cracked. I got up to get a glass of water, and I snuck back to my room. The last time I asked Daed a question about Magdelena, he got upset. God knows how many hairs I have on my head. He's pretty smart. I'll ask him about this in my prayers. He's answered a lot of my prayers." She held her chin up and grinned.

"I have no doubt God's answered your prayers." Toby smiled and stood.

Bernice came behind Charity. "Dochder of mine, it's time to go. Find Peter, and he can kumme and play with you this afternoon if Liza approves."

"Yay!" Charity waved to Toby. "Goodbye, Toby."

"Goodbye, little one." He faced Bernice. "Good afternoon."

"Have you given any more thought to our last conversation?" Bernice stared at him.

Magdelena's mamm's pinched lips and sternness unnerved him. He had made himself clear the first time. He had to remain calm and not be frustrated. She had lost her dochder, and it could be permanent. "I haven't changed my mind."

Bernice frowned and left.

He stood and scanned the thinning crowd. Most Amish had left to go home. Abram and Annie weren't in sight. They must've departed. He found Rachael heading for the buggy. "Are you and Mamm ready to leave?"

"Yes. Mamm and Liza are having a conversation about Magdelena. Liza's worried about her. Hannah has been filling in at the bakery. I love baking with her, but I miss my best friend."

"Would you like to kumme with me when I return to Mt. Hope? Magdelena and her relatives said to bring you."

"Yes! I'll look forward to it. Wait. I can't leave Hannah by herself. No. I shouldn't ask Liza or Hannah to give me the opportunity. I pray Magdelena will return and be free to marry you. I'll stay and keep the disruption to the bakery to a minimum."

"I commend you for your loyalty to Liza and Hannah. Magdelena will understand and appreciate it. I'll tell her you asked about her and wanted to kumme."

"Danki, bruder."

Mamm arrived at the buggy and put her basket on the back bench. "Toby, I noticed you and Bernice together. Anything new?"

"No. She still wants me to withdraw from the competition for Magdelena. She and Mark don't realize there is no competition. Politely, I told her I haven't changed my mind." Toby liked Bernice. To maintain a good relationship was important to him. He hoped the damage done by all this would be repairable one day.

* * *

Magdelena dug potatoes from the garden late Monday morning. She wiped the sweat from her brow with the back of her dirty hand. Toby would've had church service yesterday. Had he had any conversation with her parents or Zach? It must be difficult to be in Charm with them and the gossips. She didn't want to ever let him go, but she might have to. She realized now no bishop would condone going against her parents. What would it mean for him in Charm? She wasn't ready to face this. She loved him too much.

Aunt Gloria bustled to her. "Smile. We've got beautiful sunshine, and the lilacs and lavender blooming in my flower garden are giving off the best aroma. Were you up last night? Are you having trouble sleeping?"

"I'm sorry. I can't turn off the thoughts in my head about this mess long enough to go to sleep. I pace the floor to get rid of my nervous energy." She'd lost weight and her clothes were hanging off her. She needed to put meat on her bones.

"We'll put some lavender under your pillow tonight. It calms me and helps me drift off. Maybe it will do the same for you." Aunt Gloria held lilacs. "I'll put these on the table. They'll cheer you and the scent will be lovely inside the haus."

"I'll try anything. Danki." Magdelena stared at Aunt Gloria's back as she walked inside the haus.

Then she dropped her last potato in the basket. She had enough to make potato salad. She'd already chopped the celery, onion, and boiled the eggs. Aunt Gloria had a cheerful outlook on everything. She overheard her aunt and uncle discussing finances, and Uncle Otis had asked her advice about buying another mare. Did Daed consult

Mamm about purchases? She didn't remember him asking her opinion. They were happy. What else mattered?

Magdelena shielded her eyes. Someone had turned down Aunt Gloria and Uncle Otis's lane. She gasped and clutched her apron. "Mamm?"

Mamm drove to the front of the haus, parked her buggy, and got out.

Uncle Otis hurried to meet her. "Bernice, what a nice surprise. I'll take your horse, and you make yourself at home."

Magdelena wrapped her arms around her. "Mamm, I've missed you."

Mamm stiffened in her embrace. "You wouldn't miss me if you were home where you belong." She separated from Magdelena. "Why be a rebel? You've always been obedient and respectful until now. Is Toby worth the turmoil you've put on our family?"

Magdelena's cheeks warmed. "I won't marry Zach for what Daed surmises is the greater good for our family. Zach can take over Daed's business and not be married to me. Aunt Gloria said she was instrumental in you and Daed marrying. Didn't your daed want you to wed another man? How was your situation different?"

"The circumstances are different. Zach's a better choice for you in every way and for our family. You're young. You'll get over Toby. Our business has given you a privileged life. You won't be satisfied with what Toby can provide versus Zach in the future. You're blinded by love. I would've never defied my parents like you."

Aunt Gloria came from inside the haus to the porch. "I recognized your voice, Bernice. Then I listened to your answer. I don't believe you, and we'll never know the truth since I convinced our parents you were the woman for Mark.

I'm doing for Magdelena what I did for you long ago. Support your dochder. He may listen if you will join us."

"I will be forever grateful for what you did for Mark and me. Please don't stand in our way. Send Magdelena home. You'll not win against Mark on this one. He's grown more stubborn, but he loves us. It's not right for you to kumme between us and Magdelena. Please, Gloria, I must take her home."

Tears of frustration stained Magdelena's face. "I'm right here, but you speak as if I'm not. You, Daed, Zach, and his parents discuss me when I'm there, but you don't address me. Yes, I'm in love with Toby. Blinded by love? No. I mean no disrespect, but I'm an adult with a sound mind. I've done what you and Daed have asked of me my entire life until now. Doesn't it matter that I'm heartbroken my parents won't support me?"

Mamm huffed. "We let you accept the job at the bakery, and we made the wrong decision. You've become more outspoken and independent since you've been there."

Magdelena motioned for Mamm to sit in the rocker on the porch. "Let's take a breath and sit."

Aunt Gloria nodded. "I'll fetch some lemonade and cookies." She went inside.

"Mamm, let's not argue. I'm sick about the dissention between us. I want to fix it, but I can't do as you and Daed ask. My love for Toby is long-lasting, and I believe he's the man God would have me marry."

"You're wrong. God would never have you go against your parents." Bernice scowled.

Aunt Gloria returned and served them each a glass of lemonade and two cookies on individual plates. "We'll have to agree to disagree, Bernice. This conversation is fruitless. Otis and I are prepared to have Magdelena live with us for as long as she likes. Now, let's change the subject. How's Charity?"

"Yes, I miss my little schweschder. Please tell her I love and miss her," Magdelena pleaded.

Mamm drank half her lemonade. She set the glass on the small table by her chair and took her time to answer. "She's fine. She misses you." She jumped to her feet. "I can't pretend nothing is wrong and have a light conversation. You could be banned from Charm, and you've put a dark shadow on our family with the community. The wedding dispute is common knowledge. The gossipers say we can't control our dochder and question our parenting abilities. Your reputation is ruined. They call you the runaway bride. You've brought us such shame, Magdelena."

Aunt Gloria and Magdelena rose. Aunt Gloria circled her arm around Magdelena's waist. "Magdelena's not the problem. You're more worried about your reputation than what is best for your dochder. You and Mark are at fault, not her. And the gossips are wrong to judge others."

Magdelena held her arms out to her mamm. "Please, Mamm. Can't we mend fences? I love you, and I'm homesick. Please. I want to have you help plan my wedding. Do all the fun things together. Aunt Gloria, too. If you and Daed show you approve of Toby, the community will, too. Zach should fall in love and marry a woman who will love him back. He can manage the ranch. It really is this simple."

Mamm's scowl softened. Tears filled her eyes. "I won't go against your daed. Please, Magdelena, kumme home with me. Right your wrongs. Do as we ask. This is tearing my heart in two."

Magdelena's sliver of hope dissipated. "I'm sorry, Mamm. I can't do as you ask."

Aunt Gloria stepped to Mamm. "I am sad about the division between us. I'm not trying to take your dochder away from you. I'm giving her hope and encouragement. I respect you for obeying your husband, but there are times where we, as fraas, need to show them where they're wrong. It's part of our job as a partner in a marriage."

"I'm not you, Gloria. And I won't go against my husband."

"No, don't go against him, but reason with him." Aunt Gloria reached for Bernice's hand.

Mamm jerked her hand back. "I resent you for this. She's my dochder. You've filled her head with rebellion. She's not like this. It's you I blame."

Magdelena covered her open mouth. "Mamm. No. This is all me. Not Aunt Gloria. She loves you and Daed." The trouble in the family had grown deeper today. She didn't think it could get worse, but she'd been wrong.

"I can't understand why you would defy us like this. You should trust us." Mamm wiped a tear from her cheek.

"You showed her she can't trust you. You're asking her to give up her life for you. I won't let her do it." Aunt Gloria crossed her arms.

"This is never going to end. We can't get a bishop to marry us. My family has fallen apart. Toby's and my reputation are ruined. It's the only way to bring order back to our family." Magdelena's head hurt.

"Bernice, look what you're doing to your dochder. Fix this for her." Aunt Gloria put her hands on Magdelena's shoulders and pleaded.

Mamm's lips quivered. "I must admit I'm having second thoughts about all this. Maybe Gloria's right. I now realize I haven't voiced my opinion on important matters with your daed. But your happiness should be a priority for me. My anger at Aunt Gloria was because she hit a nerve when she accused me of not showing your daed the other side of things I've let go even if I disagreed over the years. I can't promise, but let me try. There's always a first time, and maybe it will open the door for me to express myself better in the future."

Magdelena couldn't believe her ears. She'd always yearned for her mamm to at least try to have her daed listen to reason on many things over the last couple of years since she'd become an adult. This time would mean the most. But she didn't want to cause trouble between her parents. "As much as I would like for you to stand with me, I don't want the cost to be a division between you and Daed."

"Don't worry. I won't allow for your choice to cast division in our marriage. In the end, I will stand with him. He's my husband. But if I can put our family back together, and at the same time, Toby becomes a part of it, I will." Mamm held her arms open wide.

Magdelena fell into them and hugged her tight. "Your willingness is all I ask."

Mamm released her. "If I don't return, you'll know I wasn't successful. And if so, please kumme home and do as we ask. Make the sacrifice for your family. Marry Zach."

Magdelena wouldn't commit to Mamm's request. She wasn't sure she would ever return to Charm. "Danki for your efforts, Mamm."

Chapter Twelve

Abram picked up Toby at his home around six in the morning on Friday, and they drove to Massillon. Abram glanced at Toby and then back to the road. "We should arrive in Massillon around two-thirty or three, depending on how many times we stop. You don't need to kumme to the moonshine sale. I'll be fine. The danger may be when I pay Larry Greene, if he chooses to punish me for being late with the money I owe him."

Toby didn't relish being a part of any of it, so he'd stay back and take Abram at his word about the sale. "I'll stay in town then. What time should we meet?"

"I should be done and ready to pay Larry around six. I'll meet you outside the saloon."

"Abram, I'm not criticizing, but have you noticed Annie has a lot of mishaps? Is she nervous, or does she need spectacles?" He had shown Abram he could trust him. Maybe his friend would confide in him about Annie's condition, if there was one. Or if it was something worse.

"I'm responsible." Abram stared straight ahead, his face turning red.

Toby had been afraid of this answer. He didn't condone

violence of any kind. But he would defend family or friends if someone threatened to harm them. He hoped never to be put in such a position. "What do you mean?" This needed clarification for sure.

"I'm caught in a web of deceit. She's made friends in Charm. She visits the bakery where customers may become familiar. My chances of being found out are greater each day. I have been abrupt, stubborn, and harsh around her since we married. How can she not be a bundle of nerves?"

Toby disguised his relief and looked away from Abram. "I suppose you're right."

He didn't want to scold Abram. The man had already said he planned to treat her with love and kindness after today.

Abram slowed the horses to give the dog in the road time to move to safety and then coaxed them back to a steady rhythm. "I suspect we'll notice a big change in Annie when I tell her what I've done and apologize. I have a lot of making up to do. I'm hoping she'll stay and give me the chance to show her how much I love her. She's innocent, genuine, and caring. She doesn't have a greedy bone in her body. She made me feel guilty as I fell in love with her. She sets an excellent example as a child of God."

"It's not easy to recognize your flaws and want to change them. I admire you. The payoff in your marriage will be a worthwhile and priceless reward. And God will bless you for it." Toby had known men who had left the Amish life and never returned.

"Yes. I turned my back on God. I attended church and pretended to be the obedient husband and follower. But inside, I was lying to myself. I'm feeling better already knowing this will all be over after today and I'll get my life right again."

While traveling, they stopped for restroom breaks and then ate the sandwiches Abram brought with him.

They arrived in Massillon, paid for a room they'd share at the boarding haus, and then Abram and Toby went into town.

Abram tipped his hat to Toby. "I'll meet with the moonshiners to complete the sale, and then I'll be at the saloon around six to pay Larry Greene." He pointed to the big saloon on the corner. "I'll see you there. Enjoy Massillon while you're here."

Toby nodded. "I will. Be careful."

"I'll be fine." Abram retrieved his buggy parked outside the boarding haus and left.

Toby dodged the newspaper boy waving a paper.

"Will France stay neutral in the Russian-German war? Read all about it!"

Patrons gathered around him to buy the few papers he had remaining in a pile at his feet. World War I. What would it mean for the United States? He shuddered to think about it. He darted in and out of the crowd of the busy town with shoppers. Model T automobiles, and buggies, crowded the street. Shoppers entered and exited the stores and the livery had a steady stream of customers.

A woman dropped her package. "Oh dear."

Toby retrieved it and passed it to her. "Here you go."

"Thank you, young man." She tucked it under her arm and proceeded inside the hat shop.

He searched for the canal, and he found it. He stood and watched the fishing and cargo boats loading and unloading their wheat, grains, iron and steel, machinery, and other products.

A man held a sign. "Want a ride along the canal? I've got a decent boat. I can take you for a sightseeing tour."

"No. Danki." He left the canal and went to the train station. The train whistle blew. The sound could be heard all over town. He admired the big black locomotive taking passengers to their destinations. The whoosh of the wheels click-clacking on the train tracks as it moved along the rails mesmerized him. A happy child waved to him from the train window, and he waved back.

He moved to another part of town and passed the saw, flour, and wheat mills. He stepped aside to allow two men carrying heavy burlap bags to pass in front of him. "Sorry. Didn't mean to be in the way."

One of the big husky men glanced at him. "Don't mention it. You're fine."

He found a café and enjoyed a ham salad sandwich with corn chowder soup and iced tea. He watched the patrons going by outside the window and kinner chasing each other. He wiped his mouth with the red and white plaid napkin and paid the cashier. He'd not taken the time to roam through this city before today. The day would've been more fun with Magdelena. Maybe they would've taken a boat ride or gone a short distance on the train for the experience. The rest of this month would pass at a turtle's pace for him. He missed the sound of her voice, her beautiful smile, and those deep brown eyes gazing at him and confirming he was the only man for her.

He checked the simple white painted wall clock. Abram should be at the saloon in half an hour. He'd better get going. What would he do if Abram didn't show? He hoped his friend was truthful about the sale not being a problem. He'd have no choice but to go to the sheriff if he couldn't find him.

He sat on a bench outside the mercantile next door to the saloon.

Two older Englischers stood not far from him.

The taller man shook his head. "It's sad President Wilson and his three daughters are suffering the loss of his wife and their mother, Ellen, yesterday. I went to grade school with her. We're both from Georgia."

"What took her life?" The shorter man puffed on his pipe.

"Bright's disease, which is a kidney disease."

The two men departed and went to the livery.

Toby prayed silently for the president and his family. He couldn't imagine having the responsibility of the president in having to make decisions for the United States, and then to have his fraa pass away on top of it. He hoped to someday marry Magdelena and have a long life with her.

He scanned the area for Abram and stood relieved. "Abram, did everything go as planned with the sale?"

Abram patted the bag on his shoulder. "Yes. I told my friends this was my last sale. They wished me well. They have a man in mind to take my place. One step taken to disassociate myself from this part of my life, and now one more."

The saloon had large swinging doors. Piano music and chatter rang out.

Toby didn't want to go inside. "I'll wait here."

"This shouldn't take but a couple of minutes." Abram strode inside the saloon.

Minutes later, Toby stood in front of the establishment and Abram wasn't in view. He noticed two men arguing at a table. They stood, and the other men at the table got involved. He recognized one of the men's voices. Abram? No. But who?

Abram waved him inside. "Toby, I need you. A man we know is in trouble."

Toby ran inside. "Zach, what is going on here?"

Zach's face paled. "Toby! What are you doing here?"

The men stopped and stared at them. One man snarled, "He owes us money, and he doesn't have enough."

Toby asked how much Zach owed the man, and he settled the debt. "Zach, time to go."

"You don't have to tell me. I'm ready. Why are you here?" Zach darted his eyes and looked away as they left the place.

Toby stopped in front of the ice cream shop. "Abram and I came together for the day. How long have you been a gambler?"

"This was my second time. I'm done. I won't play cards for money again. I suppose you'll use this against me to get Magdelena for yourself. Mark may not trust me again with the ranch if he knows the truth. But he'll question why you found me there. You look as guilty as me."

Abram clamped a hand on Zach's shoulder. "Toby came with me to make sure I would be safe. Take my advice. Don't ever gamble again. You will be forced to borrow from scrupulous men who will take your life if you don't pay them on time. Other players, like the ones you sat with today, may harm you. The thrill of the game isn't worth it. And I don't have to tell you what it would mean if you're found out by any Amish friends."

Toby appreciated Abram's explanation and advice to Zach. "Where did you tell Mark and your parents you were going?"

Mark would've expected him at work.

"I told them I had a friend meeting me here whom I hadn't met with for a long while. Mark was kind enough to give me today and tomorrow off. I told the same lie to my parents. Daed reprimanded me for being too casual about my job. He's already frustrated with me." Zach's shoulders slumped. "These men weren't as nice as the other players at the table for my first game. I'm done. This is my last time. I promise."

"Good." Abram removed his hand.

Toby nodded.

"Are you going to blackmail me, Toby?" Zach narrowed his eyes.

"No." He gave him a stern eye. "I'm insulted you'd ask that question." Toby wouldn't want to use this information to help him gain favor with Mark. He'd never feel right about it.

Abram pointed to the boarding haus. "Do you have a room at the boarding haus tonight, Zach?"

Zach nodded.

The three men headed across the street. A man raised his fist to them. "Watch where you're going!"

They hurried past the Englischer's Model T.

Toby winced at the man. "Sorry."

The three Amish men went inside the boarding haus. Zach took his hat off and raked thick fingers through his brown hair. "Danki for keeping what I've done to yourselves."

"Do you want to get some supper with us, Zach?" Toby gestured to the open doorway leading to the dining room within the boarding haus.

"I'm not hungry. I had a big dinner at noon." Zach hurried up the stairs and into his room.

Abram and Toby shrugged and went inside. Toby had dessert since he'd had supper, while Abram enjoyed beef and noodles. Then they went to their room with two beds. Toby described his interesting day, and Abram told Toby he was pleased his buddies let him out of the moonshine business so easily.

Abram pulled the sheet up to his chin. "I'm shocked Zach was here."

"He's the last person I'd expect to find in a saloon. I hope he keeps his mouth shut about us being there. I don't trust him. He lied to his parents and to Mark." Toby hoped this mess was over, but there was no predicting what Zach might do or say.

Abram took a deep breath and let it out slow. "My shoulders are lighter, and I can breathe easier. I'm excited about my new beginning with Annie. But I'm fearful about her reaction to what I have to say. She may resent me for hiding this from her for such a long time. I'll wait for as long as it takes for her to forgive me. I don't deserve her."

"You and she agreed to an arranged marriage. She needed financial support, and you provided her a home. She's a sweet and dear woman. You're a blessed man to have her for a fraa. Be honest and let her have time to digest what you tell her. Her forgiveness may not kumme right away." Toby prayed Annie would forgive her husband and the couple would grow together in love and have a bright future. Toby bid Abram good night and turned down the lantern.

Saturday morning, Toby went to the front desk at the boarding haus. "Has Zach Hilty checked out of his room?"

The small woman wearing spectacles smiled and nodded. "Yes. He left before breakfast."

"Danki." Toby shrugged at Abram. "I guess he didn't

want to travel behind us. Let's get breakfast before we head out."

Toby and Abram hurried to finish breakfast so they could get on the road back to Charm. They paid their bill, retrieved Abram's buggy, and traveled home.

Abram glanced at Toby. "I'm curious. Why did you try so hard to befriend me? I would've walked away from me if I were you the first time I was abrupt and rude. I'm thankful you didn't give up on me, but why?" Abram turned out of town in the direction of Charm.

"Magdelena liked Annie on the spot. She prodded me to go with her to meet you both. You and Annie were friends we made together. We know it can be difficult to move to a new town where you don't know anyone." Toby missed Magdelena being with him to visit the couple they'd befriended together. She'd have been a support to Annie after Abram delivered his news to her. She would know what to say and how to comfort Annie.

"Zach must be way ahead of us. I expected we might catch up to him. We haven't seen him even in the distance," Abram said.

Toby shrugged. "I'm sure he's upset we found out what he was up to. The men who threatened him might have also shaken him. I'm sure he wants distance from us right now."

"He may have been hurt by those men had you and I not been there. Do you think he'll pay you back?" Abram gestured to the bag between them. "I'll pay Zach's debt to you. It's the least I can do for you kumming with me. You put yourself in jeopardy for me."

"No, Abram. It's all right. If he pays me back, I'll accept it. Otherwise, I'll let it go." Toby would be relieved if Zach didn't bring up this subject again.

"How is Magdelena, my friend?"

"We agreed I shouldn't visit for this month. We were going to marry in Mt. Hope, but the bishop refused. The bishop doesn't agree to us going against her parents' wishes. We had thought her aunt and uncle's support would've been enough, but her daed had visited the bishop before we met with him. We realize no bishop will marry us unless we have her parents' approval. I believe God will intervene. I don't know how or when, but I have faith."

"Annie and I are praying for you both."

"Danki." Toby appreciated Abram's encouragement amidst the naysayers.

"What will you do if her daed doesn't give you his blessing? Will Magdelena stay with her aunt and uncle?"

"I don't know. Her roots are in Charm, but she's determined not to marry Zach." Her family split wasn't good for any of them. The more time passed, the more difficult it would be to repair.

"Have you and Magdelena discussed leaving Amish life?" Abram cast a worried glance at him.

"It's not an option for us. I don't believe God would've brought us together to have us part. We'll have to wait on God."

Toby didn't want to discuss this subject anymore. "Let's talk about something less heavy. Tell me more about archery. I had fun when we practiced."

Abram described making bows and arrows and then talked about farming and other subjects. They made three stops on the way home Saturday for restroom breaks and dinner, and then Abram dropped Toby off at Andrew's in time to do some work.

Toby bid Abram farewell. Andrew had given him the days off to help Abram. He had time to do some chores and feed the livestock before he would go home. He was sure Andrew wouldn't mind giving him a ride to his haus later.

Andrew came home from the furniture store. "Toby, I gave you the day off. What are you doing here late in the day? I can handle what needs to be done."

"I don't mind. We got an early start."

"How did your visit to Massillon go with Abram? I was worried you might end up in trouble if the men he was meeting were contentious."

"You and me both. But Abram made the moonshine sale himself, so I waited outside the saloon while Abram settled his debt with the man to which he owed money. Everything went fine, and Abram promises he won't gamble or sell moonshine again. He'll tell Annie what he's been up to, and he hopes she'll forgive him. He loves her, and he wants to have an honest relationship moving forward with her." Toby wouldn't tell him about Zach. There was no need.

"Things couldn't have turned out better." Andrew slapped him on the back. "I'm not sure I would've hung in there with Abram like you. You did, and you've gained a good friend. I look forward to getting better acquainted with Abram and Annie." Andrew smiled.

"Do you mind driving me home? Abram dropped me off."

"Of course I don't mind. Hop in. I'll take you now. You must be tired from the trip."

Toby hopped in the wagon. "Danki, Andrew."

"Help!" Aunt Gloria cried out.

Magdelena ran to her in the living room Monday afternoon. She knelt beside her. "Aunt Gloria, what happened?"

Aunt Gloria pointed to the small stepladder. "I stood on the ladder to reach the top of the cabinet and slipped and fell. My back hurts. Can you help me get up?"

Magdelena dragged a chair over to her aunt.

Aunt Gloria grunted and groaned as she raised onto her knees and used the chair to pull herself up to her feet.

"Please be careful." Magdelena faced her and held her hands. "Are you dizzy?"

"Not now, but I was before I fell." She sat in the chair.

"You stay here. I'll tell Uncle Otis. We need to take you to the doctor or have him kumme here." She didn't like her aunt's flushed face. Something wasn't right.

Magdelena rushed to the barn. "Uncle Otis, Aunt Gloria fell off a ladder. Her back hurts, and her dizziness before the fall concerns me."

"I'll get Dr. Campbell." Uncle Otis harnessed his mare to the buggy.

Magdelena hurried inside to Aunt Gloria. She walked her aunt to the bedroom and had her lie down. "Close your eyes and rest."

"All right, dear. I am tired." Aunt Gloria drifted off to sleep.

She couldn't imagine not having Aunt Gloria with her. She prayed for God not to take her aunt.

Uncle Otis returned with Dr. Campbell. Uncle Otis knelt by his fraa and put a hand on hers. "Gloria, the doctor and I are here."

Aunt Gloria's eyes fluttered then opened. "Don't worry. I'll be fine. I was clumsy. No need for all this fuss. Doctor, this is our niece, Magdelena."

"Nice to meet you, Magdelena. Your aunt and uncle are

two of my favorite patients and friends." Dr. Campbell set his black bag on the floor and opened it.

"Danki for kumming. Uncle Otis and I want to make sure Aunt Gloria is all right."

"I'll take a look." He removed his stethoscope. "Gloria, it's a pleasure, but I'd rather be here for your strawberry pie than to have you needing my assistance. Tell me what happened."

Aunt Gloria recounted to him her incident.

"Can you sit up for me?" Dr. Campbell put a hand behind her back and supported her.

"Sure." With his help, she sat up.

He examined her back and asked her questions.

Aunt Gloria answered each question. Magdelena didn't find any of her answers concerning.

"What do you think happened, Doc?" Uncle Otis asked with worried eyes.

"I'm not sure." Dr. Campbell checked her pulse again and then put his things back in his bag.

Aunt Gloria threw her legs over the side of the bed. "Except for the soreness in my back, I'm fine."

Dr. Campbell lifted aspirin packets from his bag and passed them to her with instructions. "If your back isn't better in a week, or if you have any more dizzy spells, send Otis and I'll kumme back."

"Danki, Doc." Otis put coins in the man's palm. "I'll take you back to your office." He kissed Aunt Gloria's cheek. "I'll be back soon. You rest."

"I'm ready to get up. I promise I'll be careful." She kissed his hand.

Magdelena stayed by her aunt's side as they padded to the door to watch the men leave. She had always taken for granted her aunt Gloria, uncle Otis, and her parents would be with her for a long time. This incident had been a reminder she could lose any one of them at any given time. She missed her parents and Charity more each day. She'd be content living in Mt. Hope, but not happy. Charm was home, and it always would remain so. And she didn't know if her heart would ever get over Toby if they couldn't marry. The first time she talked to him, she was interested in him. And now, he would always be her choice. She might have to accept Mt. Hope would be her new home.

Aunt Gloria held Magdelena's hand. "Before you know it, you'll fit right into our community. You'll meet more of our friends the longer you stay. We have many young people like you in Mt. Hope. I'm thrilled to have you here, but I'm sorry for the reason." She caressed Magdelena's cheek.

"Do you think Daed will kumme around in time?" Magdelena didn't understand him. Didn't he care enough about her to want her with them? Would he ever understand what a predicament he'd put her in? She wouldn't ask her child to make such a decision against his or her will. Didn't Daed realize they were missing out on making memories together and anything could happen? None of us knew how long we had on this earth. She blew out a breath. *What a sad situation.*

"Maybe not. Your mamm asking him to reconsider might have an impact. She loves you very much to go against her rule of not crossing him to speak on your behalf. I'd like him to respond to her in a way showing he values her opinion and not cause unnecessary tension between them. I was hoping since yesterday was our day off from church service they might pay us a visit."

"Me, too." Magdelena hoped Mamm would make progress with Daed.

Tuesday morning, Abram visited Toby at Andrew's place. "Danki again for going with me to Massillon." He tapped his straw hat against his leg. "One more thing. Toby, I need to meet with Mark about buying some meat, and there's also another matter I'd like to discuss with him. I need someone who knows him to kumme along. Given the circumstances, I realize this is a big ask, but would you do it for me? I don't know who else to ask."

Toby cocked his head. "I was happy to go with you to Massillon. I'm glad everything turned out well for you. As far as going with you to meet with Mark, I'm not the right man. Mark won't be keen to have me there. What is this about?"

Abram stared at the ground. "I'd rather not say."

"Is this about what happened in Massillon?" Toby didn't want any part of telling Mark anything about why they were there. It could make matters worse for him.

"I said I have something I want to run by Mark. Please make the introduction." Abram's brusque voice got his attention.

"All right, but I'd rather you go alone." Why would Abram have anything to say to Mark? They were passing acquaintances at best. "If you're wanting to buy meat from Mark, you don't need me."

"Yes. I am wanting to buy meat. You'll know if I'm getting a decent price." He nudged Toby's arm. "Now don't you want to know how Annie took my confession?" Abram raised his brows.

Toby hoped Annie had been receptive. "You seem in a jolly mood. I take it she forgave you?"

"She was quiet at first. Then she said she knew something wasn't right and she'd been afraid to find out what. She was angry at me for a couple of minutes, and then she hugged my neck and cried. I asked for her forgiveness, and then I promised I'd be the husband she deserved. I told her I've fallen deeply in love with her. She was singing when I left the haus this morning. We're giddy like newlyweds."

Toby couldn't be more excited for his friends. "This is wonderful news. I wish Magdelena was here so I could tell her. She'd be thrilled. We've been rooting for the two of you."

"You and Magdelena have been excellent examples of true friends. I'm looking forward to making many memories ahead with you. I shunned Amish in my last town to keep my secrets, and now I feel free and eager to make friends. Danki for your help, Toby. You are instrumental in me changing my life."

"You did it yourself, and I admire you for it." Toby had been worried how Annie would react to Abram's news. He was relieved she was ready to help him embark on this new beginning for them. Magdelena would be ecstatic.

Abram parked the buggy under the shade of a willow tree at the Beachys'.

"Greetings." Mark waited while they jumped out of the buggy. He tied the reins to the hitching post. "Toby, if you're here to plead your case, you're wasting your time."

Abram held up his palms. "I asked him to kumme. We won't take much of your time."

Toby stepped closer to his friend. "Abram asked me to introduce you. Abram Hook, this is Mark Beachy. You may recognize each other from church services. Abram and his fraa, Annie, are fairly new to Charm."

Abram extended his hand. "We've not been formally introduced. We have become friends with Magdelena and Toby."

"Wilkom to Charm." Mark shook his hand.

"Danki. I'm interested in buying some meat from you."

"Would you like a side or a quarter of beef?"

Toby didn't know why Mark needed him for the introduction. He'd introduced himself to Mark. And he could make this transaction by himself. He shouldn't have agreed to kumme. Out of Mark's sight was best for him.

"I'll take a quarter. I'm not in any hurry, so if you need to wait until you have other buyers for the remainder of the cow, I can wait." Abram gazed out over the herd roaming out in the distance.

"Your timing is perfect. I had a quarter left to sell from this morning. I'll have it cut and packaged, and you can pick it up tomorrow morning." Mark told him the price, and Abram agreed.

"There's another reason I'm here."

Mark quirked an eyebrow. "What is it?"

"I've not been an honorable man. I've been a gambler and a seller of moonshine. But I've asked God for forgiveness and promised Him I won't do either of them again."

Mark tilted his head. "Why tell me this?"

Toby listened with growing trepidation. *Yes, why tell Mark this?*

Abram glanced at Toby and back to Mark. "Toby befriended me when I didn't want anyone to know my business. I grew to trust him, and I confessed what I'd been doing. After I told him about my transgressions, he offered to go with me for safety's sake to Massillon to pay the debt to the man I owed. Thankfully, everything went without a hitch, until we found another Amish man in need of our help."

"Abram, don't." Toby put a hand on Abram's back. "Please stop talking. We need to leave. Now, please."

Abram ignored him. "Zach Hilty gambled and ran out of money to pay the man he owed. He had chosen the wrong table of men. They were a rough bunch. Toby paid his debt to settle them down, and we left. Toby wouldn't tell you what happened. He told Zach he wouldn't say a word or use it against him with you. I didn't make such a claim. Has Zach said anything to you about his visit to Massillon?"

Mark's narrowed eyes and taut jaw showed his frustration. "No. He did not." He held up his forefinger. "Wait here." He went inside the barn.

Toby watched as Mark entered the barn. "Abram, we agreed not to say anything about Zach being in Massillon."

"You agreed. I didn't." Abram put a finger to his lips. "Here they kumme. You don't have to comment. But this needs to be said for Zach's and your sakes. Zach shouldn't get by with his behavior at your expense. Magdelena is a friend of mine and Annie's, too. I don't want her to be like Annie and have her husband hiding things from her. I know firsthand secrets like this kept from family and friends is a bad idea. Mark needs to know what kind of man he's demanding his dochder marry."

Zach's face reddened. "Why are you two here?"

Mark recounted to Zach what Abram had told him. "Is this true?"

Zach scowled at Toby. "You're not true to your word, Toby Schlabach. What happened to not saying anything?"

Toby shook his head. "I didn't kumme here to say anything about you. I'll be in the buggy, Abram." He turned and walked away.

"Wait, Toby. I'd like you to stay." Mark followed him and put a hand on his arm. "Please, Toby."

Toby returned with Mark to Abram and Zach. Why had Abram put him in this position? He'd trusted Abram. His friend might have the best intentions, but he should've told Toby the truth about what he intended to discuss with Mark today.

Abram glared at Zach. "Toby hasn't said anything. I asked him to kumme and introduce me to Mark to buy some meat. He didn't want to kumme, but he did it because I asked him to. He may not be my friend when we're done here."

"You're one to talk. What were you doing in the saloon?" Zach flexed his hands.

Mark glared at Zach. "Enough, Zach. Abram told me about his past. He brought Toby here. He's changing for the better, but what about you? Why did you lie to me?"

Zach kicked the dirt and stared at the ground. "I have gambled twice. I won't do it again. We all make mistakes. And we don't need to tell each other everything. I have a right to privacy."

Abram sighed. "Zach, I don't want you to go down the wrong path. I've been there, and I don't want the same for you. I've been short-tempered with my fraa, Annie, and I kept Amish at arm's length who wanted to get better acquainted with us as a couple before we moved here. It wasn't fair to Annie. If you hide your wrongful actions from your family and friends, it will eat at you. In time, I hope you'll understand how I'm trying to help you. Mark needs to know you're not who you pretend to be."

Mark faced Zach. "Do your parents know what you've been up to?"

Zach frowned and shook his head. "Please don't tell them. I won't gamble again. And you can trust I'll make Magdelena happy. Nothing needs to change. Haven't you been satisfied with my work?"

Mark waited a couple of seconds before answering him. "I'm disappointed in you, and I stay away from deceitful people. But I'm relieved you won't gamble again, and I forgive you for lying to me about why you wanted the day off. I'll give you another chance by letting you work on the ranch."

Zach's eyes widened. "Danki, Mark. I won't let you down again."

"I'm counting on it. But, Zach, I no longer approve of you marrying Magdelena and don't push me on this." Mark gave him a stern glare.

Zach opened his mouth and closed it. Then he looked Mark in the eye. "Understood."

Toby couldn't believe what Mark said. He wanted to ask him to repeat it. Did this mean Magdelena could kumme home? She'd have her life back in Charm? What did it mean for him and Magdelena? Mark still might not approve of him.

Zach held out his hand to Toby. "I get the full picture now. You wouldn't have said anything. I'm not sure if the situation were reversed if I'd have kept my mouth shut. I appreciate what you did for me in Massillon. I thought I could win her heart, but it's clear she doesn't have eyes for anyone but you. It's difficult for me to accept or say this to you."

Toby shook his hand. "This situation has been trying for all of us."

"I'll pay you back the money I owe you. Will you give me a couple of weeks?" Zach winced.

"Yes. I'd like to put the past behind us and not have things awkward between us. I'm sure Magdelena will want the same. Agreed?" Toby nodded.

"Yes. You're being generous after the way I've treated you. I appreciate it, Toby." Zach shook Toby's hand and then met Abram's gaze. "Abram, it's going to take me a bit to warm up to you after you called me out to my boss and then ruined my marriage to Magdelena." Zach took off his hat and raked a nervous hand through his hair and then plopped it back on his head.

"Understood." Abram gave him a curt nod.

Mark gestured to the cattle. "Time to get back to work, Zach. Abram, do you mind if I have a private conversation with Toby for a minute?"

Zach bid them farewell and hurried to the corral.

Abram tipped his hat. "Not at all. Nice to meet you, Mr. Beachy."

"Danki for bringing Toby and being honest with me about yourself and Zach. It's not easy to admit our mistakes, and I've made my share." He glanced at Toby and back to Abram. "I'll look forward to your visit tomorrow to pick up your beef."

"Danki." Abram headed for the buggy.

"Toby, Bernice visited Magdelena, and our dochder has never wavered in her love for you. My fraa had a serious conversation with me after her visit, and she pleaded with me to reconsider giving my blessing for the two of you to marry. She reminded me when she and I had a similar circumstance and how desperate we were to wed. It was long ago, and I've trivialized it as the years have passed. Bernice has never pleaded with me like she did for you and Magdelena. She made me question myself. Now, Abram, your friend, has convinced me I owe you an apology. Can you forgive me for the way I've mistreated you?"

"Yes. Aside from our differences, I admire you, Mark. You love your family, and you're an excellent businessman. You've helped the less fortunate, and you've raised two wonderful dochders. I love Magdelena, and I promise you I can provide for her, protect her, and give her a good life." His throat constricted waiting for Mark's answer.

"You have my blessing. You are an impressive man, Toby Schlabach. I have misjudged you and, from this day forward, I won't make this mistake again. Now, why don't you go to Mt. Hope and bring my dochder home?" Mark slapped his arm.

"I'd be happy to. I'll leave for Mt. Hope in the morning." He grinned wide.

Mark stepped away and then turned back. "Toby?"

"Yes?" Toby stopped in his tracks and glanced over his shoulder.

"I'd like for you to consider working with me. And don't worry about buying a haus. We've got plenty of acreage here, and I'd always planned to offer the man who would marry my dochder a generous portion of land and help to build their home on it. Don't answer me now about both of these things. Think about my offers."

"I will. Danki for them." Toby touched the brim of his hat and joined Abram in the buggy.

"Well, how did it go?" Abram nudged his arm.

"Because of you, he changed his mind. I don't know how to danki." Toby didn't expect Abram would be the one to intervene for him and convince Mark he should let him marry Magdelena.

"You weren't too happy with me at first." He chuckled.

"But now you understand why it was worth the risk to tell Mark the truth about Zach. He had a right to know, and Zach will be held accountable by his parents, which will deter him from gambling again. He'll have the opportunity to fall in love and marry a woman who wants to marry him. The truth being revealed was better for all involved. Even me."

"Magdelena will be shocked. I can't wait to tell her." Toby felt like he could fly. The weight of the turmoil he'd carried from his daed's passing to not being granted Mark's blessing to marry Magdelena had been lifted. He hoped nothing would get in their way from here on out. He'd learned you never knew what was around the corner or how God's plan would be revealed.

Chapter Thirteen

Toby drove to Mt. Hope Wednesday morning. He breathed in the scent of the honeysuckle, hyacinth, and lavender spread across the meadows as he left Charm. Colors were more vibrant in the sunshine and the blue sky prettier than usual on this fine day. God had answered his prayers. He kept his eyes focused on the road ahead and prayed. "Dear Heavenly Father, danki for Your intervention. I would've never thought You'd use Abram to intervene with Mark on my behalf. I'm glad You brought him and Annie into Magdelena's and my life. Guide me in being a good husband and provider for Magdelena. I praise You and I love You. Amen."

On his way, he passed buggies and a Model T automobile on the road. He nodded and smiled. He couldn't remember when he'd felt this giddy. About an hour later, he arrived at Gloria and Otis's haus.

Magdelena ran from the porch to him. "Toby, I've missed you! I'm glad you didn't wait a month."

He clasped her hands in his. "I have the best news." He gave her a mischievous grin.

"Tell me!" She waved her hands with excitement.

"Your daed has given us his blessing to marry." He recounted what happened in Massillon and his conversation with Abram, Zach, and Mark.

She squeezed his hands. "I'm so happy I can't think straight. This means I can go home and back to the bakery. I can hardly believe this has happened."

"Who would've thought Abram would be the one to get through to your daed? At first, I was frustrated and embarrassed when Abram told Mark about Zach. Then when your daed said Zach could still work for him and he gave us his blessing, I was relieved and ecstatic we can finally have a future together."

"We've got to tell Aunt Gloria and Uncle Otis our story about Abram getting through to Daed. They'll be surprised and happy." Her smile faded. "Aunt Gloria had a day where she didn't feel well. She's better now. I was worried about her. Her sudden change gave me pause. I assume my parents, friends, and loved ones will be around forever. I don't think about them dying. I'm sad I won't get back this time I've been away in Mt. Hope with them." She pressed a hand to her heart. "Now, we can move forward and be together again. I'm thrilled to get back to Charm and marry you, Toby Schlabach."

He kissed her gently. "No more than me, my future fraa." Charm was their home. He'd have made any concessions to be with her, but this was the best outcome for both of them.

They stepped inside and told her relatives the news.

Gloria hugged Toby. "I knew God would work this out."

Otis rested a hand on Toby's shoulder. "Can't wait for the big day. Best news I've heard in a while." He caressed Magdelena's cheek. "I'll miss this one being here on a daily basis."

"We'll visit, and you can kumme stay with us. Toby said Daed is going to help him build us a haus. We'll make sure we have a room downstairs for you. Danki for taking me in and giving me your support through this difficult time. It has meant so much to me. You both hold such a special place in my heart." She wrapped her arms around Uncle Otis's neck and hugged him.

Toby watched them. The repair of relationships was important to him.

Gloria left the room and returned with their wedding clothes. "I can't wait to attend your wedding and see you in these clothes."

"Danki, Gloria. You've been too good to us." Toby admired the clothing.

They stayed for an hour, and then Toby and Magdelena bid them goodbye. Toby reached over and clasped her fingers. "Your family will be eager to hug you. And Charity will no doubt scold you for being away. I've missed your little schweschder. She asked me to play a game with her when all this was going on. I didn't like having to tell her no. I'll be glad I can say yes now."

Charity had been his friend from day one, and she never wavered. She was bold and spoke her mind, and he liked her spunk.

Magdelena pressed a hand to her heart. "I've missed her sweet kisses, chats, and warm hugs. I'll have some making up to do with her. And with Rachael. I can't wait to greet customers and bake again. I've longed to talk to Rachael. She'll be my schweschder-in-law soon, and I couldn't ask for a better one."

Toby loved watching her bubble over with cheer. She'd have a big wilkom home. He didn't want to wait to marry her. "Our original wedding was scheduled for September tenth. I may be asking a lot, but I'd like to keep the date."

Magdelena shrugged. "I'd like to also. We've been through enough, and I don't want to wait another minute, let alone months. We can pull a wedding and reception off by then. But having the haus completed might be a challenge. What do you think?"

"I'm sure your daed, myself, and our friends will pitch in to build a haus for us. And we can live with Mamm and Rachael until it's done." He'd rather live with his family than hers, even though the Beachys had more room. He needed time to grow his friendship with her daed.

"Yes. September tenth I'll become Mrs. Magdelena Schlabach." Magdelena raised his hand to her lips and kissed it.

"Your daed offered me a job on the ranch. I'm warming up to the idea. What would be your advice?" He liked to learn new things, and he never thought he'd have the opportunity to work on a ranch. He'd been thankful to work for Andrew, and he was sure Andrew would want him to do whatever was best for him.

"Andrew wouldn't mind if you worked for Daed. I'd like you to work on the ranch. You'll be what Daed needs. You're wise beyond your years, and organized, and you pay attention to detail. The men will respond to your voice of reason. You'll be an excellent manager when Daed is ready to retire. And you'll build a close relationship with Daed. I'm anxious for him to know you the way I do."

Toby's heart swelled. Her opinions about him were important. She was right. This new job would test his abilities and skills. He could perform the duties and cement a relationship with his future father-in-law. No one could replace his daed, but it would be nice to befriend Mark.

He'd discuss the matter with Andrew before he made a final decision. "I appreciate your kind comments about me."

"Humble in a perfect way is what you are. A trait I admired about you from the start. I want Rachael and your mamm to get close to my family. I'll help nurture our families building a bond along by having them kumme together for outings." Magdelena pointed to the white bunny crossing the road. "Don't hit the bunny!"

Toby slowed the mare, and the animal scampered off. "Rachael and Mamm would really enjoy getting closer to your parents and Charity. Your little schweschder lights up everyone's life."

Toby wished Mamm and Rachael would venture out more to make friends. They both worked hard, and they'd gotten into a routine when Daed was alive. They'd not had time to cultivate friendships. They'd both been a little shy, but they'd kumme out of their shells since Daed's passing. Rachael had especially, after working at the bakery with Magdelena.

Toby hesitated to ask, but he was curious. "In your opinion, how do you suppose our impending wedding will affect the friendship between your parents and the Hiltys?" He didn't want any dissension between the two families. It would dampen the positive way he and Zach had agreed to move forward. This was important if they would be working on the ranch together.

"I'm a little worried about the Hiltys' reaction. We'll soon find out. I'll ask Mamm about them."

"I'm relieved your daed let Zach stay on at the ranch since he loves it. His being grateful to your daed for doing so helped us move past our differences. I'm afraid he'd have been bitter otherwise." Toby didn't want any ill will with the Hiltys or Zach. They'd be at church services and socials where they would need to be cordial.

Toby pulled into the lane and halted the buggy at the Beachys' an hour later. They stepped out of the buggy, and Charity came running to them.

She hugged Magdelena. "Don't ever leave me. I missed you, and I wasn't sure if I'd ever see you again."

Her parents joined them.

Bernice wrapped her arms around Magdelena. "Wilkom home."

Magdelena hugged her schweschder and her mamm.

Mark opened his arms and she rested her head on his chest as he wrapped his arms around her. "I was pigheaded and a fool. Will you forgive me?"

She wiped her tears. "I already have."

Charity reached for Toby's hand. "I told Daed and Mamm they should let you marry Magdelena, and they wouldn't listen. I'm glad they finally did." She shot a stern glance at her parents. "Please don't upset Magdelena like this again. I was sick without her here."

"We promise." Mark tousled his little dochder's curly hair.

Bernice stepped to Toby. "I'm sorry for the trouble we've put you and Magdelena through. I admire your devotion to her, and I hope you'll forgive us."

"I'm overjoyed we'll be a family. The past is behind us, and Magdelena and I are ready for our families to join together."

Charity stared at her parents. "Just so you know, I will not marry anyone other than Peter."

Mark and Bernice chuckled. "We understand, but you have several years before making your final decision."

"Nope. He's the one." Charity lifted her chin and grinned.

* * *

Magdelena had missed her little schweschder's outspoken nature. She didn't blame her for making her wishes known after watching what had happened with her and Toby. Maybe she'd made Charity's life a little easier by softening her parents' hearts when it came to making life decisions. "Toby, kumme inside."

"I should get back to work," Toby said.

Mark studied him. "Have you thought anymore about working on the ranch?"

"I would like to take you up on your offer, but I need to speak to Andrew and give him time to find someone to take my place."

"Toby, you take all the time you need. I'll look forward to having you with me on the ranch when you're ready. I'll be training you to take over for me when I retire." Mark clapped a hand on his shoulder.

"Danki, Mark. I'll let you know a specific date soon as I can as to when I can start work." He gazed at Magdelena. "You enjoy your time with your family. I'll kumme by tomorrow." He chatted with them for a couple of minutes and then retrieved her wedding dress from the buggy, returned to Magdelena, handed it to her, and then left.

Magdelena and her mamm settled in on the back porch, while her daed returned to work and Charity played with the barn cats.

Mamm rocked in the rocking chair and gazed at Magdelena. "I'm sorry I didn't listen to you. My heart broke when you left us. Anger turned into fear. I thought I'd lost you for good. I'm sorry I didn't take up for you sooner. I reflected on our relationship as you've grown, and I regretted not speaking to your daed on your or Charity's behalf more often."

"Aunt Gloria told me you've always stood by Daed and I should respect you for it. And I do. She expresses her opinion and Uncle Otis takes what she says into consideration. I will do the same with Toby. I never understood why you didn't."

"Your leaving showed me what I might lose if I don't express my thoughts to your daed. I was taught you didn't disagree with your husband. I stand by him no matter. But the cost was too great this time. Your determination showed how much you loved Toby. I had to intervene. I pleaded with your daed to grant his blessing for you to marry Toby. Guilt ran through me at how we pushed you to marry Zach for our own desires."

"I'm relieved you and Daed finally relented," Magdelena said.

"I didn't realize how much Toby meant to you at the time. Maybe I didn't want to. I wasn't ready to risk an argument with your daed until after I visited you in Mt. Hope. He surprised me and listened to what I had to say. He was shocked when I revealed with him what was on my heart. I learned a valuable lesson, and our relationship is deeper than before because of it."

Magdelena dragged her rocker closer to Mamm. "I'm grateful you spoke to Daed. I've always thought your opinion should matter most to him." She was happy her mamm had grown her relationship with her daed in this way. She noticed a gleam in her mamm's eyes when she spoke about it. She must be exhilarated after all these years to know her husband wanted to hear what she felt about things.

"Mamm, how is your relationship with the Hiltys?"

"After your daed told me what Abram told him about Zach,

I wasn't sure how the Hiltys would treat us. I figured Zach working here might soften the blow you wouldn't be marrying their son. The Hiltys still want to maintain a friendship with our family. We enjoy Ida and Ethan's company. I stopped by Ida's, and I asked them for supper. I hope you don't mind."

"No. I don't mind now that I'm marrying Toby and you and Daed are happy about it. We need to show there are no hard feelings. I don't want to interfere with your friendship with them. And I need to speak to Zach. I want to remove any awkwardness between us." She didn't look forward to having a conversation with Zach. She'd been resentful of his interference and demands. But after Daed had let go of her marrying Zach and Toby had forgiven him, she was ready to put all this ugliness behind them.

"Danki. She might offer you the wedding dress she stitched." Mamm grimaced.

"I'm going to wear the dress I showed you Aunt Gloria made for me. I don't want to hurt her feelings, but I wouldn't be comfortable accepting the dress under the circumstances. I'll suggest she may want to keep the dress for her future dochder-in-law. Zach's handsome, and I'm sure he'll marry someday." She hadn't appreciated Ida's persistence during the turmoil, but she'd put her frustration with the woman aside.

At six, the Hiltys showed up for supper.

Magdelena greeted them, and they came inside.

Ida pulled her close and whispered in her ear, "Will you go with me to the back porch? I'd like to have a word."

Magdelena couldn't read her mood. She nodded and followed the woman out the back door. She waited for Ida to speak.

"I was furious you weren't going to marry Zach, and

I'm ashamed of my part in keeping you from marrying the man you love. Zach disappointed me when I found out about his trip to Massillon and why, but I understand we all make mistakes. I've made a big one, and I apologize for my part in it. You are mature and kind and the type of woman Zach needs to give him direction. I dismissed your wishes to satisfy mine. Will you forgive me?"

"Yes. I don't want my decision to ruin your friendship with my parents. I do ask you to respect Toby, Rachael, and his mamm if they're here at the same time as you." How would Ida act around the man she loved? She didn't want any tension. Ida had been frank with her, and she felt compelled to do the same.

"You needn't worry. Ethan and I value our friendship with your parents. Furthermore, we've run into many new friends who have nothing but praise for Toby. I can understand why you fell in love with him. I look forward to getting better acquainted with all of you. Ethan wanted to ask your daed to allow you to marry Toby after you left. He didn't like that we'd caused your family to split. I refused. I feel terrible about it now."

Magdelena's heart jumped. Ethan had taken up for her. She didn't know him well, but she was appreciative for what he'd wanted to do. "There's no need for us to discuss this any further. This is a new day and we're moving forward."

"Would you like the dress I made?" Ida grinned.

"Why don't you keep it for your future dochder-in-law? I'm sure Zach will find the woman for him sometime soon. Now he's available, I'm sure girls will be vying for his attention." She fidgeted her hands. "Aunt Gloria made us wedding clothes while I was in Mt. Hope. We've always been close. I'm sure you understand." She didn't want to lie and say she appreciated the dress. At the time, she didn't want anything to do with it.

"I was certain you wouldn't want to wear it, but I thought I'd offer. I like your idea. I'll keep it for Zach's future fraa. Hopefully he won't make me wait too long." Ida chuckled. "Should we join the others?"

"Do you mind asking Zach to kumme out here and speak with me first?" She didn't want to wait to dispel any uncomfortableness between them.

"Sure." Ida opened the door and entered the haus.

Moments later, Zach stepped out onto the back porch.

"We should talk. A lot has happened since I've returned to Charm." Magdelena was curious as to what he'd have to say. "Why don't you go first?"

Zach took off his hat and traced the brim. "I'm sorry for what I put you and Toby through. I didn't realize until you left Charm how much you loved him. You told me, and I didn't listen. Toby and I have made amends, I'm hoping to do the same with you."

"I have let go any animosity I had for you. Toby and I would like to offer our friendship, and we both wish you well in finding the right fraa for you. Our parents enjoy each other's company, and I don't want it to change. I understand Daed has offered you to continue to work here, and I ask you to treat Toby with respect if he chooses to accept Daed's job offer." She could foresee Toby becoming Zach's boss one day. He'd be better suited with his maturity to take over the ranch than Zach. She didn't want any lingering trouble between them.

"Toby and I are fine. I'm grateful for the job. I don't want to rehash any of this, nor do I want any more trouble."

"Danki. Let's go have supper. I'm hungry." She opened the door.

He followed her into the haus. "The aroma of chicken and dumplings made me hungry the moment I arrived. I'm ready to eat."

Magdelena laughed at stories Ida told about Zach when he was little, and they had a nice time. Later, the Hiltys departed, and she rocked on the porch swing. It was wonderful to be home.

Rachael's mare galloped to the haus and came to an abrupt stop. She hopped off the horse, threw the reins in the direction of the hitching rail, and ran to Magdelena. "I'm glad you're home, and I want to hear about your time in Mt. Hope! But right now, I need your help. My new neighbor, Katherine Wagler, dropped dead in her kitchen. Will you and your mamm bring four of any of your casserole dishes?"

"Of course, we will. What was the cause of her death?"

Rachael said, "The doctor doesn't know why. Nathan, her husband, said she complained of chest pains the last two weeks. Dr. Harrison suspects the cause of her death may have been her heart. Toby came home from work, and I told him about her. He drove to the Waglers' to help her husband, Nathan, take her body to the undertaker. I feel so sorry for those kinner. A neighbor is watching them."

"How terrible!" Magdelena hooked her arm through Rachael's. "Walk with me. We need some privacy." Her eyes pooled with tears as she and Rachael walked away from the haus and toward the pond. "I didn't know them since they moved here days before I left, but I'll do whatever I can." She dabbed her eyes with a handkerchief she kept in her sleeve. Magdelena gestured for Rachael to sit. "Mamm has leftover chicken and dumplings. I'll send some home with you for them. Those poor kinner."

Rachael wrung her hands. "Katherine delivered us food

to introduce herself a day after they arrived. Then she visited often with Thad and Joy a couple times a week while you were gone. I'll miss her. Those sweet kinner will be lost without her. Little Joy is five and Thad is seven. Joy has cute pudgy cheeks and Thad is tall for his age and serious but kind. They are such a sweet family."

"Toby will know the funeral arrangements when he kummes to your haus this evening. We'll prepare the casseroles and friends will contribute food dishes, too. I'll arrive early to help with whatever you need," Magdelena said.

Rachael grabbed her hand. "I should've said congratulations. I'm thrilled for you and my bruder, and I'm relieved and happy you're home. The bakery isn't the same without you. Will you return? I hope so."

Magdelena tightened her grasp on Rachael's hand. "Yes. I'm ready. I planned to go early tomorrow morning and relieve whoever is there if it's all right with Liza."

"You don't need to ask. I'll stop by Liza's and tell her you're home and ready to work. She'll be ecstatic. She's been worried about you. We all have. Now we'll be planning your wedding, and we better be fast about it. Toby said you're sticking with September tenth."

"Yes. Rachael, do you understand why I didn't tell you I was leaving?"

Rachael mustn't have any misgivings. She was her best friend.

"I didn't when you first left. Now I do. Toby explained it all to me. We tell each other everything, and your abrupt exit left me sad and worried about you."

Magdelena took Rachael's hand in both of hers. "Have no doubt. You are my best friend. Because I love you, I didn't put you in the middle. I missed you more than I can put into words."

"You did the right thing. I'm over the top about you being back. We'll be schweschders soon. I love it. Toby said Zach was reconciled with everything. I'm proud of Abram taking up for Toby. What a surprise Abram turned out to be the one to stand up to Mark and Zach and make the difference." She chuckled.

"I worked hard to befriend Abram, and then I misjudged him. Although, he did hide his bad behavior. He's made up for it, and then some. I'm hoping he and Annie will flourish in their relationship." She heaved a big sigh. "The Hiltys came for supper earlier this evening. I had separate conversations with Ida and Zach. They apologized and want to move forward without any grudges. Ida said Ethan, Zach's daed, wanted Mark to grant Toby's request to marry me after I left town. His support touched my heart."

"I don't care who brought you back, as long as you're here to stay. Is your relationship with your parents where you want it?" Rachael raised her brows.

"Yes. Mamm spoke to Daed on my behalf. Remember, I told you it's not something she's done before, and I'll never forget it. Going forward, I believe this will help Charity. Mamm will hopefully speak up more often when Daed may seem too harsh on his punishments. She said knowing her opinion is important to Daed has made her feel even closer to him." She never expected the blessings God had provided to more than she and Toby being free to marry.

"Toby may work for Daed. I doubt Zach would complain. He won't do or say anything to jeopardize his job. He and Toby are amicable. He'll be who Daed needs. And I'd like them to become close." She wanted her daed to learn he could depend on and trust Toby. She was sure Daed would be grateful for Toby once he worked with him. Zach was all right, but Toby possessed all the traits her daed needed.

Rachael grimaced. "Toby will no longer work for Andrew? I'm not sure. He loves what he does, and he's devoted to Andrew."

Magdelena sat back. "Andrew wants what's best for Toby. Their friendship wouldn't suffer if Toby works for Daed." She was certain Andrew would encourage Toby to try ranching. He'd presume Mark needed a son to take over one day, and this would be best. Toby could still handcraft furniture for a hobby.

"You're right. Andrew won't stand in his way." She took a deep breath. "I should get back to the Waglers'. I'm supposed to relieve the neighbor watching them. I'm keeping the kinner overnight. They're comfortable with me."

"I can't imagine how Nathan must feel. He's blessed to have you jump in and care for the kinner."

"Mamm said she'll watch them during the day. When school starts, she said they can kumme to our home, and she'll take care of them for Nathan. He was thankful. He's grieving Katherine's death, and he'll need time to heal. His fraa managed the home, and he's not used to having the responsibility alone for the two kinner. I'm relieved he'll let us assist him them.

"I'll go over and clean and launder the clothes. Mamm and I will have him for supper some nights and on other nights, take food over for him and the kinner." Rachael gazed into Magdelena's eyes. "I love you, and I'm glad you're back."

"I love you, too, best friend. I'll be at the bakery early tomorrow, and we can discuss what more we can do for

Nathan after work each day." She clasped Rachael's hand. "I'll run inside and get the food for you to take to Nathan and the kinner. I'll be right back." She ran inside the haus, grabbed a container of the leftovers, and went to meet Rachael. She sighed. *We're never ready for tragedy,* she thought.

Magdelena drove to the bakery early Thursday morning. She left her buggy at the livery and then walked to the bakery. She inhaled the aroma of white bread Rachael must've taken out of the oven. She entered the kitchen. "Liza!" She hugged her. "Is Rachael at the Waglers?"

"Yes. She stopped over last night and told me about you and Toby. I'm thrilled, and I'm pleased you're back. Rachael said you'd be kumming to work today. I told her to not report to work. I would stand in for her today. I wanted her to concentrate on Nathan and the kinner. I didn't know Katherine well, but she seemed like such a sweetheart. We'll bake extra goodies today to take to the funeral. We'll take those." Liza pointed to a tray of butter cookies. "How are you? I've missed you."

Magdelena slipped her apron over her head and tied it in back. "Marvelous. Ready to marry Toby on September tenth if we can get everything ready. I feel guilty being happy about our wedding when Nathan is suffering. We expect to grow old and then die, but this reminds us we don't know when our time to die will kumme."

"Remember how hard it was for Ellie to get through grieving her mamm? I didn't think she'd ever accept me as her friend and later, stepmamm. I pray Thad and Joy will heal without anger. They're younger than Ellie was when her mamm passed. They will probably mourn her loss easier. Although, it's never easy to lose a loved one. My heart aches for them." Liza kneaded the dough. "On a more pleasant note, I'm excited for your marriage to Toby. God is good. I prayed for you and Toby every night. So did Jacob."

"Danki, dear friend. This was the most difficult decision I have made. I never planned on defying my parents on any matter, or leaving Charm. I had taken my roots here for granted. Toby, family, and friends became much more important. Losing the place and those I love behind tore my heart in two. I knew I'd never be the same if I couldn't return to Charm. It was frightening, but I had faith God would work things out for Toby and me. And here we are about to marry."

"Jacob said he's willing to help Toby build a haus." Liza flipped the dough over and dug her hands into it.

"Daed offered us land, and we'll need all the muscle we can get. Tell Jacob danki for us." She had envisioned a home with Toby many times. Soon, she'd arrange furniture and share each day with him.

Magdelena recounted the details of the conversations with her parents and the Hiltys. "I'm pleased with the outcome. Everything has worked out much better than I could've anticipated."

Toby arrived. "Greetings, sweetheart." He smiled. "Liza, how are you?"

"Thrilled for you." She wiped her hands and passed him a cup of coffee. "I told Magdelena Jacob will pitch in when you need hands to build your haus."

"I could use them. Danki." He frowned. "Nathan is having a difficult time. I've arranged for the men to kumme over and arrange benches in the yard for the visitation and funeral early Friday morning. Katherine's body will be delivered back to the haus early Friday for the viewing. Rachael will wash and dress Katherine for Nathan. The kinner are with Mamm. Andrew gave me the day to help. He's pitching in to help at Nathan's after work at the store. Nathan wants it over as soon as possible. I don't blame him."

"Do we need to spread the word?" Magdelena's eyes pooled with tears.

She couldn't imagine what the kinner were going through. Did they understand? They might to a certain extent, but they would mourn her loss and ache for a long time.

"Bishop Fisher is making the rounds today, and he'll assign men and women to visit homes and tell them. Any news in our community doesn't stay private long. They're always ready to jump in wherever they're needed."

"We'll close the shop early today and all day Friday. This family will need our attention."

Toby and Magdelena nodded.

Magdelena chatted with Toby and Liza about the Waglers and then bid farewell to Toby. It was like she'd never left. And she was ready to concentrate on the Waglers and put her plans aside. She loved how the Amish took care of one another. Rachael and Nathan had both experienced losing their loved ones. Would this bond them in the future?

Chapter Fourteen

Friday morning Magdelena traveled to the Waglers' home early. She stepped inside, and Rachael was washing Katherine's body as tears streamed down her best friend's cheeks.

Magdelena hugged her. "Let me take over."

Rachael shook her head. "I want to do it. I didn't know her well, since they'd moved here recently. But I liked her from the first time we met. Little Joy and Thad were affectionate with hugs and wilkoming, too. This is such a sad time." She gently washed Katherine's feet. "I'm almost finished. I could use another set of hands to dress her."

Magdelena picked up a white dress. "Is this the dress you chose?" Katherine's lifeless body brought tears to her eyes. She'd been pretty with her slender build and cherub face. She couldn't have been much older than her.

Rachael nodded.

Magdelena and Rachael dressed Katherine with loving care. "How are the kinner?"

"They understand, and they cry, and then they stare off. They won't eat much. They cling to Mamm and me. I wish

I could protect them from all the pain and suffering as they grieve her loss."

"How's Nathan?" Magdelena circled an arm across Rachael's shoulders.

"He's a loving father. He came over last night to tuck the kinner in bed and say their prayers. I stood outside the door and listened. He's patient with them, amidst his sadness. He asked God to give them the strength to get past losing her. The kinner wept. I had to walk away before I started to weep."

"He's blessed you and your family are here for him and the kinner. What can I do?" Magdelena assumed Rachael would be reminded of the death of the love of her life, John. This would add to the grief of Katherine's passing. Magdelena wished she could erase all their pain.

"Greet guests with me. Mamm is bringing the kinner over after more families are here and there are boys and girls for them to play with outside. I don't know if they will, but maybe friends will coax them to."

Magdelena nodded. She greeted the visitors with Rachael and chatted with her friends Hannah and Ellie, who brought enough food for ten families. She loved them for always going overboard when it came to taking care of others.

At ten, the bishop rounded the crowd outside and to sit on the benches. Magdelena nodded to Toby, sitting by Nathan. She hadn't had the opportunity to speak to him. He'd been at Nathan's side. Right where he should be, and she was proud of him for always being there for whoever needed him. She prayed they'd have a long lifetime together. She sat next to Joy, who leaned on Rachael. Thad sat close to her friend's other side.

Bishop Fisher prayed and read scriptures which spoke

of Heaven. She'd not lost any immediate family. She'd been too little to remember when her grandparents died. She didn't want to contemplate what it would be like. Times like this brought the possibility to the forefront. She shoved the thought out of her mind.

The bishop led them in a hymn and then dismissed them to the burial site close by.

Joy tugged on Rachael's arm. "Please ride with us. Please."

"You ride with your daed, and I'll be right behind you with Toby." Rachael bent and kissed their cheeks.

Rachael turned to Magdelena. "Are your parents here? Do you want to ride with us?"

"They came with the Hiltys. I'd love to ride with you and Toby." They walked to the buggy and got inside. Magdelena sat next to Toby. She glanced over at Rachael. "I'm sorry. This must bring back fresh memories of your daed."

Rachael nodded. "Yes, but the assurance he's with God in Heaven makes his passing easier to accept. I'm praying the kinner and Nathan will find the same comfort in time. The difference is Katherine left them fast, and she was so young."

Toby followed behind Nathan and the kinner. "I have thought about Daed a lot through this. He'd be overjoyed we have a wedding date. I'd have loved having him there. I don't ever want to experience what Nathan is going through. He's a strong man, but this is heartbreaking for him. Even more difficult for him will be raising two kinner by himself."

"We'll check in on them. And Rachael and your mamm have a bond with the kinner. We need to be there for them for a long time." She didn't want Rachael and her mamm to shoulder this responsibility on their own. She'd be a part of their family, and she wanted to support them in tending to Nathan and his kinner.

Toby parked the buggy, and they watched the men remove the pine box and lower it into the hole already dug for burial.

Joy motioned for Rachael to join her, Thad, and Nathan in the front row.

"Kumme with me, Magdelena," Rachael pleaded.

Magdelena and Toby came alongside Rachael as she held Joy's hand and Nathan held Thad's. They all wept as the bishop prayed, delivered a message of hope, faith, and love, and then led them in a hymn.

They sobered and departed to their buggies.

Joy wiped her nose on Rachael's sleeve. "Please kumme home with me."

Nathan leaned over to her friend. "Rachael, I'd appreciate it if you would. I could use the company for the kinner."

"I'll be right over." Rachael patted Joy's back.

Magdelena cleaned dishes and straightened the kitchen. Toby popped his head around the kitchen doorway. "I'm going with Andrew and the men to unload the benches and store them in the shed where they're kept for services and socials. I'll be back. Will you wait here or should I meet you at your haus?"

"I'll stay with Rachael and entertain the kinner." Magdelena watched him until he disappeared. He always provided leadership at times like this. He'd taken the initiative with Abram, he'd given good advice to her and her friends, and Andrew claimed Toby managed his property better than he could. She'd been proud he'd mended fences with Zach and her parents without hesitation or question. She had no doubt Daed would be pleasantly surprised when he found out Toby had what it took to do whatever was needed on the ranch. He didn't hesitate to learn or take on a challenge. She found Rachael outside with Joy and Thad throwing a ball.

"Want to play?" Rachael threw the ball to her.

"Sure." She played ball with the three of them for the next fifteen minutes.

Joy flopped on the ground. "I'm tired."

Thad stood quiet.

Rachael squatted next to the little blond girl. "What would you like to do? Are you hungry?"

Joy's sad sky-blue eyes looked at Rachael. "My tummy hurts. I miss Mamm. Will it ever stop hurting?"

Thad bounced the ball. "No. We'll always miss her. But Daed said the more time passes, missing her will get easier. I'm not sure he's right."

Magdelena stood next to Rachael and faced them. "Anytime you want to talk about your mamm and how you feel, Rachael and I are always ready to listen. I would imagine you'll ache for a long time."

Rachael dried Joy's tears trickling down her cheeks. "My daed is in Heaven, and I feel better knowing he's happy, healthy, and in God's arms. Your mamm isn't in the box we put in the ground. She's with God. You can look at the sky and think of her smiling and singing with the angels. It won't make your heart hurt less, but it is reassuring. And I'm here anytime."

Joy leaned her head against Rachael. "Promise?"

"Yes, I promise." Rachael rubbed the little girl's back. "And this goes for you, too, Thad."

Thad dropped his chin to his chest, dragged his feet to her friend, and took Rachael's hand.

Magdelena watched her friend with the kinner. They had kumme to depend on her already. She would make a superb Mamm someday.

Magdelena waited on two Englischer couples who ordered cakes for their upcoming weddings on Saturday. She had fun sitting with them to put their wishes on paper. She was excited for her and Toby to exchange their vows and enjoy wedding cake on their special day.

Her smile turned to a frown. Two weeks had passed since Nathan had lost his bride. Rachael had been going to the Waglers' home each day after work to clean the haus, wash dishes, and play with the kinner. She wondered if he would consider Rachael for a fraa in the future. He was handsome, with his sun-kissed blond hair, emerald eyes, chiseled chin, and strong farmer build. Given time, would Nathan consider Rachael? She thought they would make a sweet couple, but it was early to assume anything. Nathan was still grieving.

Bishop Fisher entered the bakery. "Good morning, Magdelena. I'm glad you're back in town."

"Bishop, Toby and I would like you to marry us on September tenth at my parents' home at two-thirty if you still have the date open. Would you like coffee? How about a blueberry tart?"

"I'd love coffee and a tart." He sat and pulled out his pad of paper and pencil. "I have the date available. Consider it scheduled." He gave her a list of dates for their counseling sessions.

Magdelena marked them on a piece of paper. "Danki, Bishop."

"My pleasure." He drank half his coffee, finished his tart, bid her farewell, and left.

A half hour later, Toby came into the bakery. "I came to wish you a good day. I bought a saw blade at the hardware store. I should go and speak with Bishop Fisher about our upcoming wedding date."

"No need. He was at the bakery earlier." She reached in her sleeve and pulled out a piece of paper with the counseling dates on it. "He has agreed to marry us on September tenth at two-thirty at my haus, and I have counseling dates scheduled." She wrote the dates again on another piece of paper and handed them to him.

"You did a great job taking care of this." He beamed.

"Danki. I'm excited for our counseling sessions with Bishop Fisher, and I'm happy he had the date we want open."

"Me, too. I should go. Have a wonderful day, wife-to-be." He tipped his hat and headed out the door.

Magdelena grinned.

Twenty minutes later, Dr. Harrison and Sheriff Williams came into the bakery and plopped on the counter stools.

"What a day." Dr. Harrison shook his head. "We both had things happen and couldn't kumme in at our normal time. Do you still have Danish pastries? The ones with the strawberry jam in the center?"

Magdelena served them each two on a plate. She poured them coffee and set the mugs before them. "What happened?"

Dr. Harrison rolled his eyes and slapped the sheriff on the back. "My friend came and got me early this morning to tend to Norm Gardner. He'd sliced an apple and cut his hand. The man has done this at least three times in the past year. He's clumsy and a danger to himself. He needs a wife to take care of him."

Sheriff Williams shook his head. "He'll mourn Patrice for the rest of his life. Many a woman have brought him food dishes and batted their eyelashes at him, and he's polite but shows no interest. He's seventy-five and set in his ways. He's a kind old soul. He came over to my haus and thought Gladys would help him. She could tell he needed stitches, and I brought him to the doc."

"I'm sorry about your friend's accident. You're both kind to kumme to his aid." She wondered about Nathan. Would he ever get over Katherine and marry again? Rachael still hadn't gotten over the death of her husband-to-be, John. Maybe neither of them would marry again. She could understand it. She couldn't imagine losing Toby and considering another man. But she didn't want Rachael to miss out on finding love again.

Magdelena watched the sheriff open his paper and give Dr. Harrison the other half. She read the headline, "What's the latest news on the war?" She'd listened to the two men discuss the war. More countries were getting involved.

Dr. Harrison set his paper open on the counter. He flicked his finger at an article. "War is an ugly time. I wish I could say I don't see the United States getting involved at some point, but I suppose it may be inevitable the way things are going. I don't want our men to have to fight, and it will be difficult for the families of those men while they're away."

Sheriff Williams sighed. "If our freedom is threatened, soldiers would be fighting for a just cause. Let's hope they won't have to."

Magdelena didn't understand politics or war. She'd pray for the soldiers and their families and for peace.

Gladys bustled into the bakery. "Why, there's my handsome husband." She kissed the sheriff on the cheek. "I came to ask what I can do for Magdelena and Toby's wedding."

Sheriff Williams hugged her. "What a nice surprise." He turned to Magdelena. "I'm sorry. The doc and I forgot to congratulate you. Congratulations, Magdelena." Sheriff Williams grinned.

Dr. Harrison held up his cup. "Yes, Magdelena, I'm sorry, too. We've been rude not to say so before now. My hat's off to you. I'm glad things worked out for you and Toby. Rachael told Gladys why you were away, and she shared it with us. We missed you. Anything we can do, we're happy to."

Magdelena blushed. "You're all kind to offer. I'd love it if you'd all attend. We're having the wedding at my family's home at two-thirty on September tenth. Gladys, will you bring a dish of your potato salad?"

"I'll do it. Any special request for a gift? Don't be shy." Gladys beamed.

"You don't need to bring a gift. Having you and the sheriff there is gift enough." Magdelena returned her endearing smile.

"I'll bring something you'll love and surprise you and Toby." Gladys bought two loaves of white bread and left with the sheriff and doctor.

Magdelena bid them farewell as they headed out the door. She then checked on Rachael. "Gladys stopped in. She quizzed me on what to bring and what gift I want for the wedding. She's such a wonderful friend."

"I hope you asked her to bring her potato salad." Rachael's eyes sparkled.

"I did." Magdelena chuckled. "The sheriff and Dr. Harrison helped Norm this morning. He cut his hand again."

"Oh no! Poor Norm. He's not been the same since he lost his fraa. Gladys and the sheriff are thoughtful to watch out for him." Rachael poured her strawberry and rhubarb filling into the baked piecrust.

"He should've married again. The sheriff said women wooed him, but he wasn't interested. It's sad he lives alone." She waited a moment. She didn't want to offend Rachael, but she had to ask. She'd always assumed Rachael would consider a man if he showed interest. Maybe it wasn't so. "Rachael, you should consider marrying again someday. You have so much to offer a husband and kinner." Magdelena studied her friend.

"I don't know. John kummes to mind several times a day since he died. I'm not sure another man could fill his shoes or win my heart. And my limp sets me apart. Young men are going to choose the prettier women without a limp first." Rachael made lattice strips and set one layer and then another layer in the opposite direction.

"You're pretty, Rachael, and you possess all the traits a man would want in a fraa. Plus, you love kinner. Wouldn't you want a boppli?" Magdelena didn't want her friend to live as a spinster. She wanted more for her.

"I would've liked to have had kinner, but with John. Don't worry about me. I'm content living with Mamm, and I'll dote on your bopplin."

Magdelena didn't want to push her too hard. She'd work on her little by little. She wanted her friend to have love, kinner, and a full life. She'd keep her eyes open for the right man and play matchmaker. She wanted her best friend to find the happiness she'd found with Toby.

Toby removed his tool belt and plopped on a stool. "Danki for working on this headboard with me."

Andrew dragged a stool facing Toby. "I enjoy working with you. I'm going to miss you here. I hope you'll use the workshop."

"Your understanding about my accepting Mark's offer to work on the ranch means a great deal to me. You're a close friend, and I don't want anything to jeopardize our friendship. Danki, I'll use your workshop until I can build one of my own. I'll always want to construct furniture, but I won't have as much time. I do expect you, Maryann, and little Betsy to visit. Your place is close by, being two farms away from the ranch. We'll always have time for you. And danki for help building the haus for Magdelena and me." Toby would always invest in his friendship with Andrew. He'd be grateful for his support and encouragement through the good and bad times ahead.

"Mark treats you much differently since he came to his senses and granted his blessing for you and Magdelena to marry. The group of men he hired to construct your haus was impressive. They've worked long hours, and they're skilled handcrafters. Your haus will be done for sure by the time you and Magdelena are ready to move into it," Andrew said.

"He's treating me more like a son, and with respect. Before, I felt dismissed by him and never good enough for him to even befriend me. His new attitude is a wilkom change." He'd had to pray about his relationship with Mark and to really let any hurt or frustration about him go. He'd started fresh, and being open to Mark's newfound friendship had been refreshing.

"How do you think you'll like ranching? You're not doing it to please him, are you?" Andrew tilted his head and raised his brows.

"No. I'm surprised at myself. I wasn't sure how I'd feel about it. I'd not considered it before, but I like all aspects of it. He's an excellent teacher, and his enthusiasm for the work has rubbed off on me. His herd of cattle are healthy. He knows what he's doing to be successful." He admired Mark for his knowledge, hard work ethic, and love for the ranch. He didn't think Mark would've taken him under his wing and befriended him like he had. He was happy he truly felt a part of Magdelena's family.

Bernice was an older version of Magdelena, with coal-black hair, a slender body, and dark brown eyes. She had also made an effort to show she cared about him. She'd cooked his favorite foods and engaged him in conversations where she asked genuine questions to learn more about him. He grew more anxious each day to say his vows to Magdelena and start their life together.

Magdelena woke, got out of bed, and looked out the window September tenth. She'd had fun planning the wedding and reception these last weeks leading to her special day. Their haus was ready for them to move into after the wedding, and she was excited to decorate.

The birds chirped and a squirrel chased another around the big oak tree. The sky was clear and sunshine warmed her room. Her wedding day had finally arrived. She would be Mrs. Toby Schlabach by this evening. Her parents had more than made up for their opposition at first to their marriage. Magdelena and Toby were ready to begin their life together. She couldn't wait to pledge to love him for the rest of her days on this earth today.

Charity rushed in, crawled on top of Magdelena's bed, and jumped up and down. "Today's your wedding day!" She sang, "And Toby will be my bruder!"

"Toby will be your bruder-in-law." Magdelena grabbed and tickled her.

Charity laughed. "Please stop tickling me!"

Magdelena lay next to Charity, staring at the ceiling. "Danki, little schweschder, for loving Toby like you do."

"I always wanted Toby and not Zach, no matter what anyone said. And Toby and I agreed he'd be my bruder. Bruder-in-law is too much to say."

"I don't blame you, and I also like *bruder* better."

Charity frowned. "Will you let me spend the night at your haus? And you have to spend the night with me sometimes here."

"You're wilkom anytime, and you can bring Peter. We'll still have sleepovers, play games, and make cookies together." Magdelena reached for Charity's hand.

"I didn't like it when you were gone. I cried sometimes. I begged Mamm and Daed to go get you. I missed Toby kumming over, too. I got in big trouble for pouting when Zach was here. You loved Toby like I love Peter. I always wanted you to marry Toby." Charity met her gaze with an impish smile.

"I'm sorry I left in a hurry and didn't tell you. I missed you, too. Everything has worked out, and remember, Zach isn't a bad person. We should be nice to him. He won't interfere anymore with Toby and me."

"I'll try."

"Good enough. I love you, little schweschder." She rolled over and hugged her.

Charity rolled off the bed and landed on her feet. "Time for you to have breakfast. I made pancakes with Mamm, and she made apple pie pastries for the reception. The pancakes might be cold. I was supposed to tell you to kumme to the table." She put her hand to her mouth and giggled.

"Let's go." Magdelena moved to the kitchen and found Mamm with tears in her eyes. "What's the matter?"

"I'm happy and sad. You're starting your new life as a fraa, and I'm thrilled for you. But I'll miss you around here. Your room will be empty, and our routine won't be the same. I had a taste of it when you were living with Aunt Gloria and Uncle Otis. You light up the room, Magdelena, and so does Charity."

Charity leaned her head against Mamm. "Don't worry. I'll be here, and Magdelena promised to do sleepovers. You can kumme with me to Magdelena's whenever you want to," Charity assured her.

Magdelena and Mamm exchanged a grin. Mamm smoothed Charity's curls. "You're a dear."

Magdelena clapped her hands. "Enough of this talk. Let's get happy, starting with having these fluffy pancakes." She reached for the maple syrup.

Mamm joined them at the table and had a stack of three pancakes on her plate. "I'm splurging today and having more than one."

"May I have six then? I usually have three. They are kind of small." Charity reached over to add another to her stack.

"You can have four but not six." Mamm shook her head.

"All right," Charity relented.

* * *

Magdelena peeked out her window. It was an hour before the wedding. The yard was filled with her friends and their families. The long tables were already full of covered food dishes. She'd hoped to catch a glimpse of Toby, but she couldn't find him.

Daed opened the door a little. "Mind if I kumme in for a minute?"

Magdelena shook her head.

"You look beautiful as always, Magdelena." Daed held her hands and faced her. "I'm sorry for dismissing your wishes to marry Toby and all the heartache I caused both of you. You were wonderful to forgive me, and I'm grateful Toby and I are forming a friendship."

"Yes, Daed. You've been generous and loving to us. And I've always loved and respected you. I didn't want to defy you, but I was desperate to show you how much Toby meant to me. You've more than made up for what happened between us. I love you, Daed, and I appreciate everything you've done for us. I couldn't be happier."

"Your words are music to my ears. I've learned valuable lessons through the turmoil I've put us through. Mamm and I discuss ideas together now. She's very wise. She'd never voiced her opinion. I thought she didn't care what I decided. Toby is mature, wise, and very intelligent. I'm ashamed of the way I dismissed him. He's taught me to be a better man by his example."

Magdelena's eyes pooled with tears. She was grateful for all he'd done for them. "I love you, Daed. I always have. Toby has some of your qualities I wanted in a man. You've been an excellent provider, and I didn't doubt you loved me. You help those in need, and so much more."

He wiped his damp eyes. "I better get out of here and let you put on your finishing touches." He moved to the door and reached for something outside on the floor. He brought in a package and set it in her palm. "Something from me to you."

"Daed! You've done so much already." She opened it. It was a hand-carved trinket box with a heart on the top.

"Something special for your dresser." He kissed her cheek and hurried out of the room.

Magdelena traced the heart with her finger. He'd crafted little wooden dolls and animals during her childhood years, but it had been a while since he'd carved anything specifically for her. She'd cherish it always.

Mamm came inside. "I bought you a set of new dishes, and I snuck over and put them in the cabinets at your home."

"Oh, Mamm, I can't danki you enough." She hugged her.

"Rachael would like to kumme in." Mamm opened the door farther, and Rachael stepped inside with a package.

Mamm headed out the door. "I'll leave you two alone."

Rachael nodded and passed Magdelena a gift wrapped in brown paper with twine. "I've been working on this since before you came home. I always knew God would make a way for you and Toby to be together. I hope you like it."

"You've always been there for me, no matter what, and I love you for it." She unwrapped the gift. Her eyes widened and she unfolded the white quilt with a blue heart stitched in the middle. "Rachael, this is beautiful." She reached over and hugged her with one arm.

Rachael leaned her head on Magdelena's shoulder. "I'm glad you like it, schweschder." She grinned and picked up the corner where she'd sewn a pocket on the covering. She pulled out a note. "I'll read you what I wrote: 'Dear best friend and now schweschder. I've always wanted a schweschder, and now I have the best. I was shy and didn't have a best friend until I met you. You shine with God's love in everything you do, and the way you treat others, especially me. You've changed my life with your laughter, support, encouragement, and trust and caring about me. Toby is a blessed man, and I'm thrilled we'll now be family. I love you. Rachael.'"

Magdelena sobbed and held the quilt to her cheek. "I love this keepsake pocket quilt from you. I'll keep it forever, even when it's tattered and worn. You and I will snuggle with it when we're old and gray and talk about all our times together."

Rachael wiped her tears. "We've got to stop blubbering, or you'll have puffy red eyes for your wedding. I brought Joy and Thad to the wedding. I should keep an eye on them. Nathan and the kinner are having a difficult time adjusting to not having Kathcrine with them. I wanted to give him time alone. I'm hoping Joy and Thad will play with the other kinner to take their minds off their sorrow."

Magdelena smiled. "You're what they nced right now. You and your mamm are the bright spots in their lives."

Rachael shouldn't go through life without kinner. She was wonderful to Nathan's kinner. Magdelena hadn't given up her idea to play matchmaker once she and Toby were settled.

At two-thirty in the afternoon, the bishop delivered a message on the love and devotion spouses should have for one another, led the attendees in a hymn, and then officiated the marriage between Magdelena and Toby. He prayed for the food they were about to receive and dismissed them from the service and ceremony to celebrate and enjoy the food displayed on the tables behind them.

Toby whisked Magdelena away from the crowd and kissed her gently on the lips. "I'm about to burst with joy." He picked her up and swung her around. "Your determination to marry me showed how much you loved me, and I know it wasn't easy. I love you for it, and this day has been the best day of my life, becoming your husband."

Magdelena laughed as he set her on her feet. "My heart is soaring. You were always my choice, and I wouldn't change it for anything. I'm ecstatic at how everything turned out for us. God has exceeded our expectations. I will always be grateful."

PENNSYLVANIA DUTCH/GERMAN GLOSSARY

Amish rules	*Ordnung*
babies	*bopplin*
baby	*boppli*
brother	*bruder*
children	*kinner*
Children can choose to live in the outside world at age 16 to decide if they want to remain Amish	*rumspringa*
come	*kumme*
covering for Amish woman's hair	*kapp*
dad, father	*daed*
daughter	*dochder*
grandfather	*grossdaadi*
grandmother	*grossmudder*
house	*haus*
hymn book	*Ausbund*
mother, mom	*mamm*
non-Amish male or female	*Englischer*
sister	*schweschder*
thank you	*danki*
welcome	*wilkom*
wife	*fraa*

Recipes

MAGDELENA'S CINNAMON BREAD

Preparation Time: 20 minutes
Cook Time: 350 degrees for 50 minutes
Serves 12
Use 9 x 5-inch loaf pan
Large mixing bowl
Medium mixing bowl

Ingredients for the cinnamon bread

2 cups all-purpose flour
1¼ cups white sugar
2 teaspoons baking powder
1 teaspoon baking soda
½ teaspoon ground cinnamon
½ teaspoon salt
1 cup buttermilk
¼ cup vegetable oil
2 eggs
2 teaspoons vanilla extract

Ingredients for the topping

2½ tablespoons white sugar
1¼ teaspoons ground cinnamon
2½ teaspoons margarine

Directions

Bread

Preheat oven to 350 degrees. Grease the loaf pan. To mix ingredients, use a large mixing bowl. Combine flour, sugar, baking powder, baking soda, cinnamon, salt, buttermilk, oil, eggs, and vanilla into a large mixing bowl. Beat with mixer for three minutes. Pour mixture into prepared loaf pan. Smooth the top evenly.

<u>Topping</u>

Use a medium-sized bowl to combine the white sugar, cinnamon, and butter, mixing until crumbly. Sprinkle topping over batter already in your loaf pan. Using a knife, cut through the mixture in a light swirling motion to give the loaf a marbled presentation.

Put your loaf pan in the oven and bake for 50 minutes. Test with a knife or toothpick. When the knife or toothpick comes out clean, remove your cinnamon bread loaf pan out of the oven and let cool. Then serve.

MAGDELENA'S BLUEBERRY MUFFINS

Preparation Time: 30 minutes
Cook Time: 400 degrees for 20 minutes
Makes six muffins
Muffin pan
Muffin cups
Small mixing bowl
Medium mixing bowl

Ingredients

1 cup all-purpose flour
⅓ cup white sugar
1 teaspoon baking powder
½ teaspoon cinnamon
1 egg
¼ teaspoon salt
¼ cup whole milk
½ cup unsalted butter
2¼ teaspoons vanilla extract
1 cup blueberries

<u>Directions</u>

Preheat your oven at 400 degrees. Put your muffin cups in your muffin pan and set it aside. In your small bowl, combine flour, sugar, baking powder, cinnamon, and salt. In your other bowl, beat the egg, milk, butter, and vanilla together. Combine your ingredients in your small bowl with the ingredients in your medium bowl, and stir until the batter is moist. Pour your blueberries into the mixture and stir again.

Pour your batter into the muffin cups until they're each full, leaving about a half inch at the top of each one. Bake at 400 degrees in the oven for 20 minutes or until your knife or toothpick inserted in the middle of the muffins comes out clean. Cool for four minutes and then serve.

MAGDELENA'S JAM-FILLED COOKIES

Preparation Time: 25 minutes
Cook Time: 375 degrees for 8 minutes
    (crisper cookies: 10 minutes)
Makes three dozen cookies
Large flat cookie sheet or baking stone
Large mixing bowl
Medium mixing bowl

Ingredients

¾ cup butter
½ cup white sugar
2 egg yolks
1¾ cups all-purpose flour
¾ cup fruit jam of your choice

Directions

Preheat your oven to 375 degrees. In your medium bowl combine the butter, white sugar, egg yolks, and flour to form a dough. Roll your dough into 1½-inch balls. Set them two inches apart on an ungreased cookie sheet. Press the center of each cookie with the bottom of a small spoon about the size of your thumb. Spoon desired fruit jam in the center of each one.

Bake for eight minutes or until golden. For crisper cookies, bake ten minutes. Remove the cookie sheet from the oven when done, and slide cookies onto a rack to let them cool. Place them on your desired tray to serve.